Content Warning

This book is meant for mature audiences and contains content that may be triggering for some readers—including sex, profanity, verbal and physical abuse, domestic violence, alcohol use, pregnancy and pregnancy loss, as well as mentions of drug use and suicide.

If you or someone you know is contemplating suicide, please call or text the National Suicide Prevention Lifeline 988 or go online to www.988lifeline.org.

If you're the victim of domestic or dating violence, please reach out to the National Domestic Violence Hotline at 1-800-799-SAFE (7233) or go online to www.thehotline.org.

For the cycle breakers.

Part I

Wednesday, November 23rd

Cat

Waking up cold and alone was not what I'd envisioned when I slid into my absolute thirst trap of a boyfriend's bed last night. But alas, here I am.

I keep my eyes shut, suspended in that murky space between sleep and waking. I slowly register the soft cotton sheets beneath me, the faint sounds of traffic drifting up through the third-story window of Ronan and Shane's apartment, and the near-arctic temperature of the room. I pull the thick down comforter tighter, the skin on my arms chilled. Ronan runs hot, and when we spend the night together, it's always with the window cracked—even now that we're deep into fall. We even saw our first snow a few days ago. I don't usually mind; Ronan's body heat keeps me comfortable and warm at night.

I reach toward the right side of the bed, searching for him. I expect my fingers to be met with warm skin, with the curve of muscle under my palm. But he's not there.

Ronan's not in bed with me, and I couldn't honestly say that he slept in this bed at all last night. He wasn't here when I fell asleep. It's a disappointing realization, though not an unfamiliar one.

I blink my eyes open, noting the slatelike darkness outside the window. It's never pitch-black, not with the city lights illuminating the night sky and Ronan's bedroom. He only closes his blackout curtains when we plan to sleep in, which is rare.

My internal clock tells me it's an hour or two before I'd normally get up. I could check the time, but that would mean moving more than just my arm. All I know is it's early. Way too early for my liking.

I've never been a morning person. Ronan, on the other hand, is. I'm not sure if it's nature or nurture, but he always seems to have an easier time getting out of bed than I do. Part of it, I know, is history. For most of his life he tried to be home as little as possible, tried to escape the abuse. Even now, over a year after the last act of violence was inflicted on him, some routines have stuck.

Another reason he gets up so early is that Ronan is just really damn busy.

I sense him before I hear a sound. No lights. No footsteps. Just a quiet shift in the air that tells me he's here. My body is so finely tuned to him, warming with a pleasant current originating in my heart and spreading into every finger and toe. I turn my head and my lips pull into a smile.

What a sight he is. And all mine.

That fact is as calming as slipping into a hot bath on a cold night. Like collapsing into bed when you're bone tired. Like the first bite of food you've been craving for days.

I allow my eyes to roll over his bare torso, the dim light and shadows emphasizing every delicious dip and swell of muscle sculpted through years of conditioning and punishing workouts.

Ronan's hair is damp, mussed like he towel-dried it in a rush. Light catches on a few stray droplets clinging to his smooth skin. I have a carnal craving to lick away the single bead sliding down his chest.

I follow it with my gaze, envious of its slow caress as it traces the lines I ache to touch. My pulse quickens when both the droplet and my eyes reach the defined striations of his lower abs, those muscles leading like an arrow to the only thing keeping this from going full X-rated—a white towel slung low around his waist.

Enough staring.

"Good morning, sweet boy," I say, my voice a sleepy rasp, even though my senses—my body—are wide awake.

Ronan turns his head, gifting me a smile that could light this entire city.

"Morning, baby," he says, baritone low, a sound that sparks through me, heightening my already-stimulated senses.

He moves to my side of the bed and leans over me, resting his hands on either side of my shoulders before feathering a kiss against my lips. "I hope I didn't wake you."

"Nope. Your absence from my side did." I wind my arms around his neck and pull him down for a deeper kiss.

The groan he releases does nothing to cool the heat already pooling deep in my stomach. Want sharpens into need the moment his left hand skims over my stomach and slides underneath my tank top, inching upward until he cups my breast.

"Can't you just skip class today?" I moan softly, my breath catching as his thumb grazes over my nipple. It pebbles under his touch.

He rolls the stiff peak between his thumb and index finger, priming my body to receive him. God, he knows me so well, knows exactly what I like and how I like it.

"I really can't," he says, his voice husky, but his lips contradict the words as they press to my jawline, then trail down my neck.

"Funny," I breathe, head tilted to the side to grant him access to more of me. "Your words say one thing, but the rest of your body says something entirely different."

My hands find his hips, then the edge of the towel tucked tightly around his waist. One tug, and the last barrier between us falls to the floor.

God, he's gorgeous. Every. Single. Part. Of him.

I reach for him, circling my thumb over his tip, and watch the way his eyes flutter closed, how his breath deepens. That tiny sound he makes—desperate—tells me he isn't going anywhere anytime soon.

Whatever restraint he had vanishes. He climbs onto the bed and settles between my thighs, which fall open with instinctive ease, welcoming him in.

There's nothing I want more than to feel the weight of him pressing me into this mattress, to be claimed by his hands and cock like his mouth is already doing.

I reach between us, wrap my hand around him—thick, long, hard—and stroke. His hips jerk into my fist as I pay extra attention to the sensitive ridge just below his tip.

"Fuck, baby," he groans, his voice raw. "I'm going to be late."

"We can be quick," I whimper. "I just need to feel you for a moment."

He shakes his head, his hooded bright green eyes locked on my lips. "You know I like to take my time with you. I want you dripping for me."

"I'm dripping now, Ran," I hiss, too needy for my own good.

I gasp when his hand delves into my shorts, sweeping along my aching flesh—from my entrance to my clit—in one smooth, devastating pass.

"Good start," he murmurs darkly. "But I can do better."

Ronan strips me bare in seconds—tank top first, then my pajama shorts—before descending between my thighs, ready to feast. And then it's all tongue and teeth, his mouth a whirlwind of sensation as he licks, laves, and sucks on my throbbing flesh. Pleasure builds, slow and thick in my core, my hands buried in his damp hair as I try to anchor myself against the flood he's unleashing.

"More," I beg, barely able to breathe as he circles my swollen clit with soft, maddening swirls, winding me tighter and tighter. I need pressure. Friction. Release. But he denies me. "Please."

His hand joins his mouth, teasing my entrance, probing. I arch into his caress, my body begging to be filled.

"Tell me when you come, baby," he rasps. "I want to hear it. I want my name dripping off your lips like you're dripping off mine." Ronan sinks a finger inside me, then works in a second.

God, yes. My muscles tighten, clenching around him.

He curls his fingers just right, stroking my inner walls in a way that makes me ache for release. His tongue circles my clit again, and again. Then he sucks, hard enough to make me cry out. My body seizes, the coil snapping as pleasure explodes outward in a blinding rush. I arch my back, hips bucking, his name breaking from my lips in a desperate, breathless moan.

"There she is," Ronan growls, his voice laced with pride, his breath hot against my pulsing skin as waves of undiluted pleasure radiate through me. I bite my lip to muffle another cry, fully aware that Shane and Tori are just across the hall.

The shock waves haven't yet subsided, but already I'm tugging at his shoulders. "Now give me you."

He looks up and licks my arousal from his lips like this is the most delicious thing he's ever tasted. The hunger in his eyes, the almost feral craving carved into every line of his beautiful face… I might come again just from that look.

He climbs up my body, pinning me to the mattress with enough of his weight supported by his forearms that I'm exquisitely trapped beneath his tall, solid frame without getting smothered. I feel safe. Caught. Owned.

I feel his tip at my entrance, his eyes on mine, watching me intently as he slowly pushes inside me. I know he loves that feeling just as much as I do—that first thrust, that intoxicating rush of oxytocin, dopamine, and endorphins, that tight stretch and the resistance of my body as it works to accommodate his size.

"So fucking perfect," Ronan moans, eyes falling shut as he rocks forward, then pulls almost all the way out, only to slam back in.

And again. And again.

Each thrust is more addictive than the last. He's a drug and I'm hopelessly hooked, high on the way he moves, the way he feels, the way he worships every inch of me with his body.

Already, heat pools low in my core again, building fast and fierce. His rhythm is relentless—deep, purposeful, devastating.

"Ran," I cry, hips rising to meet his, my fingers digging into his skin, desperate for more. For everything.

"God, baby," he groans when I wrap my legs around his waist, pulling him deeper. "You feel so fucking good."

"I love you, Ran," I whimper, voice ragged as I cling to him, pleasure crashing through me again like a tidal wave. I moan loudly, back bowing, nails raking his back as another orgasm rips through me, stealing every coherent thought.

His lips crush to mine, silencing me, swallowing my moans, tasting every gasp, every cry, as he drives me through the climax and into the next.

"My turn," he pants, breaking the kiss just long enough to warn me.

His rhythm breaks, thrusts turning erratic, harder, faster. His body tenses above mine, muscles coiled and shaking as he chases his own high. I watch him, every glorious second, because I love seeing him like this—unraveling, needy, beautiful.

When he finally lets go, it's with a quiet, broken groan and a final hard thrust. His body seizes, releasing inside me as his head drops to my shoulder, breath hot and fast. God, I love him.

Ronan blinks his eyes open a few moments later, dazed and sated, a lazy smile spreading across his face.

"Sorry I made you late," I tease, brushing my thumb across the curve of his lips.

He chuckles. "Worth it," he murmurs, then dips his head to kiss me softly, like he's memorizing my taste all over again. "You're always worth it."

Carefully, Ronan slips out of me, drawing a soft whimper from my throat.

"Might need another quick shower, though," he mutters as he pushes off the bed and rises to his full height, gloriously naked and unbothered.

I let my eyes roam his body. "I should join you," I say, lifting onto my elbows with a grin.

He narrows his eyes and snatches his towel from the floor. "Stay away from me, Cat," he warns, half-laughing. "I can't resist you, and I really need to get to class."

I shrug and fall back onto my pillow. "Fine, if that's what you want."

Ronan stops mid-step, his towel by his side. "'Want' isn't exactly the word I'd use," he says. "Trust me, I'd rather spend all day in this bed with you than sit in a three-hour lecture about biochemical processes, but I really need to go because my final paper is due after Thanksgiving break, and I'm not sure I understand what the hell this class is even about."

He tightens the towel around his waist, which somehow only makes the pout on my lips deepen. Ronan chuckles as he heads out of the room and down the hall toward the bathroom.

***

"No class for you today, right?" Ronan asks upon his return from the bathroom only a few minutes later.

I stretch my arms over my head, the blanket slipping off my breasts. I grin at the way Ronan's eyes darken the moment he notices, his jaw flexing. "No class for me today," I say casually, like I don't delight at how he reacts to me, even a year and a half into our relationship. "Jealous?"

Normally I'd have my Intro to Psychology class today, but my professor decided to offer up the time for us to work on our term papers instead. I finished that last weekend—an aggressive-overachiever move I'm very proud of—and I gleefully kicked off my Thanksgiving break last night.

Ronan drags his eyes from my nipples and focuses on my face. “Very,” he says with a dry nod, and turns abruptly to open the door to his closet, which really shouldn’t be called a walk-in unless you’re a toddler. It’s *that* tiny.

“What time do you think you’ll be at my dad’s?” he asks, pulling a hoody over the black Murphy’s long-sleeve he’s already wearing.

“Not sure,” I say. “What time are you done today?”

“At three. Depending on traffic, I should be at my dad’s no later than four. But you can always head over there a little early,” Ronan says, then grins. “Stevie got home last night.”

I perk up. “I thought he wasn’t supposed to come in until today?”

“Yeah, but I guess he decided to skip class today and avoid the holiday traffic. He hung out at Murphy’s until I closed last night,” Ronan says with a smile.

I know he misses his big brother. The two of them are about as close as brothers can be, and Ronan has mentioned a few times over the past three months how weird it is that his brother lives so far away now. “You can interrogate him about his new girlfriend.” Ronan chuckles and pulls on his jacket, the hood of his sweatshirt tugged neatly out from underneath.

“Did he finally fess up to you?” I ask with a giggle. Ronan shared his suspicions with me a few weeks ago that Steve was seeing someone new.

“Nope, but I know my brother. Something’s up.” He leans over and kisses me softly. “I’ll see you later, baby.”

I watch him walk out of the bedroom, then hear the front door close moments later. I sigh. That half hour with him this morning is the most uninterrupted time we’ve had in days, and already that all-too-familiar ache of missing him begins to settle in my chest.

Ronan hasn’t stopped. Not once. He’s all motion, all momentum. He works, he moves, he avoids. He’s all go and no stop. He rarely even stops for me. And he also doesn’t talk—at least, not about the things that matter. Not about his past, and not about the future either. Not even *our* future.

Sometimes I wish he'd stop. That he'd pause long enough to see that he's safe now, that he can trust me. But no luck.

So I wait. I give him space, even when it hurts, even when I'm frustrated or lonely or angry. I wait for him to stop running from everything he's survived. I wait for him to fall into me completely.

I just hope he knows I'm here when he's ready to land.

Ronan

How I wish I could skip class today, spend the day in bed with Cat, feel her, touch her, make love to her several more times before the day is done. But I really can't. Not today.

We're steadily marching toward the end of our first semester in college, and, fuck, that shit is way more intense than high school. The workload is brutal—assignments, labs, papers all piling up on top of an already-packed schedule.

Things haven't exactly slowed down lately. The opposite is true, and though everyone, including my therapist, keeps urging me to rest, it's in short supply.

I'm taking a full course load at Columbia, which occupies my mornings and early afternoons with classes, labs, and lectures. And in the evenings, I work. Way more than I used to. Partly because I need the money. Mostly because Shane's been leaning on me hard.

Until roughly three months ago, Shane and I worked the same schedule. And then Shane took on full-time responsibility for Murphy's, resulting in him running the place during the day and me running it most evenings. I've definitely gotten a crash course in business management.

I cover Friday nights and Saturday brunch. Shane works Saturday nights. That way we each get at least one weekend evening with the women in our lives. Still doesn't give me nearly enough time with Cat, who's buried in her own full-time course load at NYU.

Our schedules barely align. Cat's definitely not a morning person. I keep telling her that her parents did a fantastic job picking out her name; I swear, if she could, she'd sleep sixteen hours a day. A good number of her classes fall in the afternoon, whereas I front-load mine so I can squeeze in a workout or a nap before heading into Murphy's.

Sundays are sacred. No classes, no work. Just us. Even then we're usually pulled in all directions—by our families, errands, or whatever else "adulting" requires of us, like doing laundry. God, I hate laundry.

But I'm not complaining. Not in the least. Life's busy, yeah, but it's also the most peaceful it's ever been.

I no longer live with the daily threat of getting my face kicked in—yay for that—I get to call the most perfect girl in existence mine, and I share an apartment with my best friend. Considering that only a year ago I barely managed to keep breathing, I'm in the best place I've ever been.

I love living with Shane; I love the freedom, the independence, the normalcy. Shane's a great roommate and we complement each other well. He's nurturing, and, bonus, he loves to cook. There's always enough food in the house not only for Shane and me, but for Shane's girlfriend, Tori—who spends probably six out of seven days at our apartment—Cat, and any of our friends who might stop by.

But Shane isn't particularly neat, which is where I come in. I had always been responsible for keeping things clean and tidy at home, lest I invoked my mother's wrath. So now, messes give me serious anxiety. I just can't come to rest if the apartment is cluttered, which luckily doesn't happen too often. Shane, Tori, and Cat are mindful of my mental health struggles and try to keep triggers to a minimum. Nonetheless, I'm typically on top of making sure things don't get too messy, so Shane and I make a good team.

I ready myself to sit through my morning lecture on biochemical processes and retrieve my phone to silence it. My jaw flexes when I note the voicemail from my dad. It's barely eight. But of course his military training is so ingrained in him, he's up before the sun rises, probably running a 5K and doing a hundred push-ups before he allows himself to have his morning cup of joe, or whatever. I don't actually know.

"Hey bud, just checking in," his message starts. Sure enough, he sounds winded. He for sure worked out. I wonder if he'll be able to keep that up with two newborns in a matter of months. But I digress. "Haven't heard from you in a few days. Stevie assured me you're still alive, but it would be nice if you could occasionally answer my calls. I assume you and Cat are still coming this afternoon since I haven't heard otherwise. I love you, Ran. Just..." He releases a deep sigh. "Yeah. I'll see you this afternoon. Bye."

A pang of guilt jabs at me. He's right, I haven't returned any of his calls or texts. I'm trying, but it's still difficult for me to allow my dad to play more than just a surface-level role in my life. It's hard to explain why, how much his efforts to be involved put me off, and how much I genuinely believe he has no right to *me*, not after he left me to fend for myself for so long.

Therapy's helped. A little. The walls are lower. But they're still there, still solid. He offers advice, and I bristle. Tries to help, and I push back. I don't let him pay for any of my crap. Not rent. Not gas or insurance. Not even my phone bill. Although I did finally relent and let him buy me a nice bed and new mattress when I moved into Shane's place. He was able to convince me with the argument that I was leaving all my stuff behind, which he and Penny would continue to use as they turn my old room into the babies' nursery, and that the least he could do was buy me a new bed.

I'm not going to lie, there's a ton of anger in general, but also specifically at him. At his failure to protect me, his absence, for not knowing. For building a whole new life with Penny while I was getting broken at home.

I never realized how much I resented my dad, how angry I was... *am*, until Doctor Seivert drilled down on something I said during a therapy session this past July—after Penny and my dad broke the news about Penny's pregnancy. The longer I sat with the news, the more it felt like confirmation: he's still not choosing me.

What makes this whole thing worse is that I see how hard he's trying. He calls me almost daily, checks in with texts, and even makes a point to stop by Murphy's when he knows I'm working. But it feels impossible to let him in. It makes me resent myself, which is a whole other issue.

Do I know how fucked up all this is? Of course. I've always known. But I'm learning to give myself grace. Especially on the hard days, which still come more often than I'd like. Days when just getting out of bed feels like a herculean task.

But the most effective medicine for my soul is Cat.

Everything about her is just perfect. From the way she looks, smells, sounds, tastes, all the way to her soul. She's beautiful inside and out and so damn good to me. She never judges, doesn't make me feel less than, doesn't hold it against me when I'm having a hard day. In fact, the opposite is true. She's the one who shows up when I'm falling apart. She'll drop everything to just lie beside me, sit in silence, hold my hand. She's talked me through panic attacks. Reframed my spirals. Helped me separate truth from trauma. Her touch calms my nerves. Her voice slows my thoughts. She was, is, and always will be too damn good for me, and nobody can convince me otherwise.

***

I make it through my morning lecture, scarf down a quick lunch, then spend a couple of hours in the library working on my biology paper before I sit through my economics class. My professor doesn't end class until exactly three; he drones on about gross domestic product or some shit, while just about every single one of us sitting through this torturous hour and a half is ready to call it a day.

I know there are a bunch of students in my class who aren't from New York and are eager to get on the road or on a plane to head home to their families for Thanksgiving. But my lecturer, whose cadence is drawn-out and monotone, lacking any inflection, seems blissfully unaware of the restless energy in the lecture hall. There's no wedding ring on his left hand, so maybe he's got nowhere to be. Whatever the reason, he's clearly not in a rush.

The moment I step out into the courtyard, I'm met with the kind of late-November New York weather that makes you want to crawl back into bed. Cloud-covered skies. A faint drizzle—not enough to soak through your clothes, but just enough to seep into your bones. I yank my hood up and steel myself to walk the two blocks to my car, already regretting not taking the subway this morning. Traffic's going to be hell.

"Hey!" a woman's voice calls behind me. I don't bother turning around. This is New York—someone's always yelling. I have no reason to believe that current someone is trying to get my attention.

"Hey! *Hey!*" she calls again, closer this time.

I glance over my shoulder, but don't slow my stride until I notice a young woman hurrying toward me, hand outstretched, long hair streaming behind her.

I come to a stop, eyebrows raised. "Can I help you?"

She holds up her hand, catching her breath before she straightens up and plasters a bright smile onto her ochre face. The color of her big obsidian eyes matches her eyelashes and hair.

"Hi," she gasps. "You're... you're Ronan Soult, right?"

I furrow my brow, digging through my mental archives, trying to recall if I've met her before. "Yeah?" It comes out more like a question.

Her smile widens as she adjusts the strap of her oversized leather satchel. Her puffy polyester coat sends the strap sliding right back off her shoulder. "I'm Rashana Yates."

Nope. Definitely not someone I've met before.

"I'm so sorry to ambush you like this. You're probably heading home. Or, that's probably presumptuous. For all I know you still have three hours of classes and are just grabbing something to eat. Gosh, I'm so ready for a few days off and all that good food." She giggles awkwardly.

The crease on my brow deepens. "Can I help you?" I ask again.

Another giggle. Rashana pulls her bag forward, opens the flap, and retrieves a notebook and pen. "I'm Rashana Yates," she repeats. "I'm getting my master's in investigative journalism."

My stomach drops.

"I've been working on a criminal justice piece, and—"

"No," I say. I turn on my heel and march away.

She flings her bag behind her and jogs to catch up, practically sprinting to keep pace. "No what?" she asks, breathless.

I stop cold and face her. Her eyes widen and her mouth drops open.

"No to whatever the fuck you want from me," I growl.

She raises her hands in surrender. "I'm working on an investigative journalism piece involving abuse cycles in families and the failures of the criminal justice system. I came across your mom's case. It took me forever to find you. I'd love to—"

"No. Whatever it is you want or think I can give you, the answer is no. I don't know how you found me—I thought my name was redacted from all court—"

"It was," she says, but smiles. "But that's what investigative journalism is. There's always a way to find a person if you're willing to dig deep enough."

This feels violently intrusive.

"Yeah, so, I'm gonna tell you right now to stop. Drop this. Take my mother, my story, *me* out of your... piece. Don't approach me again," I warn her, each word punctuated by a sharp pause.

I turn and walk away.

"You know what all investigative journalists have in common?" she calls. I don't stop. "We're determined. I have buried secrets I could share with you if you'd be willing to sit with me for an hour."

"I doubt that. And I won't," I call back without sparing her another look.

"Yeah? So you already know about your mom's sister?" she shouts.

I hesitate, my stride slowing as my thoughts stumble. My mom's *sister*?

I know she has a brother—never met the guy—but I've never heard a single word about a sister. For a second, I'm tempted to turn back, to ask what the hell she's talking about.

But I keep walking. It doesn't fucking matter. It's not like I'm going to rekindle some kind of familial relationship with anyone on that side of the family, and I sure as fuck won't sit with some investigative-reporter wannabe and do a deep dive into things I barely manage to talk to my therapist about.

She can get fucked.

Cat

"Well, well, well, look who decided to join us today," my dad says over Sam and Benny's boisterous needling of each other when the three of them walk into the house this afternoon. "A rare but lovely sighting of my eldest."

I grin. "Don't get used to it. I'm leaving in a minute."

His face sours. "You're never home anymore!"

He's not wrong. I turned eighteen three months ago and have spent most weekends at Ronan's apartment since then. Combine that with college classes and my parents' full-time jobs and they only catch the occasional glimpse of me, usually in passing.

"I was home all day," I say. "I helped Mom brine the turkey and I baked three pies from scratch, including your favorite pecan pie."

A smile brightens his expression. "I just wish you'd spend more time with your family, Kitty."

I shrug. "I'd be home more if you weren't so mean to Ran."

"I'm not mean to him." He crosses his arms over his chest, eerily reminiscent of a sulking child. But he knows I'm right. While my dad doesn't outright argue with Ronan, he's not what I'd consider even lukewarm. On the rare occasion Ronan does spend time with my dad—only when absolutely required, like for my eighteenth birthday dinner with both our families—my dad purposely ignores Ronan, speaking to him only through me.

It's exhausting, and even though Ronan takes it in stride, I know it gets to him. How could it not?

"Okay, then let Ran sleep over."

On cue, my dad's face contorts. "Not a thought I'm going to entertain."

I smirk. "Letting Ran... *sleep*?"

"In the same bed as my daughter," he says stiffly.

"You know that's already happening, right?" I say, then take a bite out of a leftover Granny Smith from my pie prep.

"Not under my roof it's not," he huffs. "You're eighteen. I can't stop you from spending the night with your boyf... with Ronan, but I can put limitations on where you guys... *sleep*," he says, his tone gruffer with each word.

"Because *location* magically changes the fact that we're... sleeping?"

My mom exhales noisily. "Oh, for crying out loud. You two need to—"

"Ignorance is bliss," my dad says.

My mom shoots me a look—the kind that begs me to take the high road.

I swallow my bite of apple. "Fine. Your house, your rules. But if you could try being nice to Ran tomorrow, that would make me happy. And in return, I'll spend the night at home."

"I'm always n—"

"No, you're not, Bobby," my mom says. "You're a curmudgeon when it comes to Ran. He's a good guy. He's good to Kitty. And if you don't want to push our daughter away, maybe try a little harder."

She shuts the pantry and walks out, leaving him standing there with his arms still crossed.

***

Ten minutes later, I spot Steve's black Challenger parked in the driveway next to Frank's Tahoe and I pick up my pace on the short walkway to the Soult house. I climb the three steps to the familiar dark-green front door and knock three times.

"Stevie!" I exclaim when Steve opens the front door and throw my arms around his neck. I haven't seen him in weeks.

Steve moved up to Boston at the end of August and has made only rare showings in New York. Between school and the four-hour drive, he's had plenty of excuses.

"Hey, Cat!" He squeezes me tightly, his chest solid and warm.

"It's so good to see you! How are you?" I step back to take him in.

His light brown hair is longer now, and his face is scruffy, probably five days past clean-shaven. It suits him. He looks relaxed and happy in dark jeans and a fitted black henley that shows off his broad shoulders. He and Ronan look so much alike, and yet completely different.

"I'm great," he says, a giant smile on his lips. "Really great. How about you?"

"Really good," I say, grinning.

"Yeah. You look good," he says sweetly, and pulls me in for another hug after closing the front door behind me. "You and Ran doing okay?"

I take off my coat, then kick off my shoes. "Yeah, we're doing great," I say, my voice rising an octave. The butterflies I feel whenever I so much as think of Ronan are the same as the day I met him. I swear, every day that passes I fall more in love with him.

"And how about you?" I ask, smirking. "Ran has a theory that you're secretly seeing someone up in Boston."

Steve chuckles as I follow him down the hallway and into the living room. "Does he now?" He takes a seat on the sofa. "Ran and his theories."

I sit down beside him. "Well, he's usually spot-on with those theories of his."

He nods. "So, where is my little brother?"

I decide right then and there that Ronan is right about Steve having met someone. "He won't be done with class until three, so he should be here at four or so," I say. "How's Boston?"

"Really good. Fucking cold right now," he says with a small frown. "But yeah, really good. I miss you guys, though." He pulls me against him to squeeze me once more.

"We miss you, too. Ran has actually told me a bunch of times how much he misses you."

Steve chortles. "No, he didn't."

"Yeah, he did. He keeps saying how weird it is that you're so far away."

"Huh." He leans back. "I should try and visit more often."

"I think Ran would like that," I say, nudging his ribs. "So, other than school and your new girlfriend, what have you been up to?"

Steve shakes his head, laughing. "Well, I've officially declared my major as pre-med."

My eyes widen. "You're going to be a doctor?"

"That's the plan. I mean, it's a long road and super competitive, but it feels right."

"Stevie, that's amazing!"

"I took on a volunteer intern position at Boston Medical just to get my feet wet, see if I could handle it."

"That's so great. I never knew you were into medicine."

He raises his eyebrows. "Honestly, neither did I."

I laugh. "So what made you choose pre-med?"

His eyes soften. "Ran."

I nod.

I don't need to ask anything else because I understand Steve's motivation for wanting to go into medicine. It was the moment he found his little brother unconscious on the living room floor, barely breathing. The moment Ronan's heart stopped. The moment Steve had to perform CPR and pray he was doing it right. That helplessness carved a path he couldn't ignore. His interest in medicine makes complete sense.

"So, have you thought of what you'd want to specialize in, or...?"

"Right now, it's trauma surgery," Steve says with a nod. "But it can change, I guess. I definitely don't want to be a plastic surgeon," he adds with a chuckle.

"Oh, no? You don't want to do boob implants all day?" I say with a giggle.

Steve's face turns thoughtful. "Well, now that you talk about touching breasts all day, maybe I was wrong." He laughs, and I join in.

"Hey, Cat," Frank says, walking in with a very pregnant-looking Penny, his hand resting protectively on her lower back.

"Hi!" I say brightly as Penny waddles over to the armchair. She lowers herself with effort and exhales like she just ran a marathon.

"How are you feeling?"

"Huge," she says with a quick laugh.

"You're perfect," Frank murmurs, rubbing her belly before taking the loveseat.

Penny kicks up her feet on the ottoman with a grateful sigh. "We had a doctor's appointment this morning. The boys are looking great."

"They both measure really big," Frank tells us. "He says he wants to try to get her to thirty-nine weeks, but he might induce her earlier. We'll see."

Steve gives a one-shouldered shrug. "Well, I guess it's not a total surprise that they're big, right? I mean, you and Athair are both tall and so are Ran and I."

Frank nods. "Yeah. Looks like those Soult genes are strong in the males. Although Ran was a scrawny little dude when he was born," he says with a laugh. "You, on the other hand, were a big boy. Over nine pounds."

Penny makes a horrified face. "No, don't say that, Frankie! I can't squeeze two nine-pound boys out of... well..."

"Maybe they'll both be scrawny like Ran," Frank says.

"Nice try," she says. "But the doctor said they already measure two weeks ahead of schedule."

"Oh, right," Frank says with a quick laugh. "Baby, you'll be fine. It's going to be fine."

"Easy for you to say. You don't have to give birth to them," Penny says through gritted teeth.

"Don't forget, there's medication," I offer.

Penny laughs. "And I'll be asking for *all* of it." She gives me a knowing look. "You and Ran are going to have big babies too, one day. You're both tall. And apparently the Soult guys have dominant big-boy genes." She rubs her belly as if in warning.

Frank chuckles. "But please, take your time with that!"

Of course I blush. "Oh, I don't think Ran and I are in any rush at all."

Ronan and I haven't ever talked about kids. In fact, we haven't really talked about our future. It's not that I don't envision us together forever, or that I don't sometimes fantasize about him asking me to marry him, our wedding, and growing a family. I just haven't brought it up to him yet. I don't want to pressure him; he's still very much in the process of healing. After all, it's been only a little over a year since the abuse stopped, and really only a few months since he's had a chance to create a new, peaceful normal for himself. And we're only eighteen, for crying out loud. There's no need to hurry things.

"I sincerely hope so," Frank says. "Not that I don't love my boys, but to say it was easy becoming a dad at sixteen would be a lie. I mean, in retrospect it's pretty cool that I had them while I was so young because I can relate to them so much more. But I made a lot of mistakes that I'm not sure I would have made if I had been older, had actually known what I was getting myself into when I had unprotected sex with a girl I had met only hours before, you know?"

Steve laughs and glances my way. "Dad, I don't know if you've noticed, but Cat's very red face suggests she's maybe a *little* uncomfortable with this conversation."

"Sorry," Frank says with a throaty chuckle. "So, buddy, how are things with your new girlfriend?" he adds, clearly catching Steve off guard.

"Not you too, Dad!"

"Your brother is absolutely convinced that—"

"I'm seeing someone. Yeah, yeah. Cat already filled me in on Ran's theories," Steve says with a huff and a shake of his head.

"Before you interrogate your son further, could you help me up, please?" Penny says, struggling to get out of her chair. "I need to use the bathroom."

Frank quickly gets up, then helps Penny to her feet before she makes her way upstairs.

"I talked to Morai yesterday," Steve tells his dad. "I guess she and Athair are thinking about taking a trip to New York this summer?"

"That's what they're telling me," Frank says with a nod. "She was complaining that we don't make enough trips to Montana." He laughs. "So, I told her she should come and visit us instead."

"Uh-huh. She told me she doesn't want to have to wait another year after your wedding before she gets to see all of us again."

"So, they'll be here this summer?" I ask excitedly.

I've only met Ronan's grandparents once—when Ronan was in the hospital, in a coma, and his grandparents flew in from Montana to be by his bedside and provide support to Frank and Steve. I love

Ronan's grandparents, and his grandma Saoirse and I really hit it off. I'm already looking forward to seeing them again in April for Frank and Penny's wedding. It's set to take place on the Soult Ranch in Montana. Just the thought of going to Montana, which has always been on my bucket list, to the place where Ronan was sent to heal, has me excited. Both my mom and I are bridesmaids. Not only that, but Frank asked Shane's dad, Seamus, to be a groomsman alongside Ronan and Steve. There was no question whether Shane and Tori would come along, too. Ronan and Shane were both pretty adamant that if Seamus came, so would Shane and Tori. I can't think of a better way to spend my spring break.

"Looks like it," Frank says with a nod. "We haven't nailed down an exact date yet, but I think they're planning to come in June and stay with Penny and me for a couple of weeks. It'll be great to have them around to help with the babies."

Just then, there's a knock at the front door.

"I'll get it!" Penny calls from the stairs. Moments later, she walks into the living room.

"Who is it?" Frank asks, analyzing Penny's concerned expression.

"It's a lady by the name of Callista Donahue," Penny says.

Frank's face instantly darkens. "Shit. That's Rica's mother." He pushes up from the couch and strides out into the hallway without another word.

The rest of us freeze, the mood instantly shifting from light to brittle.

"Hello, Frank," Mrs. Donahue says, her voice cool, refined.

"What can I do for you, Callista?" Frank replies evenly, his voice devoid of inflection, stripped of any warmth.

"I'm sorry for stopping by like this, unannounced. I was in the area, and, well, I need to speak with Ronan." She has an eloquent way of speaking, her voice slightly nasal, but dignified, proud. I remember seeing her at her daughter's trial last April, how well-dressed she was with her pantsuit and Louboutin heels. If I had to sum her up in one word, I'd say regal.

"Ronan isn't here," Frank says, his tone shifting to something lower, protective.

"Frank, I know you don't harbor the warmest feelings for me. I understand that, but I really do need to speak with my grandson."

"He isn't here right now, Callista," Frank repeats sharply.

"Well, are you expecting him at all today? Because if so, then I'll wait."

"Callista, this isn't—"

"Frank, I'm not here to argue or make your family's life difficult. I drove over an hour to visit my daughter today—the day before Thanksgiving—in prison, and I won't be making the trip again anytime soon. My husband… Brian…" Her voice falters. "He's not well, so…"

It's silent for a long moment, and I imagine Frank is weighing his options.

"Oh, is that him?" I hear Mrs. Donahue ask suddenly.

My heart lurches into my throat, beating as if it's trying to escape my body. I glance at my phone. It's just before four.

"Shit," Steve mutters and gets up. I follow him into the hallway where Frank stands facing Ronan and Steve's maternal grandmother.

She looks exactly as I remember her. Her perfectly coifed hair is pulled up and held in place by an elegant hairclip. She's thin with impeccable posture, poised, standing straight-backed as if she's perpetually balancing a book atop her head. Her elegant fingers are long, nails painted a subtle nude pink. Today, she dons a rose-pink, knee-length tweed skirt with a matching jacket, as well as her shiny pair of Louboutin high heels. A large black leather purse hangs from the crook of her elbow. I take note yet again of her pencil-thin lips and her steel-blue eyes—all so unlike Ronan with his soft, full lips and strikingly green eyes.

Steve doesn't greet her. He brushes past with a look at Frank, who nods slightly.

I peer through the hallway window as Ronan approaches. My heart tugs in two directions. I'm so glad to see him, yet so terrified of what this meeting might do, or... *un*do.

Ronan has been doing well lately, though it isn't always predictable what might trigger him. Some things bounce off him. Other seemingly small things will cause him to spiral into darkness.

Steve intercepts Ronan, who frowns at his brother. The two talk for a moment and Ronan's body noticeably tenses, his eyes flitting to the window then back to his brother. Steve puts his hands on Ronan's shoulders, talking to him intently for a second longer before the two walk up the short walkway, climb the three stairs to the front door, then step into the house.

Ronan's eyes lock on me and his face softens the smallest bit.

"Ronan," Mrs. Donahue says, scanning her grandson's face, her blue eyes wide.

Ronan doesn't immediately acknowledge her; he moves straight past her toward me. I reach my hand out for him and he takes it, interlacing his fingers with mine. That warm current fills me like he's the source of all light. I give his hand a little squeeze before he finally faces his grandmother.

"My god, you look exactly like Brian when he was your age," Mrs. Donahue says, studying Ronan's features, her gaze moving over his face, down his tall, muscular body and back again. "Same eyes, same hair, same lips."

Ronan frowns, his jaw rigid. "What do you want from me?"

She flinches, just barely. "Would it be okay if we sat?"

Frank turns his attention to Ronan. "Ran? Are you okay with her being here?" It's not about politeness. It's about Ronan. Only Ronan.

"I'm trying to figure out what exactly it is you want from me," Ronan says, his eyes locked on his grandmother. I can feel how tightly wound his muscles are, see his jaw flexing as he holds my hand firmly in his. "Why are you here?"

Mrs. Donahue takes a deep breath, working to maintain her composure. But the fidgeting of her fingers tells me she's frazzled by Ronan's reception. She lifts her chin. "I'm here to apologize," she says with a sigh, a look of defeat in her blue eyes.

Ronan's eyebrows dip, but he doesn't otherwise speak. His silence is louder than words.

"Ronan, I... Could we please sit?" she asks again, quieter now.

Ronan sighs. "Fine."

Frank nods and leads the way into the living room.

"I love you," I whisper to Ronan. He only squeezes my hand.

We take our seats—Frank and Penny on the loveseat, Steve, Ronan, and me on the couch. Mrs. Donahue sits alone in the armchair across from us. It's a stark contrast.

Mrs. Donahue crosses her ankles and clears her throat. "I think you need to understand the cards you were dealt, Ronan."

His muscles coil beside me. He's so tense, I wouldn't be surprised if he woke up sore tomorrow.

"I know you had a hard life growing up," Mrs. Donahue says, clasping her hands in her lap. "It didn't have to be this way. I very much blame myself. I don't know if you know anything about what Brian did to Rica and my son, Cormac."

"Yeah, I do," Ronan says simply.

She nods. "Brian was strict when Rica and Cormac were growing up. He very much believed in corporal punishment. Brian himself grew up with a father who regularly hit him, and his father him, and so on, from what I understand. If I tried to come to my children's aid, Brian would... well, he made sure we all understood who the head of the household was," she says, sitting up straight, her hand moving to a small scar on her left cheekbone.

My heart aches.

"Honestly, he wasn't like that before we married, but once we were and had moved to Westchester he... I think it was his work, maybe. He was under a lot of stress," she says, sinking briefly into herself.

She collects herself, plastering a proud look onto her perfectly made-up face.

"Anyways, I wanted you to understand that your mother did what she was taught, what she grew up with. She perpetuated a painful, vicious, violent cycle that had been passed down through the Donahue family tree for generations. It was always very much about respect and obeying. A failure to obey was synonymous with disrespect, which was not tolerated by any of the Donahue men," she says like she's reciting an undeniable truth.

Anger ignites within me. Mrs. Donahue's words resonate with what I learned during the trial in April, when I listened to Ronan testify—lay himself bare before strangers—for hours, and saw the surveillance video in which Rica repeatedly accused Ronan of disrespecting her, of disobeying her rules, before she viciously beat him.

Ronan's profile is unreadable, his silence suffocating.

"I should've left Brian the first time he hit me. At the very least I should have left him when he began laying his hands on our children," she says, her voice cracking. "I wasn't strong enough."

She directs her gaze to her hands in her lap, and suddenly she reminds me of myself, how I made excuses for Adam's violence, how I didn't recognize what he was doing to me as abuse, how it took Ronan's words to finally make me understand that nothing that had happened to me was my fault. She takes a few steadying breaths before she squares her shoulders, replacing the expression of sadness with a stoic determination. I'm impressed and simultaneously appalled by how well she maintains her proud composure.

"I had nothing; Brian had always provided for me. I had no job experience, no real education. I married into money, and Brian was good at reminding me that I was nothing without him. What was I supposed to do?"

She raises her thin blonde eyebrows at us as if daring us to contradict her.

"My children and I would have been homeless. I couldn't possibly tell my parents, my friends. On the outside, my family was picture-perfect. My children went to private Catholic schools, they were well-dressed, we drove the nice cars, lived in a beautiful home," she says, the words rushing from her mouth.

I wonder if this is the first time she's ever said these things out loud to anyone.

"I had no right to complain. Brian worked so hard, climbed the military ranks quickly. He was disciplined, and all he ever asked of me and his children was to obey and respect him. In fact, those words were in our wedding vows," Mrs. Donahue says with a nod. "He expected Rica and Cormac to do as he told them. Do well in school, don't slack, be disciplined like their dad, don't complain. He provided for us. It was great, except when he became physical. Cormac left as soon as he turned eighteen. I don't know where he went; he just disappeared. I haven't spoken to him in over twenty years. I don't even know if he's still alive." I note the pain in her voice as her composure slips. "I pray he was able to build a beautiful family for himself, that he was able to find peace. But those Donahue genes... I worry..."

Her words taper off, and the room falls still. Ronan's eyes are unfocused, his lips pressed together. I wonder what he's thinking.

"When Rica became pregnant," Mrs. Donahue finally continues, "Brian was incensed. She was barely sixteen. She had always been such a good girl—obedient, straight-A student, amazing volleyball player. She sang for her school and church choirs. She always did exactly as she was told, but that didn't stop Brian from always expecting more of her. Then she went to the city with her friends on her sixteenth birthday and..."

Mrs. Donahue looks at Frank, who nods grimly.

"She became pregnant. Brian wouldn't have it. He kicked her out. No money, nowhere to go. He and I fought about it, and it got ugly. He hit Rica, he hit me, and in the end, Rica left. I had no choice but to make her leave, both for her own safety and for mine."

She turns to Frank. "Thank you for taking her in. I cannot begin to tell you how often I've thought of you, how many silent thank-yous I sent to you and your parents for taking in my daughter."

"It wasn't enough," Frank says, his voice heavy with guilt.

"It was everything," she says. "You gave her so much more than we ever had. Not the material things, but the emotional. You offered her peace, you allowed her to live in a warm, loving home. But I don't think you could have done anything to change the outcome. It was up to Rica to break the cycle. It takes a lot of strength not to fall into the same patterns, not to repeat what you've been exposed to all your life, and especially during your formative years. There's a reason abuse is generational."

Ronan untangles his hand from mine.

"Rica called me one night after Steve was born," Mrs. Donahue continues, either oblivious to or disregarding Ronan's obvious discomfort. "She told me she was in Montana, that she was living with your parents, Frank. She had nothing but wonderful things to say about them, told me how loving everyone was, how they helped her with the baby. She sounded happy, especially when she told me you two married." A smile flits across Mrs. Donahue's pencil-thin lips. "She said she wanted to go back to school when Steve was a little bit older, that she wanted to be a nurse," she says, then lowers her head. "We spoke every couple of weeks or so, and then one night only a few months later, she called me crying. She was pregnant again, and she wasn't sure she could do it. She spoke about terminating the pregnancy, told me she had researched it, but that the nearest clinic was two hours away."

Ronan shifts uncomfortably beside me, and my heart breaks for him. I know it's not the first time he's heard this. Rica made it clear that Ronan was a mistake, that she thought he should never have been born. That knowledge—to know that you were so deeply unwanted—what does that do to a soul?

"But of course, I talked her out of that. Terminating the pregnancy wasn't an option," Mrs. Donahue says with a huff like the thought alone wasn't even up for consideration. "We're Catholic. It's a cardinal sin."

So is abuse, I want to snap. *So is exile. But you lived with those.*

"So I tried to assure her, told her how strong she was. And I started speaking with Brian about allowing me to help Rica. I reminded him that Rica's boys were our legacy, the only descendants to the Donahue family tree since we had no idea where Cormac was, and Brian's brother never had children. Those things always mattered to Brian, and though it took a long time, he eventually relented. You know the rest, obviously," Mrs. Donahue says to Frank and motions around the living room. "We helped you two buy your home. I remember the first time I met Steve and Ronan. They were so little, absolutely precious." She nods with a smile, looking warmly at Steve, then Ronan, whose expression remains guarded. The only sign of distress I detect—and only because I know him so damn well—is in his hands, which are balled into fists on his thighs. But other than that, and the tension sharpening his already masculine angles, he's the personification of an impenetrable brick wall.

"When Rica called me from jail last year... when she told me what she had done..." Mrs. Donahue chokes. "I felt so helpless. I had let her down, and I had let you down," she says to Ronan. "I didn't see any signs of what she was doing to you the few times I got to see you. I didn't see any marks, and you didn't let on that anything was wrong. I wish Brian had permitted me to be more involved in your lives. Though I often wonder if things would have been different. I have a feeling it wouldn't have changed anything at all." A single tear carves a slow path down her cheek.

Penny moves from her spot next to Frank to retrieve a box of tissues, which she hands to Mrs. Donahue.

"Thank you." Mrs. Donahue takes a tissue and dabs her cheeks and eyes. "After Rica was arraigned, I told Brian I was bringing her home. It was the first time I truly stood up to him. He was already sick then; he didn't put up much of a fight. So I posted her bail, picked her up, and finally brought her home with me. At first she refused to speak about anything that had happened. I would ask her flat out if she did to you, Ronan, what Brian had done to her. I asked her over and over, and finally, a couple of months before the trial, it just broke out of her. All of it. We sat for hours—just Rica and I—as she cried and told me about all the times she had ever hurt you," she says to Ronan.

His jaw is clenched, brow furrowed as he listens to his grandmother. How I wish I was privy to his thoughts. I have a suspicion it's chaos in there, even while he exudes outward control. His mother did a hell of a job conditioning him.

To my left, Steve exhales deeply and leans forward to rest his elbows on his knees. "Did she tell you why she only ever hurt Ran, but never put a hand on me?" His face reflects pain.

Mrs. Donahue shrugs with pursed lips. "No. I don't think she understands it herself. I have my theories, however," she says with an air of self-importance.

"Oh yeah? And what are those theories?" Frank asks, Penny's hand in his.

"Well, I believe that when Brian kicked Rica out, it afforded Rica a fresh start. She was finally free. And not only that, but Frank, you brought her to Montana, to your parents, who I understand are wonderful, loving people. You two got married and Rica was happy. She spoke with so much hope whenever we talked, had plans for the future, was no longer afraid. Then she became pregnant with Ronan, and you, Frank, left for the Air Force. Rica felt trapped."

She turns her attention back to Ronan. "And then you were born. And you look so much like your mother and like Brian. Those eyes...

You have the same eyes, the same mouth, the same hair," she says with renewed incredulity. "You're so much like your mother, Ronan."

He flinches. A sharp, almost imperceptible hitch in his breath. I feel it more than hear it.

Clearly, Mrs. Donahue doesn't pick up on it. "Not just on the outside," she continues. "From what I've learned about you at the trial, you're a smart young man who was always trying to be better. Just like Rica. And I believe you striving for perfection, to please Rica, only made her angrier. You were never good enough to her because she was never good enough to Brian. I think deep down she believes she deserved everything she got and so, when she hurt you, she hurt that child version of herself."

My chest is tight with grief. Not just for Ronan, but for the unbearable weight of generational pain no child should have to carry. I was aware that Rica's father subjected her to pain, but this? If these musings are even slightly correct, then the tentacles of fear and violence spread far beyond a mother parenting the way she was parented. The pain Ronan was subjected to would be deeply rooted in something way more psychological than simply "history repeating itself."

I feel uneasy, but my quick glance at Ronan doesn't provide me with much insight as to how he's feeling. He's as unreadable as ever, and I don't know if his perceived composure makes me feel better or worse.

"It became clear to me that what Rica did wasn't because she was evil, but because of the trauma that was inflicted on her. Not just the physical, but the emotional neglect and abandonment... I knew there was emotional damage. So, we fired the public defender and hired the best defense attorney money could buy, and we had her psychologically evaluated. The attorney told us it was a risky move to put Rica's mental health at issue because the D.A. would be able to request his own assessment—and he did—but it was worth it," Mrs. Donahue says, nodding determinedly. "She was diagnosed with PTSD and bipolar disorder. It was a chance to keep her out of jail, or at least to get her sentence reduced."

"Well, it worked," Frank says.

"It did," Mrs. Donahue says with a small smile.

The smile doesn't belong on her face—not here, not now. It's as jarring as laughter at a funeral.

"You probably think I'm an awful human for working so hard to keep my daughter out of jail after everything she's done, but she's still my daughter. I failed to protect her growing up; I wasn't about to let her down again. I knew it was my fault that she was at this place in her life, and it was my obligation to help her. I hope you understand," Mrs. Donahue says to Ronan.

He still doesn't say anything, his expression unreadable.

"We pushed for a trial because we wanted the opportunity for the jury to hear about Rica's trauma, but then... then you went on the stand, Ronan, and after you were done testifying... it was so emotional to witness. Rica had told me what she put you through, how much she hurt you, but hearing it from you, seeing the video footage... I don't think I understood before then what she had truly done to you. It was like hearing my own daughter talk about what Brian did to her, except... except Brian was never quite like that. Rica, sad to say, stepped it up a level. The pain she inflicted on you didn't always seem motivated by anger at you specifically. She just took everything out on you. You were her punching bag. I hadn't realized how much anger she had inside her. I felt so horrible for putting you through that trial, for making you relive everything, for making you watch the moment your life almost ended. It was obvious how much it affected you, and how much the jury tuned in to you. You could see it on their faces—several were crying. When you were off the stand, Rica's lawyer thought the best option would be to take a plea and argue the sentence with the judge. He didn't think Rica stood a chance in hell with the jury after how compelling you were. So that's what happened; Rica and her lawyer decided not to put on their case and instead make their case to the judge for sentencing purposes," Mrs. Donahue says, and is followed by silence.

She expels a shaky breath, her voice softening. "My daughter did not set out to become like her father and his father before him. But she couldn't escape her past..." She trails off before she looks around the room. Just like that, her well-practiced smile returns to her lips. "When I saw her today, she was in good spirits. I try to see her every week, but Brian is not well and is getting worse, so it's harder to make the trip now. For a while now I've contemplated stopping by to speak with you, Ronan."

"Well, you did, so you can cross that off your list," Ronan says unemotionally.

"Ronan, you need to know that your mother really struggles with what she's done to you. She is exceptionally remorseful. I cannot tell you how much sleep she has lost, how often she has cried, how hard this has been on her," Mrs. Donahue says, her voice soft, warm.

Ronan's face reflects anything but warmth; his features are hard, his jaw and brow set. If I wasn't already silent, what Mrs. Donahue just said would leave me speechless. "Uh-huh," Ronan says, his voice barely audible.

"Maybe... maybe you could find it in your heart to forgive your mother," Mrs. Donahue says. "I think it can help you heal."

Never mind. *Now* I'm speechless. Actually, no, I'm furious. How dare she suggest that healing hinges on Ronan offering forgiveness. As if absolving his abuser is some kind of cure.

Clearly, Ronan has had enough. His jaw ticks once, twice. "Dad," he says, his eyes on Frank, who is completely focused on his youngest son.

"Yeah, bud?"

"I'm done with this conversation," Ronan says. He gets up from his spot next to me and walks out of the living room.

Frank stands and faces Mrs. Donahue. "Let me walk you out."

She nods curtly, then stands, adjusting her skirt and jacket before gripping her bag tightly. "Thank you for having me in your home, Frank," she says warmly, then turns her attention to Penny. "You look lovely. I hope you have a healthy and speedy delivery when the time comes." She turns to Steve and smiles. "I'm so glad I got to see you and your brother today. You're both exceptionally handsome young men."

Finally, she addresses me, her blue eyes intent as they lock on mine. "I'm glad to see Ronan has someone wonderful by his side. I hope your love for him can help him on his road to healing. And more than anything, I wish for you that he's strong enough..."

Ronan

Fuck.

Why can't my past just stay buried? Locked up tight, keys melted, tossed in the deepest, darkest part of the ocean. Is that too much to ask?

Clearly it is, because after barely six months of trying to build something for myself that wasn't founded on basic survival, the universe served me a steaming pile of remember-how-fucked-up-your-life-is.

I was still trying to decide whether to tell my family about Rashana when I exited my car and spotted Steve marching toward me. That expression on his face was telling as hell, and up went my walls. Solidly. Funny how it takes months of chiseling away at the bricks to break down that emotional barrier, and only seconds to put them right back up. It's like muscle memory.

I've never been close to my maternal grandparents, but that didn't stop my grandmother from unloading decades of unprocessed trauma in the exact room where my own was inflicted. I knew about my mom's past to a very limited extent, knew that my grandfather hit her and her brother. But I never realized how far up the Donahue family tree it went, was never aware that he also hit my grandmother. It was a hell of a lot to take in. I wasn't prepared for this, and even less so for the moment my grandmother urged me to forgive my mother. The irony hit hard—her plea for forgiveness delivered in the same spot my mother screamed at me to beg her to kill me, feet from where I lay gasping for air while she shattered my ribs, ruptured my spleen, and broke twenty-six bones in my body.

I felt the rage rising within me like a tide, the edges of my mind buzzing with a restless, crackling energy, and I knew I needed to step away, for me and for everyone else.

That rage, that anger—that's new, and it's not something I'm willing to explore, despite Doctor Seivert's insistence.

My dad tried to convince me to stay and eat dinner with them after he ushered my grandmother out of the house. But I didn't stay. I really needed to get to work, but I also didn't feel like sticking around and discussing what the hell just happened with my family and Cat. It's still something I struggle with—talking about things that are uncomfortable or painful. I tend to swallow pain. Bottle it up. Wrap it up into a nice, neat package, then lock that shit away deep, deep inside me.

I drove straight to Murphy's, hands on the steering wheel, breathing slow. Like nothing had happened. Like I hadn't just watched my past drag itself back to life like the undead.

***

"Someone had a shit day," Shane says as soon as I walk into Murphy's and meet him in the office behind the bar. "And that someone's you, judging by that look on your face."

I shrug off my jacket. "It actually started out pretty good, but then it kind of took a turn." I dig my wallet and keys out of my jeans and shove them into the jacket pockets.

"What happened?" he asks, blue eyes narrowed as if he can penetrate my mind. Not that he needs to. He picks up on everything: tone, posture, breathing. We've known each other too long for me to fake it around him.

After losing his brother and watching what my mom did to me, Shane doesn't just read people, he scans them. Especially me. It's both comforting and claustrophobic. He's an amazing friend, but he can be overbearing. I have to remind him to stay in his lane when he gets preachy or tries to get me to open up about shit I'm not in a place to talk about.

"My grandmother decided to pay me a visit," I say simply, but Shane only looks at me confused. "My mom's mom."

"Oh, shit. Why?"

"She said she wanted to apologize, and for me to understand why my mom enjoyed beating the living shit out of me. So she spent an hour going on and on about how my grandfather was an abusive asshole, how his father was an abusive asshole, and probably his father, and so on. And then she talked about how my mom wasn't able to break the cycle and how hard that was to do when you grew up with violence and never knew any different."

Two lines appear between his brows. "Fuck, Ran."

I exhale deeply. "Yeah. It was a real fucking pep talk."

Shane winces. "Oh, yeah. Inspirational. She just decided to stop by to tell you these things?"

"Well, I guess she was 'in the area'"—I make air quotes—"because she visited my mom in prison." I can't help the rueful chuckle that escapes my mouth. "I swear, Shane, sometimes I wonder about my life."

"You do know that you're nothing like them, right? You're nothing like your mom or your grandfather," he says, holding eye contact, his hand on my left arm.

"Sure." This is as much as I want to talk about this bullshit right now, and probably ever. "Anyway, I didn't really get the chance to eat. Do you mind if I scarf down a sandwich before I get going?"

I can tell he feels the need to talk about my grandmother's visit some more, but he doesn't push it. "Yeah, sure."

I give him a nod, then walk out of the office.

Luckily it's busy tonight, and by the time Shane is ready to leave and spend his evening with Tori, my mood has lightened significantly. I'm actually pretty impressed at my ability to suppress heavy shit.

"Is Cat staying over tonight?" Shane asks, pulling the hood of his jacket over his strawberry-blond hair.

"No, I think she's spending the night at her house." I push a tray of drained whiskey glasses across the bar counter and toward Jack, who snatches them right up and puts them in the sink.

"So Tori and I might be able to get some sleep tonight," Shane says with a suggestive grin.

"What are you talking about?"

Shane's grin widens. "Well, you know, Cat wasn't exactly quiet this morning."

I guess we're doing this. "You're one to talk. I've heard Tori beg you to 'go harder, Daddy' more times than I can count," I say with a wicked grin, imitating Tori's voice.

Shane shrugs, unbothered. "She likes what she likes."

I chuckle. "Yeah, well, how about you don't comment on Cat enjoying herself and I won't mention Tori? Especially not the daddy stuff."

"Deal." He laughs, then claps me on my shoulder. "I'll see you at home."

Only ten minutes later, the front doors to Murphy's open and my brother walks in with Vada, Zack, and Summer, along with some guy I've never met. But my eyes are instantly drawn to Cat, who has the ability to make my entire world zoom in on her.

"Holy shit," I laugh when I approach them.

"Ran!" Vada throws her arms around my neck. I bend to hug her back. "I've missed you so much. I've missed everyone so much!" She squeals and lets go of me. "Ran, this is my boyfriend, Brady," Vada says with a huge, mushy smile on her face.

I throw the tiniest glance at my brother. Steve and Vada dated for almost two years before they broke things off earlier this year. But Steve appears unaffected by Vada's new beau, which is further confirmation that Steve has someone in his life. I've been suspicious for a few weeks now, but he's been tightlipped. I will get it out of him sooner or later.

I shake Brady's hand. "Hey, what's up, man. I'm Ronan."

"Nice to meet you," he says.

I let go of his hand, then hug Summer and Zack in turn, before finally pulling Cat into my arms and softly kissing her lips. She smells delicious and tastes even better. God, this girl is everything.

"How are you guys?" I'm elated to see everyone here. It's been months since we've all been together.

Zack smiles widely. "Really good, man. Summer and I are just here over Thanksgiving; we fly back to L.A. on Sunday," he says, holding Summer's hand. Summer followed Zack to California, though she attends USC while Zack is at UCLA, still in pursuit of becoming a director.

I sigh. "Man, Shane just left." I know he'd love to hang out with everyone, too.

"We actually ran into him in the parking lot," Steve says. "He just went to pick up Tori and then he'll be back. We figured we'd hang out here and watch you work. Just like old times." Steve chuckles, nudging me with his elbow.

I nod appreciatively. "Works for me."

I look around Murphy's, take Cat's hand into mine, then lead everyone to a large table. They begin throwing food and beverage orders at me, making me smile. I love how familiar this feels. By the time I return to serve their food, Shane and Tori have joined the party.

I've always loved having Cat, my brother, and my friends around me while I work, giving me the opportunity to stop and chat with them and get my fill of the people I need most in my life. Honestly, I don't think I would've made it through any of it without them. They were there when I was in the hospital fighting for my life, attended every day of that god damn trial earlier this year, and have been by my side—steady as rocks—every day since then, even over a distance. I know I can always count of them when the going gets rough. In fact, I'm pretty sure Shane would help me bury a body while my brother gave me an alibi.

The evening passes quickly with how busy Murphy's is, and I don't have as much opportunity to stop by my friends' table as I'd like, but it's nonetheless calming to have them here with me.

***

I'm making my rounds through the place, checking on patrons not only in my table section but around the pub, when I notice Cat standing at the bar counter. She's chatting with Jack when some dude approaches, his eyes dragging up her long legs, lingering on her ass, her bare midriff, then her chest, before finally reaching that beautiful face framed by her long, blonde hair. If she wasn't already mine and I'd spotted her here at Murphy's, I'd be prowling toward her exactly like that dude is doing.

I know Cat can handle herself, as became evident when she put Drew in his place last February when he made a not-so-subtle move on her while I was in Montana. I heard from Shane that Cat broke Drew's nose when he tried to kiss her even though she had made it clear that she wasn't interested.

Still, I move toward her just to make sure boundaries don't get crossed. I recognize the guy—he's in my English class at Columbia and actually pretty nice. He notices me and nods his head in my direction, causing Cat to look over and smile at me.

I come to a stop next to her.

"Ronan, what's up?" the guy asks.

"Not much, Brandon. How about you?"

"Not much. Just hanging out with some friends." He nods in the direction of a table occupied by a group of five guys, who I also recognize. "You work here?" he asks, his eyes on my black long-sleeve with the Murphy's logo printed on my chest.

"Yeah."

"Huh, good to know. Might need to make this place our regular spot. The food is bomb here" — Brandon nods approvingly—"and so are the girls," he adds with a smile at Cat.

Smooth.

I grin. "This one's kind of impossible not to look at, huh?" I say with an admiring glance at Cat, who's so god damn sexy in a pair of low-rise, ripped jeans and an emerald-green, cropped sweater that shows off her tight stomach and that belly button I want to kiss so damn badly. I'm honestly shocked there's not a line of guys waiting their turn to hit on Cat right now. I might have to beg her to stay the night with me instead of at her parents'. I'm greedy when it comes to her. I miss her in my sleep, even while she lies right next to me. And I detest waking up without her, especially now that I've gotten a taste for having her by my side at night.

Brandon nods like he's very much in agreement with my statement. I recognize that look in his eyes—like he's about to sink his teeth into a perfectly cooked piece of meat. I smile to myself, knowing I'm about to pop his bubble.

"Brandon, this is my girlfriend, Cat." I move my left hand to her bare lower back, grazing her soft skin.

Disappointment crosses his bearded face. Cat smiles at him, the faint pink hue in her cheeks making her hazel eyes pop.

"That's your girlfriend?" he asks incredulously.

I get it, man, I'm incredulous, too, that this goddess chose me.

I nod, smiling, as Cat leans back to rest her head against my shoulder.

"Yeah," I say with a chuckle at the envy lining his brow. "I'm a lucky son of a bitch, right?"

"Hell yes you are," Brandon says, making Cat blush. Fuck, I love it when she blushes like that. The way the heat creeps up her neck to her cheeks, flushing even her lips. It's sexy as hell. "And on that note, I'm going to just grab my drink here and go back to my table," he chuckles. "I'll see you later, Ronan. It was nice to meet you, Cat." He leaves me standing with the most beautiful girl in this world.

"Hey there," I say when she turns to face me, the flush ebbing from her cheeks. I glide my right hand to meet my left on her lower back and pull her toward me to kiss her forehead.

"Hey there," she giggles. "Thank you for rescuing me from evil guys who want to talk to me."

"Don't get me wrong, baby. I know you don't need rescuing. You're a badass."

"You just want to mark your territory. I get it," she laughs.

"I consider it to be more of a gentle advisory to guys to keep their hands off you. Just trying to keep the evening free of bar brawls and broken jaws," I say with a grin. "Did you need anything from me?" Obviously, she left our friends and came to the bar for a reason.

Her expression turns serious as she analyzes my face. "I just wanted to check if you're okay. We didn't really get a chance to talk before you left for work. And I know what your grandma said rattled me, so I can't imagine it was easy for you to sit through that."

Walls. Up they go. "I'm fine."

Cat's face instantly sours. "I don't like it when you say that."

I chuckle even though I'm not amused. "Why?"

"Because it's evasive, and I've known you long enough to know that you usually say you're fine when you're not actually fine."

Jesus Christ, this girl knows me too well.

"Really, baby, I'm okay," I say, turning serious. I mean, I'm not really, but I'm even less willing to get into it with her right now. I'd just as soon forget about my grandmother's visit, because thinking about it—contemplating the things she said, the implications of it all—will to take me down a rabbit hole that I have absolutely no desire to go down.

Cat studies me for a long moment, her delicate, usually soft features tight, and I can tell she's unconvinced. "Ran, you know you can talk to me."

"Yes, I know, baby." I tug her toward me, then move my mouth to hers. But she resists me, taking a decisive step back.

My brow creases at the distance.

"Don't try to distract me, Ran," she says, her words laced with frustration. "I don't want you to bottle this up like you do everything that's uncomfortable or painful."

"Cat, please don't push this right now. This is neither the time nor the place."

Her lips press into a thin line, her nostrils flaring. "Fine. But be honest with me, Ronan. Are you alright?" she asks, her eyes locked on mine. It's startling as hell when she calls me by my actual name instead of "Ran" or "sweet boy," the latter of which always makes my heart skip a beat; only she calls me that.

The deepest exhale leaves my chest. "I'm not really sure, baby." I can admit that much. "It was a lot to take in, and I haven't really had a chance to process it. But right now, in this moment, I'm alright. I promise." I hold her gaze, determined to ease her worry. She studies me a moment longer and it makes my lips tug into a smile. "I love you," I say. "And I love how concerned you are. Now, go and spend time with our friends."

She narrows her eyes, her bottom lip pulled between her teeth while she taps her foot on the wooden floorboards.

She knows not to press this issue right now, knows that any further prodding will result in me shutting down. It's a bad habit of mine, one I'm still working on, but it's a slow and rather aggravating process.

"Okay," she breathes. I can tell she isn't satisfied with the end of this conversation, but she allows me to kiss her before she rejoins our friends.

I feel Cat's eyes on me throughout the evening, boring into me from across the crowded restaurant like she's aiming a laser at me. I know she's worried. We've been through so much together, and I know how much I put her through during our year and a half together. But there's still so much I don't understand about myself, so much I don't know. I know it's there—the darkness, the shadows. I can feel it simmering behind some steel trapdoor hidden in my subconscious, hot to the touch and locked tight. I don't know what's behind it, and I'm scared to find out. But it's there. Always.

***

"Hey, sit down and take a load off. I'm gonna cover you for fifteen minutes," Shane says later in the evening. Murphy's has only gotten busier, and I haven't had a chance to so much as take a piss.

"You don't have to do that, man. You're off the clock," I say, chuckling.

"I know, but since I'm here I might as well give you a break. I know you don't usually get to take them when you're running shit at night," he says, then veers off toward two of our newer waiters who are currently more interested in each other than the tables they're supposed to be managing. The second they see Shane approach with what I can only imagine is his best boss face, they scatter.

"So, how about a nice, killer workout tomorrow morning?" Zack pipes up the moment I'm within earshot of the table. I slide into a chair next to Cat, who smiles at me before resting her left hand on my right leg underneath the table. "Just us guys. Like old times," Zack adds with a grin.

"We were thinking eight or so," Steve says. "Shane said he's down."

I shrug, then reach for Cat's glass of water and drain half of it in one gulp. "Sure." I nod at Zack and the small tripod set up at the end of the table. "I see you're still going strong with filming."

"Hell yes." Zack's eyes light up. "I'm never not filming."

"I've been meaning to ask about that, but I didn't want to be rude," Brady chimes in, his arm draped over Vada's shoulder. He's a shorter guy, clean-shaven face, with thick dark brown hair and eyes to match. If I had to guess, I'd say he's of Armenian descent. "Why are you always filming?"

I turn serious. "Oh, man, I can't believe Vada hasn't told you. We don't really like to talk about it because it makes him feel like shit, but Zack suffers from short-term memory loss."

Brady turns pale as he looks from me to Zack to Vada.

Vada nods solemnly, like she's been asked to speak at a memorial service. "Yeah, he was born that way. My brother has real trouble finding *things*."

"Oh, yeah," Cat says sweetly. "Did you ever end up finding it?"

I beam at her proudly.

"God, fuck off, you guys," Zack gripes loudly. Everyone busts up laughing. "I don't have short-term memory loss," he says to Brady, who looks like he just got released from a hostage situation. "I started filming everything when I was like fifteen. Especially when it was all of us together."

He leans forward slightly. "I actually made an admission movie instead of writing an essay for UCLA."

Brady blinks. "No shit?"

"Yeah. It was basically a short documentary about us," he says, looking around the table. "Growing up together. The dumb stuff, the good stuff. I figured if I was gonna ask a school to believe in me, they should see what made me."

Brady's body sags with relief. "Right. Vada told me you wanted to break into the film industry."

"Yep. I've been filming for three years now. I've captured some pretty amazing stuff so far; some really, really cool moments."

"So, Brady," I say, pivoting the conversation. "How long have you and Vada been seeing each other?"

"A couple of months now," he says. Vada looks at him with a mushy expression.

"Are you from New York?" I ask. I notice Cat's hand gliding an inch up and down my thigh. I can tell it's an unconscious caress, but I love it. Cat's touch is unlike anything else.

"No, I'm from Philly. My parents are out of the country for a few weeks, and Vada invited me to spend Thanksgiving with her family," he says, then looks around the table. "She didn't tell me that this apparently included seven of her closest friends," he chuckles. "I've been learning that you all go back to kindergarten or something. That's so fucking cool. I'm still trying to get everyone straight, though. You're Steve's brother, right? But you live with Shane, who's your best friend. And Cat is your girlfriend, and Vada's brother is your brother's best friend?"

Tori giggles. "Confusing, right?"

"Spot on," I say, laughing. "You coming to the gym with us in the morning?"

"Yeah, sure, if that's cool with you guys?"

"Definitely," Zack says, just as Shane returns to the table.

"Well, Ran, I tried," he says with a smirk. "But there's a table of four pretty drunk girls and they're insisting that you come take another round of drink orders."

Cat's hand glides higher on my thigh—casual, confident—until she cups my dick through my jeans and gives it a sensual squeeze.

I look at her while she smiles, her eyes donning the most seductive little gleam. "Don't forget who you belong to," she says quietly.

"Never," I say, planting a kiss on her perfect lips, and get up from the table to get back to work.

Thursday, November 24th

Ronan

I'm fucking pissed. Just fucking boiling with anger. Fuck, anger is not the right word. Rage, fury, wrath. I'm live-wire electricity. It's blinding, the heat of it rushing through my veins, adrenaline surging and fortifying my body, preparing for... I don't even know. I have no idea what the hell set me off, but I feel my entire body tense, muscles wound so tight they hurt. My fists clench by my sides and my fingernails pierce the palms of my hands, splitting the skin open.

I don't think I've ever felt this way. I can't fucking take it anymore. I need to let it out.

And then I'm swinging.

My fist crashes into her face. Again. And again. Relentless. I hear bones breaking, feel her supple skin tear open when my knuckles connect with her body. I don't let up. Even when the faceless person drops to the floor, begging me to stop, my blows continue mercilessly, violently. I am consumed by rage, by fear, by pain.

"Stop, please," Cat whimpers, her beautiful face almost unrecognizable—swollen, bloodied—her voice barely audible.

The world stops, the realization of what I've done draining my heart of all life. *No.*

The fog of wrath clouding my mind clears and I become aware of my surroundings—the living room in my dad's house. The lighting is strange, though. Why is it so fucking dark? Jesus, there's glass everywhere. Tiny, razor-sharp shards glint across the wooden floor, and Cat's lying in the middle of it, on the old rug. I recognize that rug. It's stained with blood—so much fucking blood. It's dried into the fibers, black, like tar. But wait, that rug got thrown out a long time ago. Why the hell is it here? Why the fuck is Cat here? What the hell happened?

"Please don't hurt me, sweet boy," Cat cries.

I jerk awake, my breathing out of control, my heart stumbling in my chest, desperate to find a steady rhythm. My skin is clammy, sweaty, despite the coolness in my room. Holy fuck. I had a nightmare. A nightmare so sickening that I roll out of bed with a groan, rush out of my room and into the pitch-black bathroom where I drop to my knees in front of the toilet and get violently sick.

Nightmares are nothing new. I started having them a couple of weeks after waking up in the hospital over a year ago. They were bad for a while—so bad that I'd fight going to sleep. But they had become less frequent, less vivid. I haven't had one in over a month now.

Things have been going pretty smoothly. So smoothly, in fact, that I broached the subject of taking a break from my therapy sessions with Doctor Seivert. We had tapered our sessions down to once a week after the trial. We ramped back up briefly in August, around the anniversary of the last time my mom hurt me, when I was triggered and sleepless again. But by mid-September, I'd leveled out. Three weeks ago, Doctor Seivert agreed to let me try just living life for a while. She assured me that the moment I felt I needed her again, she was only a phone call away.

I didn't expect things to take a turn so damn quickly.

In my nightmares, I'm always on the floor with my mother standing over me, her face contorted in anger as she beats and kicks the life out of me. But this? This was different. This was *me*. And holy fucking shit, it's freaking me the fuck out.

I stay hunched over the toilet, my forearms draped over the cool porcelain, my clammy forehead resting against my arms. And I try to breathe. I know it was just a dream, but it was so vivid, so fucking real. I swear I could feel the warmth of Cat's soft skin as I hammered my fist into her perfect face, heard the cartilage of her nose as I broke it. *What the fuck is wrong with me?*

"Ran, are you okay?" Shane asks, standing in the doorway to the bathroom. His voice is raspy, thick with sleep.

"Yeah," I groan.

"Are you coming down with something?"

"No." I push myself up to stand, then walk to the sink and grab my toothbrush. I hate the taste of vomit in my mouth.

"Are you sure?"

"Yeah." I squeeze some toothpaste onto my toothbrush. My hands tremble with the adrenaline that horrific dream dumped into my system. I turn to him, my jaw tense. I'm completely shaken, and though my instinct is to push it deep down inside me, I decide to confide in my best friend. "I had a nightmare."

Since moving in with Shane, I've had them only a few times, though Shane did have to wake me twice, so he knows what it is I'm dealing with.

"You haven't had one in a while," he says, watching me.

"Yeah. And this one was different. Shane"—I inhale a shaky breath—"I dreamed I was beating the shit out of Cat." The nausea rolls back through me just saying it. I stare at the floor, ashamed, like I actually laid a hand on her.

"What?"

"Yeah. God, what the hell is wrong with me?" I groan, running my right hand roughly over my face.

"Wait, so, what happened in your dream?" He moves into the bathroom and sits on the bathtub ledge.

"I have no fucking clue. I just remember being so angry and then I just started hitting her. I didn't even know it was Cat until she begged me to stop. And then she was on the floor in my dad's house, lying in broken glass on that fucking rug," I choke out, my head spinning. "Fuck, Shane, I feel like I'm losing my mind."

"Okay, deep breaths, Ran." He stands and grips my shoulders, grounding me. Cat does this, too—touches me when I'm spiraling. Shane picked it up somewhere along the way. It helps. It always helps.

"First of all, it was just a dream. It was a fucking nightmare. I bet it was because of whatever the fuck your grandmother told you yesterday. It's probably just your subconscious trying to work through it. I know for a fact that you would never lay a hand on Cat," he says intently, his eyes locked on mine. "You would never, ever hurt her. It was just a dream, Ran. Just a terrible fucking dream."

"But what if I—"

"You wouldn't," he says. "You won't, Ran. I know that like I know that the sun will set tonight and will rise again tomorrow. You're nothing like your mother or your grandfather."

He holds my gaze.

"I see the way you look at Cat, how you touch her, how you talk to her. There's not a chance in hell that you'd ever hurt her," he says. "This dream was just a manifestation of your fears, but it means absolutely nothing."

God, I want to believe him. I want it so badly.

He studies me for a moment longer, then gives me a nod. "You know what you need? Heavy weights. Go, get ready. We're heading to the gym now. I'm going to text the guys that we're leaving. They can meet us there whenever."

"Okay," I say, and start brushing my teeth while Shane walks back to his room. I glance at my watch. It's barely six-thirty. I got a whopping three hours of sleep. But Shane's right, I need to get this damn dream out of my head, out of my body, out of my system.

Cat

As I had expected, my mom is absolutely frantic today. This is a pattern of hers. My mom loves the holidays—all of them—and she loves the opportunity to get everyone together, to be surrounded by family and friends. Unfortunately, she also seems to forget how stressed she gets. She wants everything to be perfect—even though nobody cares whether things are perfect; they're usually just happy to be together. She worries about the cleanliness of the house while trying to cook way too much food that she believes should live up to the creations of a Michelin-star chef. It would be funny if her frenzy wasn't so contagious.

So I got up early this morning, even though I was bone tired after getting to bed so late last night. I honestly haven't stayed at Murphy's until Ronan closed since the beginning of September, since everyone went off to college. Last night was the first time in about three months that we were all together. My heart was full, even though I was worried about Ronan after his grandmother's unannounced visit yesterday afternoon.

I was so rattled by the things she said, and so were Steve, Frank, and Penny. Ronan, being who he is, bolted as soon as his grandmother left. He did what he always does when faced with anything about his past—he runs from it, too afraid, too traumatized to sit with it. I wish he'd talk to me. I wish he'd trust me with the thoughts in his head. Haven't I earned that by now?

My dad had the wherewithal to take my younger siblings to my grandparents' house for a few hours while my mom cooked and I cleaned. It certainly helped my mom's stress levels. When two o'clock rolls around and my dad returns with my siblings and his parents in tow, my mom cheerfully greets them.

My mom's parents show up half an hour later, and Frank, Penny, and Steve join us a mere ten minutes after that.

"Where's Ran?" I ask Steve after he introduces himself to my grandparents and comments on how incredible my mom's food smells. She turned beet red at the compliment. That's definitely a characteristic I get from her; I blush like nobody's business. I'd always hated it until I met Ronan, who always tells me how much he loves how easily I blush. It's incredible how you can hate something about yourself, and then the right person comes along, calls it lovely, and suddenly it's not so bad anymore.

"He's on his way." Steve lowers his voice. "Did you get a chance to talk to him about... yesterday?"

"Just briefly at Murphy's. He said he was 'fine,'" I say, and frown.

Steve sighs. "Ah, shit."

"Yeah, I know. I told him I needed an honest answer, and he said he hadn't had a chance to process everything. But he said he really was okay at the moment, so I left it at that. I figure there's no point in pushing him. He'll either talk about it or he won't. It's so frustrating, Stevie." I groan. "Why doesn't he trust me?"

Steve just shakes his head. "I don't know. I don't think it has anything to do with trust. And he probably really hasn't had a chance to process everything. I'm honestly not even really sure what the hell the point of her visit was..."

"To apologize."

"That's what she said, but did you hear an apology in there?"

I let my mind return to yesterday's conversation and realize Steve's right. All Mrs. Donahue did was give a speech about why her daughter did what she did and why she should be forgiven. In a way, it felt like Mrs. Donahue was seeking forgiveness, too. No wonder it left such a bad taste in my mouth. Now I understand why I felt so put off. All she really did was unburden herself. She didn't offer Ronan any comfort, or a way forward. She came, she dumped, she left.

I shake my head.

"He's been doing better, though, so let's just give him some time," Steve says, just as there's a knock on the front door.

My heart trips over itself when I open the door for Ronan. Of course, that guy is gorgeous as ever. The two-day-old stubble on his chin and cheeks is rough against my palms when I put my hands on his face, pull him down to me, and kiss him deeply. That elicits a quiet moan from him, and I pull back to look into his bright green eyes.

"Hi, baby," he says, his voice husky. For one suspended second, everything stops—my mom's chaos, the tension in my chest, even the questions I'd planned to ask.

"Hey, sweet boy." I smile and take a step back to allow him entrance to the house. "How are you?"

"A little tired, to be honest." I'm grateful he doesn't give me his usual deflection.

He shrugs off his jacket. I take it from him. "How was your workout this morning?"

"Good, but exhausting." There are indeed dark shadows under his eyes. "I was hoping to squeeze in a nap before heading over here but the damn washer in our apartment building went out, so I had to take all my crap to the laundromat down the street."

"You should have just brought it with you," I say, tipping my head up to kiss his soft lips again.

"Oh, yeah, I'm sure your parents would've loved that." He chuckles. "Hey, Bobby, mind if I throw my dirty boxers in your washer while I eat your wife's food and then take your daughter home with me, where I will very likely ravage her hot body?"

I laugh at the image. Ronan takes my hand, pressing my palm to his mouth softly. "You're so beautiful, Cat," he says with such intensity, it turns my skin to fire.

"What just made you say that?" I ask, my voice an octave higher.

He shakes his head. "I don't know. I just had this overwhelming need to tell you. I love you so much, baby."

I kiss him again, parting my lips, and giving Ronan permission to deepen the kiss. He does, sweeping his tongue slowly over mine as he lays claim to my mouth. The rest of my body responds instinctively and instantaneously, flooding me with moist heat that collects deep in my core. *Oh, yep, I'm definitely going home with him tonight.*

We reluctantly break apart, then I lead the way into the living room. Ronan politely greets my mom—who hugs Ronan tightly—then my dad, whose reception of him is much less heartfelt. Then Ronan introduces himself to my grandparents, all four of whom smile warmly at him. He looks so handsome in a pair of light-blue jeans and a gray crew neck sweater.

"Hey buddy," Frank says to his youngest son with a meaningful look. "You alright?"

"Yeah, fine," Ronan says with a nod. His smile doesn't quite reach his eyes. I exchange a brief glance with Steve before my grandparents engage the Soult guys in conversation.

We gather at the table an hour later. After my grandfather insists on saying grace, we dig into the food.

"So Penny dear, may I ask when your due date is?" my grandmother asks Penny, who already looks like she's about to pop. The fact that she's carrying twins certainly adds to her looking much farther along than she actually is.

"February sixteenth, but we're unlikely to make it that far," she says with a smile at Frank. "We're having twins, so the doctor said he'll be happy if we make it to thirty-six weeks. But to be honest, I'm ready to have these boys now," Penny laughs.

"You'll have to at least make it to your baby shower," my mom chimes in. She's been planning Penny's Christmas-themed baby shower for weeks now.

"Oh, how exciting," my grandmother chirps. "Babies are such a joy. You both will certainly have your hands full with two, but that just means so much more love. Do you have a good village?"

Penny and Frank look at each other with some confusion.

My grandmother laughs. "Family and friends to help you. Unfortunately, Jen and Bobby had moved away to North Carolina when they had Cat, so Gerry and I weren't around much to help them. Although I did go to stay with Jen for about a month after Cat was first born so I could help out."

"Yes, my parents are close. Just across the bridge, actually. Frank's parents live in Montana, but Ran is here," Penny says with a wink at Ronan.

Ronan raises an eyebrow at her. "I'm not really sure how much help you think I'll be," he says with my favorite half-smile. "I don't know the first thing about babies."

"We'll teach you," Frank chuckles.

Ronan's phone starts to buzz in his pocket. He pulls it out and takes a glance at the screen, his eyebrows creasing. "Sorry, I have to take this really quick. I'm just going to step outside," he says to no one in particular, then leaves and heads out the front door, closing it behind him.

"Not very polite to take a call right in the middle of Thanksgiving dinner," my dad mutters.

I throw him a stern look, while my mom elbows him in the ribs. My dad's dislike for Ronan has no rhyme or reason other than the fact that Ronan is my boyfriend, especially considering how fond my dad is of Frank.

"So, do you have your nursery all set up?" my other grandmother asks.

Penny nods, rubbing her tummy lovingly. "Mostly. Frank just needs to put together the cribs and then we're pretty much set."

"Good call on turning Ran's room into the nursery instead of mine, by the way," Steve says with a grin.

"Yeah, we figured it made sense since you'd need your room when you come to visit," Frank says.

"Plus, the light in Ran's room is so nice," Penny chimes in. "It has windows facing north and east; the morning light is just so beautiful in there."

"And it helped that Ran's room was already mostly empty. It was really just his bed and desk left," Frank says.

It's true. Ronan obviously took most of his possessions with him when he moved in with Shane, which wasn't too much to begin with—just his clothes and books. He even left his hockey gear behind.

The chat about babies continues for a while, and I begin to wonder about Ronan when he still hasn't returned to the dinner table fifteen minutes later. I excuse myself to go to the bathroom, and I look out the doorway window. I spot Ronan—his phone still to his ear—pacing the short walkway.

"Who's he talking to?" Steve asks me in a quiet voice when I return to the dinner table. He obviously figured I was checking on Ronan.

I shrug. "How did he seem to you this morning at the gym?"

He looks at me sheepishly. "I actually hadn't seen Ran yet today; I didn't go to the gym."

"Too tired?" I ask with a giggle.

Steve nods. "Yeah. When Shane texted us at like six-thirty that he and Ran were heading out, I just looked at my phone, shoved it under my pillow, and rolled over to sleep some more," he chuckles.

"Six-thirty? What happened to eight?"

"No idea. Maybe they were up and just wanted to get it done."

I hear the front door open, then close before Ronan walks back into the dining room. I watch him as he retakes his seat between Steve and me.

"Everything alright?" Steve asks him before I get the chance.

"Yep, all good," he says. Steve and I exchange another look. Ronan notices. "Jesus, guys. I'm fine!" he says quietly but forcefully. "Can you both stop acting like I'm a wounded animal?"

"Who were you talking to for the last half hour?" Steve asks in a hushed tone.

Ronan narrows his eyes at his brother. "My other girlfriend," he says dryly.

"Oh, Kylie?" Steve asks, playing along.

"No, Violet," Ronan whispers back without missing a beat.

"Oh, right, I forgot about her," Steve chuckles.

I've never heard either name, so I assume this is random banter between the brothers and there neither is nor ever was a Kylie or a Violet. Still, I'm not amused. I put my fork and knife down. "Not funny," I say, crossing my arms in front of my chest.

Ronan wraps his arm around me and pulls me against him. "You know I only want you, baby. Only ever you."

We get swept up in conversation again when my grandparents ask about school and classes, inquiring not only as to my progress, but

Steve's and Ronan's college experience as well. I don't get the chance to talk privately with Ronan until later in the evening.

To my dad's very obvious dismay, I inform my parents that I'll be spending the night at Ronan's place. I do offer to spend the night at home if my dad lets Ronan stay with me, but he predictably doesn't agree. Not that I could have convinced Ronan to stay; I think the thought of spending the night with me at my parents' house when my dad is home is as uncomfortable for Ronan as it is for my dad.

"So, how is the 'processing' going?" I cautiously ask when Ronan slides into the driver's seat of his Mustang, ready to take us back to his apartment.

He glances at me only briefly, but it's enough to let me know I hit a nerve. He doesn't want to talk about his grandmother. Figures.

"It's not," he says, looking intently at the road ahead of him.

I keep my eyes locked on him. "Are you doing okay? I really w—"

His jaw flexes. "Baby, please. I don't want to do this right now."

"When then, Ran? You never want to talk to me. It... Why won't you talk to me? Why don't you trust me?"

"I do trust you." He still doesn't look at me, but I can clearly see his puckered brow and the tension in his jaw with the streetlights illuminating the car's interior.

"Not with the thoughts in your head. God, Ran, I was there yesterday. I heard what your grandmother said. I felt how tense you were. I'm in this with you, don't you understand that? Or am I just a pretty body to you?"

"Of course not," he says, but an infuriating smile tugs at his lips. "I mean, it *is* a really nice body. One I plan on taking good care of in about half an hour."

I groan loudly, throwing my hands in the air. "You're always so god damn evasive."

"What do you want me to say, Cat? Because I'm not going to have a fucking therapy session right now."

His sharp words cut into me like razor blades. He never talks to me like this. It hurts. And not only that, it also bolsters my belief that his grandmother's visit affected him deeply.

I ignore the piercing pain in my heart and take a shaky breath. "I don't know, just anything. Anything other than just 'fine.' Tell me something that matters. Something that's real."

"I love you," he says with an earnestness that causes my anger at him to teeter. But no, I won't let him keep placating me.

"I know that," I say quietly. The defeat, the frustration at his stubborn refusal to open up to me causes the back of my eyes to sting with tears like it has so many times these past few months.

I understand that the trauma Ronan endured requires time—lots and lots of time—to heal from. But his unwillingness to share that pain with me feels, to a very real extent, personal. Everyone I talk to about this tells me that trust isn't the issue, but I can't agree with that. Of course it's trust. Trust that I'll be there no matter what he divulges, trust that I won't cut and run. It's the foundation of any relationship—the ability to share the deep, the dark, the painful, the good, the bad, the unforgivable. And clearly he doesn't trust me with that. There's a huge, gaping ravine of things I don't know about Ronan. And it's been like that from the moment we met. At first he hid the abuse, then he hid the aftermath of his trauma until it was almost too late, until we almost lost him, and now he's hiding... something.

"Tell me something I *don't* know. *Please.*"

He looks over at me, holding my gaze for a beat longer than is probably safe while driving. He exhales deeply. "I was talking to Doctor Seivert. At dinner. That was Doctor Seivert on the phone."

"Oh." Relief surges through me. I may have gone the ninety, but he still came the ten. Something is better than nothing. For now. I study his gorgeous profile as he navigates the road. "About what your grandma said yesterday?"

"Yeah, that and..." His jaw ticks. "And the nightmare I had last night," he says, avoiding eye contact.

I knit my eyebrows at his hesitation. I know about his nightmares; I've witnessed them a few times. He'll toss and turn, talk in his sleep, then startle awake, his chest and forehead clammy, heart pounding until he's able to focus on his surroundings and realize it was just a dream. I remember the first time I had to wake him from one and finally realized just how bad they were. It was disconcerting to see him in so much distress until he was able to come out of it. But he hasn't had one in a few weeks.

"I tried to get in touch with her earlier today, but she only called me back during dinner," he says.

The fact that Ronan reached out to his therapist on Thanksgiving when he hadn't seen her in a month gives me pause. My mom's a psychiatrist who works with victims of severe trauma. That means, aside from her regular office hours, she's always on-call and available to her patients when they find themselves in crisis. It must have been a bad nightmare if Ronan's call to his therapist couldn't wait until Monday, or maybe his grandmother's visit yesterday affected him more than he's letting on.

I'm contemplating how best to continue the conversation without inadvertently saying something that will cause him to shut down. "Were you able to get some relief by talking to Doctor Seivert?"

Ronan turns his head to look at me, eyes searching mine with something like gratitude for not forcing him to talk. "A little," he says. "I'm actually going to see her on Monday."

"Really?"

"Yeah, I think I need to."

I wish I was the woman he was comfortable opening up to, but at least he's talking to someone.

Tuesday, December 20th

Ronan

It's still dark when I wake—not from the soft patter of rain, though it's steady against my window—but from the persistent buzz of my phone under the pillow. I squint at the screen. 6:52 a.m. An unfamiliar number with an area code I don't recognize. Dread twists in my gut before I even swipe to answer.

"Hello?" My voice is raspy, like my vocal cords were raked over hot coals.

"Hey, Rony," Miranda chokes out.

I sit up fast, immediately on high alert. "Randi?" Holy shit, I haven't heard from her since she left Montana last March. "Are you alright?"

"No. I need your help," she says, her voice cracking.

Is she crying?

I'm already getting out of bed. "What happened?"

She holds back a sob, but I hear the whimper. "I... Everything is gone. My money, my phone, my truck," she says, choking on the last word. "He fucking took everything. I don't know what to do. I have no one else to call."

There's something about the way she says that—*no one else to call*—that lands like a stone in my chest.

I don't ask her who "he" is while I walk to my closet.

"Where are you right now?" I ask, switching my black sweatpants for jeans while I balance my phone—with Miranda on speaker—in my right hand.

"I'm at a motel in Pikeville, Tennessee," she says, then sniffles. No fucking clue where that is.

"Is anyone there with you?" I try to button my jeans one-handed.

"No," she says meekly. Miranda doesn't get defeated, but that's all I hear in her voice. Defeat. "I'm all alone. I don't know what to do."

I pull on a hoodie before I ask her for the name and address of the motel. I pull it up on my phone.

"Okay, listen, Randi, I'm going to head to you right now, but it's going to take me a while to get to you. I probably won't be there until tonight sometime. Can you stay where you are?" I grab my wallet and car keys from my nightstand.

"I have to check out in a few hours, Rony. I don't have any money to pay for another night," she says, clearly trying to keep her composure but failing. "He took everything. Everything." A renewed cry follows her words.

I make a split-second decision. "Okay, let me talk to the front-desk person."

Miranda must have handed off the phone, because only a second later an older woman's voice comes through. I cut to the point, pay for another night, and make sure she confirms Miranda is all set. The woman passes the phone back.

"Thank you, Rony," she says. Her voice is hoarse. Like she hasn't slept in days. Like she hasn't stopped crying in hours.

My heart squeezes uncomfortably in my chest. I've always had a lot of love for Miranda. Not in the way she wants me to—at least based on what she told me the last time I saw her—but I care about her deeply. I also know that Miranda isn't one to ask for help. She and I are so alike in that respect: way too damn independent for our own good, too afraid to ask for help because it makes us vulnerable and exposes us to pain. So the fact that she called me after disappearing into thin air, after not speaking to me for over nine months, makes me think she's in a bad place.

"Don't even worry about it," I say. "Randi, just do me a favor and stay where you are. I'm leaving now, but it'll take me a while to get to you, okay?"

"Okay," she sighs.

We end our conversation and I walk straight to Shane's closed bedroom door across the hallway. I take a second to listen, making sure I'm not about to interrupt something. Not surprisingly, no sounds emanate from Shane's room. I'm sure he's still fast asleep.

I knock a couple of times before cracking the door slowly. *Oh god, please don't be railing her right now...* I'm spared. As I suspected, Shane is still passed out, Tori in his arms, her back to his front as she sleeps soundly. The two of them haven't said anything, but at this point Tori has basically moved in with Shane and me; her stuff can be found all over our apartment. It doesn't bother me in the least. I've always liked Tori and I know that Shane feels about her exactly how I feel about Cat. And much like Cat saved my life, Tori saved Shane's.

"Shay," I whisper, trying to wake him without rousing Tori, but she's the first to blink her eyes open at me. "Sorry, Tor, can you wake your guy?"

She bumps her butt against him, causing him to open his eyes with a sleepy grunt. "Ran needs to talk to you," she mutters before shutting her eyes again.

I walk into the kitchen to wait for Shane. He shuffles in a minute later wearing gray sweatpants, his chest bare. He and I sleep exactly the same way—window open, wearing only sweatpants, boxers if it's too damn hot in the summer—which is something both Tori and Cat commented on once Shane and I started living together.

"What's up, dude?" He looks exactly like someone who just got pulled out of deep sleep, his shoulder-long, undercut hair messy, eyes squinting against the kitchen lights. The sun is only just rising and it's still dusky in the apartment.

I open the fridge to retrieve the ingredients for a turkey sandwich to take on the road with me. "Do you remember me telling you about Randi?"

"Randi, your ex?"

I nod. Shane's my best friend—I've obviously told him about Miranda. He knows we were together a few years ago, knows she was my first.

"Yeah, what about her?" he asks.

"She just called me. She's in some kind of trouble. I'm not completely sure what happened, but she isn't usually one to ask for help, so the fact that she called me worries me."

"Okay?" Shane leans against the doorframe, watching as I throw together my turkey sandwich. "Where is she?"

"Tennessee. Some place called Pikeville."

"Never heard of it."

"Me, neither. I looked it up. It's about an hour north of Nashville." I put some mustard on the slices of whole-grain bread on the counter.

Shane pushes off the doorframe and crosses his arms in front of his sturdy chest with a frown. "Wait, are you planning on heading there? Dude, that's like a twelve-hour drive."

"Thirteen," I say with a nod. "And yeah, I am about to get on the road."

"Ran, do you think that's a good idea? I mean, why do you have to head down there?" Concern lines his brow and laces his tone.

"She's stuck there; her truck was taken and so was all of her money. Randi doesn't really have anyone else she can call. I have to do this."

He studies me for a few seconds, his brow creased. "Okay." Shane finally nods. "Is there anything I can do to help?"

"I hate to do this to you, man, but are you okay covering for me at Murphy's tomorrow? I doubt I'll be back in time for my shift." I feel shitty asking Shane to take on extra hours. He's been working like crazy these past few months and I hate asking him to work doubles. "I have to see what I can do to help her."

"No problem, Ran," Shane says without hesitation. "You're a great friend, you know? I don't know many people who would just drop everything to help someone they haven't seen in months and who's hundreds of miles away."

I face him. "You'd do it for me."

He squares his shoulder. "Yeah, I would."

"Randi isn't lucky like me," I say. "I wouldn't know what to do without you, and Cat, and my brother. Vada, Zack, Summer..." I trail off. "Randi really only has... me."

"She *is* lucky to have you." A smile curves his lips. "Does Cat know about this?"

"Not yet," I say hesitantly. "I'm going to call her from the road."

"What do you think she'll say?"

I pause. Not because I don't know the answer, but because I'm afraid of it. "Hopefully she'll understand that this is something I have to do."

Things have been slightly tense between us ever since my grandmother showed up, and it's completely my fault. All of it. I still haven't opened up to Cat about it, still haven't told her about the nightmares. And yes, Cat deserves to know what goes on in my head, but I can't. I can't tell her about the dreams, can't tell her that I fear losing control, that I'm terrified of repeating history. Saying it out loud... it's like speaking it into existence. Maybe if the thoughts stay locked away in my head, I can keep destiny from fulfilling itself.

And I haven't told her about Rashana, either.

Just last week, Rashana hunted me down in the library at Columbia. I was studying for my econ final when she slid into a chair right across the table from me. I threw her a look that should have properly conveyed my unwillingness to talk to her, but she didn't budge. She just sat there, quiet, occasionally looking up at me, while I tried to focus on whatever the fuck I was reading, then rereading and rereading again. It got so uncomfortable, I slammed my laptop shut, shoved my shit into my backpack, and marched out to the courtyard. I was counting on Rashana to follow me, and when she did, I rounded on her.

"You need to stay the fuck away from me," I barked at her, and immediately felt guilty when she jumped back.

"Ronan, I promise, I'm not the enemy. I'm just trying to write a good story. And I think I could give y—"

I chuffed at her. "This *story* you're hounding me about? That's my damn *life*. It's not fucking entertainment. It's not a *piece* you get to use to get an A in your damn class or find a sweet fucking job after graduation." I took a deep breath, trying to steady myself. "Please, I'm begging you, leave me alone. Write a different story, find a different subject. I don't care. Just... leave me alone."

We stared at each other a moment longer. When she didn't respond, I turned to leave.

Cat doesn't know about any of this.

Cat

I don't think I ever truly realized that romance doesn't always mean bunches of roses, chocolate-covered strawberries, and big declarations. And then I met Ronan who, even with the smallest gestures, makes clear to me how much of his thoughts I occupy, even when we're not in the same room.

One of my favorite things is when he randomly calls me at three o'clock in the afternoon to check if I've eaten recently. I tend to forget to eat, then have dizzy spells from low blood sugar. And I love blinking my eyes open in the morning to a text message from him, usually containing only two words: "Morning Baby." To know I'm his first thought upon waking is peak melt-my-panties-right-off-my-body.

And that's exactly what I wake up to this morning. My eyes briefly take note of the time—it's just before ten—then drop to the text message Ronan sent... over two hours ago? Good god, this guy doesn't sleep even when we're on Christmas break. Always on the go, always with a mind that won't let him rest.

I open the message and smile at the intimate familiarity of it.

Ronan:

Morning, baby. Call me when you're awake.

My smile slips at his request for a call. For some reason his message feels ominous.

I dial his number as I get out of bed and walk to the small bathroom.

"Hi baby," Ronan answers, his voice silky. I swear I can feel his hands accompanying his verbal caress. I know we're young—some might even say too young for feelings this big—but oh my god, I love this boy.

"Hi sweet boy." I get out of my pajama bottoms, then turn on the shower to allow the water to warm up.

"Were you able to get a good night's sleep?" Ronan asks.

"Yes. I actually just woke up."

"Nice. Are you feeling more rested?"

Finals were taxing these past couple of weeks, and I've needed more than one night of solid sleep to recover.

"Yeah, much better. Are you driving?" The background noise and the slight distance in his voice are clear indications that he's in his Mustang.

"Yeah. Actually, I need to talk to you," he says, hesitantly.

Ominous.

"Okay? Is everything alright?"

"I got a call from Randi this morning."

I stare blankly at the tiled bathroom wall before I realize he's talking about his ex-girlfriend.

"Oh... uhh... that's... random." Wouldn't I know it, that little fuzzy monster that had lain dormant in my chest stirs. As far as I know, Ronan and Miranda haven't spoken in over nine months, ever since she confessed her love for him and then left Montana when Ronan rejected her.

"Yeah, I know. But baby, she's in trouble. I don't have any details, but it sounds like some dude she was with took all her stuff. Her money, her phone, her truck. Everything, from what Randi said. Baby, she doesn't have anyone to call. She really only has her dad, and... well..."

I nod. I know from Ronan that Miranda doesn't have a good relationship with her father. It's one of the reasons Ronan feels so bonded with Miranda—their shared experiences of growing up with parents who made them feel unloved.

"That's awful," I say as I hold my hand under the spray of the shower.

Ronan's voice tightens. "The problem is, she's in Tennessee with nowhere to go and no means to leave."

My heart drops into my stomach. "You're driving to Tennessee right now?" I ask, even though I already know. He didn't ask for my input. He's already gone. Already hours away. On his way to *her*. The monster blinks its eyes open and twists its neck in a serpentine manner. "Ran, that is so far!"

"I know, but I don't know what else to do. I can't leave her stranded. She didn't even have money to pay for another night at whatever motel she's staying at. I don't know how she'd get out of there or where she would go," he says, his baritone voice laced with deep worry.

I shake my head to clear it of the toxic, extremely unproductive, and completely unwarranted jealousy. Ronan and Miranda are childhood friends, and even though I can't be certain of her intentions, I am confident in his. He loves me.

I exhale. There's no point in arguing. Ronan has probably been on the road for hours by now, and for all I know he's already in Maryland. "So, what's your plan?"

"I honestly have no clue. I don't even really know what happened, but I guess I'll figure it out somehow. I have no idea, baby," he says.

"How long do you think you'll be gone?" Christmas is in only a few days, all our friends are in town, and I was really hoping to spend some quality time with Ronan over break.

"No idea, but I'm thinking at least a couple of nights. I should get to Tennessee sometime tonight. Depending on how quickly I can come up with a plan, I'll head home to you as soon as I can."

Home to *me*. I cling to those words like a lifeline.

"Cat, I'm so sorry for springing this on you." He knows what this might stir in me. But can he blame me? Miranda is his ex-girlfriend who, only months ago, tried to convince him to have sex with her even while knowing he was with me.

"It's okay." I mean it. Mostly.

I still don't quite understand Ronan's relationship with Miranda, that deep bond he has with her even with time and miles separating them. Do I have reason to feel threatened? Probably not. Ronan has never given me reason to doubt his commitment to me. He's always been honest with me, even while he was in Montana, on the nights when Miranda snuck into bed with him. He'd tell me about it without flinching.

I trust Ronan—and the fact that he is so willing to jump into action for a friend who kind of left him hanging while he was at his most vulnerable is one of the things I love most about him. He's been through so much pain, and still he goes above and beyond for the people he cares about. "Just, will you please check in with me? Let me know you got there okay?"

"Of course, baby."

"Okay. I guess I'll get under the shower and let you go."

A quiet chuckle travels through the phone. "Want to switch to video and let me watch?"

My lips quirk. "I don't think that's a great idea. I need you to be safe while you're driving."

"Good call. Your body is distracting as all hell. I'd wreck in a matter of seconds."

"Yeah, I definitely don't want that. Plus, I have to give you an incentive to come home to me."

He huffs into the phone as if my last sentence offended him. "I don't need sex as an incentive. I'm not with you for just your body. I love you, baby. I know this is really unexpected and definitely not ideal, but—"

"I know, Ran." I sigh again. "Just... think quickly, sweet boy, okay? Come up with a plan and then come home. And please drive safely. I need you."

"Not as much as I need you."

My lips tug into a smile. If only he knew how much I love him.

"Let me know when you get there. I don't care what time that is, just please call me?"

"I will, baby. I love you so much. You're the best thing that's ever happened to me."

"Same. I love you."

***

Less than an hour later, I walk through the doors at Murphy's and grin when I spot Vada, Tori, and Summer sitting in our favorite booth. It's the one closest to the bar and the small office frequented by Shane and Ronan—or the "man-ogle booth," as we girls dubbed it last summer. It gives Tori and me the perfect vantage point to get a visual fix on our guys.

Most days, just watching Ronan work is enough to make my blood simmer. He's such an exquisite male creature, with that perfectly fitted Murphy's shirt and his gloriously sculpted body that strains against the fabric. I'm never the only girl drooling over him, but I do take pride in the fact that I'm the one who goes home with him.

"Have you talked to Ran yet this morning?" Tori asks me with a telling look the second I slide into the booth. She obviously knows about Ronan's little getaway.

I press my lips together. "Yep."

Vada looks up from her menu. "What's up with Ran?"

"He's on his way to Tennessee," I say.

Vada's face scrunches in confusion. "What? Why?"

"His ex called him this morning. Something happened to her, and Ran's trying to figure out how to help her."

Vada's eyebrows nearly hit her hairline. "Wait, his ex from Montana?"

I nod.

"What the hell happened to her?"

I shrug. "I don't really know. I don't think Ran knows very many details, either. He just said all her stuff was taken, including her money and car, and that she's stuck in Tennessee and doesn't have anyone else she can turn to."

"So he just up and left to drive to Tennessee? Today?"

I nod again.

"And you're okay with this?" Vada asks, her eyebrows—and the pitch of her voice—rising with every question.

"Ran didn't exactly ask for my input, but yeah, I guess."

Vada cocks her head to the side. "Kitty Cat, I love you. And you know I love Ran. And we *all* know he's been through it, but..."

"But what?"

"But you do know you don't have to be okay with everything he does, right? Don't you think it's weird to help an ex out like that?"

"What are you saying?" I don't need Vada to echo my own insecurities; I need my three closest girlfriends to talk me out of my jealousy, not confirm that I have reason to worry.

"I don't want to start shit, but isn't this the same ex-girlfriend who hung out with Ran in Montana in the middle of the night? You don't worry about this at all? It just seems weird to me."

"I trust Ran." And I do. It's Miranda I don't know how to feel about.

For half a second, I imagine Miranda getting into Ronan's car, her face puffy from crying, her hand brushing his. I blink it away before it can take root. I trust him. I trust him. I have to.

Tori comes to my aid. "You'd help Steve out like that if he called you and asked for your help."

"Yes, but that's a little different, don't you think?" Vada asks.

Tori cocks her head to the side. "How so?"

Vada's jaw works for a second, like she's chewing something back. "I don't know, it just feels different." For the first time, she won't meet my eyes.

Summer shifts uncomfortably in her seat but stays quiet. I can't tell if that means she agrees with Vada or just doesn't want to get involved.

"If it makes you feel any better, Cat," Tori says, "when Shane told me about Ran this morning, he didn't seem concerned. He said Ran really just looked and sounded like he needed to help out a friend. Just like Ran would drop everything to help one of us out."

Shane wanders over to our table with a smile. "Hey, guys," he says, then kisses Tori's head.

"Shane, what the hell is up with Ran driving to Tennessee to meet up with his ex?" Vada asks.

Shane frowns. "Woah, why the hell are you so aggressive?"

"Because I find it weird that he's still in contact with this chick." Vada crosses her arms in front of her chest.

Shane narrows his eyes at her. "Are you sure you want to be starting shit again? I very vividly remember the fight you and Steve got into earlier this year after you told Cat that Ran's ex is easy."

"Seriously, nobody thinks this is weird?" Vada asks, looking around the table.

"No," Shane says. "Because we all know Ran. We all know that he wouldn't do what you seem to think he's capable of doing. You really need to consider your audience and who the fuck you're talking about here, Vada. Fuck, I mean, Ran worships the ground Cat walks on. Don't tell me you seriously think he'd cheat on her."

"Well, no, but..."

"But what?" Shane dares her to continue.

"But we don't know anything about his ex. Why the hell would she call Ran? Why not someone else?"

"Because she doesn't have anyone else," I say. As far as I know none of my friends know about Miranda's history or her strained relationship with her dad. Ronan is an exceptionally private person—he barely talks about his own shit, and definitely won't gossip or talk about other people's private details.

Vada exhales a noisy huff through her nose. "Okay, well, if you're all okay with this, then I'll just shut up and mind my own business."

"That seems like a viable strategy." Shane gives a single nod before turning his attention to me. "Cat, Ran was super forthcoming with me this morning. I could tell he's just concerned about helping out a friend. I really don't think you have anything to worry about."

"I know. I trust him."

If only I trusted Miranda with him.

Ronan

The sun has long set when I finally pull into the small parking lot of Miranda's motel in Pikeville. The town itself doesn't strike me as much larger than Redtail Ridge—the small town closest to my grandparents' ranch in Montana—and traffic was virtually nonexistent the last twenty minutes of my drive.

I briefly look around for the familiar baby-blue '88 Chevy Silverado—Randi's truck—until I remember it was taken by "him."

The parking lot is empty except for a beat-up white Ram truck parked in front of what must be the lobby, and I pull into a spot right next to it. I clamber out of my Mustang, then stretch my legs. My back and neck crack as though sighing with relief.

I look around briefly, noting not a single soul, then lock my car and walk into the small office of the L-shaped motel. The moment the door's creak announces my arrival, a heavy-set, older gentleman looks up at me.

"Checking in?" he drawls, giving me a skeptical once-over.

"No. I'm meeting a friend who's staying here. Miranda Jackson." I come to a stop in front of his counter. "Can you please call her room and let her know I'm here? My name is Ronan."

The guy raises an eyebrow, looking me up and down. He's probably wondering what my business is with Miranda, but he picks up the phone and dials a number.

"Good evening, ma'am," he says into the receiver. "There's a young man here asking for you. He said his name is..." He looks at me expectantly; he obviously already forgot my name.

"Ronan."

He repeats my name. "Would you like to meet him here or should I send him to your room?" The man nods. "No problem. Have a nice night."

He hangs up, taking his sweet time before looking back at me. "Ms. Jackson is in room seventeen. Across the parking lot, second-to-last door on the right." He points in the direction of Miranda's room. His face makes me think he suspects my motives aren't necessarily PG, especially if he saw her arrive with someone else. Judging by the condition of this lobby and the motel's exterior, I bet he sees his fair share of guests paying by the hour. It's probably on the tip of his tongue to tell me that this is a respectable family business, but he just sizes me up with a disapproving scowl.

Then again, maybe that's just his face and the dude couldn't give a rat's ass why I'm here. I nod curtly, then stride back outside and down the narrow walkway, past a number of doors and my car.

I stop in front of a white door with the number seventeen in large numerals and knock twice.

"Oh god, Rony!" Miranda opens the door, throws her arms around my neck, and buries her face against my chest.

"Hey Randi." I wrap my arms around her. Still tiny.

"I'm so glad you're here," she says into my jacket, her voice cracking. I can tell she's crying; her small frame shakes with each sob. So I hold her against me for a few minutes, not saying a word until she finally releases me and takes a step back.

Her blue eyes are watery, red, and puffy. She's obviously cried a lot, which is so unlike her. Miranda has experienced her share of terrible things in life, and like me, she's developed an extraordinary ability to swallow heavy shit. Until something happens that completely unravels her.

"What happened?" I ask as she holds the door open for me to enter the small room. It's run-down. The brown carpet is stained, and the wooden wall panels have definitely seen better days. There's a single queen-size bed pushed against the right wall, opposite a small round table and two wooden chairs. A crappy TV is mounted to the wall across the bed, and the two lamps on the nightstands on either side of the bed are the room's only source of light.

"Rony, I'll explain everything, I promise. But... can we get something to eat?" she asks, looking up at me.

It dawns on me that she probably hasn't eaten all day, seeing as she has no money. "Oh, shit. Yeah, of course." I pull the door open again. "Do you have a jacket? It's kind of chilly outside."

Miranda is dressed in a pair of light blue boot-cut jeans, a white tank top—the fabric of which is so thin her black bra is clearly visible through it—covered by a red-and-black plaid flannel, but nothing else.

Miranda shakes her head. "No. He took everything. Including my clothes," she says, despair etched into her face.

"Okay, no problem." I shrug off my hooded leather jacket. I fully expect her to fight me on taking it, and I grin when she tries to wave me off. "Just take it, Randi."

She relents with a sigh, then slips her arms into the too-long-for-her sleeves before walking out ahead of me.

I walk next to her, leading her to my car.

"That's your car?" she says, admiring my satin-black Mustang.

I smile proudly while I hold the passenger door open for her. "Yep."

"Nice," she says before sliding into the seat.

I get into the driver's seat a moment later. My back immediately protests the cramped conditions so soon after escaping them. "So, what do you feel like eating?" I ask as I maneuver out of the parking lot.

She melts back against the leather seat and sighs deeply. "Anything."

"Helpful," I say dryly. "What's around here?"

"Not much—probably just fast food. Most places are already closed. But if I remember correctly there's a twenty-four-hour diner in Dayton, about half an hour west of here."

I look up the place on my phone, then start driving down the deserted highway.

It's silent in the car. I know her well enough not to push her into talking. She's just like me when it comes to stuff like that—we have a tendency to shut down if we're forced to talk about crappy shit too quickly. I figure she'll talk when she's ready. So I just let the music play quietly in the background and wait for Miranda to make the first move.

She finally breaks the silence, though her eyes are shut. "I can't believe you're here."

"You sounded pretty desperate."

She turns her head to me but doesn't respond to my comment. "When did you get back to New York?"

I briefly meet her gaze before focusing back on the road. "Mid-April."

"Did you end up testifying at the trial?"

My chest tightens at the recollection. Those ten hours of being in the same room as my mother, talking about all the beatings I took and watching a year's worth of surveillance of every time she hurt me cracked me wide open. "Yeah."

"I'm sorry, Rony. I bet that sucked."

"It did," I say with a nod. "But it was also cathartic."

Her lips tug into a smile. "I told you you needed to talk about it. Remember what I said: it sucks in the moment, but afterwards you—"

"Feel a little bit lighter."

She nods. "Yeah. Do you feel lighter?"

I shrug. "In some ways, yeah. I don't have to lie so much anymore. Don't have to come up with excuses or stories..." The shit that weighs me down now is the fear of... myself.

I don't need to look at Miranda to know her gaze is locked on me. I feel her eyes boring into my head. "And your mom? What happened to her?"

"After she made me sit through ten hours of testimony, she changed her plea to guilty and made her case to the judge," I say in an unaffected manner.

I note the dip of her eyebrows out of my periphery. "I didn't know that was an option."

"Well, it is. She ended up getting three years."

Miranda recoils as if I just zapped her with electricity. "What? Three years? After... after putting you into a god damn coma?"

I just nod.

"Jesus, that's... completely fucked up," Miranda huffs. "She tortures you for seventeen straight years and only gets three years?" She crosses her arms in front of her chest and gets back to analyzing my profile. "Are you angry about it?"

"I don't think so," I say with a tiny shrug and a quick shake of my head.

"You don't *think* so?"

"No. I guess I don't think about her enough to be angry. I honestly don't want to spend my energy on that," I say, my jaw tight.

Miranda falls silent, studying me for a long moment. "Are you still with your feline?"

Guilt flickers in my chest for leaving so abruptly. I need to call Cat ASAP. Still, my lips curve into a smile. I can never control my body when Cat comes up, when I hear her voice or lay eyes on her. I have an instinctive and immediate physical reaction. Fuck, I've been with her for just over a year and a half now and I'm as crazy about her as ever. "Still with her."

"That's... good," Miranda says, then falls silent again. She turns her head to watch the dark nothingness fly by.

We don't speak again until I pull up to the small diner about ten minutes later. The parking lot only has one car, and for a moment I wonder if the place is closed. But then I spot a handful of people inside, and the sign on the door clearly indicating that they're open. Good thing, too, because I can actually hear the hollow growl of Miranda's stomach.

I hold the door open for her and she slips in past me. The smell of warm food is in the air, immediately assaulting my senses, and I realize how damn hungry I am. I haven't really eaten today other than that sandwich early this morning.

"For two?" a waiter who looks to be about my age asks, then leads us to a small booth. Miranda shucks off my jacket, placing it beside her as she slides into the booth. She grabs one of the menus tucked behind the salt and pepper shakers and eagerly flips it open.

I pull my phone out of my pocket. "Randi, I'll be right back."

"You calling your feline?" she asks with a tired smile.

"Yeah. I'll just be a minute."

I step outside into the nearly empty parking lot and am met with a cold breeze that skillfully finds its way underneath my gray long-sleeve, causing goosebumps to erupt on my arms. I dial Cat's number, then leave her a quick voice message when she doesn't answer the phone. New York is an hour ahead of Tennessee, so Cat is probably asleep. Or maybe she's still out with Vada, Tori, and Summer, and just didn't hear her phone ring. Regardless, I tell her that I made it to Tennessee okay, that I will call her tomorrow, and most importantly that I love her.

Back inside the diner, I take a seat opposite Miranda just as the young waiter stops at our table. I raise my eyebrows when Miranda orders enough food to feed a small army.

"When was the last time you ate?" I ask her after ordering a turkey burger and fries.

"I don't know. Two days ago?"

I frown at her. "Okay, Randi, time to spill it! What happened?" I lean forward onto my forearms, holding eye contact. I've had enough of the small talk.

She sighs deeply. "God, Rony," she begins, her voice already cracking. "It's so bad." Her eyes water and spill over, tears silently rolling down her cheeks.

"Just tell me, Randi," I say softly.

She takes a shaky breath, then another. "When I left Montana, I basically just went back to what I was doing before I went home last December."

A small, involuntary groan rumbles in my chest with the thought that Randi did what I begged her not to do only months ago. She put herself at unnecessary risk for... *Nope, not a thought I'm going to finish.*

She picks up on my energy and furiously wipes away her tears. "No, I didn't do that," she says. "I promised you I wouldn't do it again, and I didn't. I swear." I nod, and she says, "I just went back on the road, tried to hook up with bands. I played small shows and gigs, auditioned, did open mics and stuff. In July I ended up in Georgia and actually got a job waiting tables at this little country-western place. They'd pay me to play on the weekends and then I'd wait tables during the week. The owner let me stay in a room above the bar. It was really nice because I was able to save up most of my money, you know?"

I nod without interrupting her.

"A couple of months ago I met this guy, Jordan. He was a musician and was sort of doing the same thing as me—just driving around, auditioning, playing gigs. We hit it off, started messing around with each other."

I raise my left eyebrow at her. "Messing around?"

She smirks, the grin on her lips such a stark contrast to her red-rimmed, tired eyes. "Yeah, well, you know," she says meaningfully. I do know. After all, I've "messed around" plenty before I met the love of my life. "Anyway, Jordan suggested we go back on the road together, and it just felt like something I wanted to do. I knew I didn't want to be a waitress forever. So he sold his piece-of-shit truck, I quit my job, took my savings, and on the road we went."

Miranda pulls a sour face. "It became pretty obvious to me right away that this wasn't a good idea. We had been on the road maybe six weeks before Jordan became super possessive and jealous, and he'd always want to start shit with me. When I got a gig playing somewhere he'd try to tell me that I only got it because of my looks, not because of my talent. And maybe he was right, but whatever. I still got the gigs," she says with a rueful laugh through her tears.

"A couple of days ago, we decided to head to Nashville. It was a total spur-of-the-moment decision. We drove until I just couldn't keep my eyes open anymore. We stopped in Pikeville yesterday morning and checked into the motel at five. We ate something really quick and then we just slept most of the day. I was so tired, Rony."

"Is that when he took all your stuff?"

She picks up her water, then sets it down again without drinking, her fingers trembling just slightly.

"No, but when we woke up yesterday afternoon, Jordan was already in a shitty mood. I don't know why or what set him off, but he was such an asshole, nagging and trying to provoke me. It just got worse throughout the afternoon. He started telling me how going on the road with me was the worst decision he had ever made and then he started calling me names and shit," she says, anger tingeing her voice. "I don't do that crap. I've had to listen to that shit from my dad for way too fucking long to let some asshole I've known for two months treat me like that. Anyway, I told him off, and you know what that motherfucker did? He fucking hit me." She chuffs.

"What?" I growl, my reaction as visceral as always when I get wind of some lowlife piece of shit putting hands on someone I care about.

"Yep. Punched me right in the ribs," she says, resting her left hand against her side. "Man, if he thought I was going to back down, he was sorely mistaken. I kicked him in the balls so fucking hard, I brought him to his knees. And then I told him to get the fuck out of my room or I'd call the cops on him."

I smile at her. That's the Miranda I know—never taking shit from anyone.

"But what I completely forgot was that Jordan had a key to my room," she says, her face contorting in pain again. "He snuck back in while I was sleeping and, Rony, he took all my stuff. I mean, he took everything. Everything. When I woke up this morning, my bag with my clothes was gone, my purse, and my truck. My mom's truck," she chokes, fresh tears spilling from her blue eyes as she buries her face in her hands. Miranda's mom died when Miranda was twelve and the only thing Miranda had left of her mom was her mom's baby-blue '88 Chevy Silverado. I reach across the table to rest my hand on her forearm.

She looks up at me. "He even took your old guitar. The one you gave me on my seventeenth birthday. The only things he left are the clothes on my body and my ID, which just so happened to be in my jeans pocket. But everything else is gone. All the money I had saved up, my phone, my guitar, my truck," she says again, her voice strained. "What am I going to do?"

"We'll figure it out, Randi," I say calmly, then pull my hand back when the waiter arrives with a large tray balanced on his left hand and shoulder. He carefully sets several plates of food in front of Miranda, who works hard to compose herself, wiping her flushed face with a paper napkin.

My phone begins to buzz in my back pocket. "I'll be right back," I tell Randi as I slide out of my seat to retreat into the parking lot. "Start eating!"

Once again, I step outside to answer Cat's call. "Hey baby."

"Hi, sweet boy." God, I didn't realize how much tension I carried in my jaw until just now; I feel myself relax the second I hear Cat's voice. "How's Randi?" she asks sweetly, expressing real concern for a girl she's never met.

"Not great," I say. "We're just grabbing some food right now. Apparently she hasn't eaten in two days."

"What? Oh my god, Ran. Did she tell you what happened?"

"Yeah, right before you called, actually." I sigh. "Some asshole she had traveled to Tennessee with came into her room last night and took all her shit. Just everything. She literally only has the clothes on her back and her ID left, baby."

"That's awful. What are you going to do, Ran?" She knows me, knows I won't be able to come to rest until I've figured out some way to help Miranda.

I rake my hand through my hair. "Not totally sure, but I can't leave her here like this."

"No, you can't."

I don't know how I deserve her. I exhale loudly through my nose. "I'll figure it out," I say, more to myself than Cat.

"I know you will, sweet boy. You always do."

"What are you doing right now?" I miss her; I wish I could pull her into my arms, wish I could sleep next to her tonight.

"Just got home a few minutes ago. Tor, Vada, Summer, and I got our last bit of Christmas shopping done today. I'm about to climb into bed. I'm exhausted," she says with a yawn.

"I'll let you go so you can get some sleep. I miss you, baby," I say and close my eyes, pretending for a moment that I'm right next to her.

"I miss you, too, sweet boy. Will you call me tomorrow?"

"Yeah, definitely. I love you, baby."

"I love you, too," she says, and we end our call.

I'm astounded when I slide back into the booth and notice that Miranda has already devoured her stack of pancakes, all her chicken strips, and is halfway through her own burger and fries while I haven't even touched my food.

***

"Are you feeling better?" I ask, falling in step behind Miranda when we walk back to my car thirty minutes later.

"A little bit." Exhaustion lines her face and grates her voice. "I'm so tired, though."

The moment we're in my car, I tell her to close her eyes. She does so without protest, then falls asleep within minutes. I only rouse her once I shut off the ignition after arriving back at the motel.

She sways slightly, so I wrap my arm around her shoulder and draw her against me, allowing her to use me as support while we walk.

"Where are you going?" she asks, two small lines visible between her eyebrows, when Miranda unlocks her door and I turn to walk back toward the small office.

"I still need to get a room."

She takes a step toward me, a hand reached out. "No, Rony, don't leave me. Jordan still has a key to my room. I don't want to be alone. What if he comes back?"

I consider her for a moment. The fear in her voice is real. Raw.

"Please, Rony!"

"Okay."

Miranda visibly relaxes, then leads the way to her room. *God this place is such a dump.*

I lock the deadbolt in place behind me while Miranda disappears into the tiny bathroom.

The soft mattress on the bed sinks and the cheap metal frame squeaks when I sit down. I briefly wonder when this mattress was originally bought, then decide against going down that rabbit hole. No good comes from thinking too hard in a room like this. The carpet looks like it hasn't been replaced since before I was born, maybe even since before my dad was born. My lips curl. *Nope, not gonna go there.*

I take off my chucks, then send a quick text to Shane to let him know I made it to Tennessee okay. His response comes through almost immediately. It's short, steady, like a tether I could grip if I needed to.

I feel Miranda climb into the bed behind me and instinctively turn toward her just as she gets under the burgundy duvet. She's taken off her flannel and jeans, leaving only her thin white tank top and a red, lacy thong.

My head snaps away. Hard. I stare at the wall. The nightstand. Anything but her.

I know exactly how this would look if someone were to walk into this room right now. My last interaction with Miranda—back in March, in Montana—has left me admittedly guarded. I no longer trust that I'm able to properly read her and her intentions. I used to think I knew her, knew what her endgame was, then found myself completely caught off guard when she told me she loved me.

But she pulls the blanket up and over herself, then faces me, her blue eyes still puffy, red, and tired, her forehead creased.

"What am I going to do, Rony?" she whimpers. "I have nothing left and nowhere to go. I have no family. I have no one at all," she says, a desperate sob breaking from her chest. She begins to cry again.

Without thinking, I move to her. I position myself next to her and pull her into my arms. She buries her face against my chest, her arms tucked between us, her pain palpable.

"You have me," I say softly. "I'm here, Randi. We'll figure something out, I promise," I tell her over and over again as she cries in my arms. She doesn't stop for a long time.

I just lie next to her—Miranda underneath the blanket, me on top of it—holding her close, whispering what I hope are the right things. Eventually, her tears taper. She exhales, deep and heavy, then shifts to rest her head on my chest. One last breath, and she's asleep.

I listen to the slow rhythm of her breathing. Even, steady. Unlike mine. My mind won't still.

I try to think of a solution. Some way out of this for her.

I guess I could bring her back to New York with me, but where the hell would she stay? She can't stay with Shane and me—we don't have the space and I'm not sure this idea would go over well with Cat and Tori. Miranda couldn't stay with my dad either, with Penny about to give birth. I could give Miranda some money, I guess. I have a good chunk sitting in my savings, but man, everything was taken from her. She'll need a car, a place to live, food, clothes, and all the shit that comes with living on your own. I don't have that kind of money just sitting around. What I'd be able to give her would probably get her through a few weeks, but then what? Miranda will need something more permanent for a while, something that'll allow her to get her feet back under her and start over.

I reach behind me to turn off the nightstand light. My movement causes Miranda to conform her body to mine, and she hitches her right leg over my thigh just like she would when she'd sneak into my room in Montana. And then it hits me. Holy shit. I can't believe it took me so long to think of this.

I carefully unravel myself from Miranda's hold on me, pull my arm out from underneath her, then glance at the watch on my right wrist. It's almost two in the morning—1 a.m. where my grandparents are.

Wednesday, December 21st

Ronan

I didn't sleep much last night, but I did finally doze off for a few hours after I came up with the rough outline of a plan. It was just enough to ease my mind a little, to let me get some rest.

I sit up, my hands on either side of my hips, and fuck if my back isn't pissed at me. Between the eight-hundred-mile drive and this shitty lump of fabric stuffed with creaky springs calling itself a mattress, I'm in desperate need of a chiropractor—or one of those medieval rack devices that pull your limbs apart. Honestly, sounds kind of amazing right now.

The few hours of shuteye I did get were piss-poor, partially because of my ruminating mind and partially because Miranda's slightest shifts caused the bed to squeak and the mattress to ripple like we were on a raft on the open sea. None of it was conducive to good rest. I'm actually shocked that Miranda is able to sleep as soundly as she does, but then again, she was probably wiped out from all that adrenaline coursing through her veins and the waves of powerful emotions she had to brave most of the day. I'm glad she slept. She needed it way more than me.

I half expect my joints to creak like the damn bed frame when I finally roll out of bed at just after five. The tightness in my back is rivaled only by the stiffness in my knee, which I suspect has more to do with the cold temperatures than the sleeping arrangements. My knee has been getting progressively more "difficult" with the change in seasons, locking up when I don't spend enough time warming up before a workout, or just deciding to ache for no apparent reason. Good times.

After the briefest, quietest trip to the bathroom during which I try to focus on anything but the mold-riddled grout cementing the yellowed tile to the wall, I put on my shoes and jacket, grab the room key, then slip out the door.

It's frosty, but not nearly as cold as New York, where I'd have to scrape the ice off my windshield right now. Still, I find the contact I need in my phone, then shove my right hand into my jacket pocket while holding my phone to my ear with my left.

"Soult Ranch," my grandma answers on the third ring, making a giant grin appear on my lips.

"Hi, Morai."

"Baby boy? Oh my goodness, hi!" she says with such glee, one would think she just received the most incredible news of her life. But her inflection changes to concerned in an instant. "What's wrong? Why are you calling us in the middle of the night?"

I chuckle. "Well, it's not the middle of the night where I am."

"True, but it's still very, very early in the morning. Is everything okay?"

"Yeah," I say. "Actually, no. Morai, I need to talk to you and Athair about something important."

"What is it, baby boy? Did something happen? Are you okay?"

"I'm okay, Morai, but Randi isn't." I tell her about Miranda's phone call to me the day before, what happened to her, and that I'm in Tennessee right now.

"This asshole took everything from her, Morai. I mean, everything. She literally only has the clothes on her body and her ID. No money, no phone, no car."

"That's terrible," my grandmother says. "What kind of person would do that?"

"I mean, I think we can agree there are a lot of not-so-great people in this world," I say dryly. "Morai, I know I'm asking a lot, but do you think Randi could come back to the ranch for a while? Maybe she could help you and Athair for a few months, get her bearings while she tries to figure out what's next? She'll need a place to stay and a way to earn some money so she can start over."

I shut my eyes tightly. Miranda always had it tough with my grandma, though she did warm up to her a little while Miranda worked on the ranch for a few months earlier this year before she just up and left overnight. I hope my grandma has thawed enough to agree to take in Miranda for a while.

"Yes, of course," she says, and my eyes snap open. "She can stay in the same cabin she stayed in last time. This is actually great timing. We're approaching calving season and we're expecting a few guests over the holidays. As you know, there's never a work shortage on the ranch, so we can certainly keep her busy."

My lungs expand with a cleansing inhale of the crisp morning air. "God, thank you, Morai. You're the best."

I continue to talk to my grandmother for another ten minutes as we figure out the details of Miranda's arrival on the ranch.

"Okay, I'll talk with Randi and let you know how it goes. Hopefully she won't fight me too much on this idea." I sigh, knowing how damn stubborn Miranda can be. "Hyper-independent" is probably the word Dr. Seivert would use; that's how she's described me and my total inability to ask for help from... well, anyone.

"She won't," my grandmother says with conviction and a smile in her voice. "She's strong-willed, but she knows when to accept help, especially from you."

"I hope you're right. I love you, Morai. So much."

"Oh, baby boy, I love you more. Call when you've had a chance to talk to Miranda and we'll get everything ready," she says. "And then get home to Cat as soon as you can."

I chuckle. "I'm planning on it." I say my goodbyes before ending the conversation.

Instead of heading back into the room, I decide to find a place to grab some breakfast for Miranda. I stop first at a gas station, fill up my tank, then grab a toothbrush and a touristy *Tennessee—the Volunteer*

State hoodie for Miranda. That girl needs some clothes, but I'm not comfortable picking out anything but a sweater. It takes me a few minutes to find a decent-looking coffee shop where I stop and order some breakfast for takeout along with some coffee for Miranda. I'm still not a coffee drinker, and I don't think I ever will be. It's fucking disgusting to me, though Cat swears by it. I just make a face whenever she offers me her cup, which makes her giggle every time. Man, it's only been forty hours since I've seen her, but already my entire being yearns for her.

It's weird how fast I can flip between feeling responsible for someone else's survival and craving the touch of the one girl who makes me feel like being in her orbit is the only thing that keeps my bullshit from swallowing me whole. As always, I send her a quick text.

Me:

Morning, baby. I have a plan on how to help Randi. I just hope she agrees to go for it. Fingers crossed that she does, and I should be home by tomorrow night. I love you so damn much. Miss your perfect face. And body…

***

When I get back to the motel, Miranda's up and the bathroom door is closed—clearly, she's in there. So I walk to the round brown table and set the coffee cup down, then take the food out of the plastic bag.

A moment later, the bathroom door unlocks. "Holy shit," Miranda squeals. I turn my head in her direction just as she quickly whirls around, turning her back to me. She's completely naked and I catch a glimpse of the familiar, dainty tattoo of scripture that stretches the length of her spine from her neck down to her tailbone before my head is turned resolutely in the other direction. "Fuck, I didn't hear you come back," Miranda grumbles and hastily grabs her clothes from the bed.

"Sorry Randi, but didn't you expect me to come back at all? Why the fuck would you walk out of the bathroom naked?" I ask her through gritted teeth.

"I figured I'd hear you. I forget how fucking quiet you always are," she mutters. I hear her slip into her clothes.

The flash of her tattoo—the same one I used to trace with my fingertips—burns behind my eyes, even after I slam them shut. I turn my back to her like it might erase the image. But it doesn't. I hate how easily memory slips past defenses. "Yeah, well, it's a habit I formed when I realized being noisy around my mother would result in pain," I growl. "I'll try to make more of a fucking ruckus next time."

"Okay, you're safe now," she says with a laugh. "No more sexy naked babes."

I open my eyes and turn to her. "Maybe next time just take your damn clothes into the bathroom with you. Just a suggestion," I say, the crease still deep on my brow. "I brought you breakfast." I nod toward the food on the table. "And a toothbrush and a hoodie."

"Aww, thank you Rony," she says, her voice much less tired-sounding than yesterday. "Is that where you went? To get me breakfast, a toothbrush, and a sweater?" She opens the small paper bag, pulls out the croissant, and inspects it briefly before taking a large bite.

"Partially." I sit down on the creaky bed. "I came up with a plan."

She stops chewing. "Oh, yeah?" she asks, her mouth full. "Care to share it with me?"

"So, I spoke to my grandmother earlier," I start. Miranda's eyes widen. "I told her what happened, and she said she'd be happy to have you." At this, Miranda's brow furrows, but I don't give her the chance to argue. "It's not a handout, Randi. You'd be working on the ranch, just like last time. You'd stay in the same cabin. You'd earn your keep. I think it's the best option to give you the chance to start over, get your feet back underneath you, save up some money and figure out your next steps. You'll have my truck available to drive around while you're there. You'd have a place to stay, you'd have work, you could even check in on your dad from time to—"

Miranda throws herself into my arms, holding on to me for dear life.

"Rony, I don't know what I'd do without you. Thank you..." she sobs.

I blink at her. I honestly thought she'd fight me, would protest, would argue about going back to Montana to live on my grandparents' ranch. This was way easier than I expected. But I'm not complaining.

I pat her back as she buries her face against my neck, her hot tears rolling down my skin. "I wish I could do more, but—"

Miranda pulls away from me, shaking her head. "Are you kidding me? Rony, I can't even tell you how much I appreciate this. You're incredible," she says, wiping her tears.

"So I looked, and there's a flight going from Nashville to Missoula tomorrow morning. It leaves at five. I haven't booked it yet because I obviously wanted to get your okay first, but if you want to go, I can get it lined up right now."

More tears escape Miranda's blue eyes. "Okay."

I smile. "Alright, go eat."

She sits down to eat her breakfast while I take care of the details, then call my grandmother back to give her an update.

"You're all set," I tell Miranda after hanging up the phone. "I figure we'll check out of this fucking dump and then just head to Nashville. I reserved a hotel room by the airport for the night. We'll get you some essentials today—you obviously need some clothes and a bag, and probably a phone."

Miranda shakes her head at me, her eyes full of emotion.

"What?" I ask.

"You're such a good guy, Rony," she says. "You always were, but really, you're amazing. I wish..."

I raise my eyebrows at her, waiting for her to continue.

She sighs. "Nothing."

But the pause lingers. And the way she looks at me? It's familiar in a way that makes my spine tighten. I shift away slightly, not enough to be rude, just enough to make it clear that those kinds of wishes can't live here anymore.

Cat

I reach for my phone, feeling desperate. The sight of Ronan's name on my phone this morning settles something in me.

I did not have a great night. As much as I want to convince myself that Vada's words didn't feed into that seed of jealousy in my chest, I can't deny that it jabbed at my insides throughout the day.

I keep telling myself that I don't have anything to worry about, but the fact that Ronan just up and left to see Miranda irks me a little. Or a lot. Maybe it's because of what Vada said, or maybe it's because I know how Miranda feels about Ronan. Is it normal for a guy to drop everything, drive hundreds of miles, and sleep in a motel room with a girl he hasn't spoken to in months if there's truly nothing between them?

I want more than anything to believe that Ronan is just being Ronan. I've always known he's exceptionally giving to the people he cares about. It's one of the many things I love so much about him. But I've never met Miranda and, yeah, maybe I feel threatened by what she has with Ronan, especially because I still don't understand what exactly that is. Obviously she still has a some kind of hold on Ronan's heart.

I tried to push my doubts out of my mind. After all, Ronan has never, ever given me a reason to question his love for me—but my efforts were marred by visions of Ronan and Miranda spending the night together. I kept reaching for my phone, checking if Ronan had sent me a message before bed or throughout the night, until I finally fell asleep from exhaustion.

To say I woke up grumpy is putting it mildly. But the second I see the notification—and Ronan's text message that he sent me hours ago—a smile breaks across my face. Elation floods me; he has a plan and promises to come home tomorrow. A familiar little flutter expands in my chest when I read that he misses me and my body.

Stop being so damn insecure, Cat. Not once has Ronan given me reason to doubt his love for me, even with the gaggles of girls vying for his attention every waking moment, and during his five months in Montana.

***

"Hey Jack," I greet the Murphy's bartender with a giant smile. I braved the city this morning to hunt down birthday gifts for Vada and Zack, then swung by Murphy's to go over plans for their New Year's Eve birthday bash. Honestly, how cool is it to have a birthday on a day that's always guaranteed to have a party?

Jack gives me a bright smile, his white teeth an exquisite contrast to his tawny skin and the dark stubble on his cheeks.

"You're in early," I say. Jack usually tends the bar in the evenings.

"We're short waiters. You know, people take time off to be with family or run off to Tennessee. So I work doubles," he says with a grin.

I return his smile. "Ah, so you know about Ran?"

"Only that he ditched us for a couple of days to, you know, run off to Tennessee. You're not with him?" Curiosity twinkles in his brown eyes.

I shake my head. "Nope. He just had to... take care of some business," I keep it purposely vague. "But hey, is Shane around? I tried to call him, but he didn't answer."

"That's probably because he forgot his phone." Jack grabs something from the counter, then holds up Shane's phone with a chuckle. "He's picking up some supplies we ran out of last night. Did you need something from him?"

"Nothing that can't wait until I see him."

Jack nods, then motions his head just behind me. "So, there's a lady sitting in the booth behind you just to your right. I just overheard her ask Casey if Shane was in, and then she said something about Ran," Jack says, the smile vanishing.

I turn and spot a dark-haired young woman sitting in a two-person booth, studying the menu. "She asked about Ran?"

Jack nods. "Yeah. I didn't catch the whole thing, but she asked if Shane was in. Casey told her he wasn't, that he was expected back and that she could wait. When Casey was leading her away to the booth, I overheard her saying something about Shane being friends with Ran. That was all I could make out, but I definitely got the impression she wanted to talk to Shane about Ran."

Well, that's... odd. I study her from across the room. She doesn't look much older than me, maybe about Jack's age—early twenties. Her black hair is tied up in a loose bun atop her head, and her expression is studious on the menu through her black-rimmed glasses on her nose. *So she's waiting for Shane so they can talk about Ronan?*

"Do you know her?" Jack asks, his gaze also directed at the woman.

I shake my head. "Never seen her before."

"Huh," Jack grumbles, crossing his arms in front of his chest as he cocks his head to the side.

Fuck this. There are entirely too many random women coming out of the woodworks for Ronan. I make my way over to the small booth, coming to a stop right in front of her table.

It takes her a second to notice me. "Oh," she says, startled, and lays her menu down. "I'm not quite ready to order." She gives me a tentative smile.

"I don't work here," I say, but don't move from my spot.

Her lips part as if to speak, then her eyes narrow. "I've seen you before," she says, and her eye widen with delight. "Oh my gosh, I've seen you before," she says, louder. *Alright, well, this is taking an unexpected turn.*

She pulls open a large black bag and rummages through it before pulling out a manilla folder stuffed with papers. She retrieves a single piece of paper. "You're her, right?" She taps her index finger on the paper. "You're Ronan's girlfriend? Or at least you were back in November. This was the last photo I could find. I think I pulled it from Shane's profile. It's the last image I was able to find of you with Ronan. He doesn't have social media, so it's hard to confirm relationship status. And yours is private, so..." She pushes a paper printout across the table toward me.

I recognize the photo. It was actually taken last summer here at Murphy's. It was the last time all eight of us were together before Zack and Summer left for California and Vada left for Philadelphia. In the picture I'm standing next to Tori, and Ronan is just behind me, his left arm draped over my left shoulder and across my chest.

"I can't quite figure out if you're still together and how long you've known him. Your yearbooks don't have any photos of the two of you together. It looks like you maybe only started attending East Bay High during your senior year? Gosh, I can't believe I'd run into you here. I was coming to chat with Sha—"

I blink at her, trying to find my way through the onslaught of information and questions, then finally find my voice. "Who are you?" I ask with a shake of my head.

Her eyebrows shoot up as though she's only now realizing how strongly she's coming on. "I'm so sorry." She stands and reaches her hand out for me to shake. I don't take it. "I'm Rashana Yates. I'm a grad student at Columbia. I'm getting my M.A. in investigative journalism and I'm working on a piece involving abuse cycles in families and the shortcomings of the criminal justice system. I did a bunch of initial research over the summer, you know, trying to come up with a good idea for a story, and I came across Rica Soult's case. It immediately spoke to me. It's kind of the perfect example of cyclical violence, you know? So I've been doing my sleuthing"—the word leaves a bitter taste in my mouth—"and I'm going to incorporate it into my story," she says with such enthusiasm that I have to take a step back from her.

My mind is made up. I don't need to hear anything else, don't need to learn anything about Rashana, couldn't care less about her background and accolades. I don't like her.

"You're... You've been researching?" I ask, trying to wrap my head around everything she just said.

She nods.

"And you've been searching social media?"

She nods again. "I have a lot of threads going at the same time. I've reached out to Rica Soult in prison to see if she'd agree to an interview, but nothing yet. It's not a surprise, to be honest. But there's a lot I can gather just from news reports, lots of public information and documents. It was a little harder figuring out Ronan's name, but obviously not impossible. And then there's social media, which is hugely helpful. Nothing is truly private anymore," she says with a delighted smile—while my frown deepens.

"I wanted to get a good understanding of exactly what I was dealing with before I made contact with Ronan. The fact that he attends Columbia is just... chef's kiss," she says, touching her fingertips to her lips.

The monster in my chest is wide awake and roaring, but this time it's not one of fear or jealousy. It's pure, primal protectiveness. I couldn't shield Ronan from his mother, couldn't stop the darkness from swallowing him whole... but I can stop *this*. I *will* stop this. "Don't contact him!"

Her mouth clamps shut for a moment. "I already did. Well, I tried. A couple of times." She shakes her head.

"When?" I ask before I can stop myself. I don't want to give this chick the impression that Ronan doesn't share things with me, even though it's not a lie. He very obviously doesn't—a fact that makes my stomach feel hollow.

"The day before Thanksgiving. He shut me down so fast," she says with a half-hearted laugh. "I tried again last week but I didn't fare any better. I figured I'll give him time to come around while I follow up with my other potential leads. Shane is obviously tied to Ronan, so I thought I'd try my luck here," she says with an expectant smile.

"Not gonna happen," I say. "If Ronan doesn't want to talk to you about this then neither will Shane, nor I, nor any of our other friends."

Her mouth opens, but no sound escapes.

I shrug. "I'd recommend you come up with a different story."

"But, I—"

"Let me guess, when you talked to Ronan he asked you to please leave him alone, right? And he probably told you not to pursue this story, that he doesn't want anything to do with this?" I don't wait for her response. I know Ronan; there's no way he'd even consider going into detail about his upbringing with a stranger when he can't even fathom it with his closest friends. "You won't have any luck going after Shane, or me, or anyone else who's connected to Ronan because we won't talk to you. You're better off forgetting about this story, forgetting about Ronan."

Her face contorts. "I can't do that," she says. "I've already invested so much time. And this is part of my master's degree."

I shrug. "I guess you better find a new story quickly, then."

She leans back in her seat, crossing her arms. "I'm not going to do that."

The roar in my chest increases. I place my palms flat on the tabletop, then lean into Rashana's space, tilting my head to the side. "You're in the investigative journalism master's program at Columbia?"

She narrows her eyes at me but nods.

"Great. Can't be that difficult to figure out who your advisor is then, right? And your professors? I don't know a ton about investigative journalism, but I have a feeling you stalking the victim of severe childhood trauma and relentlessly hounding people who have told you they won't talk to you wouldn't go over well. Aren't there ethical guidelines? So unless you want me to do my own 'sleuthing,' I'd recommend you find a different story to write."

I'm met by a shrieky laugh. "Are you seriously threatening me?"

I straighten. "Yes. And I promise you that if you don't let this go, I won't be the only one. One thing you need to know about Ronan is that he has a hell of a force behind him, and we're going to make damn sure that people like you don't undo the peace he's worked so hard for."

We stare at each other silently, her eyes bouncing between mine as if to determine the seriousness of my warning. I feel someone move up behind me, and a large, warm hand comes to rest on the small of my back.

"Hey, Cat, everything alright over here?" Shane asks in his deep voice. I turn to him, noting his thick bomber jacket. He obviously just got back from wherever he was. He turns his attention to Rashana, giving her a polite smile. "My bartender said you were looking for me. Can I help with anything?"

I shake my head without taking my eyes off Rashana. "No, she doesn't need any assistance, Shay."

I see him look at me out of my periphery, his eyebrows raised.

"This is Rashana Yates. She's an investigative journalism student who was trying to get the inside scoop on Ran for a story she's writing," I tell him, teeth gritted. "But I already informed her that none of us have anything to say to her."

Shane directs his gaze at Rashana. "You're trying to get information about Ronan from me? Like, about the things that happened to him?"

Rashana begins to stammer. "Yeah, well, I tried to speak with Ronan directly, but he's reluctant. I'm really not trying to ruffle feathers or—"

"Sorry, but I can't help you," Shane says, his hand still on my low back. "I really don't think this is the story you want to write unless you want to do a half-ass job, because if Ronan won't agree to talk to you, then neither will any of us," he says with a tip of his head in my direction. I gotta give it to him, he's a heck of a lot politer than me. But then again, he probably doesn't want to scare off any customers, either.

"I already told her that," I say, my focus on Rashana.

Rashana nods and gathers her things, shoving her manilla folder back into her satchel before she stands. Shane and I take a step back, giving her space to exit the booth. "I can appreciate your hesitation. I told Ronan I had some information I'd be happy to share with him if he was willing to talk to me. Hopefully he'll come around, because you're right—without his input, it would be a half-baked, one-sided story," she says. "I really don't mean any harm."

She allows her gaze to linger on Shane and me a moment longer before she walks away and out of Murphy's.

"What the actual fuck?" Shane punctuates each word with a sharp pause and turns his arctic-blue eyes to me.

I prop my hands on my hips. "Your reaction makes me think Ran hasn't told you about Rashana either."

"No. Did he tell you?"

I shake my head, dismayed. "No. But apparently she tried to talk to him twice already—once the day before Thanksgiving and again last week. He's doing it again, Shay. He's not talking to us."

Shane exhales so deeply, his chest concaves. "The day before Thanksgiving? The same day his grandmother showed up?"

I didn't even make that connection. "Yeah."

"Shit." The word escapes Shane in a hushed whisper. He rubs his neck. "I'll talk to him when he's—"

"No," I say. "*I* will talk to him."

Shane's jaw flexes as his eyes lock on mine. He's as protective of Ronan as I am, and the way he's studying me right now, his features hardening, blue eyes icy, gives me the impression a small part of him feels the need to protect Ronan from *me*. I won't lie, I'm pissed that Ronan hasn't told me about Rashana, especially after his unwillingness to talk about his grandmother's visit.

"I'm serious, Shay. This... doesn't it bother you? Doesn't it irk you that he doesn't open up to you? That he doesn't feel he can share his pain?"

Shane's forehead creases, his eyebrows dipping. "Yeah, but I also know there's no forcing Ran to open up. He copes the way he copes, and I'll be at his six whenever he's ready to share. Ran's been my best friend for-fucking-ever. I love him like a brother. We've been through some deep fucking shit together; he's been by my side when I was at my absolute lowest, never wavering, never questioning. That guy... he's never been anything but patient with me even when I definitely did not deserve his patience. Trust me," Shane says with a steadfastness only a lifelong best friend can bring, "I owe him the same unwavering, unquestioning patience."

"Except you know Ran doesn't share unless he's forced to. Unless something horrible happens and he's no longer able to hide it all. That might work for you, but it doesn't for me. You're not in an intimate relationship with Ran. You're not trying to... I don't know, build a life with him, I guess. I can't do that—can't build a future—if Ran never lets me in. You know he still won't talk about his grandmother's visit? It's been a month, Shay. And I'm not stupid. I know it's eating at him. We can't build a strong foundation if he..." I shake my head, throat thickening. "If he won't let me *see* the parts that scare him."

I don't know why it hurts so much, but it does.

"So, before you give him a heads-up about this, before you tell him about Rashana's visit, I want the chance to talk to him first. *Please*, Shay. Just... keep this between us."

Ronan

"I'm no germaphobe," I say to Miranda's suggestion that I take a quick shower before we check out of the motel. "I have no problem getting down and dirty, but this bathroom is a no-go zone for me. No way am I going to get buck naked and stand under that shower. I'll catch something the moment the air makes contact with my bare skin. No thanks, I'll wait until we make it to Nashville."

"Oh my god, Rony, you're not serious," she wheezes, her right hand pressed against her abdominals as if she's trying to hold them in place. "Are you telling me you didn't even relieve yourself in there this morning?"

I shake my head. "I'm *very* serious. I brushed my teeth, then booked it to the next gas station and took a piss there."

Her laughter turns into a high-pitched squeal. "You *chose* a gas station over this bathroom?"

"Like I said, very serious."

"The bathroom isn't *that* bad," she says through a guffaw. "I've had much worse."

I shake my head at her. "Sorry my dick's not as thick-skinned as you. I have no doubt I'd catch an STD just standing in there," I joke, nodding in the direction of the bathroom.

"You're concerned for your cock Mister Slept-With-Over-Fifty-Chicks?"

I narrow my eyes and tilt my head at her. "Only ever with a condom, and I'm not about to put on a rubber to take a fucking shower."

"You know, I did use the toilet in there and I'm perfectly fine," she says, her blue eyes watery with laughter.

"Nah, you for sure contracted something. I'd recommend you find the nearest clinic when you get back to Montana. Get ready to ruin your intestinal lining with some harsh antibiotics to kill whatever worked its way into your system while you peed."

That results in a new wave of laughter. She composes herself, then smiles at me with a sanguine look. "I've missed you. Only you manage to make me laugh until I want to puke," she says, then ties her red flannel around her waist. "Alright, let's leave this beautiful five-star resort and get on the road."

I pull on my jacket, grab my backpack, and follow Miranda out the door and to the small lobby to check out. We're in my car and on the road just minutes later. Miranda immediately starts messing with the stereo, trying to find suitable music for our short road trip.

"So, when can I finally see a picture of your feline?" she asks with a grin after she settles on a bluegrass station of all things.

I smile, then quickly pull up a picture of Cat before handing my phone to Miranda.

"Holy shit, Rony. This is her?" Miranda's eyes are huge as she looks at the photo I took of Cat at Murphy's one evening. My smile widens. To say that I'm proud—and immeasurably undeserving—to have landed Cat would be the understatement of the fucking century.

"Yeah," I say, my focus on the road.

"Good god, she's"—Miranda searches for the right words—"fucking gorgeous. No wonder you go all goo-goo when you talk about her."

Miranda begins swiping around on my phone, probably looking through more pictures. "You two are so cute together," she says as she continues to scour my phone. "Oh, fuck, Rony. She's got a perfect body, too. Nice, perky boobs." Miranda grins and turns my phone for me to see a topless picture Cat sent to me when I was at work one night a couple of months ago.

"What the fuck, Randi," I grunt and snatch my phone from her hand. That is definitely not something I'm willing to share. Not with Cat's history. She only started to trust me with intimate pictures of her in September. It was a huge surprise to receive a text message with an extremely provocative and equally sexy picture of Cat. I called her the second I opened it—even though it was well past midnight—wanting to gauge her feelings about the step she had just taken. It was important to me that she knew I never expected her to send me nudes, that I'd never pressure her. It had to be her idea. I mean, was I going to complain? Fuck no, but I needed her to know that I only move at her pace, always.

Cat assured me that she had thought about it long and hard, and this was something she wanted in our relationship. She's definitely gotten more comfortable, and I have a small, nicely curated collection of intimate pictures of Cat on my phone. I just didn't expect Miranda to start looking for it.

"I know all about hidden albums, Rony." She grins at me.

I frown. "You ever heard of privacy?" I lock my phone with the push of a button.

Miranda only laughs. "But seriously, she's stunning. I love her eyes."

My face softens. "Yeah, me too. There honestly isn't any part of her that I don't love," I say, then sigh.

"Oh yeah, I bet you love every. Single. Part. Of her." Miranda wiggles her eyebrows at me.

I shrug. "I mean... yeah." I can't help but smile. Cat seriously is the most beautiful, perfect girl I've ever laid eyes on. "She's honestly way too good for me, Randi."

"Why would you say that?" she asks, studying me.

"She always has been. I knew it right from the moment I met her, and I felt like such shit for dragging her into my bullshit. And even now..." I trail off, shaking my head. *Okay, Ran, why the hell are you going down this path right now?*

"But it's over, Rony," Miranda says. "Your mom's not able to hurt you anymore."

"Yeah." I sigh.

I feel Miranda's eyes boring their way into my head.

"You're doing it again," she says. "You're bottling shit up. I told you to stop doing that. It's not healthy, Ronan. Tell me what you're thinking!"

There go my walls, up and up, brick by fucking brick. Except I was the one who cracked open the door. Why? Maybe because being silent is starting to feel worse than bleeding. "Last I checked, I drove thirteen hours to help you out. Not talk about my shit again."

"It's not just a one-way street, Rony. Talk!"

I stay silent for a while, battling the weight of what's transpired over the past thirty days. It's been getting heavier and heavier—the nightmares, the spiraling thoughts, the intrusion by that damn journalist...

Up until August of last year, Miranda was the only person who truly knew what my mother was doing to me. Miranda and I have known each other since I was ten and she was twelve, and we bonded over having parents who treated us badly. Her father—the pastor of my grandparents' small church in Montana—is a verbally, emotionally abusive. And my mother would regularly beat the living shit out of me while reminding me that I was utterly, fucking worthless.

So, I open the door a little wider; maybe I can relieve just a tiny bit of the burden. I tell Miranda about my grandmother's unannounced visit, the way she rationalized what my mom did to me, and her suggestion that I search my soul for forgiveness.

Miranda chuffs loudly next to me. "So what I hear you telling me, Rony, is that your grandmother came to the house where your mother inflicted almost two decades' worth of torture on you, just to make fucking excuses for your mom's behavior." Her blue eyes are ablaze with anger.

I nod. "That night I dreamed that I was beating the shit out of Cat, Randi. And I've had several more of those fucking dreams. It freaks me out so much. I swear it felt real. What if I hurt her, Randi? I can't do to my family what my mother did to me, what my grandfather did to his family." My stomach churns. Each time I have a dream like that I wake up not only drenched and clammy, but overcome by nausea that brings me to my knees. I've thrown up twice after that nightmare, but I've managed to keep from purging my stomach the last few times by sitting on the edge of my bed while hugging my knees and concentrating on slowing my breathing.

"Rony," Miranda says with an air of amusement, "you can't seriously think you'd be capable of doing that."

I clench my teeth, my jaw flexing. I have no idea what I'm capable of. I've lost control before, have found myself in situations where I saw nothing but deep, dark red, where violence seemed the only reasonable response to whatever the fuck triggered me. Who's to say I won't find myself in a situation like that in the future, that I won't be set off by something as yet unknown to me? From what I understand, my grandfather didn't lay a hand on his wife until they were married. Maybe it's only a matter of time before I... snap.

"What does Cat have to say about all of this?" Miranda asks when I don't respond.

"I honestly don't know," I say sheepishly. "I haven't talked to her about any of it."

"Ugh," Miranda groans. "Why not, Rony? You talk to me about it."

I throw my hands up, then grip the steering wheel tightly. "You two are so different, Randi. You know what it's like; you understand the darkness, how fucking broken I am. Cat is... Her love for me is so pure. She's... whole, and unbroken, and... not... stained like me."

"You think you're stained?" Miranda asks, a note of sadness in her voice.

"I don't... I can't burden her with this shit," I say without responding to her question. "I just want to protect her. She's... God, she cares so much about me. She's always so considerate and I... I don't want her to forget herself or be anchored down by me or..." I don't think my ramblings make any sense at all.

Heavy silence engulfs us for what feels like an eternity while Miranda studies me. “Can I tell you what I think?” she finally asks.

My jaw ticks. “Since when do you require my permission to word vomit all over me?” I ask dryly.

“I just thought I’d be polite,” she says with a small giggle, but immediately turns serious again. “Two things, Rony. One, when it comes to Cat, you have to remember that she’s been through the thick of it with you already. She’s not ignorant to your pain. You guys have been together for quite a while now and she’s seen you when you were at your most broken, right?”

I shake my head. “Not really. I was gone; I was in Montana. Those months when I couldn’t drag myself out of bed, when I couldn’t eat, when I had nonstop nightmares, when I tried to figure out a new normal, a life without fear and violence—I was in Montana, away from Cat. I didn’t even get to talk to her while I was at my lowest. She may have an idea, but she doesn’t really know how bad it was, how close I got to just... ending it all.”

“She knows, Rony,” Miranda says. “And if she doesn’t, I’d say she deserves to know. What’s the point of swallowing it all? If she loves you the way you love her, then she’ll also love the not-so-perfect pieces of you, the broken parts, the darkness that’s still inside you that I know you’re working hard every day to keep at bay, because I do it, too,” she says, her voice warm. “And two, when it comes to the shit your grandmother piled onto your already overburdened shoulders, you have nothing to worry about. I’ve known you for a long time, and you don’t have violent tendencies.”

Except I do. It just has to be drawn out of me, which obviously can be done. It’s happened before, and it can happen again. “But what if I just fucking snap one day? What if something happens and I lose control? I could never undo that.”

“Rony, you were so sad when your grandpa hauled off that cow for culling when we were little. Do you remember that?” she asks with a smile, and I nod. “You have such a good heart. You’ve always been there for me. For crying out loud, you saved my dad's life! You really think someone capable of hurting the person they love most would drop everything to drive thirteen hours and do *this*? I don't. Someone like that wouldn't do mouth-to-mouth on a drunk person who was choking on his puke."

"You've always been like that; you've always been there for the people who needed you, even while your own life lay in ruins. That's... that's so damn selfless. How many times have I told you how damn good you are, Rony? That wasn't just bullshit. I know I say a lot of stupid shit, but I don't lie. You know me, I say it how I see it, and I know you're good. You don't have a malicious bone in that sexy-ass body of yours," she says with a grin and a wink.

I'm not convinced, but I also don't want to argue her point right now. I know none of us are only ever just good or evil. My grandfather obviously had some redeeming qualities, and even my mom was respected and well-liked by others.

My mom never touched my brother. And even when she hurt me, she'd clean me up after. Apologize. Say she didn't want to hurt me. That's what fucked me up the most: how abuse and care came in the same breath. That's what made life with her such a damn mind-fuck. It wasn't just black and white. It was very, *very* gray. And I'm well aware that I, too, have a switch that can be flipped under just the right circumstances. The problem is, I don't know myself enough to understand what those circumstances are. I can't guarantee that I'll never lose my shit on anyone I love.

I only shrug. "Alright, if you say so."

Miranda studies me a moment longer, then flashes a grin that's equal parts mischief and mercy. "Okay. Mood reset. Can I see more sexy pictures of your girlfriend?"

I shake my head at her with a half-smile on my lips. "You'd like that, huh?"

"Well, yeah. I don't discriminate, and she's really nice to look at. How tall is she?"

"I've never asked her, but probably around five nine?"

"Damn, she's tall!"

"Yeah, I definitely don't throw my back out trying to kiss her," I say with a smirk.

Miranda laughs. "I bet that's convenient."

"Definitely is."

Out of my periphery, I notice Miranda running her hand over the conditioned leather seat as she looks around the interior of my '69 Mustang. "You know, I really, really like this car of yours. I bet it's a real panty-dropper. How many girls were you able to hook up with because of the car you drive?"

I chuckle. "What do you think I did, take a survey after I finished? 'Oh, hi, now that I've climaxed, please tell me exactly what it was that convinced you to let me fuck you.'"

Miranda giggles. "You ever have sex in this car?"

I shake my head at her. She really has no respect for my privacy. She never has, though.

"Come on, Rony, you know how nosy I am."

"I'm well aware."

"Glad we have that understanding. So? Sex in this car? I can't imagine a reason why you wouldn't. It's so sexy in here," she purrs, her right hand gliding along the black dash.

I still don't answer but can't hide the grin tugging at my lips.

"I knew it," Miranda says victoriously. "With your feline? Of course with your feline. She sends you pictures like that, she's definitely had you in this car."

I laugh at her ability to carry an entire conversation without me even saying a word.

"I'd love to meet her some time, Rony." She turns her attention to me. "Bring her to Montana with you one day. Or maybe I should come visit you in New York."

"One thing at a time, Randi. Let's get you set up first, okay?"

"Whatever you say," she says, then sighs. "Thank you again for being here. It's been a rough couple of days."

"Don't even mention it," I say, merging lanes.

"You know what I could really go for right now?" she asks. I briefly look at her, bracing myself for another random subject change. "Some weed." She sighs. "I'd really just love a couple hits to calm my nerves. You wouldn't happen to have any on you, by any chance?"

I nod toward the passenger side. "Oh yeah, right there in my glove compartment."

Her blue eyes widen as her brows move toward her hairline. "Seriously?"

I snort a laugh. "Fuck no. Of course I don't have any weed on me, Randi."

"Don't get my damn hopes up like that, Rony," she says, making me laugh even more. "Jordan took my last bit, too."

"You still smoke?"

"Not as much as I used to, but occasionally. It helps me sleep. You?"

I shake my head. "Not since before I met Cat. But, if you're desperate"—I chuckle quietly—"I still have a bag in my room in Montana. Not sure if it's still any good since it's like three years old, but it's taped to the underside of the second dresser drawer in my room."

"Are you lying to me again?"

I laugh. "No, I'm serious. Have at it. Just don't let my grandmother catch you. And if she does, don't tell her where you got it from."

"I'd never rat on you." She giggles and draws a cross over her heart. "So did meeting your girlfriend change your ways then, lover boy?"

"Not really. I just haven't smoked much after moving back to New York; a handful of times with my best friend and Steve, but I don't know, I just stopped, I guess. No particular reason."

“That’s good,” Miranda says. “It’s just a crutch anyways. I should really stop, too. After I dig through your bedroom in Montana,” she says with a mischievous laugh.

***

We get to Nashville a little while later and grab some lunch before I check us into the hotel for the night.

“You have standards,” Miranda says as we step into the room, which is bright, modern, and clean.

“Didn’t want to risk catching some disease.” I throw my backpack on one of the two queen-sized beds. I made sure to book a room with two so we each had our own.

“I’m just glad there wasn’t a blacklight in that Pikeville room. Aside from the bathroom, I’m pretty sure the bed, the carpet—hell, the walls—would’ve lit up like a Jackson Pollock painting,” I say with a disgusted face. “There were probably fluids all over that damn place. Did you see those lampshades?” I shudder.

“Ew, Rony,” Miranda laughs. “On the lamps and walls?”

“Not everyone has great aim.” I shrug, and she dissolves into a new fit of laughter. That’s something I’ve always been able to do—make her laugh. No matter how bleak things got for either of us, I could always crack her open just enough to let in some light. When you’re freefalling, that matters. I *know*.

“Gross,” she wheezes.

“I swear there are documentaries about how nasty motels are. I bet the one we stayed at last night was featured in one of those. You know they’ve found semen on remote controls?”

Miranda struggles to catch her breath from laughing so hard.

“Stop, Rony,” she screeches, tears streaming down her face as she holds her stomach, doubled-over. “That’s so nasty.”

“I’m truly sorry to burst your bubble about how clean last night’s place was.”

“You don’t even know if it really was as bad as you think it was,” she says, desperately trying to catch her breath. “Okay, the place was old, but—”

“Dude, I could *smell* the stale cum on the sheets. And those pillows were way too stiff and crinkly.”

Miranda folds her arms over her stomach like she did this morning. “Rony, seriously, you need to stop. I can’t breathe…” she squeals.

I stretch my arms over my head. “Fine. I’ll shower, and then maybe we can grab you some clothes once you catch your breath.” I grin and pull a fresh pair of boxers and a clean long-sleeved henley from my backpack.

When I walk into the bathroom, the white tile looks clean and the space smells fresh. Much better.

I stand under the shower for a long while, relishing the hot water, my muscles relaxing with the warmth. I wash myself thoroughly and brush my teeth for a second time today before finally drying off and slipping into my fresh boxers and shirt, then pull on my jeans again. Incredible what a hot shower can do for the body and soul.

***

Miranda and I set out and spend a couple of hours getting some basic necessities for her to take to Montana, along with a temporary phone and some new clothes.

I shake my head with a groan when Miranda holds up a lacy thong-and-bra set and notes how unsatisfactory the selection is at the store we’re in.

"I took your virginity, Rony. Stop acting all shy around me," she says with a wicked grin before she throws the underwear into her shopping basket, then drags me onward.

Half an hour later, we leave the store with the essentials. It's not much, but it'll get her by until Miranda has the chance to stock up.

Once we're back at the hotel, I fall stomach-first onto my bed, send off a quick text to Cat with only the words "I love you," then pass out. I didn't get great sleep last night, and this is the first real chance I've had to rest since getting Miranda's call yesterday morning. I only wake up when Miranda rouses me a couple hours later, telling me she's hungry. I'm too damn tired to go anywhere and happily agree when Miranda suggests room service.

I check my phone, but there's neither a message nor a missed call from Cat. I haven't heard from her at all today and it's making me surprisingly antsy. It's not like I can't go a day without hearing from Cat. I can and I do. All the time. We're both busy people; we don't constantly expect check-ins. Still, I'm oddly restless. I texted her twice today without a response.

"So, how are things back home?" Miranda asks, then takes a bite of her dinner that just got delivered to our room.

"Pretty good," I say with a nod as I inspect my club sandwich. I take off the ham I had specifically asked them to leave off. *Yuck.*

"Do you still work at that bar?"

"Yep."

"And Columbia? Is it everything you dreamed it would be?"

I chuckle. "Umm, sure."

"Not very convincing, Rony!"

"I mean, it's more school." I shrug. "It's fine."

"What's your major?"

"I'm still undeclared. Just doing the general ed stuff right now. I'm not totally sure what I want to major in, to be honest."

"That surprises me," she says, studying me.

"Why?"

Miranda shrugs. "I don't know. You're really good at making it look like you have it figured out."

"I have absolutely nothing figured out," I say dryly.

"Had me fooled."

Yeah, I guess that's kind of the point.

"Well, what do you see yourself doing in the future?"

"I don't know. I've been trying to figure it out." I take a bite of my sandwich.

"Does your feline know what she wants to do?"

"She's majoring in psychology."

Miranda nods. "That's what I'd want to study if I ever went to college. I like figuring out what makes people tick." Then she giggles. "Has she been trying to psychoanalyze you?"

"Not yet, but I'm sure it's coming soon," I chuckle.

"Don't worry, Rony, you're really fucking good at shutting down. You're like Fort Knox when it comes to your psyche."

"It's a hard-earned skill." I take another bite.

"Skill? More like bad habit."

"Whatever you want to call it," I mumble and shrug. My phone starts buzzing in my pocket and I pull it out. Cat's perfect face lights my screen.

"Ah, speak of the devil?" Miranda laughs.

I nod and answer Cat's call. "Hey baby," I say, elated.

"Hi sweet boy. How are you?" Cat's voice doesn't give me any indication that something's wrong. The restlessness in my bones ceases.

"Good. Eating some dinner right now. How about you?"

"I just got done with dinner and I'm getting ready to head to your apartment. I'm hanging out with Tori and Vada tonight."

"Any plans?"

"No, I think we'll just relax, watch a movie or something," she says softly. "So, any news?"

I fill her in on the plan, letting her know I'm in Nashville now. "Randi's flight leaves at five tomorrow morning. I'll drop her off and then I'm heading home to you," I say with a sigh.

"So, you'll be home tomorrow evening?"

"Yeah. Are you around, or do you have plans?" Cat has been spending a lot of her evenings with Tori, or on schoolwork, or just with her family lately.

"No plans. Want me to meet you at your apartment when you get home?"

"Yeah. I want to see you badly." I feel Miranda's eyes on me. "Can you stay the night?" I ask Cat. I need to spend some uninterrupted time with her.

"I can," she says with a smile in her voice. "Did you know our families will be spending Christmas Eve together?"

"Nope," I say with a chuckle. "Good to know, I guess. I *love* spending time with your dad." Try as I might, Cat's dad isn't particularly fond of me. I'm not totally sure why. I don't think I've ever given him a reason to dislike me, other than the fact that I have sex with his daughter, which I hope isn't something he actively thinks about. That would be... weird. But maybe it's just a dad-thing rather than a me-thing. No idea.

"Oh, yeah, I know. You and him are basically best buds," Cat giggles.

"Might just have to ask him to move into the apartment with Shane and me," I say, making Cat giggle more. I fucking love the sound of her laugh.

"I'd love to see my dad's reaction to that question."

"Me, too," I say. "How was your day?"

Silence follows. "Uneventful," Cat says. My brow creases. That pause didn't feel natural. Something's up. I've always been good at picking up on these things, thanks to my mother's volatility. But before I can overanalyze the one-breath-too-long pause, Cat continues. "I picked up a birthday present for Zack and Vada. And my mom's in

Christmas prep mode, so I've been trying to help her—and distract myself from missing you so much."

My heart gives a jolt and I close my eyes. "I miss you, baby."

"Really?" she asks like she doesn't quite believe me.

I blink at her question. "Yeah."

It takes a second for Cat to respond. "I miss you more," she finally says, a tone of sadness, or maybe it's disappointment, tingeing her words.

"Baby, is everything okay?" I ask, very aware of Miranda's gaze on me.

"Yeah, I'm fine," she says quickly.

"Are you sure?"

"Yes, I'm sure. I just really, really want you home."

"I'll text you as soon as I get on the road in the morning."

She sighs. "Okay. Mind if I call you while you're driving?"

"Of course not. Nothing better than your voice. I love you, baby."

"I love you, too, sweet boy. I'll talk to you later."

"She's really lucky to have you," Miranda says, sitting cross-legged on her bed when I hang up with Cat and toss my phone onto the pillow next to me.

"No." I shake my head and pick my sandwich back up. "I'm lucky to have her. She's honestly the best thing that has ever happened to me."

"I can tell." Miranda gives me a vigorous head nod. "I can actually see your whole body relax when you talk to her. I could always tell how much she means to you. Just by the way your eyes light up, the way your face softens when you talk about her. I'm so glad you have something this good in your life, Rony. You deserve it," she says, her voice soft and warm.

"You'd deserve something this good, too."

Miranda smiles but doesn't look at me. "Yeah, I'd love to have something this good, but I don't think it's meant for me." Her eyes lock on her dinner plate. Before I have an opportunity to contradict her, she says, "What time does my flight leave again?"

"Uh, 5:05 tomorrow morning," I say, pulling up her flight info on my phone.

"So, we should be at the airport no later than maybe four, huh?"

I nod. "Yeah, probably. Just to give you time to check in an all that stuff."

"So maybe no crazy partying until the early morning hours, then?" she says jokingly.

"Probably not." I take another bite of my food.

"So, what should we do tonight?"

I chew and swallow quickly. "Uh, sleep?"

She grins mischievously. "Your bed or mine?"

I shake my head at her. "How about you sleep in yours and I sleep in mine?"

"Aww, but who's going to keep me warm?" she asks with a giggle.

"Your blanket," I say, and take another bite while Miranda laughs.

Thursday, December 22nd

Ronan

"Randi. Dude, you really have to wake up now." I sit on the edge of Miranda's bed, nudging her shoulder.

She grunts, face buried in her pillow, body wrapped like a burrito in the thick blanket. I've been trying to wake her for the last thirty minutes. Once before my shower, again after brushing my teeth, and one more time while getting dressed. It's three-thirty in the morning and she seriously needs to get her ass up so we can grab our things, check out of the hotel, and get her to the airport in time for her flight to Missoula.

"Fine. You leave me no other choice."

I flip on every light in the room, then yank the blanket off her.

"Nooo, Rony!" she whines, curling herself into a ball, trying to shield her tiny body from the cool air suddenly assaulting her skin.

"Get up, Randi!"

"Ten more minutes," she rasps, reaching for her blanket. I keep it out of reach, standing at the foot of the bed like a sentry.

"We don't have another ten minutes. Come on. Up!"

She rolls over and climbs out of bed, her light brown hair a freaking mess.

I chuckle. "There you go."

She flips me off. "You're way too damn energetic for this time of... what is it? Night? Morning?" she grumbles as she shuffles into the bathroom where she grabs her toothbrush. "How are you so fucking chipper?"

"Well you know, just happy to be alive, see another sunrise or some shit like that."

"Ah, yes, all the positive affirmations." She starts brushing her teeth while I throw my stuff into my backpack. "Do you think I have time for a quick shower?" Miranda calls to me from the bathroom.

I check the watch on my wrist. "Yeah, if you make it a really fast one."

"Great," she says and turns on the shower faucet.

"Woah, woah, before you get all naked and shit, please grab your clothes so you don't flash me again."

She pokes her head out and rolls her eyes. "Oh, please. Stop acting like you didn't like it." But she still grabs fresh clothes and disappears again, hips swaying provocatively.

I shake my head. She hasn't said a word about what happened between us in Montana. Not once. Still, it's the elephant in the room. She's been flirty, suggestive even. But Miranda's always been like that. I can't tell if she's testing me or if this is just Miranda being Miranda. All I know is I need to stay out of my own head and pray she doesn't pull anything again. Last time was too damn close, and she knew how much Cat meant to me. Means to me.

By 3:55, Miranda's dressed, hair damp, eyes still half-lidded. We check out of the hotel and hit the road. Traffic is practically nonexistent this early. We're at the airport fifteen minutes later.

She gets herself checked in and I walk with her all the way to the security checkpoint where we have to part ways. Miranda turns to me, then slings her arms around my neck and pulls me in for a tight hug. I wrap my arms around her tiny waist, hugging her back. She smells like wildflowers and hotel shampoo.

"Thank you, Rony. For everything," she sighs against me. "I don't know what I would've done without you."

"You're welcome, Randi. Just let me know when you get to the ranch, okay?"

"I will." She steps back, stands on her tiptoes, and kisses my cheek softly. "I'll see you around, Rony."

"Yeah. See you."

She hikes her new backpack onto her shoulder and walks toward the TSA line.

I turn to leave, already itching to be home, even if the thirteen-hour drive is going to suck.

"Hey, Rony," she calls. I pause and look back. Her expression is serious now, open in a way I'm not used to seeing.

"I'm sorry," she says quickly. "For leaving you like that. And for what I did before I left Montana. I'm sorry."

"It's okay," I say, because I don't know what else to say.

She nods, gives me a soft smile, then disappears into the line.

I pull my phone out of my pocket and send a quick text message to Cat.

Me:

Getting on the road. I love you.

God, I can't wait to pull her into my arms.

Cat

"It honestly never occurred to me that you don't have a key," Tori says unlocking the front door to Ronan and Shane's apartment. She pushes the door open, and I step into the narrow hallway behind her.

I nod with some dismay. "Yeah, I guess I've never needed it before tonight because I'm usually either here with Ran or you."

It's just past six. Twenty minutes ago, Ronan sent me the shortest of texts—just his ETA: six-thirty. I made my way to his apartment, intent on meeting him there, only to realize I couldn't get in. With Shane working Ronan's shift tonight, my only hope to get in was Tori, who luckily, had only just left and was kind enough to swing back.

Tori cocks her head to the side, her long dark hair following the motion. "You should ask Ran for a key. Shane gave me one the day he moved in. I don't see why Ran wouldn't give you one."

I've thought about that, too. About the fact that Shane made sure Tori had a key right away, and about how Ronan moved into the apartment months ago and hasn't even hinted at wanting me to have a key. And yes, I've thought about asking him, but a very real, very stubborn, and probably irrational part of me doesn't want to have to ask him.

"I kind of want it to be Ran's idea," I say, kicking off my shoes. "I don't want to bring it up if he hasn't thought to."

Tori raises an eyebrow. "This sounds oddly familiar."

"How so?"

"Oh, you know, like how you didn't want to tell Ran you were in love with him until he told you first. And then you almost didn't get to tell him at all," she says with a sassy twist.

I expel a weird snorty huff at her.

"Cat, if you haven't noticed, guys aren't super perceptive. You're not doing either of you any favors by staying quiet."

My brow furrows. If anyone's staying quiet, it's Ronan.

"Just ask him for a freaking key when he's home."

"You don't think he wants to talk to Shane about this first?" I ask. "I mean, it's not just Ran's place. And what if Ran doesn't want me to have free roam of the apartment? If I asked him for a key and he gave it to me, I'd just feel like I'm pressuring him into something he doesn't actually want."

"You're making excuses," Tori says, waving me off. "Shane won't care. As far as he's concerned, four of us live in this apartment. And do you really think Ronan is worried about you having the run of the apartment when he's not here?" She giggles as if the mere thought is absurd.

But I'm not so sure. Lately I've been riddled with questions, with doubts that have only compounded. Ronan's still holding back. Even after everything, even after a year and a half together, there are parts of him I've never touched. Parts he won't let me near.

"Alright, I can tell I'm not convincing you, so I'll head back out. I'm meeting my dad for tapas. But seriously, Cat, it's okay to ruffle feathers sometimes. You won't know the outcome until you do. So please, ask Ran for a key."

Then she's gone, and I'm left alone in the stillness of the apartment. Everything's quiet.

Too quiet.

***

I'm on the sofa, trying to think of the best order in which to broach what I consider to be the uncomfortable subjects with Ronan once he's back. Should I ask about the key first and then Rashana? Or the other way around? Or just pick one and save the other for another day?

When I hear Ronan's key in the lock, I get up and meet him in the hallway as he walks in. His face illuminates with a beautiful smile the moment his eyes find me. He drops his backpack to the floor, then pulls me into his arms. His body is firm but warm, and I bury my face in his jacket, inhaling his clean, familiar scent. Ronan smells like home, like comfort, like love. *God, I never want to lose that.*

He mimics me, his face in my hair, taking a deep inhale before he exhales with a soft, sated groan. "Hey baby."

"Hi sweet boy," I say without moving my head from his shoulder. This right here—Ronan's arms wrapped tightly around me, the feel of his body, his scent, his warmth—is exactly what I needed. It doesn't matter that he was only gone for two days. It may as well have been two years; the ache was the same. I'm convinced it was his sudden departure that caused my insecurities to rattle around my brain these past couple of days, because it all suddenly feels so much less significant. Miranda, Rashana, stupid keys. Who cares. He's here. He's mine. He loves me.

"How was your drive?" I ask, taking a small step back without breaking physical contact. I just want to be able to look into his face.

That smile on his soft, full lips hasn't vanished, and his beautiful green eyes are bright and happy.

"Long as hell. I tried to stop as little as possible. I wanted to come home to you." He tugs me close to him again, unwilling to allow even the smallest bit of space between our bodies. His words make my heart flutter. "I feel gross, though." He shifts slightly as though suddenly feeling uncomfortable in his own skin.

I grin. "How about you take a quick shower," I purr, "and then we can pretend to watch something while I climb on top of you?"

A low groan emanates from Ronan's chest. "I like the sound of that, but I'd like it even more if you suggested *we* take a quick shower."

I giggle. "Smooth. Real smooth, sweet boy."

"All I heard was 'yes.' Unless you actually mean 'no,' then of course I'll respect that," Ronan says and releases me from his hold. He takes his backpack, then motions for me to lead the way into his bedroom.

I take a seat on his bed and open my food delivery app while Ronan pulls some clothes out of his backpack and deposits them in his hamper. "What are you feeling?" I ask him, scouring the restaurant options.

Ronan hangs his jacket on a hanger in his cramped closet. "How about Thai?"

I smile. He knows Thai food is my favorite. That and barbeque.

"The usual?" I ask, already selecting the small restaurant four blocks west from here, then quickly add our favorite dishes to the cart for delivery.

Ronan nods. "The usual. I'm going to start the shower," he says with a smirk and a wink. My body is already heating in anticipation.

I hurriedly finish ordering the food. Delivery time is an estimated thirty minutes—plenty of time to have a little *snack* before dinner—then toss my phone onto Ronan's bed. I can already hear the water running in the shower. I pull off my oversized knit sweater and drop it on the bed, heat blooming deep in my core. T-minus too many seconds until I'm naked, wet, and pressed up against him.

But before I can get too excited, my gaze lands on his desk. His phone lights up, buzzing against the wood. And the name on the screen sends my pulse skittering.

Miranda.

Guess she really is back in his life. Suddenly, it feels significant again.

I take the phone, the vibrations traveling up my forearm as if tiny bugs are crawling beneath my skin, and walk into the bathroom. Ronan is already half-undressed, shirtless—and perfect; always so perfect—his jeans unbuttoned and hanging loosely on his hips, giving me the perfect view of his beautiful chest, those abs, and that delicious V leading to his manhood. I just learned in my biology class that there's an actual term for the muscle group in his lower abs, the grooves that run diagonally from his hip bones to his... groin. It's the Adonis belt, and I'd say that's a pretty damn perfect term. I salivate every time I see it, my fingers itching with desire to trace it. It's enough to temporarily distract me from the phone buzzing excitedly in my hand. That's until Ronan turns to me with a smile and his eyes move to his phone.

I hold it out to him. "Your phone," I say, even though it's completely unnecessary.

"Who is it?" he asks, already reaching for it.

I don't respond, watching instead as recognition flashes in his eyes and his lips tug into a small smile. I don't think his smile is as big as the one he gave me when he saw me walking into the bathroom five seconds ago. Or is it? Does he seem excited? I find myself listening intently to the pitch of his voice as he holds the phone to his ear.

"Hey Randi! I take it you made it?" His lips curl into something soft.

Just hearing her name makes my heart twist.

Ronan moves around and past me. "Get under the shower. I'll be right there," he whispers to me, gives me a quick kiss against my temple, then leaves, closing the bathroom door behind him.

I stand for a moment, the muscles in my back tensing with the rigidity of my spine. Ronan left me to speak with Miranda in private. Does that mean he doesn't want me to hear what they talk about? *God, what is wrong with you, Cat? Why are you so sensitive lately. Stop being ridiculous. The water's running. He probably left to escape the background noise. His smile wasn't any wider than the one he gave you.*

I strip off my clothes, then step into the tub and under the warm shower. My muscles relax immediately, my eyes closing with the warmth. I let my head fall back and allow the water to run over my head, drenching my hair. I run my hands through it slowly.

Ronan's voice comes as a needy rasp. "You're a ten on a normal day, a damn twelve naked, but *fuck*, naked and wet? There isn't a scale high enough to measure how fucking perfect you are, baby."

My eyes fly open just in time to see him step into the shower with me.

I didn't hear him get back to the bathroom or undress himself, didn't even hear him pull aside the shower curtain. The look on his face tells me he means every word he just uttered. Ronan steps in, the water catching the edges of his shoulders, but his attention is fully on me. He reaches for my hips, tugging himself closer to me until my nipples brush against his chest. They harden immediately at the sensation running straight to my core. My inner muscles clench as if searching for something to squeeze, searching for him.

He lowers his head and ghosts a kiss against my cheekbone, then my ear, then the spot right below on my neck. My eyes shut with his caress.

"Are you happy that you got to see Randi again?" I manage to moan as Ronan's lips traverse the side of my neck, slowly but surely making their way toward my collarbone.

"Yeah, sure," he groans against my skin, but he doesn't stop kissing me, licking the water off me slowly.

I'm torn between my desire to lose myself in Ronan and seeking enough information about Miranda to still my insecure thoughts, at least partially. The latter wins. "You missed her, huh?"

Ronan doesn't break the contact with my skin. "Not as much as I missed you," he growls, his breath hot against my skin. Every inch he kisses feels claimed. When his mouth skims the swell of my breast, I arch toward him involuntarily, my nipples already aching, straining for his tongue. A couple more inches and he'll reach the stiff peaks.

I moan and move my hands to his hair, grasping his wet strands just as he reaches my areola and begins circling his tongue around the pebbled bud.

"Ran," I whimper when he takes my nipple between his teeth, carefully nipping at my sensitive skin before drawing it deep into his warm mouth. "Did you sleep in the same bed with her?"

He retreats. The sudden loss of Ronan's physical contact causes me to open my eyes. He stands, naked—and very hard—in front of me. His green eyes, though lidded and filled with want, also carry confusion as his brows dip. "Why are you asking me all of this, baby?"

Despite the warm water, a cold shiver runs through me. He's right in front of me, but I miss him. This makes no sense at all. *What am I doing?*

I shrug. "Is this not a question I should be asking?" I truly have no intention of picking a fight, but something inside me is needling. Maybe it's Vada's words about not having to be okay with everything Ronan does, or Tori's suggestion to ruffle some feathers occasionally. I don't like any of this, hate the feeling of dread settling in the pit of my stomach. *What if I push him away?*

Ronan's face sobers, the lust draining from his eyes as his gaze remains pinned on me. "You can ask me anything, baby. Anything, anytime," he says, unwavering.

Relief lightens my shoulders. "Okay then."

"The first night, yes, we shared a bed. Randi asked me to stay in her room with her because she was afraid the guy would come back. Her room only had one bed, so… The second night, in Nashville, I got us a room with two beds and we each slept in our own."

The information definitely eases my mind.

"And even when we slept in the same bed, I was fully dressed and slept on top of the blanket while she slept underneath it."

I'm immediately taken back to the morning I woke up on Shane's couch after some guy slipped me a roofie. Ronan lay next to me, fully dressed and sleeping on top of the blanket that was draped over me. Ronan did for me then what he did for Miranda these last two days. He was an amazing, supportive, protective friend. He did what I've always loved him for, and I need to get a damn grip.

"Honestly, baby, I don't want to talk about Randi. I want to talk about you and me, or better yet not talk at all"—he steps toward me again—"if that's alright with you." *Always seeking my consent. Still moving at my pace.*

I just nod, my skin heating with a delicious tingle at the sight of Ronan's pupils widening as his eyes gloss once more. My "yes" served as the drug hitting his bloodstream. "I missed you, Cat. I hate being away from you, hate physical distance between us. It's like I leave my heart behind."

"Yeah?" I breathe.

"Uh-huh," he groans. His body comes flush with mine, and I gasp with the swiftness with which Ronan spreads his palms over my butt cheeks, then hauls me up and against him, only to shift and press my back against the tiled wall. His mouth is on my breast a fraction of a second later. "And you know what else?"

"What?" I whimper.

His left hand glides under my thigh and between my legs, slickening his fingers with my arousal before he begins to sweep them up my sensitive flesh. "I've been hard for you since the second I left. I didn't touch myself once. Not even this morning. I wanted it to be unbearable by the time I had you under me again. And now? Baby, I'm fucking starving for you."

I let my head fall back and against the tile, breathing heavy with the feel of his fingers circling my swollen clit. "Can I ask you something else?" I breathe barely loud enough to be audible through the water.

"Anything," he groans, his breathing just as deep, just as labored as mine.

Ronan slips a finger inside me, and I gasp, white-hot pleasure surging through me. "C...can I... God, Ran," I break off with a moan when he sucks hard on my nipple. He works a second finger inside me, curling them to stimulate my inner walls in the most delicious way. "Can I have a key?" I manage to squeak before a moan tears from my throat and reverberates loudly through the bathroom.

"To the apartment?"

How Ronan is able to formulate complete sentences while giving me such unspeakable pleasure is beyond me. Unlike him, I don't manage to form a coherent word and make do with a simple nod.

He stills, just for a second, as if the weight of the question hits him. Then his lips curl into a bright smile. "Fuck, yeah. Of course you can, baby."

I don't know if it's my brain—high on all the sexy, feel-good hormones—or if he really is as excited about me having a key as I think he sounds, but I decide to take this as a win. I finally allow myself to melt into him, letting reason slip away, giving in to need, to love, to him.

Sunday, January 1st

Cat

It's just past midnight on New Year's Eve, and rather than spending it at Shane's mom's beach house, we're all gathered at Murphy's.

"End of a damn era," Shane sighs, looking around at us. He brings his glass to his lips and takes a forlorn sip of his whiskey.

Ronan chuckles. "Don't be so dramatic. It's not like we won't be able to hang out at the beach house again." He runs his hand through his hair to muss it, only to put his black ball cap right back on.

Ronan and Shane have been working all evening while Tori, Steve, Zack, Summer, Vada, and I have been hanging out, eating, and celebrating. Just before midnight, Ronan and Shane joined us at our table for the countdown. At exactly midnight, I collected a deep, sensual kiss from the most perfect guy in this world. The heat brought on by Ronan's tongue sweeping over mine for a solid sixty seconds is only just dissipating from my body, and the grin is still prominent on my face.

"Not for an epic New Year's party," Shane laments. From what I understand, it's the first time my friends have spent this occasion at Murphy's rather than at Shane's or his mom's beach house. "God, I miss throwing parties."

I can't help but laugh. It's only been a few months since Shane threw a party with what I'd estimate to be over a hundred people.

"So plan one, then," Steve says with a shrug.

Shane shakes his head. "No, I think the epic party days are behind me," he says almost wistfully. "We've all graduated."

"But Lauren is a senior," I say of Shane's sister. "I'm sure you'd still get a great turnout."

"Baby, please don't encourage him to be one of those dudes who still wears his letterman jacket with his beer belly hanging out when he's forty-five," Ronan groans.

That earns an offended huff from Shane. "I will *never* have a fucking beer belly." He flexes, causing the fabric of his already fitted long-sleeved shirt to strain against his chest and biceps.

Tori pats Shane's butt. "Of course you won't. No dad bod for you, Daddy."

"Oh god," Ronan groans while Vada and I dissolve into fits of laughter.

Shane shrugs. "But regardless, it's not like there's a ton of time to throw parties anymore. Not now that I've taken on full-time responsibility for Murphy's. And definitely not on New Year's Eve. It's one of our busiest nights after St. Patty's. I have to be here for that."

"And so do I, apparently," Ronan grumbles. He's dressed in almost exactly the same attire as Shane, the only difference being the small black apron tied around Shane's waist—Ronan never wears an apron—and the black ball cap covering Ronan's dark-blond, freshly-trimmed hair. Other than that, they blend in perfectly with all the other Murphy's waiters and the four bartenders.

"I told you, Ran, it's all hands on deck tonight." Shane nudges Ronan's shoulder.

"Uh-huh," Ronan mutters, looking worse for wear. He's been on his feet since Murphy's opened for brunch, and he won't be done for at least another couple of hours. He'll for sure be sleeping until past noon tomorrow. I can see it in his face. He's beat.

"I know it's a long day, man, but at least the tips are good, right?" Shane asks. "I scored a solid Franklin on top of a sixty-three-dollar tap."

"Don't get cocky, Shay. Jack tried to beat me yesterday, too, and at the end of the night his take-home was over two hundred less than mine." Ronan swipes his left hand over his right palm as though he's sending dollar bills flying. "I have every intention of walking out of here victorious tonight."

Steve chortles. "Alright, before you boys start whipping out your dicks to measure whose is bigger—"

"Mine," Shane says.

"Yeah, okay, wishful thinking, Shay." Ronan pats Shane's shoulder before he turns to his brother and raises his scarred left eyebrow. "Tell us about your new girl!"

Steve throws his hands up. "For fuck's sake. Why are you so convinced there's a girl?"

"Uh, let's see." Ronan taps his index finger to his lips, making a contemplative face. "You never come home. You're super fucking secretive. And whenever anyone asks you if you're seeing someone, you're evasive as all hell. You never just straight up say 'no,' which is as good as saying 'yes.'"

"Yeah, that and the fact that you came back home with a giant fucking hickey on your neck," Vada says so drily—and unexpectedly—that instead of sipping his drink, Zack inhales the liquid and begins coughing violently.

"I did not!" Steve grumbles, clapping his best friend's back in a half-hearted attempt to aid his intake of oxygen while both Tori and Summer screech with delight.

"Actually, you did," I giggle.

"Traitor," Steve throws at me, making me laugh out loud. "I thought you of all people would have my back, Cat. Guess I was wrong about you." He tsks loudly, then folds his arms over his chest.

"Case in point!" Ronan shouts at his brother. "E-fucking-vasive."

Steve looks anywhere but at Ronan.

"Stop the bullshit," Ronan says with a chuckle. "We all know you're seeing someone."

"Come on, Stevie," I say. "Why aren't you telling us about her?"

"I don't know what you're talking about," Steve says, still refusing to make eye contact with, well, anyone.

"Holy shit, dude, at this point she better be married with three kids and a mafia boss husband," Shane says.

Everyone's eyes are on Steve, looking for the tells he's unable to hide, try as he might.

I bump him with my shoulder and smile. "If we promise not to ask for specifics, will you at least tell us whether you're seeing someone?"

There's a long moment of silence—well, as silent as it gets, considering we're in a crowded Irish pub with hundreds of patrons loudly talking and singing along to the music playing on the speakers. It's honestly a surprise the eight of us are still managing to hold a decent conversation.

Steve exhales deeply, his shoulders sagging. "Fine. Yes, I'm seeing someone."

Zack chuffs in offense. "Are you serious? You fuck, why haven't you fucking told me?"

"Sorry man, it's just... it's still really, really new and... it's..." Steve trails off, but his eyes snap to his little brother, a dark determination hardening his face. Something settles in his jaw, and his voice lowers. "Stop, Ran. I can already see it in your face that you're trying to figure this out, okay? I know you're trying to read me and shit, and I'm asking you right now, as your brother, to please respect me when I ask you not to. All I'm willing to share with you guys right now is that there's a girl. I'll even tell you that her name is Ember and that, yes, I'm fucking head over heels for her, but that's all you're getting right now. If you love me at all, Ran, please don't prod, don't... think. Don't do the thing where you piece the puzzle together, okay? I promise, I'll tell you everything once I'm ready. But that's not now, so... please."

Ronan's expression mirrors his brother's, his brow and jaw set. I too can practically see Ronan's wheels spinning, his eyes narrowing as his gaze drills into Steve's head.

"Yep, definitely a mafia husband," Shane concludes with a chuckle.

"Fine," Ronan grits out. "I do love you, and I—" He pulls his phone from his back pocket. It buzzes in his hand, and his expression neutralizes.

"You're not doing anything dangerous though, right?" Zack asks Steve, visibly upset at his best friend's failure to tell him about this new girl.

Ronan leans toward me, his lips close to my ear. Goosebumps erupt down my neck and back with the warmth of his breath feathering against my skin. "I'll be right back. It's Randi." He places a soft kiss on my temple.

He turns and begins to walk away from the table I'm occupying with Steve, Vada, Tori, Summer, and Zack.

"Where the fuck are you going?" Shane calls after Ronan, who just points at his phone. "Break's over in five minutes, Ran!"

There he goes, leaving me to talk to Miranda in private. Again.

I hate that this is starting to feel familiar.

Ronan

"Hey there, Rony," Miranda says. "Happy New Year!"

"Yeah, you too! How come you're awake?" I ask her, pushing open the steel backdoor to Murphy's to step into the narrow alley behind the building. It's the quietest place I could think of.

Murphy's is always lively, but occasions like New Year's, St. Patrick's Day, and the Super Bowl and Stanley Cup games are a whole different level of crazy. It's still noisy out here with the sounds of typical New York traffic and the bangs of distant fireworks exploding in the night sky, but at least I can understand Miranda without changing the call to a video conference and attempting to read her lips.

"Couldn't sleep," Miranda says.

"I figured. I didn't think my grandparents' roaring New Year's Eve party kept you up," I chuckle. I shrug my shoulders up. It's chilly out here without my jacket.

"Well actually, your grandma is out here bumpin' that nineties R&B, so," Miranda says, making me laugh out loud. I'm about 99.9

percent sure my grandparents have been asleep for the past couple of hours. Ranch life isn't conducive to staying up until the crack of dawn to ring in the New Year.

"Oh yeah, I can totally see that," I say, trying to imagine exactly that. "So, what are you up to then?"

"Not much, honestly. Elias and I just got back from Sterling's a little while ago. We would have stayed longer, but that guy can't hold his liquor," she laughs.

"Oh, I'm very aware. Did he try to take you home with him again?"

"You know it," Miranda says mischievously. "But I told him I was tired. So he tried walking me to my cabin. It didn't go so well. He threw up in the bushes," she laughs. "He's honestly so sweet, Rony. He has absolutely no idea what he's doing; it's kind of cute."

"I bet 'cute' is exactly what he was going for," I say, making Miranda laugh again.

"How about you? What are you up to? Sounds like you actually are at a party?"

"No, I'm working tonight. I'm just making sure the people inside get to have their party?"

"I'm sorry," Miranda says earnestly.

"Don't be. I still get to be with the people I care about and I make great bank tonight. It's a win-win."

"You sound tired, though."

"It's been a long day, but it's fine. Any news about your truck?"

Miranda sighs loudly. "Nothing. I doubt I'll ever see it again. It's probably burned out or disassembled for parts or..."

"I'm sorry, Randi." I know how much that truck meant to her.

Another loud exhale travels through the phone. "It's alright. I'm going to save up to get myself another truck. In the meantime, I'm making good use of yours," she cackles. "How's your feline?"

The smile on my lips is immediate, as always. "She's good. I think... I don't know, I've been misstepping lately."

It feels safer to say it like that—to admit to something vague, instead of the things I actually can't face.

"What do you mean?"

"I don't know. I think maybe I'm not communicating right with her, or—"

"Uh, duh," Miranda huffs. "You're definitely not communicating right with her, Rony. I mean, you haven't been really talking to her about the stuff in your head, right? You're not letting her in!"

"Right, yeah," I say, even though that's not what I was talking about. But she's not wrong. That's the part that stings.

The slam of the door crashes through the quiet, jarring me like a punch. For a second, I forget where I am. Shane steps out, all business.

My heart gallops in my chest. "Fuck, are you trying to give me a fucking heart attack?"

"Sorry, dude. I just need you back inside." He disappears again.

"I gotta let you go, Randi."

"Back to the grind?"

I chuckle. "Yeah. Happy New Year, Randi."

"Happy New Year, Rony. Oh, and you know what a good resolution might be?"

I chuckle quietly. "What?"

"Talking."

I shove my phone back into my pocket, thinking about how only Miranda finds a way through my armor. And how that might be the whole problem.

***

At ten minutes until three in the morning, Vada is passed out with her head resting on her arms on the table, while Summer's asleep with her head in Zack's lap, her legs tucked onto the leather seat of the booth.

Shane locks the front doors behind Jack, closing Murphy's for the night.

I groan when I pull a chair up next to Cat's seat in the booth, then fall gratefully onto it. Holy hell, my entire body aches. I better not allow my eyes to shut or I'll pass out like Vada and Summer.

"Damn good night." Shane pulls up his own chair next to Steve, whose expression is sleepy, body relaxed. Shane is amped, even hyper, but that's nothing new. He's always like this. Crowds and noise don't wear him down like they do me—they invigorate him, which is probably why he misses throwing parties so much. I grin at his exuberance while draping my arm over Cat's shoulder to pull her toward me.

Even though she leans into me, her body feels stiff, unconforming. I angle my face to look into her eyes. "Everything okay, baby?"

"I'm fine," she says, her words cool. My eyes bounce between hers. I haven't had a chance to stop by her table again after the ball drop, after I got off the phone with Miranda and went back to work. She was fine when I kissed her at midnight. What the hell happened in the last three hours to cause her to be this short with me?

"How much did you make in cash tips?" Shane asks, pulling a long, rolled-up receipt from the pocket of his apron.

"For the entire day?" I ask.

Shane just nods, his eyes on the receipts.

"Seven hundred and forty-seven," I say, suddenly aware of the thick wad of bills in my jeans pocket. "Brunch was kind of slow today."

Shane grumbles, "Damn."

"You?"

"Six hundred and ninety-six," he says with a note of defeat.

"At least it's a sexy number, baby," Tori says, her eyes bloodshot and glossy. I'm surprised she's not asleep, too.

Shane grins at her. "Very sexy. Okay, well, Jack made nine hundred and fourteen in cash tips."

"Holy shit," Steve says, his eyes wide. "You guys make *that* much in tips? Why didn't I know about this?"

"And that's only the cash," Shane says with a nod at the paper in front of him. "Alright, so Ran, you got an additional eight hundred and eighty-seven in electronic tips. I got nine hundred and one. And Jack got..." Shane's face falls. "Eight hundred and thirteen. Without doing the exact math, I think Jack won this one."

I shut my eyes and crack my neck. God, I need sleep. "Yep. But to be fair, he ran the bar. On New Year's Eve. Drunk people tip more than sober people. It's all good. It's still a great fucking night."

"Yep, that's rent right here." Shane nods and taps his index finger on the paper receipt on the table.

I kiss Cat's temple, inhaling her. She hasn't moved out of my arms, but she still feels rigid. Like I'm holding a statue instead of a person. I tell myself it's just fatigue, but I've known Cat long enough to know the difference between tired and tense.

I kiss her temple again, trying to smooth whatever tension there is, but she stays still. And I start counting the seconds of silence between us.

Cat

Yes, I'm aware. I'm aware that I should tell Ronan how much it bothers me that he walks away whenever Miranda calls him, how much it bothers me that he obviously doesn't want me to hear what they talk about. Heck, that it bothers me that she calls him in the first place—after trying to convince him to cheat on me, then abandoning him while he was at his most vulnerable. But the words feel petty in my mouth. So I swallow them. Again.

The rational, unemotional part of my brain constantly reminds me that I don't have anything to worry about. Each time Miranda called Ronan it was noisy, and I'm sure the only reason Ronan walked away was to be able to hear her. I also just don't want to get into it with him right now. I will tell him eventually, but not tonight, not when we're surrounded by our friends, when this is a night to celebrate.

"Is something wrong?" Ronan asks me for the second time since sitting down with me.

I look into his beautiful green eyes and force my body to relax against him. I love him. I've always loved him. But I'm also irritated.

"Nothing's wrong. Just getting sleepy." I force a smile.

"Ran, I wanted to ask you something," Zack says, hesitation prominent on his face as he leans forward and rests his elbows on the table, careful not to jostle Summer in her slumber.

Ronan diverts his attention to Zack. "What's up?"

"So, I have this opportunity to submit a film of mine for a national competition," Zack says. "My film professor at UCLA has been mentoring me. I'm trying to come up with a concept and then work on it this next semester. I'm hoping to get it finished by June or July and submit it for judging."

"Okay?" Ronan says. "And how do I play into this?"

"Well, if you'd be okay with it, I was hoping to make a film about you," Zack says hesitantly.

Ronan's brow creases. "What do you mean?"

"Okay, Ran, please just hear me out, okay?" Zack says raising his hands.

"Sure," Ronan says calmly.

"I have all this footage, like of all of us and stuff, and, obviously, a lot of you. And... I mean, I still have that footage from... from when... when everything hap—"

"Yep," Ronan says with a nod, urging Zack to move past that point.

"Your story, it's super compelling, Ran. And I mean..."

I feel the tension in Ronan's body, and I wrap my arm around his waist, scooting a little closer still.

Ronan shakes his head. "Zack, I don't think—"

Zack moves his hands as if to rebuff Ronan's reluctance. "Hold on, okay? The documentary won't focus on like, specifically what happened to you. It's more about how you came out of it on the other side, you know? Like, how you overcame it and where you are now and stuff. You don't have to really do anything," Zack says, ignoring the rather harsh look Shane's throwing his way. "I'd just keep doing what I'm doing. Like, just film stuff and put it all together."

Ronan inhales and exhales deeply. "I don't want to be an asshole, man. I don't want to tell you not to do this because, I mean, I know this is your passion and stuff, but... I don't really want... I can't..." Ronan trails off.

Zack deflates, sitting back in his seat. "It's okay, Ran. I figured you'd say that," he says warmly, though the disappointment is visible on his face. "I just wanted to ask because, well, I really think that your story would touch a lot of lives, you know?"

"I'm sorry," Ronan says with a guilty look. "I just don't think I'm ready for this."

Shane shakes his head. "You don't have anything to feel bad about, Ran. You're not fucking obligated to talk to anyone about anything, okay? Not some investigative journalist, not even one of your best friends. You don't owe anyone anything,"

Ronan's face blanches. "What?"

"You don't owe anyone anything—not Zack, not that investigative journalist chick."

Ronan's eyes flare for the briefest of moments. "What investigative journalist chick?"

"The one who..." Shane trails off, realization dawning, and levels a dismayed look at me. "You haven't fucking told him?"

I shake my head at Shane.

"Why the fuck not, Cat? It's been like two weeks!"

I shift out of Ronan's hold, creating some distance between us as shame, guilt, and anger clash in my chest, each fighting for pole position. I know how this looks. Like I'm the one who kept a secret. I'm the one who made Shane raise his voice.

"What are you guys talking about?" Ronan asks, his gaze moving from Shane to me, then back again. I think I recognize fear flaring in his emerald-green eyes, and the guilt inside me takes the lead.

Shane squares his shoulders and crosses his arms in front of his puffed-out chest, his jaw ticking twice while he waits. And now I know, without a shadow of doubt, where Shane's loyalty lies. Not with me. Never with me. Always and forever with his best friend, no matter how unreasonable, how obstinate, how stubborn Ronan may be. Shane has his back, and nothing and no one will change that. Not even me.

I hold Shane's eye contact for a moment longer before he raises his eyebrows at me, and I turn my attention to Ronan.

"When were you going to tell me about Rashana Yates?"

Ronan pales even more, his full lips losing their soft pink coloring and I see the bob of his Adam's apple as he swallows what I imagine must be akin to ash. To his credit, he holds eye contact. But his breathing is noticeably elevated as he works to maintain his outward composure, just like he's been conditioned all his life.

"I wasn't," Ronan finally says, his tone even. "I wasn't going to tell you or Shane or anyone."

"I'm sorry, I missed something," Steve says. "Who in the world are we talking about?"

Ronan exhales deeply, then directs his gaze at his brother. "Rashana Yates. She's in the investigative journalism program at Columbia. She's been... She reached out to me about a story on... on..." The words get stuck in Ronan's throat. He looks back at me. "But you're right, I should have told you. I'm sorry. I had thought about it when Rashana first talked to me, but I got sidetracked when my grandmother showed up, and... I don't know how to explain it, but... I'm trying to be careful with what I give my energy to. Telling you guys about Rashana when I have absolutely zero intention of talking with her is not where I want to put my energy." He shuts his eyes. "It's just that there's so much damn noise, and if I give a voice to all of it..." He trails off. The anguish on his face completely desiccates the anger in me. It crumbles, leaving only the guilt and shame in its wake.

Of course Ronan hasn't told me about her—wasn't going to tell me about her—because it's all still so raw, so painful, so fresh for him. He's nowhere near done purging his past. While a year without violence may seem like a long time to me, it's probably nothing to Ronan.

"Ran," I say softly. He opens his eyes. "I love you. I love you so much, but you need to talk to me. I'm trying to be patient. I'm trying to be understanding, but I need you to talk to me. Don't leave me in the dark. It's not fair! It's not fair for me to find out about Rashana from anyone but you. She just showed up at Murphy's and started asking about you and... it's not fair!"

He nods. "Yeah, I know."

His voice is even, but the words are heavy. Like he's said all he can say without promising change.

Friday, January 20th

Ronan

Me:

Stay with me tonight.

I text Cat while I grab a quick bite to eat at one of the campus coffee shops in between classes. Break's over, and both Cat and I are back to our regularly scheduled programming of trying to squeeze in some quality time between our class schedules, Murphy's, and Cat's new job.

If you asked her, she'd tell you her job isn't a real job, but it definitely is. Yeah, she may be working for her mom three days a week for a few hours in the mornings, but it's honest, paid work. I also think Shane would very much disagree with the assessment that just because you're working for your parents, means you're not working a real job.

Cat's mom broached the idea with her when both our families were gathered at my dad's on Christmas Eve. She explained that her receptionist asked to reduce her hours in the mornings due to some childcare issues and that this might be a good opportunity for Cat to get some experience.

"Plus, you need something to do other than your boyfriend," Cat's dad said. It was meant as a jab—he hardly ever talks to me directly and often will just refer to me as "Cat's boyfriend"—but Penny and Steve's snorts of laughter quickly made him realize that his statement came out different than he meant it.

"I'd prefer she stick to doing her boyfriend," I muttered under my breath, earning me a nudge from Cat, although the grin on her face gave her away.

Cat's dad didn't pick up on my comment and just continued to grumble. "You used to play softball and hang out with your friends."

"Sure," Cat said with an unimpressed shrug. "But I'm not in high school anymore, and my girlfriends are busy. Vada is in Philly, Summer is in California, and Tori is either with Shane, at school, or at work. And I *do* hang out with them whenever they're around." She turned her attention to her mom. "But I would absolutely love to help you, Mom."

So since the beginning of the new year, Cat has been working at her mom's office three mornings a week—answering phones, scheduling appointments, and keeping patient records. From what I can tell, she loves it, which makes me love it in turn. I love that she has something that's entirely her own, something that gives her purpose outside of school and me, I guess. And she's definitely bubblier, her mood boosted after I know I've done—or maybe *not* done—some things that have led to tension between us. I've been fucking up. I'm aware. I'm *always* aware. Nothing bothers me more than the knowledge that my actions negatively affect the girl I love more than life itself. All I ever want is to make her happy, to keep her safe. It's just that sometimes those things are mutually exclusive, and, fuck, I'm struggling to figure out a way to give her everything, because she *deserves* everything.

Cat:

Only if you'll promise to wake me the way I like you to wake me...

The grin on my face is instantaneous. I know *exactly* how she likes me to wake her when I get back from Murphy's in the middle of the night. It's those stolen, quiet hours when the rest of the world sleeps that feel especially intimate. Sex with Cat is always completely consuming, but when my body melds with hers in the middle of the night, it might as well be only us in the entire damn universe. Nothing and no one exists but us.

Me:

I wish it was tonight already so I can (a)rouse you properly.

Cat:

Why is it that just reading your words, I can feel your hands on me, sweet boy. I miss you.

I'm about to write back that I miss her, too, that I want my hands and mouth all over that delicious skin of hers—preferably right fucking now—when I note movement out of my periphery.

I glance up and tense when my eyes meet Rashana's. I groan—partially frustrated, partially resigned. I can't escape her.

"Hi Ronan," she says, more reserved than the last few times she's accosted me and spouted off like a damn waterfall.

"I'm still not talking to you," I say, keeping my voice neutral. "Especially after you invaded my sanctity and talked to my girlfriend."

"To be fair, she started talking to me."

I cock an unimpressed eyebrow at her. "Fine, but you tried to talk to my best friend, and I have no doubt you would have hunted Cat down eventually. She just got to you first."

Rashana gives me a sheepish shrug. "Fair."

I consider her for a moment. I don't know if it's her calmer, less intrusive approach today, or the fact that those closest to me know about her now, but those brick walls that sprang up from the ground the first few times she talked to me are slower to assemble themselves today.

I exhale deeply. "I assume you're not here to sit and enjoy a cup of coffee." I nod at her empty hands. "You trying to get me to talk about my life growing up?"

She shrugs. "It's a compelling story."

There's that word again—compelling. Zack used it, too. And yeah, maybe it is. There are plenty of people who don't make it out the other side, plenty of people who die at the hands of their abusers. But there are just as many people who *do* live a life after the violence, some more, some less successfully so. What I have yet to figure out is if those people are truly the lucky ones.

I shrug. "Maybe. But it's also painful and private. It's not just a story—it's my life. It's… my entire childhood. Seventeen years." I really want to put this into perspective for her.

Rashana nods. "I'm aware of that. Ronan, I'm not trying to tear open old wounds or retraumatize you. But… I mean… is there any chance at all I could convince you to sit down with me?"

I lean against the back of my chair, forcing my shoulders to relax, then shake my head. "I can appreciate what you're trying to do. This is obviously an"—I search for the right words but come up short—"interesting story for you. I get it. There's a reason true crime documentaries do so well. People get invested in other people's drama. But… look, I'm not trying to be difficult, okay? My refusal to talk to you has nothing to do with you personally."

She looks at me doubtfully, and I chuckle.

"I'm serious," I say with a nod. "One of my best friends just asked me if he could do a story about me and I told him no. I've known this guy since I was three years old. We went to preschool together. He's like family and still I told him no." I'm really trying to soften the blow. "And you know what, I could sit here and explain my reasoning to you again—how my 'story' isn't just a story, that it's my whole damn life, that it's painful and that I still have a really hard time talking about it. Maybe I could tell you that I'm sorry for shutting you down like this, but I'm finally learning that I have a right to set boundaries, that I have a right to protect myself. For so long I had no agency over my life, over the things that were done to me. And I'm just getting to a point where I get to say *no* without having to brace for pain. I empathize with you about how this affects your work. I'm sure it sucks, but I don't feel bad. I'm not sorry for not setting aside my own needs, my peace, so you can write a story."

Rashana takes in my words. Then she nods. "I figured you'd say that, but I thought I'd shoot my shot one last time."

"Consider it shot," I say, a hint of a smile on my lips.

"There's nothing I could do to convince you, huh?"

Jeez, relentless.

"You could tell me what you know about my uncle... and what you meant when you talked about my mom's sister," I say with a small shrug, careful not to change my facial expression. If there's anything I'm good at, it's maintaining a poker face. *Thanks, Mom.*

Her eyebrows rise hopefully. "And then you'll talk to me?"

I chuckle quietly. "No, but you have information about *my* family. You dug into *my* past. I think it's only fair that you share."

She studies me, her eyes bouncing between mine. Then she nods. "Okay. Mind if I sit?" She nods at the chair across the small table from me.

I give her a shrug-nod.

The chair scrapes against the floor when she pulls it back. She takes a seat, shoulders slumped forward.

The low hum of people chatting around me falls away like a curtain.

"Is it bad?" I ask, a definitive, fearful edge to my voice.

"Well, you have to understand that a lot of it is conjecture, you know? Facts, like puzzle pieces, that would need to be pieced together, but..." She hesitates, eyes flicking to mine before dropping to her hands. "It's... yeah. I think it's probably not good. I'm sorry, Ronan."

I nod, warring with myself. I want to know and not know; I'm curious and simultaneously terrified of what I'm about to learn.

Before I can stop her, Rashana dives in. I let her.

By the time she finishes, all I can think is I should've walked away. I should've never asked her to tell me what she found out. Because now, all I can see when I close my eyes is blood and lineage, rage passed down like inheritance. And in just a few weeks, there will be two newborn babies in my family. Brand-new, innocent lives. And I'm suddenly convinced that I cannot be trusted around them. After all, I'm descended from monsters.

Cat

My eyes flutter open, but the smile that wants to take up residence on my lips at the sight of a sleeping Ronan next to me doesn't get the chance to blossom. I didn't hear him come in or feel him slip beneath the covers. And he didn't wake me the way he usually does—fingers, lips, that slow seduction in the dark. His face is contorted, pained, lines sharp in the shadows. I can tell by his erratic breathing, his tossing and turning, the clamminess of his skin, that he's in the throes of a night terror.

He's been having them more frequently lately, though I'm not totally sure why. He first told me the nightmares had started up again after his grandmother's visit in November. But unlike the last flare-up back in August, this time they aren't tapering off. They're getting worse.

"Ran?" I say quietly, my hand on his chest. He's drenched in sweat yet cool to the touch; his breath rises and falls fitfully. I've witnessed him have these nightmares several times since the trial, know how distressing they are to him, especially when he's unable to come out of them by himself.

"Sweet boy, wake up," I say, a little louder. I move my hand away from his heaving chest and to his cheek. I'm surprised when my skin is met with wetness. I lift my head to find tears staining his face. He's crying in his sleep. I've never seen that before, not like this. Not silent tears slipping down his face while he fights some invisible terror. *What in the world has him so freaked out?* "Ran, come on, wake up," I say, wiping his tears away, but they keep coming. There's so much pain on his face, it guts me.

I sit up and kiss his lips gently. "Ran, wake up!"

He gasps and startles awake, shooting up on his elbows, breathing labored as his eyes dart over the room. When they land on me, they're full of despair.

"I'm sorry, baby," he chokes out. "I'm so sorry."

I reach for him, my hand against his cheek. "No, it's okay." I move my left hand to his chest. His heart is hammering against his ribs at a brutal pace. "Are you alright?"

He takes a second, then nods, though the crease on his brow doesn't soften and the sadness in his eyes remains.

"Nightmare?" I ask simply. He nods again.

I analyze his face a moment longer, desperate to make him feel better, to distract him from whatever pulled him into the darkness of his night terror. I know what he needs. Not words, not logic. He needs to feel safe again. And if I can give that to him, even just for a little while, I will.

I pull my shirt up and over my head, discarding it on the floor.

Relief floods me when the tension bleeds from his face. "Baby," he breathes and pulls me into his lap. I straddle his hips, then dip my head and ghost my lips over his, doing the one thing that I know will take him out of his head, out of his pain, out of this world.

Monday, January 23rd

Ronan

I officially became a half brother last night.

My dad texted Steve and me early yesterday morning, letting us know that he and Penny were at the hospital, that Penny's water broke, and she was going to stay at the hospital until she delivered the twins.

After that the updates from my dad were sporadic, which I don't fault him for. I'm sure he was preoccupied with, well, Penny's labor and all of that. Cat received regular updates from her mom, who ended up going to the hospital to provide Penny and my dad with support. So it was actually Cat who told me at just before ten last night that my twin brothers were born via C-section half an hour earlier.

The babies and Penny are doing well. So well, in fact, that the three of them will be able to go home in a few days, despite the babies being born three weeks early.

"Oh my god." Cat swoons, a love-struck look on her rosy face the moment we walk into Penny's hospital room this afternoon and she spots the tiny babies wrapped like burritos in light blue blankets. My dad holds one of the boys while Penny holds the other, a tired smile on her face.

"How are you?" Cat leans over the bed to give Penny a gentle hug.

"Surviving," Penny laughs, her long dark hair wrapped into a messy bun atop her head.

"Are you in pain, baby?" my dad asks her, concern in his eyes.

"I'm okay right now," she says. "Do you want to hold him?" Penny asks Cat, who smiles widely, then carefully takes the baby from Penny's arms into her own.

"Oh my gosh, he's so tiny," Cat croons, her voice probably three octaves higher than usual. She gazes at the little bundle in her arms, gently rocking from side to side, instinctively knowing how to soothe a baby.

"So, who is who?" I ask my dad.

My dad chuckles. "This is Dean." He motions his chin at the baby in his own arms. "And that's Kellan." He gives a quick nod toward Cat.

"I love their names," Cat sing-songs quietly, still swaying, the baby securely cradled in her arms. She lowers her face to Kellan's head and inhales, her lips tugging into a sated smile.

"How can you tell them apart?" I ask. "They look exactly the same."

"Yeah," my dad says. "We're dressing them differently until we start to recognize their physical features more."

"Their little onesies have their names on them," Penny says with a giggle.

"Oh, okay, so it's not just me then," I say, relieved.

"No, it's not just you," my dad laughs. "I'm really worried about mixing them up and never being able to tell them apart," he says. "Do you want to hold Dean?" he asks with a smile in his brown eyes, his voice warm.

I hesitate. "Uhh..." I feel everyone's expectant gaze on me.

"Come on, Ran, hold your little brother," Penny says.

I awkwardly hold my arms out for my dad to place my brother in them. Dean hardly weighs anything at all, and I can't help but notice how fragile he feels in my arms. I suddenly feel too big, too muscular, too strong, too volatile to be holding something this... breakable. Like one wrong move could shatter him. What if I'm not wired for gentleness the way Cat is?

"Aw, you two," Penny chirps, looking from me to Cat, each of us holding one of the babies. "You're going to make great parents one day."

Cat smiles, but I'm overcome with unease. It's only made worse when Dean begins fussing in my arms. I eagerly return him to my dad.

"Babe, I think Dean's hungry," he says with a chuckle, moving to Penny's bed.

"Again? Jeez, I feel like a cow," Penny laughs.

Cat giggles. "Do they eat at the same time?" She's still holding Kellan, looking utterly comfortable as she sways with the sleeping baby.

Penny huffs. "I wish." I divert my eyes when she unbuttons her hospital gown, then moves Dean to breastfeed him. "No, they definitely don't eat at the same time, which means I'll never sleep again." Penny laughs ruefully.

"I'm sure we'll figure out a rhythm soon," my dad says with an expression that I can only describe as a mix of pride and contentment.

"You're awfully optimistic for someone who didn't have to give birth and doesn't have people sucking on their boobs all day and night," Penny says only half-jokingly.

My dad chuckles. "Hey, I'd do all those things for you if I could, but seeing as I'm biologically incapable of doing so, I'll just provide you with all my love and emotional support whenever I can."

"Maybe you could pump some milk and then Frank can take some night shifts for you when you guys are home," Cat says.

Penny beams at her. "That's a great idea! Please keep your wisdom coming! Honestly, you're going to be a fantastic mommy one day. You already have this figured out."

A faint blush warms Cat's face. "I had the advantage of being quite a bit older than my younger siblings, so I saw how my parents handled the newborn stage. My parents definitely teamed up," Cat says. "My dad would take every other feeding so my mom could get some sleep. My dad also did most of the work at home for the first few months so my mom could rest when my siblings were asleep. So that helped, I think."

"Well, looks like you'll be doing all the laundry," Penny says with a grin to my dad, who raises one dark eyebrow.

"Babe, I already do all the laundry."

"Oh, right," Penny laughs.

"Ran, do you want to hold Kellan?" Cat asks, taking a couple of steps toward me.

I shake my head. "I'm okay; knock yourself out, baby. Kellan looks perfectly content in your arms." I smile at her even though my body feels tense. "Have you talked to Stevie?" I ask my dad, desperate to distract myself from the restlessness growing inside me.

"Yeah. He's coming home in a couple of weeks to meet your brothers," my dad says, his voice full of warmth and love as he looks at Penny.

Cat and I stay at the hospital another fifteen minutes. Only reluctantly does she transfer a still-sleeping Kellan into my dad's arms when I suggest we head out to let Penny get some rest. To be honest, I'm eager to get out of here. Hospitals make me twitchy. Too many memories. Too many sharp smells and hushed voices. Too much... history. So after saying our goodbyes with promises—especially from Cat—that we'd stop by my dad's soon to visit, I follow a happy and smiling Cat outside and to my car.

Her beautiful smile doesn't fade from her lips the entire drive back to my apartment.

Cat

I won't lie. I'm a total girl when it comes to babies. They're just so cute and tiny and cuddly. And they smell so good. I remember when my siblings were born. They were like living dolls. I was always so eager to help my parents with feedings, dressing them, and bathtime. Okay, maybe I wasn't as eager about diaper changes, but I still think I was a pretty great big sister. Still am.

"Kellan and Dean are just the cutest little guys with their heads full of dark hair and chubby pink cheeks," I tell Ronan as he lets me into his apartment ahead of him, then closes the front door behind us.

"Uh-huh," Ronan says.

I kick off my shoes, hang up my coat, then meander into the living room.

"You know what's interesting? That even though they were born a bit early, they don't look super skinny," I say with a nod. "Skinny babies tend to look like little old people," I jabber on as Ronan walks into the living room. "Hopefully any babies we have will be chunky." I move to the couch. "But having twins can't be easy. Can you imagine how little sleep we'd get? Twins don't run in my family though, so, I don't think we'll have to worry about that."

Ronan doesn't say anything at first. He just kind of hovers near the arm of the couch, like he's weighing whether to join me.

"I don't want kids, baby," he says matter-of-factly.

I stop to look at him. "I don't want to have a baby now, either."

He shakes his head. "No, I don't want them *ever*."

His words hit me like a shove to the chest.

"Oh."

I don't know what to say to him. In our year and a half together, we've never expressly talked about our future together. I had always just assumed that if Ronan and I stayed together—which is obviously my deepest desire—we'd eventually have children. The thought that he may not actually want them never even crossed my mind.

"Why?"

He shrugs. "I just don't want them." He's trying to sound unaffected, but I must have hit a nerve because his face darkens and his body tenses.

I frown. "That's not a reason."

"Why not?"

"It just isn't," I say with a shake of my head. "Why don't you want to have children with me?" I'm hurt for some reason.

"It has nothing to do with you."

"How can you say that? Of course, it does."

"I don't want kids regardless of who it's with," he says, and again I feel offended.

"So, you don't even see a future with me at all?" I'm escalating our discussion, and I know it.

He grits his teeth and his jaw flexes. "I do, just not one that includes children."

I fold my arms over my chest. "Well, I *do* want kids. I've always wanted them," I say with a decisive edge. "What does that mean for us?"

He hesitates, but his brow and jaw are set. "What do you want me to say, Cat? I'm not budging on this. I don't want kids. If you do, then... I don't know," he says with a dismissive shrug.

His words pierce my heart. I stare at him incredulously. "Then we break up? Is that what you're saying? Why are you so set on this? Don't you want to be with me?"

"Of course I want to be with you, Cat. But I don't want kids. I don't want to be a dad." I can tell by the tone of his voice that he really wants this conversation to be over, but I'm agitated and dig in more. I know I'm provoking a drag-out, blow-up fight, and I'm not sure why, but I'm already invested and double down.

"But I do want to be a mom eventually. I want kids with you, and you're saying that I can't have that. You're going to withhold that from me because... because 'you just don't want them?' That's not good enough for me," I yell at him.

"What do you want from me, Cat?" Ronan yells back at me, raking his hands through his dark-blond hair.

I chuff loudly. His refusal to just talk to me summons a potent anger in my chest. "I want you to tell me what's going on in your head for once, Ran. Just once, you could fill me in on your thought process. You're always so damn closed off. Why don't you want kids with me?" The pain in my voice is audible.

"It's not that I don't want kids with *you*, Cat. I don't want them at all."

His vague response only pisses me off more. "Yeah, you've made that clear by now. But why, Ran? Why?"

"Because I just don't—"

I jab my index finger at him. "Don't you dare say 'because I just don't want them' again. That's fucking bullshit, Ran. You always do this; you never open up to me. You leave me fucking guessing. Why?"

We are all out shouting at each other now.

"Fuck, Cat. Just fucking stop," Ronan growls at me. He's pissed and hurt and frustrated; his entire body is tense as he paces the living room.

"No," I say. "You have to give me something. I bet you talk to Miranda about the stuff that goes on in your head."

And just like that, we're no longer arguing about babies. It was never just about babies.

Confusion mixes with his angry expression. "What the hell does Randi have to do with this?"

I exhale loudly. "You obviously talk to her, Ran. I don't get it. Why don't you ever just talk to me? I'm your damn girlfriend, but won't ever talk to me, but you're okay talking to your ex? It's unfair," I yell at him. "Do you still have a thing for her?"

He stares at me, flabbergasted, before he runs his hand roughly over his face with a shake of his head. "What the fuck are you talking about?"

"Well, you just up and drove to Tennessee to see her."

He looks at me, his brow creased, his eyes bouncing between both of mine. "Are you seriously worried about Randi?"

"Obviously," I say. "You talk to her on the phone randomly; you went and spent two nights in Tennessee with her. You just up and left me a few days before Christmas without even getting my opinion on the matter. And I know you talk to her about stuff you'd never talk to me about," I say, hurting my own damn feelings.

"You can't be fucking serious, Cat," he says. "You know I love you!"

"I am serious, Ronan," I say, using his full first name. It feels weird on my tongue, unnatural, wrong. "Do you love her? Would you want kids with her?"

His mouth drops open as a myriad of emotions flash in his eyes, from bewilderment to amusement to hurt. "No, Cat. Shit, you're being ridiculous."

"Don't call me ridiculous. Don't fucking gaslight me. How do you expect me to feel any different when you never let me in? Ever!" I yell so loudly that I'm certain the neighbors across the hall can hear.

He stares at me, his eyes darkening like a rising storm, yet I don't stop. In fact, I want to push more. Even "angry Ronan" is more than I usually get, and I will gladly take whatever breaks out of him, will gladly absorb the shock waves of his emotions if that means he'll finally open up to me.

I take a quick breath, then continue my barrage, allowing my feelings to flow freely as I wish his would, just once. "You never, ever, *ever* talk to me. About anything! You kept the abuse a secret. You didn't tell me you were struggling with thoughts of suicide. And even after you came back last year, you never allowed me into your head. You refused to talk about your grandmother's visit—which, by the way, I *know* has affected you. I'm not blind, you know? I've noticed that you have more nightmares. And, god, then you didn't even bother to tell me about Rashana. And you know? It's getting really fucking old, Ran. This... this not talking to me? Old."

My body feels too small for the frustration in me. Ronan is just as tense, his hands grasping his hair as he paces back and forth. It's eerily reminiscent of a lion roaming its steel cage.

"And I try to give you space. I want to be there for you. I know it's not... it's not easy, but fuuuck"—I draw out the last word—"I can't always be the one doing the giving, Ran. It's been like this from the moment we met. You and your damn secrets. You know how that makes me feel? It makes me feel like shit. It makes me feel like you don't trust me. I've never given you a reason not to trust me, Ran. I've been by your damn side through it all. Don't you think the least you could do is share your thoughts with me? Don't you think I *deserve* the *real* you? Deserve to see you from all angles. I mean, you've seen me break apart, you've seen me cry, you've seen... *everything*. You know my deepest, darkest secrets, Ronan. It's so damn one-sided and I'm so. fucking. sick of it!" I yell, my voice pitchy, serrated.

I don't expect his next words not to hurt. In fact, I welcome it. I welcome this entire argument because it's more than what Ronan usually gives me, at least when it comes to the painful parts of his life. This is raw. It's real.

He rakes his hands over his face and down his throat like he can force the tension out. "What the fuck are you talking about one-sided? You keep secrets from me too, Cat."

"Liar!"

He recoils as if I slapped him. "You don't get to call me a liar. I'm a lot of things, but not a damn liar."

"Oh no? How am I keeping secrets from you, Ronan? By telling you that I'm insecure about your weird relationship with your ex? Or telling you that all I want is a damn future with you?"

"I don't know, how about the fact you sent nudes of yourself to your ex during *our* relationship?" What a low blow. I can't believe he's bringing this up. "And you know what? That shit I can forgive because you didn't have a damn choice. What I can't forgive is that you didn't tell me you talked to Rashana."

Pain is replaced with fresh outrage. "You didn't tell me about Rashana either! You didn't tell me that she tried to talk to you twice. You didn't tell me that she talked to you on the same damn day your grandmother showed up. You hide way more things from me than I do from you," I say like it's a damn competition. "Me not telling you about Rashana was just giving you a taste of your own damn medicine. Sucks having someone hide things from you, right?" My voice is undiluted venom.

Ronan glowers at me, his chest rising and falling with fitful, shaky breaths. "Yeah, it sure as fuck does. But you know what the difference is between my secrets and yours? I don't keep mine to weaponize them against you. I don't hide shit from you to 'give you a taste of your own medicine.' I keep them to make sure you're safe."

I throw my hands in the air. "From what, Ronan? What the fuck are you trying to keep me safe from?"

"From me! God damn it, Cat, I'm trying to protect you from *me*. You're so damn hung up on me just... breaking apart in front of you, on... losing control. You want me to be such an open fucking book for you. But you have no fucking idea how damn dangerous that is." If I didn't know better, I'd almost think I see devastating pain in his green eyes.

His words make zero sense to me; the anger, the hurt, the frustration are bringing me close to combustion. I bring my hands to my hair, yanking it with the Poseidon waves of emotions.

"What the *fuck* are you talking about Ronan? Use normal words and just. fucking. talk. to me!"

He abruptly stills, ceasing his pacing. His expression is cold, gaze icy, and it sends a shiver through me. "You want to know why I don't want kids?"

We are both completely outside of our comfort zone, way beyond the bounds of normal conversation. It's unnerving and scary, but god, I'm so, so angry at him, and he's right there with me. We're opposing poles, battling it out right here in Ronan's living room.

"Duh," I huff with a mean attitude.

He frowns at me. "Because people like me... I'm very fucking likely to hurt my own kids, and maybe even you. Because I refuse to continue this bullshit cycle of abuse that has been part of my family for fucking generations, Cat."

I'm too upset, too worked up to see reason. "So, you're going to let what your mother did to you dictate your future with me?" A tiny voice in my head screams at me to back off. This is obviously not about me, but I don't. "You have to let that go and move on," I say like a wise-ass, knowing full well it's not that easy.

"Oh really?" Ronan laughs, not even an iota of amusement reflected in the sharp angles of his face. He's all tempered steel. "Fucking great, Cat. You're right. Why didn't I think of that before? Just fucking let it go. Got it," he chuffs.

Guilt rises in my chest, but I still don't back off.

"Stop being an asshole. You know what I mean. I mean stop allowing your mother's ghost to be a part of our future. Stop letting what happened to you affect what you do with the rest of your life. Just stop!"

"I'm trying! I fucking try every god damn day."

"Try harder!" I stomp my foot on the floor loudly.

Ronan comes to a dead stop in front of me and searches my face, his own hard, expressionless.

For an excruciating few seconds he simply studies me, his eyes pinned on mine before he shakes his head. "Fuck this," he growls, then marches to the hallway where I see him grab his keys.

"Are you fucking walking out on me?"

He doesn't turn around and instead walks out of the apartment. He slams the door with such force that that the picture of me and him on the entry table falls. It hits the floor and splinters. I flinch at the sound. It's just glass, just wood, just a picture. But it feels like so much more than that.

I stand in the silence. I'm dazed, shellshocked. What the hell just happened? Ronan and I hardly ever fight, and we've certainly never yelled at each other like this. We've bickered, sure, have disagreed, have needed a time out, but we've never had a falling out like this. And we've never, ever just walked out on each other.

Wednesday, January 25th

Ronan

I jerk back as Shane lets out a high-pitched shriek the second I yank open the apartment door on my way to Murphy's.

It's only three o'clock—too early for me to head into work and too early for Shane to come home—but there he stands, his hand pressed to his chest where I assume his heart hammers against his ribs at our mutually unexpected face-to-face.

"Holy shit, what the fuck?" He sounds like he spent the night screaming into a mosh pit.

I skim his face, noting the light sheen of sweat, and cringe. "Oof, yeah. You look like shit, Shay." I step aside to grant him entrance to our shared home.

"I'd flip you off if I wasn't also feeling like shit." The way he grimaces tells me his body aches with fever. "Thanks for jumping in early."

I was still suffering through my anthropology class when Shane's text came through only a couple of hours ago.

Shane:

I don't want to be dramatic, but I think I'm dying.

Me:

???

Shane:

I feel like I swallowed shards of glass.

Me:

Maybe stop deep-throating the customers in the back alley?

Shane:

Aww, but the tips are so good...

I snorted a laugh in the lecture hall, earning me a "shh" from a studious-looking guy in the row ahead of me.

Me:

I have no comeback for this one. Seriously, though, what's going on?

Shane:

As much as it pains me to say this, I think I'm coming down with something. I'm fucking shivering, Ran. Like, teeth chattering. Didn't feel great this morning, but all I want is to lie down in the middle of 17th and let some Prius take me out of my misery... Do you think you can relieve me early?

Shane doesn't bail on work. On the contrary, that guy is a damn workaholic, which I know has caused tension between him and Tori in the past. Which meant he really was feeling like death. I grabbed my stuff—not even a little sad about leaving this riveting lecture on the social orders of chimpanzees—and texted him that I was on my way home to change and take over for him.

Looking at him now, I know I made the right call. I don't think he would've made it another five hours without collapsing. "You know I got you, Shay. Need me to do anything before I head out?"

His motions are sluggish as he takes off first one shoe, then the other. "Yeah, talk to Cat," he says hoarsely.

My lips flatten. "I texted her last night." I admit it wasn't much of a text message. Only that I got home from work okay because I didn't want her to be worried. Not that I thought she was.

Cat and I haven't spoken to each other since I left her standing in my apartment after our fight two days ago. It wasn't my proudest moment, but no good could come from me staying. We needed to step away from each other, to cool down. We were both worked up, slipping into a vicious fight. We were on the verge of saying things we could never take back. In fact, I'd already set a toe over that line. I hit below the belt. And so did she.

I hate myself for bringing up Adam. It was uncalled for, mean, just plain wrong. I know what happened with Adam wasn't Cat's fault, but man, when she called me a liar, I short-circuited.

My mother constantly accused me of lying, even though I never did. She'd provoke me, lay into me, get a rise out of me, then use it as a reason to hurt me. So when Cat said I was lying about her keeping secrets, it wasn't just a disagreement. It threw me right back into a beatdown from my mom. I was defensive. Panicked. Raw. And I went low. Too low. Not a minute has gone by when I haven't regretted bringing up Adam, haven't regretted raising my voice at Cat like that. In a sense, this entire thing feels like a self-fulfilling prophecy.

Shane raises an unimpressed eyebrow. "Texting isn't talking."

"You gotta tell her that. She's the one who isn't answering my calls."

Neither of us tried to make contact with the other on Monday, but I did finally dial her number Tuesday afternoon. Our extended radio silence was beginning to make my skin crawl. But Cat neither picked up nor returned my call. She's clearly pissed at me. And rightfully so. As I said, self-fulfilling prophecy. At least I know she's alive and well from Tori, who—according to Shane's report this morning—hung out with Cat last night.

"Tor does that to me, too," Shane says, his blue eyes empathetic even though they're red-rimmed with exhaustion. "When we fight?

She'll just go off-air for a few days, make me grovel and beg before she'll give me the time of day again," he says with a grated chuckle. "Must be a girl thing."

"I guess it's deserved. I was kind of a dick." My gaze drops from Shane's to my black chucks.

"From what Tor shared with me, Cat's hands aren't all that clean either."

I lift my eyes. "Cat told Tor?"

He shrugs. "Must have. Tor was pretty well apprised of what went down between you and Cat. For what it's worth, Tor and I have fought much worse than that." Shane moves his hand to my shoulder. My reply dissipates as his body heat seeps through my hoodie.

"Holy shit, Shay, you're burning up. Get the fuck to bed, man. I'm gonna get you some shit to get this fever down and then I'll head into work."

I usher him down the hallway where I veer into the bathroom to grab the meds.

I pop open the Tylenol and wish undoing the damage I did with Cat was as easy as swallowing a couple of pills.

Cat

A single loud knock makes me aware of my dad standing at the threshold to my room. I look up from the laptop perched on my thighs.

He holds his arm out to me with my buzzing phone in his hand. "Your boyfriend's persistent. That's four times in five minutes."

My nostrils flare with a deep inhale. I move my laptop, then walk over to my dad. He tips his head, eyes narrowing as though looking over the rims of his nonexistent glasses at my leisurely pace. I'm in no hurry to take my phone from him, in no rush to answer Ronan's call.

I'm still pissed—at his unreasonableness, his unwillingness to talk to me. As uncomfortable and painful as our fight was, and as much as I hate how we left things on Monday, I also refuse to be the first to tuck tail. I need him to understand that I meant what I said, that my feelings are valid. I'm frustrated he still won't confide in me. I'm still confused about Miranda. And then there's his total refusal to consider the idea of having kids with me. Why doesn't he at least allow for that possibility? I mean, there's no rush. Maybe in ten years? Fifteen? We're so young, how can he make this decision for us now?

I hold my hand out to my dad, who places my phone in my palm, his eyes pinned to me. "Everything alright between you two?" he asks when I don't follow my usual pattern and immediately return Ronan's call.

"Yep." I return to my bed and retake my seat.

He still doesn't retreat, leaning against the doorframe, settling in. "Trouble in paradise?"

My eyes flit to my dad, but I refuse to give him the satisfaction of knowing Ronan and I hit a rough patch. "Nope."

My phone begins to buzz again. Even though I'm still mad, the second I see his name on my screen my heart does that stupid flip it always does. And just like that, I'm smiling—against my better judgment. I pick up my phone, push the answer button, and demonstratively move my phone to my ear.

My dad gets the hint and shoves off the doorframe so I can speak with my *boyfriend* in private.

I take a deep breath. "Hey."

"I miss you," Ronan says.

And just like that, I fold into myself. "I miss you, too. But I'm still mad."

He chuckles dryly. "I figured as much. Thanks for picking up this time."

"I left my phone downstairs. I wasn't ignoring you on purpose. Well, your last four calls at least," I say with a giggle.

“I deserve that.”

Ugh, why does he have to be so self-sacrificing? I’d deserve for him to ignore me, too.

I decide against dredging up our argument over the phone. “What are you doing?”

“I just got to Murphy’s. Shane’s sick as a dog.”

“What? Oh no!”

“Yeah. He looks like death himself. Just before I left he started coughing so hard I thought he was going to throw up,” Ronan says. “How about you? What are you up to?”

Our conversation feels stilted, chilly even, but what do I expect? We need a second to rewarm to each other. “Just doing some school stuff. Do you… I probably shouldn’t come over then and wait for you tonight, right? With Shane sick?”

“No, definitely not. I don’t want you to catch whatever Shane has. I already texted Tori, too. I doubt she’ll stay away from her sick guy, but I at least had to give her a heads-up.”

“What if I don’t want to stay away from you?”

He chuckles, and I smile. He sounds like himself already. “Then you can come see me at Murphy’s anytime you like, but I’d prefer you not go to the apartment right now.”

“Okay. Want me to stop by tonight?” Relief eases the ache I hadn’t realized I was feeling in my bones.

“If you’re asking me if I want to see you, the answer is always yes. But I gotta be honest, I don’t know how much time I’ll have tonight. From what I can gather, Shane’s not the only one sick. Whatever is going around has me down three waiters,” Ronan grumbles. “We might have better luck tomorrow.”

It’s not perfect. But it’s a start.

Saturday, January 28th

Cat

Saturday morning, I call Ronan on his way to Murphy's. "Please tell me Shane's finally feeling better?"

Shane's "plague," as Ronan called it, has had him down all week. Even Tori warned me to steer clear of the apartment.

"I'm relying on the random coughs I hear from Shane's room to assure myself he's still alive," Ronan told me during our phone call while he was on break at Murphy's. Because of Shane's sickness, Ronan has been filling in for Shane, working crazy hours, going straight from class to Murphy's where he works until closing the place down, then does it all over again the next day.

I made it a point to stop by Murphy's on Thursday and again last night just to catch a glimpse of Ronan. But we barely had a minute to ourselves, and we still haven't had a real conversation about the fight. The unresolved tension gnaws at me, even though he's been sweet, stealing kisses like nothing ever happened. But something *did* happen. And I need us to stop pretending it didn't.

Ronan chuckles. "Well, he did finally emerge from his bedroom this morning looking a little less like the undead, so I'd say he's on the up and up. He actually told me he's feeling well enough to work tonight. I think he might just be going stir-crazy, but I sure as fuck ain't going to fight him."

"Oh good," I say, a smile breaking across my face.

Vada's in town this weekend and she and Tori talked me into going to a party with them in Greenwich tonight. It's an NYU party, and Vada has already announced she intends to "find some yummy frat guy to go home with" tonight.

When I asked her about Brady, she just shrugged. "We're in this sort of on-again, off-again relationship."

"And right now you're off?" I checked while Tori laughed.

"Exactly," Vada said.

I'm looking forward to having Tori and potentially Ronan at the party with us tonight, not least to act as a buffer to Vada's prowling.

"You'll come to this party with us, then?" I ask Ronan. I brought it up last weekend, but that was before our fight and before Shane got sick.

Ronan's deep exhale through the phone tells me that's a big fat no. "I'm sorry, baby, I don't think I can swing it. With Shane sick last week, I've done fuck-all for school. I need to catch up tonight; I really want to spend the day with you tomorrow without having to worry about reading a million pages or some shit," Ronan sighs.

It's a perfectly valid reason. But that doesn't stop the hollow feeling that settles in my chest.

"Okay," I sigh.

We're quiet for a few seconds. I really wanted to see him tonight, to reconnect after this past week. We're in desperate need of connection, both physical and emotional. We need to talk.

"I'm sorry baby," Ronan says. "But at least you'll get to enjoy a girls' night. And then tomorrow it'll be you and me, okay? Maybe think of something you want to do. Unless you just want to stay in bed with me. Won't say no to that," he says mischievously.

"Okay," I say again.

"Who's driving tonight?"

"Vada. She's going to pick up Tori, then me."

"And this party is where again?"

I give him the address and details about where Vada, Tori, and I will be spending our evening.

"Be safe," he finally says.

"I will, Daddy."

I giggle when I hear Ronan groan.

"You know what, that may be Shane's kink—at least from what I've involuntarily overheard—but it's *not* one of mine."

"I bet I can make anything your kink if I try hard enough."

Ronan chuckles, but I hear the distance in it. We're laughing, but we're still not okay. Not really. And I'm not sure how much longer we can pretend we are.

***

As promised, Vada and Tori stop by to pick me up at seven-thirty.

"Ooh, look at you and your red lip," I say to Vada when I slide into the backseat of her car.

Vada cranes her neck to look into her rearview mirror, dabbing her pouty, bright-red lips together. "Yeah, well, studies have shown that men are attracted to red. Red dresses, red lipstick. Sluts for red."

Tori laughs. "Can confirm. Shane goes absolutely nuts when I put on red lipstick." She turns in her seat. "Hey, when are you officially starting your R.A. position?"

My Intro to Psychology professor from last semester had two open research assistant positions, and when classes started up again earlier this month I decided to apply. I didn't really expect to get it, given the rather large applicant pool, but was happily surprised when I received a call from Professor Meyers on Thursday.

When I told my mom I was actually offered the job, she did her familiar happy jig, then gushed about her own time as a psychology research assistant while an undergrad at Duke. "It really solidified my interest in the field, setting me up to pursue my medical degree. And it was ideal as far as jobs go. Super flexible hours—you could work on the evenings when Ran works. All you really need to worry about is getting your hours in and your research done. What an incredible opportunity, Kitty."

"I'm meeting with my professor Monday afternoon for onboarding," I say.

"Dang, look at you, Kitty Cat. Full-time student, two jobs," Vada nods, impressed.

I hesitate. "I guess."

It doesn't *really* feel like two jobs. The work I do at my mom's practice barely counts—answering calls, rescheduling patients, keeping charts organized. It's easy. And even as an R.A., I'll only be putting in twenty-something hours a week, max. Ronan's the one clocking forty hours at Murphy's *plus* classes.

"Between you and Tori hustling your little butts off, I look positively lazy," Vada says.

Tori, too, picked up a part-time job halfway through our fall semester at NYU. She works at a small bagel and coffee shop close to campus, nixing Shane's idea to wait part time at Murphy's; she was convinced having her boyfriend also be her boss would lead to nothing but trouble in their relationship. She's probably right. I've seen Shane when he's in boss mode, have heard Ronan grumble about it on occasion, and I can't imagine it would be easy to leave work squabbles behind and then be cutesy and intimate with each other at home.

Tori waves Vada off. "I wouldn't be working if I didn't feel so guilty about mooching off Shay and Ran. I'm at their apartment way more than I'm at my dad's. Least I can do is chip in for the occasional grocery haul and their internet."

Tori's right. She's at the apartment all the time, even when neither Ronan nor Shane are there, and she's certainly added her feminine touch to the place. That framed photo of Ronan and me on the entry table was her idea. The only things I've added so far are some of my clothes to Ronan's closet, and a toothbrush and some of my "girly" products to their bathroom.

After making our way to Greenwich and finding a spot to park we immerse ourselves in the party. Vada saunters off in search of "some hot single guys" while Tori and I grab drinks. Some very potent drinks, as it turns out; it takes hardly any time at all for us to get tipsy—or make that drunk.

We stand giggling as Tori describes in hilarious detail, how she once caught Shane masturbating. This would be way too much information for me if I were sober, and I know Tori wouldn't ever share such intimate details with me if she weren't equally tipsy. But seeing as we're anything but clearheaded, Tori's drunken retelling of the time she walked in on Shane "rubbing one out" and decided to lend a hand—literally—has me in stitches.

"Oof, I gotta pee," Tori finally says, looking around until she spots the bathroom. "Be right back, Kitty Cat."

I watch Tori sway while she makes her way through the crowd of party attendees, bumping into people and apologizing profusely each time.

"How come you're not here with some guy?" a tall, dark-haired guy with a bright smile asks me as he saunters in my direction, his eyes already undressing me. Under normal circumstances this would make me supremely uncomfortable, but I'm too inebriated to care. I haven't had this much to drink in a long time, but I needed something to distract me from my fight with Ronan and the tension between us.

I observe the guy, letting him approach without protest. The closer he gets, the more his features come into focus—the deep brown of his eyes, his slender nose, a freshly cut shock of dark hair. I won't deny that he's attractive. I shrug. "My boyfriend couldn't make it tonight." The words drip out of my mouth like glue.

An appreciative smirk curves his lips. His eyes are glossy like he's had his fair share of alcohol as well. "Some kind of boyfriend, letting you come to a party all by yourself looking gorgeous like this."

A giggle bursts from my lips, but the guy seems to take it as a compliment.

"I like your laugh," he says. "What's your name?"

"Cat."

He smiles and takes a step closer to me, leaning in to rest his hands on either side of my head.

"I'm Alex," he says in a low drawl. "And if you don't mind, Cat, I'm going to kiss you."

Somewhere in the back of my brain, alarm bells go off, alerting me to protest, to move, to push him away and leave. But I'm too far gone, too slow and sluggish, too indifferent to comply.

I stand there rooted to the spot and let some random guy kiss me.

His tongue darts out, demanding entrance to my mouth while his hands come off the wall and grasp at my hips, tugging me to him. I should pull back. I *know* I should. But my limbs feel heavy, my brain powered down. So I let him. Not only that, I actually kiss him back, my tongue sweeping over his like his sweeps over mine.

This is all wrong!

His lips are dry and hard. His hands dig greedily into my skin. He tastes like cheap booze and stale cigarettes. He's not gentle and soft. He doesn't taste like love and comfort. He doesn't smell like ocean air, fresh laundry, and just Ronan.

Oh god, Ronan.

"Cat?" Ronan's strained voice comes from behind Alex—who's kissing me, who I'm kissing back.

My eyes snap open, and I'm immediately stone-cold sober. Ronan looks like he took a one-two punch right in the stomach, his expression contorted with pain and betrayal. I shove my hands against Alex's chest, pushing him away from me.

He stumbles back, his eyes wide. "Hey, what the hell?" He tries to grab at my arm, but Ronan yanks him back so hard that the guy falls flat on his ass.

"Back the fuck off," Ronan growls, and the people in our vicinity fall silent.

Alex makes no attempt to get up, raising his hands. "Okay, man, sorry. It's all good." He staggers upright and away from me and Ronan, leaving me to face Ronan, whose attention is squarely on me.

My heart rips at the edges with the devastation in his green eyes. For a moment we just stare at each other. Regret, guilt, and shame flood my insides with ice as the moment begins to catch up with my drunken self and I realize what I just did.

I cheated on the one person I love most in this world. I cheated on Ronan.

A jumble of words demand to be released from my mouth, but the only thing I manage to express is surprise at his presence. "What are you doing here?" I whimper.

The edge in Ronan's tone makes my blood run cold. "Are you drunk?"

Hot tears prick at the back of my eyes. My heart beats so wildly I can feel it in my temples. I nod. I'm so ashamed. I know myself better than to allow myself to get this out of control, to drink to the point of losing all inhibition, of risking situations I'm not prepared to handle.

Ronan opens his mouth as if to say something—

"Ran! You made it after all," Vada cries as she arrives at the scene of the crime, her arm hooked under Tori's. Both are oblivious to what just happened. Vada takes one look at me, then Ronan, and her expression falls. "What happened?"

Ronan's eyes remain pinned on me. "Vada, how much have you had to drink?"

"Nothing, why?"

"I think you should take Cat home. And probably Tori, too," he adds with a softer, more evaluative look at a swaying Tori.

A shiver runs down my spine. Ronan's tone is too cool, too calm, too collected. The tears collect on my waterline, rising with each second. I want him to yell, want him to be pissed; he'd have every right to be. Instead he acts detached, distanced, putting a cavernous gap between us. It's crushing.

"Hold on, Ran. What's going on?" Vada asks, no doubt thrown by the suffocating silence between him and me as we continue staring at each other.

"Have Cat tell you what happened," Ronan says.

Without another word, he turns and walks away, leaving me standing there in the middle of a crowded party, stone-cold sober and drowning in shame. This time, I know I'm completely at fault.

All I want is for the earth to open up and swallow me whole.

Sunday, January 29th

Ronan

I have the worst headache. It travels all the way down from the back of my head to my neck and shoulders. I'm tense and stiff. *What a shocker.* I had a piss-poor night with sleep so light I'd be surprised if I logged any REM time. It was all tossing and turning. No rest. I'm hungover without having had a single drop of alcohol.

I don't even remember my drive home from Greenwich last night. I was dazed, the image of Cat's lips sealed to another guy's mouth branded into my retinas as though I stared into the sun too long. I couldn't get it out of my head. I still can't, and fuck if it doesn't strangle me from the inside out.

I hadn't planned on going to that party, but I found myself working through my class work surprisingly fast, churning out one assignment after another, and in just over three hours I was caught up. Given how sparse my time with Cat had been over the past week, and the festering impasse we had found ourselves at just days ago, I decided not to wait until today to see her.

I was over the tension between us, the small talk on the phone. I wanted to see her, pull her into my arms, kiss her. I wanted to move past our disagreement in a real, substantial way.

Now I wish I had never left my apartment; then I'd still be blissfully unaware, my heart would still be intact, and I wouldn't find myself in the position I'm in right now.

I'm run-down, drained, and achy. If I didn't know better, I'd say I'm coming down with whatever virus plagued Shane last week. But I *do* know better, know that what ails me is psychosomatic rather than physiological. I've been here before, recognize the signs, that deep fatigue that demands I seek sleep. I fight it. My body is merely manifesting the emotional pain.

It's only eight a.m. I usually sleep in on Sundays—my one true rest day—but I've been up for thirty minutes already. I have nine missed calls and fifteen text messages from Cat. All the texts and seven of her calls are from last night, two from this morning. I didn't talk to her after leaving her with Vada and Tori last night, and I also didn't read or respond to her messages. I couldn't. I didn't know what to say to her, didn't want to hear what she had to say to me—not in that moment, when she was obviously impaired. And we were both in a heightened emotional state, which can only lead to disaster. Not that today won't be equally as destructive...

I shower and get dressed, but none of it feels real. Seeing Cat with some dude pushing up against her felt like an out-of-body experience, like I was just witness to someone else's life, and that feeling has not subsided in the past eleven hours. Maybe this is just a dream, one of my too-vivid nightmares, one of those I can't wake up from myself. Fuck, I wish it was. I wish Cat or Shane would yank me out of my dream already, would tell me to wake the fuck up, that all of this was nothing more than a night terror. But it isn't. I know it isn't, even though it sure as fuck feels like it.

Vada did as I asked last night—she drove Cat home, then dropped Tori off at the apartment where I was desperately trying to think of a way to shut off my brain. In true Vada fashion, she immediately wanted to discuss the incident with me, wanted to hash out the painful details while Tori was in the bathroom throwing up. I just told Vada to go home, making it very clear that I wouldn't discuss anything with her that night. So, she left.

I checked on Tori, helped get her into bed, then sat on the couch trying to figure out what to do. I aptly ignored my phone each time the screen lit up with an incoming call or text from Cat. She stopped trying to get ahold of me at two in the morning.

Shane got home just before three, obviously unaware of the shitshow that had unfolded earlier that evening.

"Tori's asleep. She's trashed," I told him. Shane chuckled knowingly, but my next words wiped his grin off his face. "Cat kissed some dude at the fucking party."

He froze mid-step. "I'm sorry, what?"

"Cat kissed some guy at the party. I walked in on this asshole with his tongue in her mouth," I said, nearly choking on my words.

"Did she kick the motherfucker in the balls like she did Drew?"

I shook my head and narrowed my eyes at him. "She wasn't fighting him off, Shay. She was kissing him back."

Shane spent the next hour trying to talk me off the ledge, telling me—over and over again—not to do anything rash, to sleep on it. "I know it hurts like hell, Ran, but I'm sure it was just a mistake. I'm sure it really didn't mean a damn thing to Cat. She was drunk. It was a mistake."

Yeah, he's probably right, but what he doesn't understand—what no one truly understands—is that the issue goes way, *way* deeper than Cat kissing another guy at a party while she was drunk.

And it's exactly that realization that causes me to pull up in front of Cat's at just before ten this morning.

I put my Mustang in park and slowly shut off the ignition. I linger in my seat, breathing deeply. There's a tightness in my throat, squeezing my windpipe as if I have a noose around my neck. It only gets worse when I step out of my car and force myself to walk up the short walkway, then the steps to her front door. I stand for a second, trying to gather the strength to knock.

Cat must have heard my car, must have seen me approach, because she opens the door before I can announce my presence.

"Hey," she says meekly, her hazel eyes huge, full of emotion. I can tell by the red rims around her eyes and her blotchy skin that she's been crying. A lot. She looks as beautiful as ever, even with her hair pulled into a messy bun, her oversized sweater—*my* sweater—and her pajama pants. It doesn't matter what she does, what she wears, she will always be utterly perfect to me.

Cat stands back, bidding me into the house. It's quiet. Her parents and siblings must be out. It's a good thing, because we really don't need an audience.

I stand in the hallway, unwilling—or unable—to move deeper into the house, to walk to her room. I need to get this over with before the paper-thin resolve I built dissolves and we're right back where we started. "I... We need to talk."

She looks as tired as I feel. I bet she didn't sleep any better than I did last night. The dark circles under her eyes make that obvious. "Yeah," she says. I hear the regret and shame in her voice.

"Ran, I'm so sorry," she says, her voice cracking, her shoulders heavy. She directs her gaze to the floor.

I nod. "I know."

She lifts her eyes and searches mine. The emotions are etched into her face, reflected on her brow, her mouth, those beautiful hazel eyes. "I don't know what came over me. I shouldn't have been drinking. I know myself better than that. I promise it was meaningless. I didn't want this; I... I'm so sorry." The words spill from her lips as if the speed with which she says them can stitch up the emotional wounds, could halt the damage done last night.

I want her to stop being so hard on herself. I didn't come here to yell or make her feel even shittier about her obvious slip in judgment. "Listen, Cat, I'm sure you were still in a weird place after our fight last week."

She nods hesitantly, like she can't believe I'm letting her off the hook this easily. "But that still doesn't excuse my behavior."

Every part of me yearns to pull her into my arms, to tell her it's alright. It would be so damn easy, too. It would be so easy to ignore last night away, to avoid the painful, uncomfortable conversation. I could just tell her that it's fine, I forgive her, we all make mistakes. Part of me truly feels that way. I know what happened last night was a mistake, that Cat didn't set out to hook up with another guy, to... cheat on me. I'm sure it meant nothing. We had a terrible fight a week ago that we never worked through; she was drunk. I get it. Shit happens.

But I can't ignore it away. I can no longer avoid it; what happened last night was just what I had anticipated all along. It was inevitable. We've finally arrived at the point that I instinctively knew we would reach—the moment my mother always predicted.

I allow my eyes to close for a moment, to inhale Cat's scent—lavender and rosewater—and really feel her presence. She was the absolute best thing to ever happen to me.

I take a deep breath, bracing for my next words.

"I think... I think we should break things off."

My words are a black hole, pulling all oxygen from the room and into a vortex of darkness as I let the one thing that makes me truly happy slip from my hands. Saying it out loud hurts more than anything my mother ever did.

Cat recoils from me, her eyes wide with panic. "What? No! Ran, please," she chokes, her eyes filling with tears. "I'm so sorry I hurt you. I know I messed up last night. I—"

"Cat, I'm not good enough for you," I say. She falls silent. "I've never been good enough for you."

"You keep saying that, but it's not true," she sobs.

"But it is. There are things that you want, that you *deserve*, that I can't give to you. You deserve to have everything; you deserve to be happy."

"But I *am* happy with you," she says through her tears, her voice off-pitch, cracking.

"You say that now, until you're ready to have a family, for example. Then you'll start to resent me when I can't give you what you need."

She shakes her head adamantly, tears spilling down her face and dripping off her chin. "No, I won't."

She reaches for me, but I take a step back, closer to the door, away from Cat. I know if I let her touch me, if we make physical contact, I'll change my mind. I know I won't be able to keep a clear head because I never can when I'm with her, when she's touching me.

I want nothing more than to be with her forever, but I'm convinced I'm doing the right thing. All I've ever wanted was to keep her safe. And I've finally realized that the biggest threat to Cat's health and happiness is me. It's always been me.

"Yes, you will. And you know what? I think instinctively you know it, too. I think you letting down your guard and allowing that guy to kiss you last night was you subconsciously realizing that I'll never be able to make you truly, undeniably happy. There are things..." I exhale a shaky breath. "There are things you don't know about me, and—"

"Ran, please," she whimpers.

I try to say more, but the words get trapped in my throat. A painful lump presses on my vocal cords, making my eyes sting. It's fucking tearing me apart. She's everything to me—has been everything to me since the moment I met her just over a year and a half ago.

"Please," she says again, her voice barely a whisper now. "I don't even know who I am without you."

I swallow what feels like rocks and sand. "You deserve to find out, Cat," I tell her softly, because she's right. She's been so invested in me—my trauma, my recovery—I think she forgot herself in the process. And Cat isn't someone who should have to live in my darkness, in the shadows cast by my past. She is light and goodness. She's incredible, smart, amazing, kind, with a whole beautiful life ahead of her. I know I have to let her go so she can build the future she wants and deserves without someone as broken and fucked up as me holding her back—or worse, perpetuating my family's destructive history.

"Thank you for loving me through the dark," I croak. "I never deserved you."

She reaches for me again, but I take another step back and take hold of the door handle.

Wild panic resides in her eyes like she knows I'm only seconds away from walking out of her life. "Please don't do this," she says with a desperate sob.

My entire world breaks apart underneath me. "It's already done," I say, choking on my words.

"No. Please, I need you," she cries. "I love you so much, sweet boy, please..."

With the battle raging inside my chest, I gather all determination and I do the worst possible thing. I turn, walk out of the house, and drive away, damning myself to an existence without light, without love, without Cat.

Cat

He's gone.

Ronan is gone. Just like that. He slipped from my hands like sand, no matter how tightly I tried to hold on. He left and took my heart with him. He reached into my chest and tore out that bleeding, beating organ like it meant nothing.

For a moment, I'm suspended in a state of disbelief. This has to be a bad dream. It just doesn't feel real. It can't be real. I love him. He loves me. We're tethered, forged in pain and trauma. We've been through darkness and emerged into light. He can't just... leave like this. It can't be that easy to walk away. Not after everything. Not after the hell we clawed our way through together. If it was that easy, then what would that make me? He'll be back any second. He'll come to his senses. He's just hurt right now—has every right to be wounded—but he'll be back and pull me into his arms like always.

But he doesn't come back.

The dull ache in that spot where my heart used to be sharpens as the seconds tick by. The door stays shut. No footsteps. No click of the door handle. No breath catching on my name. Just silence that screams. I stand and stare, and the ache begins to throb, then pulsate, then hum until it's no longer just an ache but a vortex of agony that brings me to my knees. Darkness creeps into the edges of my vision, blurring my surroundings, and an uncontrollable sob tears from my throat, shattering the stagnant silence in the empty house.

It's over.

He left me.

Ronan is gone.

***

10:27 a.m.—I force myself to move, to walk up the stairs and to my room, to retrieve my phone. I'm dazed, shivering even though it's seventy-three degrees in the house. All I feel is oppressive emptiness, like there is not a person left in this world. Not a person I care about, at least. Am I going into shock?

I dial Ronan's number like I have a million times in my life. His beautiful face—alive with the brightest smile that translates even to his green eyes—lights up my screen, making a mockery of my pain.

"Please pick up, Ran," I whisper with my phone clutched in my hand. But the unemotional, robot voice of his mailbox answers the call: "The number you have dialed is unavailable. Please leave a message." Ronan never personalized his voicemail, didn't even bother recording his name. Always so damn private, robbing me even of this opportunity to hear his voice. It's stupid, but even a recording would be something. Proof he's still real. Still mine.

Me:

I'm so sorry, Ran. I'm so sorry for what I've done. Please, can we talk? Please!

11:43 a.m.—my text shows as delivered but remains unread. That hole in my chest expands, gaping now.

I call Vada and Tori. I break the news to them. The words that slip out of my mouth feel foreign, muted. Each react exactly as I thought they would. Vada begins huffing and puffing, talking about marching over to Ronan's apartment to kick his ass. Tori says Ronan isn't at the apartment, that she'll call Shane, who only just opened Murphy's for Sunday brunch. Maybe Ronan is there, too.

"Great. Then I'll call my annoyingly handsome ex and tell him to talk some sense into his little brother. Such bullshit," Vada mutters.

She means well, but her outrage only widens the rift inside me. I don't want Ronan talked into anything. I just want him to want me back.

I shake my head. "*I* messed up, Vada. *I* cheated on Ran." And with those words, I sink to my knees again, no longer solidly rooted to the ground or myself.

1:19 p.m.—my parents and siblings get home, filling the house with noise that travels up the stairs into my room. I've been lying on my bed, paralyzed. I've tried to reach Ronan twice more, sent him another handful of text messages, but the result hasn't changed. As far as I can tell, he hasn't even read the messages I sent him last night when I was drunk and desperate. I'm no longer drunk, but I'm still desperate.

I hear footsteps approach and a quiet knock on my door before my mom pokes her head into my room. The soft smile fades from her lips the second she spots me curled up in bed.

She storms into my room. "Oh my god, Kitty, what happened?"

My mom has a special touch, a special way of talking, a warmth that is soul-sustaining. The second she reaches me, sits down next to me, and pulls me into her arms without even knowing what I've done, what's transpired, I break wide open.

She sits and listens as I lay myself bare, recounting—to the best of my abilities—last night's happenings, and the devastating consequences I'm now made to suffer. Like she did when I finally came clean about Adam's blackmailing, about my thieving and lying, she remains calm and supportive, talking to me softly. She strokes my hair, my back for an eternity while I cry against her shoulder.

My dad walks into my room, completely flabbergasted. My mom shoos him away with a swish of her hand and a decisive head nod toward my door. "I'll come talk to you in a few minutes, Bobby."

Eventually, my tears ebb and I'm left with a bone-deep exhaustion that begs me to close my eyes. I don't want to be awake for this anymore. Sleep is the only mercy left.

Tuesday, January 31st

Cat

I looked up the five stages of grief on my phone today. Denial, anger, bargaining, depression, acceptance. Clearly one doesn't move through them in a linear fashion; I've mostly been living in a state of denial, bargaining, and depression, moving from one to the next seemingly within hours. I have yet to be angry, and I most definitely have not arrived at acceptance.

I skipped classes today and yesterday. I was supposed to have my onboarding for my research assistant position yesterday, but my eyes were red and puffy with the tears I've been shedding and I didn't have the energy to get myself dressed, let alone face people. So I emailed all my professors that I was sick with the flu. I know I'll need to get myself together eventually, but today's not that day.

Vada has called me several times a day. Zack and Summer have been texting me, and even Steve called me Sunday night and again yesterday evening.

This morning, Tori stopped by before class. It was the first glimmer of hope since Sunday. I pounced and bombarded her with questions. Had she been staying at the apartment? How was Ronan? How did he seem? Upset? Sad? Unaffected?

"I honestly saw him only twice for about thirty seconds," she told me. "But he looks sort of like I'd expect him to look... like shit, like he's not sleeping much or very well. But he won't talk to me about... you. And he won't really talk to Shay, either," she told me with a shrug.

That seed of hope in my chest evaporated like a drop of water on a hot stone.

***

It's just before six o'clock in the evening when I wake from the kind of nap that makes you forget what year it is. My body is heavy, my mouth dry, and the ache in my chest is momentarily replaced by confusion. But only for a moment.

My dad's voice is clearly audible downstairs.

"God damn it, Frank, get ahold of your son and talk some sense into that boy or I will."

I shoot up in my bed. My dad is talking to—make that shouting at—Ronan's dad.

Frank must be on speaker; I can hear his clipped voice clearly. "I respect you, Bobby, but don't fucking talk to me about Ronan that way. From one father to another: I understand you're ticked off, but I won't tolerate you threatening my kid."

My dad chuffs. "You know my daughter has hardly left her room since your son decided to come to my house and break her heart?"

Yeah, he did break it, but not until I gave him a reason to.

"You know full well it's not as simple as that," my mom chimes in, her tone much calmer, more reasonable.

"What are you talking about, Jen? God, I always knew this would happen. Didn't I tell you this would happen?"

My mom doesn't respond, but Frank does. "Ran hasn't shown up here. He doesn't answer my calls—"

"Yeah, because he knows he fucked up, but he's too chicken to face the music. Here's a suggestion: go find him!"

A tight exhale travels through the phone. I imagine Frank is working to maintain his composure. "I will talk to my son, okay? I'll go see him and make sure he's alright."

"You'll make sure he's alright?" my dad bellows with an incredulous laugh.

"Yes," Frank growls. "I will make sure *my kid* is alright. Just like you're making sure *your kid* is alright. And I promise you this, Bobby, Ran didn't set out to hurt Cat. He lov—"

My dad laughs maniacally. "Don't tell me your son loves Cat. Don't you da—"

"Okay, that's enough," my mom says sternly. "Frank, thank you for taking Bobby's call. I'm sorry for this entire situation. Please, check on Ran and make sure he's okay. This can't be easy on him. Please give Penny a hug from me and let her know I'll stop by tomorrow to cuddle the boys."

And with that, my parents end their call with Frank.

My dad's footfalls are poignant, a restless clomping through the living room. "I want to fucking kill this kid, Jen. I want to..." He trails off, his voice as tight as a bowstring.

"Robert Stevenson, you're a good dad, but you're also infuriatingly ignorant," my mom says.

The pacing ceases. "How am *I* ignorant?"

"You're ignorant of the deep psychology behind Ronan's actions. You've always been hell-bent on disliking him. You don't bother trying to understand. You look at the facts with a surface-level understanding of the relationship our daughter had with Ronan."

My mom, the quiet warrior, defending the boy who left me. It should sting. For some reason, it doesn't.

"Cat is my daughter. Ronan is *not* my son. I will always choose my daughter's well-being over the well-being, the emotions, the feelings of some boy."

"As you should, Bobby, but don't forget that Cat isn't entirely innocent here, okay? It wasn't Ronan who kissed another girl. It was our daughter who hurt Ronan."

My dad stays silent.

"But regardless, I believe there's probably more to Ronan's actions than just the kiss. I think he's working through his trauma and—"

My dad huffs. "Jeez, Jen, always the trauma. How long has it been? How long is that boy going to use that as a reason to act like an idiot?"

"Oh my god, Bobby. You know what, never mind. You don't want to understand this. And that's fine. You do you. I'm going to go have a chat with our beautiful daughter," my mom says so forcefully, I'd think she was on the verge of yelling at my dad.

She makes her way into my room moments later, taking her spot on the edge of my mattress.

"Hi sweet pea," she says with the soft tone that makes me want to revert to calling her mommy rather than just mom, like I did when I was five. I'm so lucky to have her.

I just blink at her.

"I'm going to need you to get up and get dressed," she says with a small smile.

"Why?"

"We're going to the grocery store," she says so enthusiastically, I wonder if I misheard.

"I don't want to."

"It's not about what you want. You need to get out of the house. Let's go. You have ten minutes."

***

"I expect you to go to class tomorrow, Kitty," my mom says when we're perusing the bread aisle at the supermarket thirty minutes later. "I know life feels topsy-turvy right now, but what we're not going to do when we find ourselves in situations like this is neglect our own well-being, okay?" She tosses a loaf of pre-sliced multigrain bread into the shopping basket I'm using to support my body weight as I trudge after her through the store.

"Okay," I drawl.

"And you'll also come back to the office tomorrow morning. I have two patients back-to-back and really need you to be available."

I sigh with the heaviness of someone who's carrying a fifty-pound rucksack. Honestly, that's exactly how I feel. Weighted down. "Okay."

"And you know what I was thinking? You could stay at the office all day Fridays. You can work on some of your research for your professor and I could give Kimberly the entire day off."

"Okay," I say yet again. Maybe if I keep saying yes, I'll eventually remember how to mean it.

My mom stops and looks at me for a long moment. She just nods, then continues walking, quietly pulling me forward with her like she always does.

Wednesday, February 1st

Cat

"Come on in," I hear my Intro to Psychology's professor call from behind his closed office door.

I open it and peek my head inside his stuffy office. I'm familiar with how cramped it is because I took advantage of a number of his office hours last semester.

"Hi Ms. Stevenson," Professor Meyers says with a smile, his eyes crinkly behind his thick horn-rimmed glasses. He motions for me to take a seat across from him at his desk.

I step into his office. The chair next to mine is already occupied. The moment I take a seat, I recognize the guy sitting next to me, though I'm not certain which class I may have shared with him. A lot of my intro classes last semester were held in rooms that could accommodate 300 students. I wasn't exactly able to ascertain everyone's name, nor would I be able to recognize everyone's face, but I've definitely seen this guy around more than once.

He has dark hair, short enough not to look unkempt, yet not so cropped that one can't immediately tell it's curly.

"Miss Stevenson, this is Mr. Campo."

The guy smiles, reaching his hand out to me. "Levi."

I shake his hand. "Cat. You were in the Monday and Wednesday afternoon Intro to Psych class, right?"

Levi nods. "Yep. We also had Stats for Behavioral Sciences together on Thursdays."

"And both of you were some of my top students." Professor Meyers chuckles, his bearded face bright. "Thank you for applying to become my research assistants this coming semester. I'm so glad you both accepted the position. I know it doesn't pay much, but I promise it'll be a worthwhile endeavor. And if all goes well, you'll even get publication credit."

He beams and dives into an exhaustive explanation of what exactly will be required of Levi and me while Professor Meyers works on his latest research paper.

Levi says something funny, and I laugh—really laugh—for the first time in days. It feels good... and immediately wrong. Like I'm betraying someone.

I leave the office forty-five minutes later with a general understanding of the research topic—something about the effects of codependency on dyadic coping and relationships—and Professor Meyers's expectations when it comes to work product.

The first thing I do is look up what in the world dyadic coping is. I've never heard that term. Come to think of it, I'm not even sure exactly what codependency is or why it's apparently a bad thing. It should make for an interesting research topic, maybe one I could even repurpose for a paper down the line.

Out of my periphery, I notice Levi approach and fall into step with me. He grins at me. "I'm glad to know I have a research partner by my side because I have no clue what the hell dyodopic coping is," he says with a chuckle.

I laugh. "I think it's dyadic. And yes, same," I say wholeheartedly. "It'll be a nice kind of checks and balances before we have to submit our stuff to Professor Meyers at the end of each week."

"Yeah, so I was thinking of spending a couple of hours in the library on Tuesdays and Thursday from like five to seven. I'm usually way more productive here than trying to get shit done at home where I'm distracted by... well, kind of everything," he says sheepishly.

I nod. "That's actually a good idea. I tend to get distracted, too. Mostly by my phone."

"Well, maybe we could research together," he says with a shrug. "What's your class schedule looking like?"

"I'm done by three-thirty on Tuesday and Thursday, so I could totally make it to research hour."

Levi's smile widens. "Research hour. I like that. Okay, it's a date then. Start tomorrow?" he asks, breaking away from me to hang a left in the courtyard.

"Sure. Wait, Bobst, right? On Main?" I double-check.

"That one. Meet you at four on the first floor," he says, already walking backward with a grin. "Try not to research everything without me."

I laugh and wave, then turn toward the train station, where the weight of the day starts to catch up to me.

I pack myself into the crowded train, cramped between people commuting home after a long day. While my mom was right—it was good for me to get out of the house—and I was surrounded by people all day long, the moment I'm no longer distracted by classes or conversation, the reality that I haven't spoken to or heard from Ronan in days now crashes in on me. How is it possible to live in a city among millions of people, yet feel so alone?

My text messages to Ronan from Sunday, Monday, and yesterday are still unread. Or maybe he turned off his read notification so I wouldn't know he read them? I really should try a hell of a lot harder to stop thinking about Ronan, what he's feeling, what he's up to every waking minute, but I just can't.

The closer I get to my house, the heavier I feel.

"Hey, Kitty," my mom calls from the kitchen the moment I enter the house. "How was your day?"

I take off my shoes, then hang up my coat. "Living the dream."

She gives me an empathetic look, then nods. "I know, sweet pea. Come help me trim the green beans.

"Tell me about your meeting with your professor today," she prompts as soon as I begin cutting the ends off the large pile of green beans, then toss each bean into the pot with a quiet clank.

“It was good. He’s working on an article about the effects of codependency on dyadic coping and relationships, and another student and I are going to be helping with the research,” I say, proud that I pronounced the word correctly.

My mom turns to me, her left hand on her hip, the other grasping a large wooden spoon. She smiles. “Well, well, how apropos.”

I crease my brow at her but don’t bother asking for further explanation. My chest is a collapsed balloon, and my brain feels like static. I don’t ask her what she means. I just keep trimming green beans and let my mind go quiet.

Saturday, March 4th

Cat

"Just please come out with Vada and me," Tori pleads over the phone.

I glance at the mess of research papers strewn across my bed. Journal articles, my own annotated notes, printouts from PubMed. I've been living in this stuff for weeks now—codependency, dyadic coping, emotional enmeshment. The deeper I go, the more hooked I get. Not just academically, either. I can't quite say why, but it's like the topic has claws in me.

Tori's still talking, trying to tempt me with food and booze and Shane's face, of all things. "We can just grab something at Murphy's, have a drink or two. I'll ogle my man and then we'll be on our merry way."

I hesitate, tugging a spiral-bound notebook into my lap. "You're sure it's Shane working tonight?"

"Very much so,

I nod to myself. That's something. "Okay, I'll go," I say with more conviction than I actually feel. "What are you up to right now?"

"Heading to the animal shelter. I didn't make it yesterday, so I told them I'd swing by today."

I blink. "Wait, why are you going to the shelter?"

Tori hums innocently. "Because I didn't go yesterday?"

"Uh-huh. And why were you going yesterday?"

A laugh chimes over the line. "Because it's what I do on Fridays, remember?"

"I gotta be honest here, Tor, I really don't."

"I go to the animal shelter on Fridays to take pictures of their new arrivals. You know, so they can put the pictures on their website? Cat, I've been doing this for months!"

Well, color me totally dumbfounded. "Really? I... Why didn't I know about this?"

"You're not serious, right? You did know. I've asked you to come with me before, but you were always so busy making sure you were at Murphy's when Ran was working."

That sentence lands harder than it should. I stare down at the notebook in my lap, my thumb caught in the coil.

I used to clear my Friday nights for Ronan. Just like I used to clear them for Adam. Only with Adam, it was about fear. Fear of what he'd say, what he'd accuse me of, what kind of fight he'd start if I said no. With Ronan, it didn't feel like fear. Not exactly. It felt like love. But maybe... maybe love shouldn't feel like obligation. Maybe that buried, clenched-up feeling in my chest isn't just heartbreak. Maybe it's old trauma flaring under new light. Ronan shuts down. I perform. I contort. I people-please until I don't know where I end and someone else begins.

I gather the papers on my bed into a neat stack and exhale, soft and shaky. "Would it be too late for you to come back and pick me up? I kind of... want to tag along."

There's a moment of stunned silence before Tori squeals. "What? Yes! I can flip a U-ey. Be there in ten. But I gotta warn you, you better have a strong constitution because you're going to want to take one or seven kittens and puppies home with you. It's serious cuteness overload in there. Tell me now if you don't think you can handle it," she says laughing.

I try to smile, but the corners of my mouth barely lift. They feel too heavy. Everything does lately.

But if there's any medicine to soothe an aching soul, it's animals. And Tori. And doing something that has nothing to do with grief.

"Bring on the kittens," I say quietly, and go to find my shoes.

***

I was right—going to the animal shelter with Tori gave me the mood boost I didn't know how badly I needed. While she flitted from pen to pen, snapping photos of the newest arrivals, I found myself curled up with a litter of purring kittens. Then came Mad Max, a squat-legged, wide-eyed pug with the energy of a caffeinated toddler and the snort of a grumpy old man. I couldn't stop laughing.

By the time we left, my hoodie was covered in fur, my cheeks ached from smiling, and I'd somehow committed to volunteering once a week to socialize the animals. I might not have Tori's eye for lighting or angles, but I'm an expert-level cuddler—and apparently, that's a skill in high demand.

It's exactly seven o'clock when Tori and Vada pull up in front of my house that evening. Vada launches herself out of the car and wraps me in a bone-deep hug, the kind that feels like it's trying to squeeze all the sadness out of you. I close my eyes and let her.

It's the first time we've seen each other in person since the breakup, and the look on her face tells me she's taken it nearly as hard as I have.

"I just can't wrap my head around this whole thing," Vada says once we're driving, twisting in the front seat to look at me. "You two are *made* for each other. And I *know* Ran loves you more than life itself. What the hell happened?"

She said the same thing over the phone, just after it all fell apart. But hearing it again now stirs something sharp in my chest.

"I fucked up, Vada," I say softly. "So badly."

She shakes her head, brows drawn together. "Okay, sure, yeah, you made a mistake—but it's not like you *slept* with the guy, right?"

Her eyes dart to Tori for backup.

Tori doesn't miss a beat. "You know, the more I talk to Shane about it, the more I think it was just the perfect storm. Ran was already in a weird place, right? With Frank and Penny having twins, and then you two"—she looks at me through the rearview mirror—"had that fight about Ran not wanting kids ..."

My stomach twists. I told them about the fight, how I lost it, how I yelled and he yelled back. I told them how I said things I didn't mean. How I turned every word into a weapon. The more I think about it, the more horrified I am. I sharpened my words on purpose, made them into knives I knew would cut deep. And then I used them. I watched him bleed and *kept going.*

My throat tightens, a hard knot forming behind my sternum. "I shouldn't have pushed so hard," I whisper. "I don't even know why I did. I saw how much it was upsetting him, but I just... pushed. And then I said he just needed to get over what his mom did to him."

That part is the worst—the way I said it, the cruelty in it. I don't regret finally telling him how much Miranda bothered me, or how much it hurt that he kept shutting me out. But I do regret going for the jugular. Tearing open a wound I *knew* was barely healing, then digging my hands into it and twisting like I wanted him to hurt as much as I did.

That's the part I wish I could undo. The part that keeps me up at night, whispering, *You went too far.*

Maybe one day I'll get the chance to say that to him. Maybe not.

***

I wonder if there's ever a moment—day or night—when Murphy's isn't packed. Saturday nights, though? A different beast entirely. The place is chaos masquerading as community, a pulsing, overstimulated organism of clinking glass, shouted orders, and bodies squeezed too close together.

It's not just loud—it's *loud*. Voices ricochet off the walls, tangled up in the bassline of whatever indie band is playing overhead. Waiters dodge and weave through narrow spaces with the grace of ballerinas and the stress levels of air traffic controllers. There's barely an empty chair in sight.

No wonder Ronan and Shane always look like they've gone twelve rounds with a hurricane by the end of a shift. Even the most extroverted person would be drowning in this much noise, motion, heat.

"Well, shit, do you see an open table?" Tori asks, elevating her voice above the noise as she looks around. Her face breaks into a smile with Shane's approach. He, on the other hand, looks anything but pleased to see her; he hurries toward us like he's trying to intercept a car crash.

"Babe, what are you doing here?" Shane says through gritted teeth, low and urgent.

Tori blinks at the cool reception. "The three of us thought we'd grab some dinner, and I wanted to see you. I'm sorry if my presence is off-putting to you."

Shane shakes his head as if to clear it. "No. Shit, no, of course I'm not—"

But I'm not listening anymore.

My heart plummets into my stomach, like my stupid, traitorous body is programmed to know he's close. My gaze rolls past Shane and I spot him mid-stride. Ronan. Sleeves pushed up to his elbows, showing off his forearms—those delicious veins—muscles flexed as he carries a case of glass bottles to the bar. He looks so good. *Too* good.

"Oh..." I breathe, my eyes fixed to him, my heart pounding like it's trying to break loose from my ribcage and find a way into his arms.

Tori follows my line of sight and gasps. "You said Ran wasn't working tonight," she snaps at her boyfriend.

"He wasn't supposed to, but he's adamant about working a double. I'm not just gonna send him home when he wants to be here. Especially right now," Shane hisses back. "I didn't know you were planning on bringing Cat tonight. Fuck."

"Kitty Cat, do you want to go somewhere else?" Vada's voice is soft, her hand gentle on my shoulder. The concern in her eyes nearly undoes me.

I tear my gaze away from Ronan like it physically hurts, like I'm unhooking barbed wire from somewhere deep inside me. I swallow the ache, breathe through the shaking.

"No," I say, quieter than I mean to, then try again with more strength. "No. I can't avoid him forever. Especially not with his dad's wedding coming up."

I pause, then force a half-hearted smile that even I don't believe. "Might as well get used to being around him... and not *having* him."

I miss him so much. I want to see him, even though it's painful as hell right now. And maybe a part of me hopes that him seeing me tonight will make him realize how much he misses me, too.

Ronan

My phone vibrates twice in rapid succession from deep within my jeans pocket. I don't have to retrieve it to know it's my dad sending me a sharp text message, telling me to call him since I've been ignoring him all damn day. He's tried to call me three times in the last hour alone. He's been even more difficult to ignore since I ruined the most perfect thing in my life.

I make my way behind the bar, mumbling a quick apology to Jack when I jam past him while he's in the middle of pouring some fancy purple drink, then set the plastic crate of beer bottles on the nonslip floor. I crouch to stack the bottles on their designated shelf, the glass clanking as I set it down, then yank my phone from my pocket when it vibrates yet again.

Sure enough. My dad's second-to-last message reads,

Dad:

Call me, Ran!

Then,

Dad:

Ran! Don't think I won't call Morai! I will deploy whatever weapons I have in my arsenal.

I can't believe he'd threaten me like this.

Me:

I'm working. Been working all day. Won't get off until two. I'll call you tomorrow.

Maybe. Probably not, though.

I barely manage to pull one bottle from the crate and place it on the shelf before his response comes through.

Dad:

You have until noon tomorrow to get in touch with me or I will call your grandparents.

I shake my head. I get why he's so antsy. I wasn't exactly the picture of mental stability in the past, but threatening to get my grandparents involved is a bit much. I hammer out my reply.

Me:

You do know I need sleep, right?

I don't appreciate being pressured like this, especially by him.

Dad:

Fine, 1400 hrs. And that's final. Set an alarm if you must, but I swear to god, Ran, if I don't talk to you again tomorrow, if you keep ignoring me, not answering your phone or your damn door, I'm going to report you missing to the authorities. I don't play!

Leave it to him to use military time.

Me:

And by authorities you mean Morai and Athair?

Dad:

Exactly. And you know that shit is way worse than law enforcement, so keep that in mind if you're planning to pretend you don't hear your phone or aren't home.

I guess my dad's right on both fronts. My grandparents—especially my grandma—*can* be worse than law enforcement. They sure as hell know how to layer on the guilt. And I *have* been ignoring him.

It's all I can do to keep my mind busy, to stop myself from thinking, from feeling that deep, gaping emptiness that opens up every time I pause. The moment I let my thoughts drift, I get pulled under. It's a darkness so heavy it presses against my airways, suffocating me. I don't want to think. I don't want to feel.

I grab another bottle from the crate and set it on the shelf with a dull thunk. Cold glass against my palm. Simple. Tactile. Safe.

It's been back to the basics without Cat. Or whatever "basics" means, since before her I wasn't really living. I was surviving. Wake up, get through the day, keep my head down, stay busy. That was it. And maybe I never really stopped doing that. Maybe I'm destined to keep repeating those cycles.

Now it's school and work. An hour or two of weightlifting squeezed in five times a week. Anything to stay in motion.

At first, Shane pushed back at my insistence to work extra hours. Even when I told him he didn't need to pay me. He wasn't having it.

"Since when do you complain about free labor?" I tried to joke. It didn't land.

He kept insisting I go home, rest, blah-blah. He didn't fucking get how dangerous the quiet apartment was until he found me absolutely fucked up one night about three weeks ago.

I have to admit it was bad. Not only had I pounded back half a bottle of Jack, I was also high as a fucking kite. I hadn't been this drunk in... fuck, I couldn't even remember. And I hadn't smoked weed in years. I didn't think it would hit that hard, but I had barely eaten and the combination was... not great. I ended up on the bathroom floor after trying to purge the alcohol, too out of it to stand, too tired to care.

Somewhere in the middle of all that, I hit my head on the toilet bowl hard enough to bleed. I didn't notice. It was dark, and I was exhausted. So I just... went to sleep right there.

Sure, not my best decision, but hey, at least I was at home.

I have a sneaking suspicion there was a moment Shane thought I had done something really stupid because that look on his face when he finally managed to rouse me spoke volumes. He looked like a damn ghost. Between my sluggish awakening and the blood, I obviously did a great fucking job scaring the absolute living shit out of my best friend, who not only lost his little brother to an overdose but also came *this* close to losing me in the past.

Needless to say, he stopped fighting me on the work hours.

He barely even mentions Cat unless I do first. I know he thinks I made the wrong call ending things, thinks my reasoning is irrational and not based on facts or logic. But even when he disagrees, he still has my back. Always. Even when it means trouble for him. He runs interference when Tori decides to lay into me, works out with me whenever he can, and lets me keep him up until all hours of the night, even when I don't have anything to say.

I was supposed to be done at five today, but the closer I got to being done, the more apprehensive I got about going home. There were really only two options for me: stay and work until closing time, or go back to the apartment and spend the night with only a bottle of Jack to keep me company. I know I would have spiraled, just like I have almost every single night since I last saw Cat. My fingers would have itched to dial her number, my voice trembling to tell her that I fucked up, that I want her back, that I need her in my life. But then what? All those things are true, but they don't negate the fact that I'll never be good enough for her, and that she deserves only good things rather than being with someone as fucked up as me.

So, work it was.

I finish stocking the bottles, move the crate back in its rightful storage area, then look around for something to do because, well, I'm not actually supposed to be here. There's no designated table section for me, so I've been keeping busy bussing, restocking, cleaning—anything to keep my mind off Cat.

Shane appears in my periphery, and I turn my head, my brow creasing at the look on his face.

"What's wrong?"

"Sorry, dude," he says, pressing his lips together. "Tor's here. With Vada. And... Cat."

My eyes search the room before I can stop them. It's like Cat walks around with some kind of beacon, because I find her immediately. My heart lurches—too fast, too hard—and my whole body tenses with this sudden, unrelenting urge to go to her. To just walk over and hold her. I close my eyes, give my head a shake, try to reset something in my system, try to push back against the realization of how fucking much I miss her.

"Sorry, man," Shane says again, softer this time.

I open my eyes and force myself to look at him. "It's all good," I lie, even though I'm already failing to keep my gaze from drifting over his shoulder. She's here. She's close. And everything in me lights up like it's been waiting for her.

Cat is, as always, the picture of perfect. I haven't seen her in weeks and somehow she's even more beautiful. Her long wavy hair falls soft and shining over her shoulders, and that cherry red knit sweater she's wearing? I've seen it before. Peeled it off her body before, too. It hugs her in all the right places, stops right above the waistband of those curve-hugging jeans, and I swear my lungs stop working.

“I gave them a booth in Casey’s section,” Shane says gently. “So maybe just... you know. Don’t go over there.”

“Sage advice,” I mutter.

He squeezes my shoulder, throws me a look of sympathy, then disappears into the little office to the right of the bar.

I take a deep breath and get back to whatever the fuck I was doing before the world’s biggest distraction walked into the restaurant. Except my eyes don’t cooperate. I keep glancing at her table. It’s strange having her here and having to deny myself when everything in me yearns to grab that quick kiss, catch a sweet smile meant only for me, tell her I love her as I pass her table. Ever since Cat first walked into Murphy’s after we met, having her around while I worked became my favorite part of the job. Now? Excruciating.

And it only gets worse thirty minutes later, when I glance over and clock two college-age guys are now sitting at the table. One of them is clearly smitten with Cat, leaning toward her, full-on beaming like she hung the damn moon. Can’t fucking blame him, I guess.

I know it’s no longer my business what Cat does with whom, but I’m not going to deny that the prospect of her with another guy makes me want to tear my own face off. I know it’s hypocritical, I know it’s fucked up. I was the one who broke things off, but not because I didn’t love her anymore. She deserves peace, stability, a family, and uncomplicated life—all things I’m incapable of ensuring. Not with the family I come from.

But that doesn’t mean I don’t want to throttle the guy talking to her.

“What are those two dudes talking about?” I ask Casey when she grabs a drink order at the bar.

“What dudes?”

“At Tori’s table.”

Casey clearly doesn’t buy my bullshit; her eyebrows rise to meet her hairline, her eyes widening empathetically. She doesn’t know specifics, but she knows enough. "Oh, yeah, the one with the dark, curly hair's definitely trying to take Cat home tonight."

I know I shouldn't, know that I'm going against my resolve, but *fuck it.* I walk over to Cat's table, my heart jumping into my throat when her eyes find mine, filling with mirrored longing. That's all it takes. One look. Everything inside me goes tight and desperate. I want to fall to my knees. Tell her I'm sorry. Tell her I still love her. But I can't—not if I mean to protect her.

The guy Casey mentioned is straddling a chair backwards, leaning in as he talks animatedly at Cat. He doesn't realize that he no longer has her attention. I do.

"Tell me what you're drinking again?" Vada asks the guy just as I step up to the table.

"It's called a Jedi Mind Trick," he says, swirling his drink so hard it sloshes over the rim.

"Looks like it's working," I say from behind him.

The guy whips around before looking down at the drink in his hand and where it's spilled on the table.

"Oh shit, damn," he mutters.

"I got this, man," I say, nodding at the table. "Maybe you should go and grab yourself a new drink."

"Yeah, cool, thanks." He stands, motions for his friend to join him, then turns back to Cat. "Really awesome to run into you, Cat. It's always a little weird to run into people outside of school."

So they know each other from NYU. Perfect.

"If you guys don't have plans, Dusty and I are heading to the Foxtail Lounge in a little bit..." The guy trails off.

"Okay. Good to see you, Levi," Cat says.

Okay. But what kind of *okay*? Is she being polite? Curious? Noncommittal? Fuck.

"You guys alright?" I ask the girls—mostly Cat, actually—when this Levi and his buddy Dusty are out of earshot.

Vada's eyes go sharp. "Not really any of your business, Ran."

Her line's clearly drawn, side chosen. Not that she was required to.

"Woah, what the fuck was that for?" I chuff, irritated. I didn't snap at her or Steve when they ended things, but I guess I shouldn't expect Vada to remain neutral. That girl has never been Switzerland about anything.

"For being an asshole, Ran."

"Fine, whatever." I turn to Cat, dialing my voice down. "Are you alright?"

She nods, her hazel eyes wide. "I'm fine."

I hold her gaze a moment longer—just long enough to remember what it feels like to belong to her—then wipe the table clean and turn to leave.

"You need to get your head out of your ass, Ran!" Vada calls after me.

I glance back, jaw tight. "And you need to butt out of shit that doesn't concern you."

This earns me a derisive look from her. "Cat is one of my best friends. You think you can shatter her heart and walk away like it's noble? Fuck that, Ran. That *does* concern me."

Her words cut into me, adding to the self-inflicted wounds in my heart—which, by now, is barely even beating.

She nudges Cat. "You know what? Let's go. Levi and Dusty actually seem like decent, emotionally available guys," she says loudly, no doubt for my benefit. *Wow.*

I march toward the back door and straight past Shane. "Taking my break," I mutter, my words grating against gritted teeth. He doesn't stop me. Just nods, eyes full of concern.

God fuck, I should've gone home and gotten wasted. Then I wouldn't have run into the most perfect girl in this world, wouldn't have had to watch some dude hitting on her, wouldn't have had to wonder if she's going to hook up with this guy tonight.

I shove the heavy steel door open, putting more weight behind it than necessary. It slams against the brick. I pace, hands in my hair, my heart shouting in my chest. Man, it's so fucking easy to fall in love, and fall I did. Hard. But nobody warned me how fucking hard it is to claw my way back out, how devastating it is to strip yourself of the person who holds your heart in her hands. I don't want it back. It's hers to keep until the end of days. I'm resigned to walking around with a void where my heart—where Cat—used to reside.

I pull my phone out of my back pocket and stare at it, battling with myself. How far gone am I right now? Far enough, apparently, for me to unlock it, then dial Doctor Seivert's number.

I never manage to have an anxiety attack during her office hours. Nope, I save those for when she's supposed to be at home, enjoying the rest of her evening. I decide against letting her answering service connect me to her cell and just leave a message for her instead.

She's told me time and time again that she's always available for emergencies. Except I don't know what counts anymore. Does this? Surely my inability to emotionally regulate myself doesn't amount to an actual crisis.

I don't connect to her cell. I just leave a message like I did back in November, the morning after my grandmother showed up, after that nightmare. The one where I hurt Cat in my sleep. Shane was the one who told me to call her then. He's not here now, but his voice still echoes in my head.

So I call. I call because I'm scared of myself. Because I can't keep bleeding out in silence. Because for all my noble bullshit, I still want to be better.

For her.

Even if I can't have her.

***

I take a few cleansing breaths, then wander back inside, chuckling to myself. Funny how I held my shit together through years of terrible abuse, but I give up the love of my life and fold like a bad hand at poker.

Shane's eyes lock on me as I approach, his expression cautiously neutral. "Tori said Vada and Cat went off to the Foxtail Lounge to meet up with those guys from earlier," he says, testing the water.

My jaw tightens. "Okay." It's all I can force out.

"Ran, what can I do?" he asks, his hand on my shoulder. "What do you need?"

"Nothing."

"Don't do that. You look like you're about to punch a hole in the wall. Tell me what you need right now. A shot?"

I exhale through my nose. "I need to get back to work." I'm desperate for a distraction from this bullshit day.

Without another word, I leave Shane standing.

My attention is drawn to a couple of girls sitting a little further down the bar. One of them waves at me.

"What can I get you two?" I ask them, adjusting my ball cap.

"I'll have a mai tai," says the girl on the right, tucking a strand of long blonde hair behind her ear. "How about you, Audrey?"

The brunette looks me over with warm brown eyes that flick briefly to my mouth, then my chest, and back again. "Jack and Ginger," she says, and adds with a playful grin, "And we'll take your number, too."

I let out a short laugh, one side of my mouth tugging upward. "You'll *both* take my number?"

"Uh-huh." Audrey nods, nudging her friend. "Allie's my best friend. We share *everything*."

"Huh, that's a great friend," I say. "But sorry, I don't give out my number."

"How about your address?" Allie asks, cocking her head.

Brazen. "Also no."

"Well, that's no fun," Audrey pouts. "Tell you what, how about I give you *our* address and you can decide if you're up for some fun with us tonight?" She plucks a napkin from the holder and reaches for a pen clipped to my jeans pocket, fingers brushing the side of my thigh. "We live within walking distance," she says with a wink.

I chuckle. "You're not worried I'm some psycho serial killer?"

Allie snorts. Audrey just smirks. "Are you?"

"No."

"Good, now that we've cleared that up." Audrey scribbles something on the napkin.

I'm taken aback by their forwardness. I've been hit on before. Plenty. But I can't recall ever being propositioned for a... threesome?

"Let me go get your drinks."

"What. The. Fuck," Shane whisper-shouts at me, his eyes huge when I reach him and Jack. They were obviously eavesdropping.

"You're taking them up on their offer, right?" Jack says, a prominent grin on his lips.

I chuckle. "What? Fuck, no!"

Shane gasps audibly, his eyes wide. "And why the fuck not?"

"Ran, seriously, why wouldn't you?" Jack looks past me to the two girls. "They're both hot as fuck and they're literally inviting you to have a threesome with them!"

"You used to live for that shit!" Shane says.

I frown at him. He can't possibly believe I'm ready to start hooking up with random girls again. "Damn, guys, why don't you two hit them up?" I growl.

Jack shrugs. "Can't. We're currently under female supervision, remember?" Is it me or do I detect a note of envy in his voice?

Shane nudges me with his shoulder. "Could be the perfect distraction tonight. I mean, if Cat's out there moving on, why shouldn't you at least pretend to try?"

What's left of my withered heart squeezes in my chest at the image his words conjure—Cat's mouth on someone else's, her fingers touching someone else's body.

"Did you really have to say it like that?" The memory of her kissing that frat guy at the party is still prominently featured in my head.

"Sorry, but—"

"You made your point, guys." I turn my attention to Jack. "Can I get those damn drinks now?"

He holds up his hands in surrender, already reaching for the bottles. "Suit yourself, man."

A minute later, he slides two glasses toward me, an imploring look on his face. I shake my head at him and Shane, then go deliver the drinks.

Audrey and Allie are already watching me.

"Here you go, handsome," Audrey says. She takes the napkin, folds it with slow, deliberate fingers, and slides it into the back pocket of my jeans, her hand lingering far too long. "I promise we'll make it worth your while. What time do you get off?"

Fuck it. "Two."

"Great. Maybe you'd like to *get off* a second time tonight," Allie purrs, raising an eyebrow.

"You have both our numbers." Audrey places a hundred-dollar bill on the bar, smiling as she pushes it toward me. "Text us if you're up for some company."

I nod, mostly out of habit. The napkin burns in my back pocket.

As I said, patterns. Cycles. Can't escape them.

Cat

"Alright, so here's the thing," Vada says the second we're sequestered in the ladies' bathroom at the Foxtail Lounge. She reaches for my wrist and whirls me around to face her. "Dusty is really freaking hot," she says with a nod. "And I want to get laid."

Vada hasn't been shy about putting herself out there since college. Once she was over Steve, she dove headfirst into dating. Even Brady hasn't slowed her down much. "I'm young, I'm hot, I want to have fun," she told me recently. That was right before launching into why I should "go get some college dick."

"Uh-huh, so what are you telling me?" I ask, wiggling myself free from Vada's hold.

Her lips pucker while she rests her hand on her popped-out hip. "That we should take them up on their offer to go back to their apartment..."

I get the impression she has more to say. I flatten my lips between my teeth and wait for her to continue.

"...and that Levi is really cute, and you should get laid, too."

There it is.

I turn to the mirror and begin to mess with my unruly hair. Not totally sure if it's the added moisture in the air, but the long blonde strands are a mess today. A pang of longing shoots through me. Ronan loved my hair, especially when it was big and messy like this. "You look like a damn lioness, baby. It's sexy as hell," he'd always say.

I freeze, my fingers still in my hair. It doesn't feel sexy now. Just wild and untamable. Like my emotions.

I sense Vada step up next to me, her face and body turned squarely toward me. I stare at myself, ignoring her intense gaze. "Come on, Kitty Cat. You've only ever experienced one cock, right? *And* you and Ran are broken up. That means, one, you wouldn't be cheating, and two, it's valuable life experience. It's not like you're 'saving yourself for marriage.'" She shrugs, then turns, leaning onto the sink counter and closing the distance between herself and her mirror image. "So, you might as well go and live life a little. Get your rocks off, you know? Nothing wrong with that. Plus, you'll be doing me a favor," she says with a smirk, then retrieves her trusty red lipstick from her black bag and applies it to her pouty lips.

My fingers rake through the mop on my head, acting as a makeshift comb. It's useless, though. I'll need heat to straighten the waves. "And how exactly would I be doing you a favor by having sex with Levi?" I ask, half-amused.

"Well, I'd feel a lot less guilty having an orgasm if I knew you were in the room next to me having one, too, rather than just sitting on the sofa watching an episode of *Friends*, waiting for me to finish."

"You know, for someone who was so intent on Ran and me getting together, you're awfully pushy about me having a one-night stand."

Vada doesn't take the bait. "Well, Ran's acting like a complete douche-canoe and you deserve a good time. Come on, don't tell me you don't find Levi attractive." She tosses her lipstick back into her purse.

I shrug. "I mean, he's not—"

"Yeah, I know, he's not Ran aka Adonis," Vada says with an eye roll.

I stifle the sigh before it has the chance to escape my mouth. "That's not what I was going to say. I was going to say that Levi isn't bad looking."

Vada smiles triumphantly. "Honestly, that's all that's required: not bad looking. And you can always close your eyes, too. Look, I don't expect you to fall in love and start a deep relationship with Levi. I don't even expect you to fall *out* of love with Ran. But I do expect you to try and have a few minutes of fun and get yourself a big, screaming *O*."

She hooks her arm under mine, then pulls me out of the bathroom and back to our table occupied by Levi and Dusty.

***

The cab ride back to Levi and Dusty's place is... awkward. I never sit in the front passenger seat, but would have gladly traded places with Levi once Vada and Dusty began making out in the backseat next to me. *Man, to have Vada's unabashed confidence and self-assurance.*

Levi kept looking over his shoulder at me, communicating his apologies with his eyes. The forced smile on my lips was both for his benefit and mine.

I'm not convinced that Vada and Dusty's lips disengaged or that his hands retreated from Vada's body while they clambered out of the cab and up to the apartment, only to disappear into Dusty's room. Vada pulled her tongue from Dusty's mouth only long enough to throw me a meaningful look before the bedroom door slammed shut behind them.

Levi motions for me to take a seat on the sofa, then walks no more than five feet to the kitchen. This place is even smaller than Ronan and Shane's apartment, but I'd bet anything their rent is half of Levi and Dusty's. That's the difference between living in one of the boroughs, like Queens, versus "the city."

The suction noise of the refrigerator opening sounds from the kitchen. "Want anything to drink?" Levi asks. "We have... water, Gatorade, beer, chocolate milk? What the fuck?" he mutters that last part, making my lips curve. What an eclectic mix of beverage choices. The fridge door shuts. "And vodka." Levi's head appears around the corner, a miffed expression crowding his face.

"Uhh—"

He expels a short laugh. "I can't even make you a mixed drink with that stuff."

I contemplate just asking him for some vodka. I hate that stuff, but it's miraculous at lowering my inhibitions. That and tequila. They're my kryptonite. I could probably benefit from a little dulling of my thoughts. Problem is, I don't know that I *want* to heed Vada's advice from earlier. I decide against the alcohol. Whatever decisions I make tonight, when tomorrow comes around I want to be certain those choices were clearheaded and all mine.

"Don't worry about it. Maybe some water," I say.

The sofa cushions concave with Levi's weight when he sits down next to me, handing me a bottle of water. "So, Vada isn't the shy type, is she?" he asks over the sound of the bottle cap separating from its plastic ring.

I shake my head, my bottle to my lips. I hastily swallow the sip. "No. She never was."

"Good for her. And Dusty."

The plastic bottle in Levi's hand crinkles when a soft moan emanates from one of the bedrooms.

Levi and I sit awkwardly, the silence growing thick. I keep taking sips of my water even though I'm not thirsty.

"You look really nice tonight," Levi says, a sweet smile on his lips.

I don't thank him for the compliment. It feels like a mandatory step for him to take in the societally accepted process of hooking up. It's all so forced and uncomfortable, especially with what Dusty and Vada are doing only feet away from us. The air is heavy with expectations and wondering where this is going to go tonight. I can practically see Levi calculating what he should do and say next. It's such a delicate balance—say the right things, push enough to test, but not so far as to be off-putting. Poor guy.

"Vada thinks you and I should hook up tonight, too," I say, then promptly take another sip of water.

Levi's dark eyes flash briefly. He was not expecting me to cut the chase short like this. His Adam's apple bops with his dry swallow. "She does, huh?"

I twist the cap back onto my water and place it on the floor, directing my full attention to Levi. I still don't know whether I want this, but I guess I'm going to find out really quickly. I nod.

Levi searches my eyes while I sit unspeaking. He slowly leans toward me, millimeter by millimeter. I inhale and shut my eyes, waiting for his lips to make contact, which they do a second later.

His kiss is hesitant, nothing like Ronan's, who knew my mouth like his own. Just the thought of him sends a throbbing ache through my chest and threatens tears. I try to stay in the moment, praying for the ability to ignore the pain and seek the pure physical pleasure. I'm verging on thanking Levi for the nice evening, yanking Vada out of this bachelor pad with me, and heading home to drown in my sorrow.

"God, you're so hot, Cat," Levi breathes against my lips, gently pushing me back against the pillows. He meets no resistance. His hands roam, but my body won't follow. It doesn't light up. It doesn't want this. My skin stays silent, numb. If this was Ronan's hand, I'd already be tingling all over. My skin would be covered in delicious goosebumps while moist heat rushed to my core. Nothing feels better than Ronan's body on mine; nothing will ever compare—but still, I don't push Levi off me.

Instead, I follow his lead, running my hands underneath his shirt and up his back. He sits back, then pulls his hoodie and shirt off, discarding them on the floor. My eyes take stock of his build. Levi obviously works out, but isn't nearly as muscular, as cut as Ronan, whose body is so damn perfect, even scarred. *God, I need to stop thinking about Ronan.*

Levi takes my hand into his and carefully pulls me up to a seat before coaxing my sweater off me. Once again, I allow it, allow his lips back on mine while his hands work to unhook my bra and slide the straps off my shoulders.

I feel naked, exposed, vulnerable. I fight the urge to cover my breasts. It's just a hookup. I'm not betraying anyone... except maybe myself.

"Jesus, fuck, you have a perfect fucking body," Levi growls before he descends toward my chest. His lips find my nipple, and he sucks it into his mouth, his tongue flicking while his hand glides down my side, over the apple of my hip and between my thighs. The heat of his palm seeps through my jeans. I can no longer pretend. My eyes open with the sting of the building tears. My heart is racing. I want to crawl out of my skin. Poor Levi is clueless, his mouth still on my breast, his hands rubbing, kneading, caressing in an effort to get me worked up and ready for him.

I can't do this. I don't want this. I don't want this with anyone but Ronan. "Levi, please stop." Either I didn't say it loud enough or Levi's hearing is muted with sex, because he begins to unbutton my jeans. I set my hands onto his shoulders and push him back gently. "I'm sorry, Levi, but please stop," I say again, louder.

He sits up, his breathing hectic. His erection tents his loose-fitting jeans as he looks at me with concern in his glossy eyes.

"I'm sorry, Cat. Did I do something wrong?" he asks sweetly. I feel so bad for leading him on like this, for allowing it to get this far.

I cover my breasts with my left arm, snatching my bra off the floor with my other hand. "No. It's just... I can't do this," I say with a tremble in my voice. A small part of me is worried about his reaction. I just did to Levi what I did to Adam, whose dismay at my rejection swiftly turned violent. "I'm really sorry. I didn't mean to lead you on, but I—"

Levi retreats, scooting back to give me space. The smile on his lips is warm, his eyes soft, unthreatening. "Is it that guy from the restaurant? That waiter?" he asks, trying to steady his breathing. My eyes widen, and so does his smile. "I saw the way he looked at you. And the way you looked at him."

I hesitate, then nod. "Yeah. He's... he's my... ex-boyfriend." I nearly suffocate on the word. "We just broke up a few weeks ago and..." I pull my sweater over my head, swiping the fabric over my face and soaking up the single tear spilling from my right eye.

"I get it," Levi says. "Who ended it?" His eyes are still full of empathy when my face emerges from my sweater.

"He did."

Levi nods. "Well, Cat, for what it's worth, I think he's a damn fucking idiot for letting you go." He replaces his own shirt. Instantly, I'm more at ease.

"I think Dusty and Vada are still busy in there," Levi says with a noncommittal nod toward Dusty's bedroom. "Do you want to wait for your friend to come out or do you want me to call you a cab?"

There's no way I'm leaving Vada here by herself. "I'll wait for her, if it's okay with you."

"Of course."

We sit and chat about school with the TV running in the background until Vada and Dusty join us in the living room twenty minutes later. Dusty grins widely, while Vada—a sated smile on her rosy face—pulls her hair into a quick ponytail.

Levi calls a ride share, and he and Dusty walk us down the stairs where we wait for the car to pull up.

"I'll see you at research hour on Tuesday, right?" Levi asks as I'm about to get into the car behind Vada.

My eyebrows rise. "Oh, uh, yeah. I mean, is that still okay with you?" I wouldn't hold it against him if he felt like we could no longer research together.

He flinches with a small frown. "What? Yeah, of course. Cat, I promise, this"—he points his index finger toward the sky, obviously indicating what happened in his upstairs apartment—"doesn't change anything. I respect your choices. We can still be friends and coworkers and all that. And honestly, I'd be so screwed if you didn't want to work together anymore." He pinches a deep exhale off with his lips, his cheeks puffing up.

I give him a grateful smile. "Okay. Thanks, Levi."

He nods and he shuts the car door behind me.

"So?" Vada accosts me the second the driver pulls away from the curb. "Tell me everything!" she squeals, her entire body turned to me.

I shrug. "There's nothing to tell."

Her brow wrinkles. "What do you mean? Are you telling me you didn't hook up with Levi?"

"I didn't."

"What? Cat, why the hell not?" Her tone makes it sound as though I threw away a winning lottery ticket.

"Because I didn't want to, Vada. I'm not ready." I take a shaky breath. "I'm not over him."

I don't say Ronan's name out loud. Even forming the syllables to let them roll off my tongue hurts as though I'm eating thorny cacti.

Vada chuffs. "You don't have to be over Ran to have single-serving sex! You can get your rocks off and still miss him. You're allowed to have fun."

She doesn't get it. "Vada, I've only ever slept with Ran. For me, it's not just sex. It's not just bodies grinding, okay? For me, it's me giving myself—wholly, body and soul—to someone else, and I only want to give myself to Ran." My voice breaks, and tears flood my eyes. "I miss him so much, Vada. I miss him so much, and nothing I do makes it better."

Friday, March 17th

Ronan

"Morning, Ran!" Tori chirps when I walk into the kitchen this morning.

I have to give myself credit for how I scheduled my classes this semester. Unlike last semester—when I had classes starting at eight a.m. five days a week—my Fridays are now short and sweet. It's almost like I knew I'd need a built-in recovery day, because I'm running on empty.

"Hey, man," Shane says, leaning his solid body back against the kitchen counter on which Tori sits, her short legs crossed and dangling off the edge.

"Hey, guys," I say, my voice tired.

Shane's eyes follow my movements as I fill a glass with water from the tap. "How was last night?"

I grab my pre-workout and scoop the powder into my glass. "Normal. We're running low on Jameson, though."

Shane pulls his phone from his pocket, no doubt to make a note to have his dad stop by the supplier and drop some off at Murphy's this morning. Funny when you think about it: Shane is old enough to run a damn business, but not old enough to buy alcohol. "Which one?"

"Black barrel."

"Got it." He studies me for a moment. "Are you doing okay?"

I blink at the concern in his voice. "No." No point in lying to him. He knows me better than I even know myself.

"I didn't think so," he says with a nod.

"What can we do, Ran?" Tori asks empathetically. I know she thinks I'm an idiot for breaking things off with Cat. I also know she spends a ton of time with Cat. So, I appreciate her checking on me when I'm sure she'd prefer to kick my ass instead.

"Nothing really," I say with a shrug. "Oh, actually, Shay, can you cover me for about an hour this afternoon? I have a therapy appointment at four, but I should be at Murphy's by six."

Shane doesn't hesitate. "Of course."

"This might actually become a more regular thing again," I say hesitantly, looking from him to Tori and back again. "I think I'm going to pick up more sessions."

Shane takes a scoop from the jar of pre-workout and adds it to his own water. "Do you feel like you need it?"

I pinch my lips between my teeth while I nod. "I think so. I can't get out of my head. It's starting to affect my sleep again." I omit the little tidbit about the nightmares I've been having almost nightly for the past few weeks, the 4 a.m. anxiety attacks fracturing my sleep for the past month and a half.

Nothing helps. School, Murphy's, even the gym no longer provide me with the longed-for distraction. Then again, they never did provide an effective cure. The only thing that ever eased the hellfire within me wasn't actually a thing at all. It was Cat. She's the only person who can make it better, and she's the only person I cannot allow myself to have.

Of course, that knowledge doesn't keep my thoughts from turning to her every waking—and sleeping—second. The sleeping seconds are the worst; so often I'm a soulless monster in my dreams. Then I wake, and the shame and guilt dissipate only long enough for me to remember that I've cut Cat out of my life. And the pain of hurting Cat is replaced by the pain of hurting myself *and* Cat.

"I promise, I'll try to make my therapy work around my schedule at Murphy's." I know how important it is to Tori that Shane doesn't overextend himself—which he definitely has a tendency to do—that he takes a step back to spend quality time with her, and I hate asking Shane to work extra hours.

Shane waves me off. "Dude, do what you gotta do."

"Yeah, Ran. It's fine," Tori says.

It hits me yet again how lucky I got in the friends department when the universe completely failed me in terms of parents. I guess there's an innate balance to everything. "Thanks, guys. Shay, I'll work your shift tomorrow night, if you want. You can take Tor on a date."

I grin at the way his blue eyes widen with happiness.

"Seriously?"

"Yeah. I got nothing better to do."

"Dude, that would be great!"

My phone vibrates in my pocket. "Yeah, you got it." I retrieve my phone, noting the area code of the incoming call. It's a Montana area code, but definitely not my grandparents.

I walk out of the kitchen and answer. "This is Ronan."

"Hey there, Rony," Miranda sing-songs on the other end.

"Hey Randi!" I walk the fifteen feet down the hallway to my room. "Did you get a new phone?"

"Yep," she says proudly. "And not only that, I bought myself a new truck." She squeals with delight.

I shut my door, grinning. "Way to go! What kind?"

Miranda giggles. "A sexy, cherry red Ram Rebel."

"Wow, that's a big truck for a little girl like you," I tease. "Are you even able to see over the steering wheel?"

I'm met with an offended huff. "I can handle big things very, very well," she says in a suggestive tone. "I know how to handle you, for example. Handled you really nicely for a while there."

I shake my head and chuckle. *Good to know some things never change.* "You always know how to make things awkward as fuck."

"Sorry, I've been stuck on the ranch for too long. Been a minute since I've ridden a cowboy rather than a horse."

I pick yesterday's shirt off the floor and toss it into my hamper. "Well, what about Elias?" I ask. "Wasn't it your mission to pop his cherry?"

"Who's making it awkward now, Rony?" Miranda laughs.

"I'm just checking up on your prior plans, that's all."

"He's not really my type. I like them tall, blond, and green-eyed."

I can all but see her wiggling her eyebrows from two thousand miles away. "Is this a competition over who can make things more awkward? Plus, I specifically remember you telling me you don't discriminate when we were driving to Nashville."

"That's when I was looking at a topless picture of your feline."

My breath hitches at her mention of Cat, my vocal cords constricting in my throat. "Right."

"Your aunt told me. She told me you broke things off with Cat. Sorry, Rony," Miranda says quickly, obviously picking up on my tone.

"It's okay." I'm straight up lying through my damn teeth because absolutely nothing is okay. I fall back onto my bed. "So, what's new with you?"

"You mean aside from me getting my life back together like the badass bitch that I am?"

"Yeah, aside from that," I chuckle.

"Oh, not much. Things are slowing down a little after calving season, which means your grandparents are fully transitioning into wedding prep mode."

I run my right hand over my face. "God, I keep forgetting about my dad's wedding."

That's also a lie. I know full well his wedding is in exactly eighteen days. While I miss Montana, the ranch, and my grandparents, I'm no longer excited to go back like I was only two months ago. And not because my dad is getting married to the woman he lived a whole different life with while my mother was abusing me, but because the stabbing pain in my heart is sure to reach bleed-out levels the moment I come face-to-face with Cat, have to stand across the aisle from her while my dad and Penny exchange vows.

Nothing made me more ecstatic than the idea of getting to share the ranch with Cat, live with her for a short time in a place that symbolized almost unadulterated peace. It was there where I began to emerge from the darkness, where I found the strength to pick myself up by my bootstraps and began to heal. Now I'm about to stain one of the only places in this world that I don't immediately associate with pain.

"Well, you kind of have some other things in your head right now," Miranda says. "I wanted to call you earlier, but things have been crazy and I figured you wouldn't want to talk about it. You probably don't want to talk about it even now."

I chuckle dryly. "You know me well."

"Just like you know me, which means you also know that I'm not going to let this go. So, at the risk of making you shut down, can I ask you what happened?"

I exhale deeply. "Well, it all started roughly nineteen years ago on the day my mother found out she was pregnant with me."

Miranda's rueful laugh makes its way into my ear. "Yeah, yeah, I figured it had everything to do with the incredibly loving relationship you had with your mom. But seriously, Rony. What changed? What happened? You were so fucking happy with her."

So, I remind Miranda of the day my grandmother showed up at my dad's and told us all about the Donahues' violent family history, tell her again about the dreams I've been having, then tell Miranda about the birth of my half brothers and my fight with Cat over having kids. And then I tell her about *that* kiss, the moment I found Cat locked in embrace with some dude whose face resembled a glossy, ready-to-be-pounced-on punching bag.

The part I leave out—the part I haven't told a single soul about—is what Rashana shared with me the last time she and I spoke.

The piece of my family's atrocious history that took my nightmares to a previously unreached level of terror.

The piece that was the last straw, the final drop, the ultimate point at which I knew that Cat and I could never have forever. Not in the way Cat deserves.

Miranda stays silent for a long while, her breathing whooshing in and out of the phone. "You didn't break it off because your feline kissed someone," she says like it's a given thing.

She's right, I didn't. As much as it hurt to find her like this, I always knew the moment would come eventually. The moment when Cat—consciously or not—would realize she's better off without me. "The kiss was just a symptom of a bigger issue," I say so quietly, I'm surprised Miranda even heard me.

"The bigger issue being that you're afraid your mom was right. That you're not enough and can never be enough, no matter how hard you try, right?"

I nod but don't say a word.

"You're afraid of hurting her," Miranda says, her voice diminishing to barely above a whisper. "Of being incapable of breaking the cycle."

"I need to keep her safe," I mutter.

"Have you talked to your therapist about your dreams and stuff?" Miranda asks, echoing Shane's words. They really do think Doctor Seivert is some kind of miracle-guru-Ronan-Soult-psyche-whisperer.

"Yep," I say matter-of-factly.

"And what about that you're scared of doing the same to your family as your mother did to you?"

"That, too," I say. "But it's different than talking with her about shit that has happened to me in the past, because that is what it is. But the future... I just can't convince myself that it's going to be okay. I have no reference point, no proof that..." My breath stutters as I inhale. "I can't risk hurting her, or..." *Nope, I won't say it.*

Her next words catch me so off guard, I'd stumble if I wasn't sitting on my bed. "Maybe you should try to find your uncle."

I blink. That thought has never even crossed my mind. "Why would I do that?"

"To see if he was able to change things. I mean, you're so afraid of doing what you think is, like, ingrained in your DNA. You literally broke up with the love of your life over this," she says like it's the most absurd thing she could ever fathom. "Maybe finding him could be helpful."

I don't reject her idea outright, but there's one problem. "I don't even know if he's still alive."

"I'm sure that can be found out pretty easily, don't you think?"

I shrug with the phone to my ear. "I have no idea. And, okay, let's say he is alive. He obviously doesn't want to be found. I mean, his own mother hasn't heard from him in over twenty years." Not to mention that Rashana was able to dig up some deeply buried shit but was unable to find even scraps of information about my uncle after he turned eighteen.

"But did she try to find him?"

Again, I find myself unable to answer her question. "I don't actually know."

"It might be worth a shot, Rony."

"But Randi, I wouldn't even know where to start. How do you find someone who's been missing for two decades?"

"Uh, doesn't your dad work like, really fancy intelligence in the Air Force?" she asks me like I've temporarily lost all my brain cells.

"Oh." I didn't think of my dad as a person to ask for help. *Does that make me a shitty son?* I don't stop to examine that question now. I have enough shit to feel bad about.

"Yeah, so maybe start there," Miranda says. "I'm sure he has access to stuff that us normal folk don't have access to, right?"

"Probably."

Faint whinnying comes through the phone. I close my eyes, pretending for a moment that I'm on the ranch with her. I can almost smell the mountains.

"So, are you going to do it?" she asks giddily.

The mountains dissipate when I open my eyes to the four walls of my small bedroom. "I don't know. I... I'm kind of scared."

"Of finding out that maybe he's alive and wasn't able to break the cycle of abuse?"

She's hitting the nail on the head.

"Yeah."

"That's definitely a possibility. But if you think about it, it's a no-lose situation for you."

"How?"

"Well, nothing really changes for you if it turns out he's dead. Just like nothing will change for you if it turns out he's still alive but also an asshole. As far as you know, the Donahue family consists of a bunch of abusive assholes. That's your baseline even before you find out about your uncle, right? On the other hand, if it turns out he's alive and a great fucking person, that's a win for you. It gives you hope, or whatever. If he's alive and a dick, then you'll just be where you are now—status quo so to speak. Not better, not worse. The way I see it, you honestly have nothing to lose."

Well shit, she has a damn point. "Yeah, maybe," I say, nodding.

"Do it, Rony. Try to find him."

I shut my eyes tightly and exhale the apprehension settling on my chest. "Okay." I guess Miranda's right—I already lost the best thing in my life when I broke up with Cat. I have nothing else to lose, even if it all goes sideways and my uncle is a very-much-alive abuser.

"Great. And I'll tell you what, if shit turns out, well, like shit, then you can come back to Montana and marry me instead. I'm well aware how fucked up you are, I have my own bullshit to deal with, and I don't want kids either. So we can just live out the rest of our lives fucking each other."

A laugh bursts from my lips. "Oh, Jesus, Randi."

"Hey, I'm just looking out for you. Wouldn't want that gorgeous, silky cock of yours to wither away from lack of usage. I only have your best interest at heart."

"Oh, yeah, obviously. Thanks for looking out for my cock."

"Anytime, Rony. Remember, I'm a regular Mother Teresa."

"I almost forgot," I say, still laughing. "Alright, Randi, I'll let you go. I'm gonna head to my dad's and see if he'll help me."

***

It's striking how strange it feels to let myself into my dad's house. I only moved out a few months ago, but already it doesn't feel like home. Maybe it never did.

Even now, nearly two years after the abuse ended, I still tense whenever I pull up to the curb. I fully expect my mom's white Camry to be parked in the driveway, to walk in on her waiting for me in the kitchen, ready to dish out punishment for some minor transgression, like sneezing or saying "hi" incorrectly.

That car, of course, is no longer around. My dad sold it a long time ago. In fact, there are essentially no traces of my mom left inside the house. He packed up all her belongings, bought all new furniture—pillows, bedding, and linens included. He even threw out that damn broom that hung on a hook in the kitchen. The surveillance the D.A. played at the trial made it obvious that my mom favored that broom as her weapon. She used it a lot there toward the end, and the day my mom changed her plea to guilty, my dad yanked it off the wall—hook and all—and bent that metal handle with brute force before marching it out to the trash can.

Still, old habits die hard. I enter the house making virtually no sound. I hang up my jacket, then take off my shoes and quietly deposit them in the shoe closet, finding a spot between my dad's running shoes and Penny's black pumps. I walk down the hallway, careful to avoid the spots where the floorboards creak, then turn right into the living room.

My dad's sitting back on the sofa, working on his laptop. He's not alone; resting against my dad's solid chest is one of my baby half brothers—Dean, if I had to guess, but I'm still not great at telling the twins apart.

Like the career soldier he is, my dad catches my movement out of his periphery and turns his head in my direction. "Ran?"

"Hey, Dad."

He narrows his eyes at me, gaze sweeping over me as if to assess my well-being as I sit on the loveseat.

"Not that I don't love the surprise visit, but I'd be lying if I said I was expecting to see you today, bud. Are you alright?" His voice is a low, soothing hum. I know it's for the benefit of my sleeping brother, but I can't say it doesn't have a calming effect on me, too.

"Yeah," I say quickly, then nod at the baby. I figure a little small talk is a good idea before I ask my dad to take advantage of his security clearance and deep dive into my mom's family history. "Is it nap time?"

He expels a breathy laugh. "You could say that. Dean really only sleeps well when he's being held, which means Penny doesn't get great sleep at night. She's upstairs right now resting with Kellan while I'm on Dean duty. He conks right out when I have him on my chest. I get a pretty solid couple of hours of work done this way."

I cock an eyebrow. "And Kellan doesn't want to be held the whole time?"

"Not when he's sleeping. Kellan's a solid sleeper. Dean not so much. But when the boys are awake, it's the complete opposite. Then Kellan wants to be held all the time while Dean wants to do his own thing."

I nod, contemplating how different Kellan and Dean are, despite them being twins. "How much longer are you on leave?" My dad took advantage of the twelve-week paid paternity leave offered by the Air Force, which I imagine is coming in handy with the twins, one of whom is apparently a terrible sleeper.

He moves his laptop onto the sofa cushion. "I go back the week after the wedding." His eyes narrow analytically again. "Alright, Ran, you haven't stopped by in weeks now. You haven't responded to my texts. I literally had to hunt you down at Murphy's a few evenings ago to assure myself you're still breathing. There's a reason you're here, and that reason is not to ask me about my leave. Feel like spitting it out?"

If only he had been this discerning when my mother was still beating the shit out of me. I brace myself and exhale deeply. "Well, I kind of need your help with something."

"Okay?" He stands, carefully moves to a motorized baby swing, and successfully transfers Dean into it without waking him. Then he retakes his seat on the sofa across from me and gives me his undivided attention, his brows raised.

"I think I want to try to find Mom's brother."

His eyes flare while his eyebrows knit. "Wow, Ran, that's... why?"

"Because I need to know if it's possible for me to break the cycle of abuse, Dad."

It's the most basic explanation, the most watered-down response. I practiced it on the car ride over here. Of course, it's way more nuanced than that, but hey, baby steps.

His features soften. "Of course it is, Ran. And you will," he says like he doesn't harbor a single doubt. I knew he wouldn't fucking get it. I mean, how could he? He's never had to live in my damn head, never had to breathe with my lungs, hasn't had to wake from those dreams, hasn't ever had to wonder whether he'd snap one day and hurt the people he cares most about.

I rake my hands through my hair, that familiar feeling of powerlessness pricking my skin. "No, Dad, you don't understand."

"Okay, then explain it to me," he says, his deep voice soft, his brown eyes warm as he studies me.

I tell myself to heed Doctor Seivert's advice, to give my dad a chance to be my dad, to lower my walls and let him in. Not just because he's my dad and has been making an unreciprocated effort to be a part of my life, but because he's in the best position to help me find my long-lost uncle.

I take a deep breath. "I'm scared, Dad," I admit out loud. "Remember when you called me in Montana and you told me Mom was going to push for a trial? That her lawyer was going to put on evidence about the abuse Mom had suffered?"

He nods, his brown eyes pinned to me. "Yeah."

"And you told me that you knew she and her brother had been abused?"

He responds with another nod.

"That was the first time it occurred to me that I might turn out just like them, Dad," I say through gritted teeth. "I mean, aren't there studies about this sort of stuff? That if you grow up with violence, you're more likely to become violent yourself?" It's a rhetorical question, and he doesn't answer. "I tried not to think about it, but... then it turned out the abuse went way up the family tree, and..." My voice betrays me and breaks.

I swallow once, twice, to push down the lump rising in my throat. "Dad, I'm fucking scared," I choke. He still doesn't speak, letting me ramble on. "I'm scared that I might, one day, do to my family what Mom did to me, and what Mom's dad did to her and his dad to him, and so on. I just... I need to know what happened to him. I need to know if he..."

He rubs his neck. "Ran, I don't even know if he's still alive. As far as I know, nobody's heard from him since before you were even born, bud."

"But, can't you find out? There's gotta be a way to see if he's still alive."

"Yeah, but Ran, what if he's still alive? What if you find him? Then what?"

"Then I'll reach out to him or, I don't know." I haven't actually gotten that far in my brain. I always got stuck on the initial hurdle of even finding my uncle.

He groans, dragging his hand through his hair like he's trying to tug the answer out. "God, Ran, I just don't know if it's a good idea."

He runs his right hand across his face. "I don't know if this is a risk I want to take. I can't let you get hurt again."

I exhale loudly, frustrated. I don't stand a chance in hell of finding someone who doesn't want to be found without my dad, and his unwillingness to help me is yet another reminder of how little control I have over my trauma or my recovery.

"Fine," I huff, stand, and walk back to the hallway.

My dad jumps to his feet. "Ran!" He reaches for my arm, stopping me from walking away, from shutting down on him. "I fucking worry about you, do you understand?" he says, his voice strained, brow furrowed. "Look, finding Cormac—it could turn out really great, but it could also turn out absolutely fucking terrible. I'm trying to protect you, Ran. I've failed you before. A lot. I won't let that happen again," he says, his gaze warm despite his rigid posture.

Our eyes meet. He used to tower over me when I was little, but at 6'5" my dad is only three inches taller than me now. He can't protect me from the realities of my life anymore. He never did before, and now it's too late.

"I appreciate that, Dad. I really, really do. But I need this. I need to know. I need to know if I'm destined to repeat history."

"Ran, you are not going to repeat the cycle!"

I groan loudly. "Fuck, Dad, you don't know that, okay? You don't know how fucking scared I am. I need... I keep going down a rabbit hole, Dad," I choke, my emotions threatening to get the best of me.

"Buddy, just, please talk to me. Let me in. Please. Tell me!"

"Fuck." I cover my face with both my hands, then breathe deeply to steady myself. "After Grandma showed up last November, I started having nightmares."

He raises his eyebrows, confused. He knew I was having nightmares; he spent many nights sleeping on the floor next to my bed, waking me when I couldn't wake myself up, when the terror went on and on. But he doesn't know about the new dreams—neither the ones that started after my grandmother's visit nor the ones that came with the revelations from Rashana.

"In my dreams... I'm beating Cat, Dad." My heart constricts just as it does every time I say those words out loud. "I've had those dreams a bunch of times. And I know, *I know* they're just dreams. But... they freak me out so much I can't breathe sometimes. I wake up with this feeling... like... I've done something I can't undo. I can't fucking shake them," I croak. "I... They feel like premonitions and..."

My dad rubs his hand over his jaw. "Ran, I—"

"I told Cat I don't want kids," I continue. "After Kellan and Dean were born... we fought about it. Dad, I'm so scared of hurting her. I'm so scared of hurting my family..." The sob breaks out of my chest before I can strangle it, making this exactly the second time I've cried in front of my dad in almost twelve years.

He doesn't miss a beat. He pulls me into his arms, holding me like he did after I testified. "Is that why you broke things off with her?" he asks in that low, soothing tone.

I nod against him, unable to speak while I try to rein in my emotions, to quell the tears, to stop the heaving of my chest. I know everyone thinks I ended things with Cat because I caught her kissing someone else, but it's honestly not even in my top five reasons. It sucked, yeah, but it's not something I couldn't work past or forgive her for.

We're silent for a minute while he holds me and I try to compose myself.

"Buddy, I want to keep you safe. I worry about what could happen if we find Cormac, what it could do to you," my dad says, then takes a deep breath. "But I'll help you find him."

I step back, quickly swiping at my tears while I search his face through hazy eyes. "Really?" I ask, my voice raw.

"Yeah. If this is what you need, I'll do it. But Ran, promise me that if and when we find him, you'll let me go with you. I'll be damned if I let you walk into this alone."

I consider him for a moment, then nod. I guess I owe him that much.

Part II

Friday, March 31st

Ronan

"Wanna just keep driving and get shit-faced by the creek?" Miranda asks.

The cabin of my truck is dark, but the moon does a good enough job illuminating the interior that I immediately notice the smirk on her face. I grin back at her; this aspect of my life, at least, has remained the same. Miranda still doesn't give a single fuck about anything, including the fact that we're both expected to be up and at 'em in only a few hours.

"Dude, I've been back on the ranch for exactly four hours and you're already trying to get me in trouble."

I arrived back in Montana this afternoon and the moment I stepped foot on my grandparents' ranch the ache on my heart eased a little. It still throbs with the reality of my breakup from Cat, but still, being here has the same effect it had a year ago—all the heaviness is just a little less so.

I slow the truck in front of Miranda's cabin. She's already in the process of opening her passenger door. *No patience.* "And I will once again remind you that I've never cared about the rules," she says, and hops out of the cabin the second I throw the truck in park. She waves at me to follow suit. "Come on, Rony, you gotta walk me inside to make sure some mountain lion isn't going to eat me in the next five seconds."

I chuckle. My grandma insisted I drive Miranda to her cabin after dinner this evening because they've had an unusual amount of mountain lion activity on the ranch. The cattle are always at risk of falling prey to Montana's natural predators, like grizzlies, coyotes, and mountain lions—that's just life out here—but my grandpa told us that they spotted a mountain lion roaming awfully close to the barn about fifty yards from the house only two nights ago.

"Maybe you need to get a little bigger so the mountain lions see you as a threat rather than their evening snack."

She giggles, bouncing along ahead of me, her light brown braid swaying. "I could eat all the food in the world and I'd still be a damn *snack*, Rony."

Walked right into that one. I laugh while Miranda blows me an air-kiss over her shoulder, her eyebrows wiggling. "So, about getting shit-faced." She steps through her unlocked front door and waits for me to enter behind her before locking it.

I raise my eyebrows. "Am I your hostage now?"

She raises her hand to pat my shoulder. "Pretty sure you know how to unlock a door, Rony. Stop ignoring my question."

I shuck off my jacket. "Fine. What do you got?"

She scoffs at my question. "Whiskey and soda water." She tosses her jacket onto her couch, then meanders the ten feet to her small kitchen.

I fall back onto her sofa. "Perfect."

Miranda joins me on the couch a minute later, handing me a glass half-filled with deep amber liquid. I cock an eyebrow. "Did you forget the soda water, or are you trying to get me drunk?"

She shrugs and raises her glass to her lips, which does nothing to hide her grin. I shouldn't be surprised—after all, she did suggest we get shit-faced tonight.

I take a small sip, the familiar burn of the whiskey heating my throat as I work it down.

"So, I never thought I'd say this, but your dad holding both your baby brothers after dinner tonight? Panty-drenching." Miranda fans herself with her free hand.

The frown on my face is instantaneous.

"I mean, sheesh. Your dad's like… a *Daddy*," she says. "Made my ovaries—"

"Fuck, Randi!"

She snorts. "I'm serious. Your dad's always been hot, but there's something about seeing a mountain of a man holding a baby. It's sexy. Big and strong, yet soft and gentle." She pauses, deep in thought. "You know, your dad's not all that much older than me…" Her eyebrows begin to dance mischievously.

I sink my teeth into my bottom lip with a deep growl. "Don't fucking go there, Randi. That's an image I'll never be able to get out of my head." My imagination has always been too vivid. Already my face contorts.

"Oh no? You don't want the girl you used to fuck fucking your daddy? Or better yet, you and your dad both? At the same time? A Soult sandwich, so to speak. Wait, Stevie is getting here tomorrow, right? You know, I *do* have three holes to stu—"

Holy shit. I throw my arms up. "Nope." I get up off the sofa, ready to walk out on her.

She grabs at my sleeve, pulling me back down with a laugh.

"I'm just kidding, Rony," she wheezes, her eyes shimmering with tears. She inhales sharply. "I don't like butt stuff, so maybe just you and your da—"

I yank my arm free and make to stand once more.

Miranda reins in her guffaw. "Stop, Rony. I'm totally joking. I'm joking!" She pats the seat next to her.

With a shake of my head, I retake my spot.

"Are you sure you don't want kids one day? Because I'll guarantee you, you'll have the same effect as your dad has on the female folk. Just, woof."

"I'm sure." Cat's face flashes through my mind, her sad eyes when I told her I don't want kids, the tears rolling down her cheeks when I ended things. I'll never be like my dad because I refuse to become like my mother.

Miranda doesn't let off the pain point. "They look really happy. Your dad and Penny. Your dad's, like, glowing with love," she says with a contemplative nod.

"Yeah, I know. I don't think I've ever seen my dad this happy before."

Miranda watches me while my gaze is glued to the patterns of the wood fibers on the coffee table.

She scoots closer and hitches a leg onto the sofa cushion, facing me. "You deserve that, too," she says. "You deserve to be happy like that. Like glowingly, stupidly happy."

I sit back, sinking into the cushions with a deep sigh. "I have a feeling that's not in the cards for me."

"It takes a long time, you know?"

I raise my eyebrows at her. "What does?"

"Unlearning the negative things that have been hammered into your head all your life," she says, her voice heavy. "You keep thinking there's something wrong with you that you can't just tune out your abuser's voice in your head telling you, like a fucking chant, that you're not good enough. You're not alone in that, Rony. I still struggle with it, too."

"Do you believe it?" I ask her. "Do you believe the things your dad's voice tells you?"

Her blue eyes hold the weight of the world as she nods. "Sometimes. Some days it's easier to tell that voice to shut up. Journaling helps. I get it all out of my head, and when I read it back, I always realize that none of the shit my dad said holds water."

My gaze falls to my hands. "I believe it. I believe the things my mom's voice says—the things my own voice tells me. I don't know how to stop it." Miranda doesn't respond, watching me instead, her eyes soft. "I wish I could shut it off. I wish I could believe, like truly, honestly believe that I'm enough. That I'm not destined to..." I swallow.

Miranda's fingertips graze my chin. "Rony, look at me."

I lift my eyes.

"You wouldn't ever hurt anyone," she says with a conviction I'm envious of. "You're good, Rony. So damn good. You deserve happiness, and love..." The last word comes out breathy and a subtle blush heats her lips, then her cheeks. I notice her eyes flitting to my mouth, feel the tension between us rise, and I know what's going to happen before it does.

I do nothing at all to stop it.

Not this time.

I shouldn't. I know I shouldn't. But my body moves before my mind catches up, because I'm tired of fighting the ache that never lets up. Miranda's lips are on mine a fraction of a second later, my tongue meeting hers. Her hands glide underneath my shirt, her fingers outlining my abdominal muscles as she slowly pushes up the fabric.

"Randi, I..." I mutter against her lips. I want this to mean something. Or maybe I just want it to *feel* like something. Anything.

But it doesn't.

Not really.

Still, I let her pull my shirt off. I let her guide us back through old, familiar motions. Her touch is soft, warm, even reverent in its own way—but I'm already aching with the knowledge that it won't be enough.

She slides off her flannel and I follow, lifting her tank top over her head, my hands moving automatically. Her bra is on the floor a moment later, my left hand cupping her breast, my thumb carefully grazing over her taut nipple. Muscle memory.

With my right hand on her back, I pull her toward me, shifting us to feel her bare skin against mine.

I know what Doctor Seivert would tell me. That this is unhealthy coping. I'm reverting to old patterns of dealing with pain. But what does it matter? Why should I stop this now? Randi and I are both lost in this world, drowning in our fucking pain, our loneliness. Why not provide each other with an hour where we can get lost in each other?

Where we can get pulled into a void of sex rather than more darkness? At least we're not strangers, some random hookup. We know each other, know that we're safe and healthy. It's familiar. It's easy. It's all physical and completely unemotional.

I go through the motions with Miranda, letting her touch me as I touch her. No sweet nothings are exchanged as we undress each other. We're merely following the steps it takes to reach the few seconds of pure fucking ecstasy drowning out our sorrow. That's all. There's an endgame to this, and it's not happily-ever-after.

Miranda takes me into her mouth, tastes me like she used to when we were together a few years ago. She sucks and swirls her tongue over my cock, but loses patience quickly, just as she always did. No one's ever gotten me off with oral sex, and I have no illusions about tonight. This is not some declaration of love, not even true intimacy.

I shift us again, laying Miranda back to work my magic. Funny thing is, I still remember exactly how she likes it; I get her to climax in no time at all. She moans quietly, breathing labored, her hips pushing up as she comes apart with my hand between her thighs. When she regains control, she retrieves a condom from I don't know where, tears the packet open, then puts the latex barrier on me, her hands soft, gentle on my sensitive skin. My eyes shut when she pulls my body down and I thrust into her.

But even as I do, I feel like I'm standing outside myself, watching it all from somewhere far away.

Miranda doesn't feel like Cat—of course she doesn't. Doesn't sound, smell, or taste like her, and for a moment my heart squeezes so tightly in my chest, the pain of it threatens to pull me back into reality. But I'm good at compensating, skilled at pushing those feelings down. So, I focus on the raw feeling of sex—just like I used to when I had one-night stands before I met Cat. It's just a casual fuck, two bodies colliding, creating friction, and soon my world begins to shrink down to the sensation of a beautiful girl's soft, warm body underneath me.

I drive us on, thrust into Miranda again and again, my muscles wound tightly as her legs snake around my waist to pull me deeper, urging me to go faster, harder.

Her breath brushes my ear—but for half a second it's Cat's voice I hear, soft and sweet, whispering my name in the dark. I blink, and it's gone. My hips move at a relentless pace, desperately chasing the apex, seeking to snuff out all thought, all doubt, all guilt tearing at the edges of my conscience at the knowledge that it's Miranda's body I'm allowing mine to meld with rather than Cat's. There's a nagging conviction that what I'm doing is wrong, is a deep, unforgivable betrayal of my love for Cat, who is still in sole possession of my unworthy heart, even though she's probably moved on by now. After all, she went to some bar with that Levi guy and, from what I've heard, she even went home with him...

My insides contract with the mental image. *Focus, Ran!*

Sweat beads at the nape of my neck, but I don't let up. I slip my left hand between us, circling my thumb over Miranda's clit. Her shallow breath stutters to a momentary halt, her body stilling for the fraction of the second she teeters on the edge, and then she falls into pleasure.

"Fuck, Rony," she moans without restraint as her orgasm tears through her. She rides the high for a long moment while I continue to piston. But I'm losing steam, the thin cloud of sex dissipating and forcing my surroundings back into focus.

My steady rhythm breaks, stumbling with the knowledge that I won't reach the high, won't get anywhere near it. For the first time in my life, I'm unable to numb myself this way, to replace pain with pleasure. Not with Miranda, who is beautiful and kind, and who I know so damn well. I will never again experience pleasure, bliss, undiluted happiness. Not with anyone who isn't Cat. I know that now. I've always known it.

Miranda blinks her eyes open at me. "Are you okay?"

I stop moving altogether, then shake my head. "No. I... Randi, I don't think I—"

"You're not gonna get there, huh?"

I meet her gaze, my shoulders sagging when I shake my head again. "No. I'm sorry."

She nods, but her smile falters just for a second. A tiny fracture. It's gone quickly, covered by her usual confidence, but I catch it. I catch the glint of something that might have been hope.

I push myself off her, get up, and discard the used condom in the trash. I'm back in my boxers and jeans in seconds.

I'm ashamed in a million different ways and would pay good money to turn the clock back twenty or thirty minutes. If it wasn't such a shitty thing to do, I'd bolt out of Miranda's cabin and pretend I didn't just try to use her to numb myself like I've done so many times in the past, like I've done to so many other girls before I met the damn love of my life. *God, the love of my stupid, lonely, worthless, fucked-up life.*

Miranda stands from the couch, still naked, her skin heated and damp from the physical exertion, though she doesn't rush to get dressed. "Rony," she says, taking a tentative step toward me.

"I'm sorry, Randi. You deserve better than this."

Her warm smile and soft eyes disarm me. "Maybe. But trust me, I knew exactly what I was getting myself into."

She stoops to pick up her jeans, slipping into them without bothering with her underwear first. "Thank you for that, Rony. I forgot how incredible you feel. Fuck, you really are good at this," she sighs contently, pulling her shirt back over her torso. What comes out of her mouth next takes me by surprise. "Now, make sure you patch things up with your feline when she gets here."

I shift beside her, my eyes flitting between hers with dipped eyebrows.

She chuckles quietly. "I love you, Rony. I really hoped things would be different with us this time around, but I finally understand that I can't have you. You're hers. You've been hers. She owns your heart. And you know what? I'm completely okay with that. But what

I'm not okay with is the way you're hurting when you don't need to be, at least when it comes to your relationship with Cat. Get out of your head already. You're more than enough, Rony. You are extraordinary."

Then she kisses me softly on the lips and disappears in the small bathroom.

I finish getting dressed, then fall back on the couch. What a shitshow my life is, and this time I have only myself to blame.

The moment she returns, I apologize again.

She takes a seat next to me, her head on my shoulder, her right arm draped across my chest. "This was completely mutual, Rony. No need to feel bad in any way. I promise I didn't have grand dreams of becoming your wife," she says, then hesitates. "I'm glad I got to feel you like that one more time, though. It really was proof to me that you and I can't work—that you belong to Cat," she says with a smile.

I raise a doubtful eyebrow. "You can tell that from having sex with me?"

"Yeah. You weren't with me. Not really. Like, your body was, for a while, but not your head. And then even your body decided you didn't really want this." She moves to face me, her expression stern. "You do have control, you know? You worry so much about... everything. But you *do* have control. I know you've been hurting, but trust me when I tell you that you don't need to be. Allow her to love you, allow yourself to feel it and to love her back. It's really the only worthwhile thing in this world. Love. Things will turn out alright in the end, Rony. You'll see. You'll be okay."

Her voice has weight, but there's a letting-go in it, too. Something honest. Something final.

***

I end up staying with Miranda until well past three in the morning, sitting on the couch silently, watching reruns of some black-and-white

TV show Miranda has always loved because it's mindless and makes her giggle.

Eventually, she falls asleep. After tugging the ornate Native American blanket over her, I leave her cabin to drive back to the main house.

The lights are on in the kitchen, shining through the downstairs windows like a lighthouse, guiding me home in the darkness. Nights out here are thick, all-enveloping, like they swallow life.

I didn't expect the majority of the Soult crew to be awake, but when I walk into the house, three adult heads turn in my direction. There stand my dad and grandparents. My grandma and dad each hold a baby, giving them bottles, while my grandpa pours some coffee into two mugs.

Judging by the surprised looks on their faces, they likewise didn't expect me to be walking in through the front door at this time of day... night... whatever. And more, I get the distinct impression they were talking about me.

My grandma cocks her head to the side. "Where are you coming from?"

Suddenly, I'm fourteen again rather than two months shy of nineteen, my heart prancing as though I just got caught doing something I shouldn't. Probably because I actually *did*.

"Randi's," I say simply. For all intents and purposes it's an innocent fucking answer, but by the way my dad shifts his weight, my grandpa's eyebrows flatten, and my grandmother's lips press together, I can tell they suspect Miranda and I didn't play a round of Monopoly.

"And what? You got lost on your way back after dropping her off at her cabin"—my dad checks his watch—"almost eight hours ago?"

Awkward silence settles so completely, the entire house seemingly holds its breath.

"You look tired," I say to my dad.

He huffs a laugh at my piss-poor attempt at a diversion.

My grandma steps toward me, those familiar brown eyes of hers warm, soft. Without warning, she transfers the baby she was holding into my arms. A quick glance into his sleeping face and I know it's Kellan I'm holding. He looks virtually identical to his brother, but their little faces are already full of expression. Where Kellan generally looks content, his features relaxed, Dean always looks a little bit like he's plotting world domination. I also know—from sitting on the plane with my dad, Penny, and my brothers for eight hours today—that the babies' cries are different. Kellan whines when he's tired or sleepy. Dean sounds like someone is attempting to amputate a limb without proper anesthesia.

"I look forward to seeing Cat tomorrow," my grandma chirps. My eyes snap to hers, which are conveniently locked on Kellan, a small smile on her face.

I knew they were talking about me when I walked in. This is an intervention-style, middle-of-the-night gathering, and I bet that baby in my arms is my family's way of ensuring I don't just run out of this kitchen. *Ugh.* I crease my brow. "Morai, please don't meddle."

Her face settles into a rigid frown. "Ronan Perry Soult, you leave me no other choice." *Jeez, always with the government name.* "I've had enough of watching you punish yourself for what your mother did to you."

I flinch at my grandmother's words. Few people so brazenly bring up my mother in front of me. Most everyone avoids talking about anything that even remotely hints at my mom or her violence, but not my grandmother. She's a huge proponent of facing the bull head-on and reminding me that none of what happened to me was my fault. It's a constant refrain in our bi-weekly phone calls, though I've admittedly been avoiding her these past two months.

The bricks around my heart begin to cement themselves. "I'm not punishing myself."

Her hands find the curves of her hips, fortifying her small frame. Unlike my grandpa, my grandma is a tiny thing—over a head shorter than me—but holy Jesus, I don't know anyone who's willing to mess with that woman once she gets going. "You know what, you can keep trying to convince yourself of that. You can lie to your friends, to your dad all you want, but trust me when I say none of us are buying your crap. Good god, baby boy, we all see what you're doing. The problem I see, though, is that you're not only hurting yourself, you're also torturing this lovely, beautiful, smart, kind, wonderful girl who is just so perfect for you."

I'd rake my hands through my hair if I wasn't holding a sleeping baby. So I settle for chuffing out a verbal reply. "But I'm not perfect for her, Morai."

"Did she tell you that?"

"No," I say sheepishly. "But I know it to be true. There are things that Cat wants—that she deserves—that I can't give her."

"And what would those things be?"

"She wants a family. I don't. I don't want kids, ever."

"Because you've got yourself convinced that you will abuse your children like your mother abused you?"

That woman does not mince words.

"Exactly."

My grandma raises her eyebrows at me. "So, you're worried about being a good dad."

I shrug. "I guess."

"Ronan, abusers don't worry about being good parents," she says matter-of-factly.

My brow knits. Before I can argue, my dad says, "Ran, can I ask you something?"

"You just did," I say like a smart-ass.

He just nods. "You told me you and Cat fought, right? After Kellan and Dean were born?"

I nod.

"Did you yell at each other?"

I break his eye contact, shame washing through me at the memory of how I lost my shit with Cat, how I raised my voice at her, how I walked out and slammed the door behind me. "Yeah." My voice is tiny with the admission.

"She yelled at you?"

I nod again.

"And you yelled back at her?"

My jaw hurts with how tense it is. "Yeah."

Despite his interrogation, there's not a hint of accusation on my dad's face. "Would you say you were angry while you two were fighting?"

"Yeah. Shit, Dad, why are you—"

"And what did you do?"

"What?" I huff out.

"What did you do? When you and Cat were fighting, when you felt angry at her. What did you do?"

"I... I told her to stop. She didn't. She was so pissed at me. Rightfully. So... I walked out on her. Slammed the damn door."

"You walked out on her," my dad says, his tone conclusory.

Is that a smile I see dancing in his eyes?

"Yeah."

"You walked out on her," he repeats.

"Yes!" The edge in my voice is audible now. I don't need him reminding me of how much I fucked up.

"Ran, did you have even the slightest urge to hit Cat while you two were arguing?"

My frown deepens, making my forehead hurt. "No."

"How about right now, bud?"

"What about now?"

"Well, I'd say this is a pretty agitating conversation we're having with you. I hear it in your voice how much you'd like to shut this down. But I'm looking at you, evaluating your posture, how you're holding that very vulnerable, fragile baby in your arms, and I detect not even a hint of volatility in you. In fact, you're doing everything you can not to wake Kellan," he says with a nod at my chest—against which the baby is cradled, sleeping soundly.

It's only now that I realize I'm gently bouncing my brother in my arms, and while my shoulders are tense, I've subconsciously, made sure that my arms remain soft and relaxed rather than rigid and flexed.

My dad lessens the distance between us, a smile on his face. "Buddy, you are so damn scared of repeating Rica's cycle of violence that you're blind to the fact that you've already started breaking it. You're already doing it, Ran."

His right hand moves to my cheek, his thumb softly sweeping over my scar as if to erase it.

My grandpa sets the coffee mug he's been sipping from down, then squares his shoulders while his arms fold across his sturdy chest. Like my dad, that man is a damn beast—6'5" and all corded muscle honed by a lifetime of hard, heavy ranch work. "You're feeding the wrong wolf, Ran."

I'm not sure if it's the late hour or the Mount Everest-sized lump in my throat, but his words make no sense to me. "What?"

He chuckles. "You're feeding the wrong wolf."

"Okay, repeating the same words doesn't help me understand what you're saying, Athair."

His brown eyes bore into mine. "The Cherokee believe that inside each man live two wolves. One dark, the other light. One represents our anger, our anxiety, our fears. The other represents love, kindness, hope. The question is always: which wolf wins? The answer—"

"The one we feed," my dad says quietly, his eyes on my grandfather.

A whole lot of nonverbal communication happens between them; their gazes stay locked on each other for a moment before my grandpa's eyes crinkle at the corners and his lips curve into a smile. He gives my dad a proud nod, then turns his attention back to me. "The one we feed," he says with a slight tip of his head. "And Ran, you're feeding the wrong wolf."

My grandma nods. "Ronan, you have to try to heal. If you never heal from what hurt you, you will bleed on people who didn't cut you. And right now, you're bleeding on Cat."

I take a deep, settling breath. "Okay, let's say Cat and I fix things"—*that's if she'd even consider taking me back*—"but then, later down the road, Cat starts to resent me because I don't want children. What then, Morai? We had one fight about it and she literally made out with some random guy at a party. What does that mean for us?" I ask, the hurt resurfacing. Every time I recall seeing Cat kiss that dude at the party, my heart threatens to shatter all over again.

"Maybe you'll change your mind about having childr—"

"I won't."

My grandma pinches off a sigh between her lips. "Fine. But, Ran, she made a mistake. Your grandfather kissed another girl once to make me jealous after we had a vicious fight. Forty years later and he still randomly apologizes for it," she says with a smile. "Relationships aren't easy. We all make sacrifices; it's constant work, a constant give-and-take. And as for you giving me great-grandchildren: you are young. You don't have to decide right now. And even if in a decade or two you decide you really don't want children, then you should allow Cat to decide what to do with that. Or maybe you'll end up changing your mind, which, quite frankly, I hope you do, because you two would make gorgeous babies," she says and I frown again. "You have to trust that Cat is capable of making her own decisions and telling you what she needs."

"You sound exactly like Shane," I say, exhaling loudly. Kellan stirs but doesn't wake.

"Shane's a great friend," she says with a smile.

"He is."

"Ran, you've shouldered a lot of pain in your young life. We know you're one hell of a fighter. You're strong. But I speak from experience when I say you're even stronger with Cat by your side. Now, answer this question for me: do you still love Cat?"

I don't need to think about this one. "Of course I do."

"And do you want to be with her?"

"Yes, but—"

"Great, then I expect you to fix this. And you better do it fast because, girls like Cat don't stay single for long. Don't let her get away, Ronan! Stop bleeding on her. She didn't cut you."

Saturday, April 1st

Cat

The pretzel bounces off my forehead, jolting me from the sea of data compiled by Professor Meyers—the same data I'm supposed to analyze over the next few weeks.

"Hey!" I yank the earbud out of my right ear. The sudden onslaught of airplane engine hum, airflow, and passenger chatter assaults my ears. Just a second ago, the ambient sounds flowing into my ears from my phone had my body convinced I was sitting by a babbling river, the wind rustling leaves while I tried to find correlations in my professor's survey responses.

I crane my neck right, past my mom, in search of the culprit. I fully expect my little brother Benny to look back at me with a victorious smile. Benny's attention, however, is on a superhero movie playing on the small seatback screen in front of him.

But a seat down, my dad grins triumphantly, a crinkly bag of airline-brand pretzels in hand.

I frown. "What was that for?"

"Just making sure you heard the announcement that we're starting the descent. You might want to put away your work and fold up your tray, Kitty," my dad says with a nod at my makeshift desk.

"We should be landing in Missoula in about thirty minutes," my mom chimes in, smiling.

"Great," I mutter, shoving my papers back into a cohesive stack. It's all numbers related to codependent behavioral patterns, life satisfaction, and dyadic coping. I never realized obtaining a degree in psychology would involve so much math.

I shut my laptop and slide everything into my backpack. Now what am I supposed to do for the next half hour? Just sit here and not think about the fact that I'll be face-to-face with Ronan in a matter of hours? *Yeah, that's guaranteed to end in tears or a panic attack.*

I've been a bundle of nerves for days now with the approach of Frank and Penny's wedding, my family's trip to Montana, and the prospect of being around Ronan twenty-four hours for an entire week. Three months ago, this vacation was something I looked forward to with giddiness. This morning, it took every ounce of willpower just to get on the plane. All I know is, being near Ronan is going to hurt like hell. He'll be there with me, but he won't be mine. It's a good thing Steve, Shane, and Tori will be there to buffer any awkwardness, at least for a few days.

We touch down half an hour later and are met in the arrivals lounge by a burly man holding a sign with "Stevenson" printed in neat letters. He introduces himself as Thomas as he shakes first my parents' hands, then tips his cowboy hat—yes, an actual, real-life cowboy hat—at my siblings, both of whom giggle.

"And you're Cat, I take it," he booms with a smile on his rugged face. Thomas looks almost exactly as I had pictured him whenever Ronan talked about him. He's of average height, but wide-backed, his jaw scruffy, skin sun-tanned and wind-chafed. He offers me his hand and I shake it, noting the thick patches of calloused skin on his palm even while he squeezes my hand gently. "Kinda weird, I'm just meeting you, but I feel like I've known you for years."

I raise my eyebrows, eliciting a throaty chuckle from him.

"Saoirse is a huge fan of yours," he says. "She talks about you all the time. You're basically part of the Soult clan."

My spine straightens.

"Not anymore. Ronan made damn sure of that," my dad says, lugging a large suitcase past me.

If my looks could kill, my dad would be a pile of ashes now.

Thomas just smiles, then lowers his voice conspiratorially. "She's been working on Ronan. That little shit," he says with a chuckle before raising his voice once more. "Alright, let's get you to the ranch, folks." He collapses the pull-out handles and lifts the awkward suitcases like they weigh nothing. "Follow me."

Thomas leads us out to the parking structure and to a large, shiny black Ford pickup. I'm not exactly short, but I still have to take a giant step up to hoist myself into the backseat. The moment I slide onto the leather bench seat, my cheeks heat with Ronan's clean, masculine scent. He's been in here. Recently.

"This truck is huge," I say, hoping the unaffected chill in my voice will lower the temperature in my face. My eyes remain firmly on the latch of my seatbelt.

The front doors slam as my dad and Thomas shut them simultaneously. "Yeah, it's roomy," Thomas chuckles. "It's actually Ran's truck." *I knew it.* "Mine's been having some issues. Not super reliable at the moment, so Ran insisted I take his. Wanted to make sure we wouldn't get stuck on the road out in the middle of nowhere."

Rather than dissipate, the warmth in my face deepens as my heart flips in my chest, hopelessly tuned to him. Seems Ronan hasn't completely written me off, at least not enough to stop caring whether I make it to the ranch in one piece.

My mom's head swivels from left to right, eagerly taking in the landscape as we maneuver onto the road. "How long is the drive out to the ranch?"

Thomas turns the knob on the radio, lowering the volume of the music. I didn't pay attention to it before, but I realize now it's EDM. Not country or something I'd suspect Thomas to listen to on the daily. This is Ronan's music—lo-fi. I looked it up one time, something about calming frenzied brainwaves.

"Couple of hours. The ranch is north of Missoula, pretty cut off from most everything except Redtail Ridge—tiny town about an hour from the ranch. You'll love it, though," Thomas says.

My dad continues to make small talk. “So, what do you do, Thomas?”

“Oh, I’m the ranch hand, wrangler, assistant manager,” Thomas says, then chuckles. “I’m Perry’s right hand on the ranch, just help him manage the day-to-day, take some of the load off, you know? My son Elias and I live on the ranch. I’ve worked for the Soults since I was eighteen—Frank was only a boy.” Another laugh rumbles in his chest. “They’re a great family. Saoirse and Perry have hearts of gold. Never met better people, especially when you find yourself in need,” he says with a decisive nod.

I listen to Thomas describe his daily work, watch the landscape fly by, and inhale Ronan’s familiar scent.

***

An hour and a half later, Thomas pulls off the paved highway onto a dirt road, and it’s another half hour before he arrives at a large, gated arch donning a giant letter *S*. Thomas throws the truck in park just long enough to hop out and open the gate for us to drive through. He repeats the process to close the gate, then continues the drive slowly. It’s not nearly as smooth of a ride now, but the truck handles the rougher terrain with ease.

“Yikes, you can’t speed down this road unless you want some serious whiplash,” my dad says.

I can’t help but roll my eyes, then lower my window. I might’ve grown up in a small town, but clearly that didn’t make me “country.” I fully expected the air to reek of livestock, but instead it’s crisp, earthy, mixed with pine and snowmelt. The breeze whispers of peace and memory, and for a moment it feels like I’m aging in reverse.

Thomas’s laugh reminds me that I’m not the only person in this ethereal place. “Oh, yeah. That’s why nothing out here will do but four-wheel-drive trucks. You’ll bottom out quickly otherwise. It’s worse after a good rain or snow. You gotta know how to handle the terrain and the weather."

"My god, it's beautiful," my mom breathes, her eyes wide.

She's right, this place is incredible. In one breath, I understand why Ronan feels safe here. I have arrived in his world.

The road is flanked by endless green pastures, the mountains behind them fading from lush green to icy white—a breathtaking backdrop. Cattle and horses graze lazily, some in the distance, others closer to the wire fence line. I delight in the sight of calves napping in the grass next to their mothers.

"The babies are so cute," Benny coos.

"Another month or two and the cattle will be moved up the mountains. We just need the snow to melt a bit more. They'll spend the summer months in higher altitude and then we'll bring them back down for the winter," Thomas says, and is met with expressive *ohs* from my parents. "You see those houses in the distance? Those are our guest cabins." Thomas motions toward some smaller homes ahead of us. While clustered, they're sufficiently spaced out to provide whoever is staying there adequate privacy. "We have ten of them. Well, nine at the moment. One's occupied by another one of our on-again, off-again ranch hands."

I bet I know who that is. Has Ronan been spending all his time with her since he got here?

"Oh, so, it's like a dude ranch?" my dad asks.

Once again, my instinct is to roll my eyes at him.

Thomas nods graciously. "We don't call it a dude ranch, but yeah. We have guests here. That's only a small part of the Soult family business. The main source of income is cattle, but we do get really busy, especially in the summer months. Last year, all guest cabins were occupied from May through September. Erin—Perry and Saoirse's daughter—and her husband Martin run that side of the business. They live in that house up there with their kids, Riley and Colin." Thomas points at a ranch-style house about a hundred yards to the right of a much larger, two-story log cabin. The driveway ends there, framed by tall grass, pastures, and mountain light.

"And that beautiful home right in front of us is Perry and Saoirse's house," Thomas says as we climb a small incline and pass a large barn on our left. He drives about fifty yards more, then comes to a stop. I spot Saoirse already waiting on the stoop of the wraparound porch; the smile on my lips is instantaneous.

She bounds down the steps like a teenager. I'm still struck by how young she looks. Mid-fifties isn't old, sure, but "grandmother" feels like the wrong word for the vibrant woman pulling me into a tight hug.

"Oh, Cat, it's so, so good to see you!" She holds me at arm's length to examine my face. "I don't know how it's possible, but every time I see you, you're even more stunning."

My face heats up again. *Great. Living furnace mode activated.*

Saoirse turns to my parents. "Your daughter is such a beautiful young woman. Inside and out."

My dad nods. "We'd have to agree."

She waves us toward the house for a tour. Inside, it's even more incredible. The rustic interior should feel heavy, all wood and stone, but thanks to floor-to-ceiling windows and an open floor plan, the space feels bright, spacious. Free, not confined.

I glance left, where a wide-open kitchen flows into a long dining room anchored by a table big enough to seat a small army. I can practically see the extended Soult family occupying each chair, the air filled with noise and clatter and the smell of hearty Irish food in the air.

A door stands open to my right. Boots are neatly lined against the wall, and jackets and hats hang from hooks above a sturdy bench. Mudroom, clearly. But somehow even that feels warm and lived-in.

Straight ahead, the living area unfolds like something out of one of my mom's home design magazines. A woven Native American-style rug centers the space, topped by a thick wood coffee table blooming with wildflowers nestled in a vase. Dark leather sofas and chairs ring the table invitingly. But what pulls me most is the staircase. It's wide and inviting, and yet I can't look at it without remembering.

Ronan talked about this staircase at the trial. One of his earliest memories of abuse involved his mother pushing him down those stairs. Another time, she locked him in the barn outside after beating him. It was the middle of Montana winter.

Surprisingly, the house doesn't feel haunted. Not like Frank's. The air here is unadulterated. Steady. The hairs on my arms don't stand like they do in that awful kitchen back in New York. Maybe the difference is that I *know* Ronan feels safe here. Maybe that's enough to shift the energy.

Saoirse leads us on a practiced tour, her voice warm. "Guests are always welcome to come and go. The kitchen's open twenty-four hours. I mean that. If you find yourself craving brownies at two in the morning like Stevie always does, come on in." She winks. "You'll get a key to your cabin, and to this house too. Just let yourselves in. You won't bother us."

She rattles off meal times: seven-thirty for breakfast, noon for lunch, six for dinner. "We're early to rise and early to bed," she says. "Well, except for the boys. I swear they run on fumes."

She gestures to a door beside the staircase. "That's Perry's and my quarters," she says, before beckoning us upstairs.

I hesitate at the side table by the stairs, drawn to a cluster of picture frames. My fingers find one instinctively—a simple silver frame holding a photo of baby Ronan.

"His second birthday," Saoirse says softly behind me, a smile curling on her lips. "Wasn't he just the cutest little stinker?"

The grin on tiny, chicken-wrangling Ronan is so mischievous it punches the breath right out of me. Blond hair, wide green eyes, arms wrapped around a bird almost as big as he is.

"I still remember this." Saoirse laughs. "I don't know how, but he caught that chicken and schlepped it into the house like he'd just found himself a new pet. He was so proud of himself."

"He still smiles like that when he's up to no good," I say.

Saoirse laughs. "Isn't that the truth. That grin gives him away every time." Then she nods toward the staircase again. "Come on. Let me show you to your room."

"Isn't Cat staying with us?" my mom asks.

"Well, I tried to figure out how to best accommodate everyone," Saoirse says, folding her hands. "The cabin you'll be in only has three bedrooms, and I figured a young woman like Cat might enjoy a little privacy. Unless that's objectionable to you, of course."

"Oh no, of course not," my mom chirps, already trudging up the stairs beside my dad.

We follow Saoirse upstairs into a sunlit hallway. Four doors—two on each side—lead to the bedrooms, and at the very end another floor-to-ceiling window glows with golden light from the west.

Saoirse stops at the first door on the left and lowers her voice. "That's Stevie's room. Poor kid got in on a red-eye this morning. Looked like he hadn't slept a wink on the plane. I haven't seen him since he vanished in there." She glances at her watch. "He'll be up soon, I imagine."

The next door opens to a sleek, spacious bathroom with a glass shower, a big soaking tub, and double sinks, all sparkling clean. "Shared bath," she says with a smile. "But plenty of space."

Finally, she opens the last door on the left.

"Here's your room."

It's beautifully simple: a queen bed with a soft white comforter, a dark wood dresser, and a matching desk beneath a wide window that frames a stretch of pasture.

"Thomas will bring your bag up in a minute," Saoirse says. "Jen, Bobby, let's get you to your cabin. Give Cat a minute to freshen up."

My parents offer their thanks and file out, but Saoirse lingers at the door. She turns to me, a twinkle in her eyes, then says in a hushed tone, "Ran's room is right across the hallway. He warned me not to meddle, but I can't help myself. I think you two need a proper talk. And knowing Ran, he's the kind who needs to be trapped into it."

She pats my cheek and disappears down the hall.

***

Fascinating what an extended, warm shower can do for the body and soul. I'm refreshed when I emerge from the bathroom, dressed in a t-shirt and freshly washed jeans. The house is quiet as I pad down the hallway, hair still damp, bare feet muffled against the floorboards.

The door to Ronan's room is wide open. I stop at the threshold, not daring to cross it, just... taking it in. His scent is in the air—clean, masculine, a little wild. My heart stutters. There's a white t-shirt tossed carelessly on the bed, and something in me wants to pick it up, press it to my face, maybe even slip it on like it could somehow bring him closer. *If this isn't stalker behavior, I don't know what is.*

"Cat!" Steve shouts from behind me, scaring me half to death.

I jump and whirl around.

He strides toward me, then throws his arms around me and lifts me off the ground in a back-cracking hug. "Is it weird that I missed you? It's kind of weird, right?" he chuckles.

"Not weird," I say, hugging him back. "I missed you, too. How have you been?"

"Really, really great," he says enthusiastically. I beam at him, at how happy he seems to be. "What are you up to right now?"

I stammer awkwardly. "Uhh, I'm not totally sure."

"Has anyone given you the tour of this place yet?"

"Thomas pointed out some stuff when he drove us up."

Steve shakes his head. "Nope, that won't do. Come on, I'll give you the *real* tour."

We're out of the house and in a dark-blue truck five minutes later, the tires kicking up dust with Steve's quick acceleration down the uneven dirt road.

We ramble along for a while, along dirt paths and off-road, with Steve pointing out random spots, each accompanied by a story. He gestures at the remains of an old wood shed, barely standing, roof caved in.

"Ran and I used to jump off those support beams. I sprained my ankle so bad once I thought it was broken."

A bend later, he points toward a break in the trees. "The creek's great for fishing. And really nice to cool off in during the summer, but you have to be careful because the rapids can get crazy with the winter runoff."

We pass a narrow stretch of trail, and Steve laughs, shaking his head. "I got bucked off my horse around here once. Inkspot took off like his tail was on fire and ran all the way back to the barn. I had to limp a mile on foot because Ran, that asshole, refused to let me ride double with him on Reaper."

"Inkspot?"

"My horse. Black-and-white paint. He looked like someone splattered ink all over his coat. He was old. Usually bombproof unless he randomly decided to flip the hell out and—"

Steve abruptly slows the truck to a crawl. I glance past him, out the driver's side window. A girl rides toward us on a brown horse, another following behind on a lead rope.

Sunlight filters through the clouds, lighting the copper-gold strands in her braid as it falls over her shoulder. A felt cowboy hat shields her eyes, though I can see the smile playing on her lips as she approaches. She's wearing a blue-and-black flannel shirt, light-wash boot-cut jeans, and scuffed brown boots. Effortless. Totally at ease.

Steve stops the truck and rolls down the window, throwing me a quick look. It's almost sheepish. "So... you're about to meet Randi."

My stomach drops. *Oh god. She's even prettier than I imagined.*

She's petite, but there's a quiet confidence in the way she rides—the fluidity of her posture, her sure grip on the reins. I scan her face: big, ocean-blue eyes fringed with lashes, a delicate nose, pouty lips.

That jealous monster in my chest jerks to life as though awoken by storm sirens. But I force it back into hibernation; it's just one more thing I've learned about myself over these past few months, one more thing I realized was preventing me from giving an unadulterated version of myself to Ronan. Jealousy. The need for control, to be so in tune with every aspect of him because I feared he'd abandon me. Except my failure to leave him be, to trust that he was doing what was best for him in the moment, that he loved me and wouldn't purposely hurt me, totally backfired.

It only dawned on me recently that Miranda isn't a threat. Never was a threat. And if I had stopped to truly listen to Ronan, had chosen to believe him in all the ways he told and showed me he loved me, then maybe, just maybe, things would be different.

Miranda pulls her horses up to the truck. "Hello, sir. Long time no see!" she says in that soulful voice I've heard before.

"I know!" Steve says. "Feels like it's been forever."

"I mean, it kinda has been. What, like four years? You're like... a total man now," she says, then laughs. "I was actually just telling Rony about how you Soult guys are, like, really hot."

Steve chuckles, clearly unsure what to do with that.

"What are you up to? Trying to find Rony?" she asks.

"Nope. Just giving Cat here a tour of the ranch." He leans back slightly, shifting in his seat to give me center stage. "Randi, this is Cat. Cat, this is Randi." His voice is wound like a bowstring, ready to snap.

I raise my hand in a greeting.

"Holy shit," Miranda breathes. She looks... genuinely stunned. "Rony's feline? Jesus, you're even more beautiful in person than in the pictures I've seen of you." Her tone is so earnest, so void of sarcasm or disdain, that it renders me momentarily speechless. My body reacts, though, just like it always does at compliments. I could fry an egg on my face.

"Nice to meet you," I say.

"Nice to meet you, too," she says boisterously. She's so opposite to me. I met her two seconds ago and already know her personality is gargantuan. "Jesus, it's so weird to actually see you in person. I've been hearing about you forever now," she says, her eyes wide. "Nice to know Rony didn't just invent you," she giggles, making me smile.

"Nah, Cat's very much a real person," Steve chuckles. "Have you seen my little brother?"

"Last time I saw him he was getting ready to head to the airport to pick up his best boyfriend," she says, smirking.

"Okay, good," Steve says.

Miranda raises her eyebrows, briefly glancing at me before her eyes settle on Steve again. "You're trying to avoid him?"

Steve takes on a sheepish expression. "Well, just for now, I guess."

"Huh." She considers that for a beat, then nods. "Well, have a good tour then." Her eyes swing back to me. "I'll see you later, Cat-like-the-feline." She grins at me, gives her horse a squeeze with her legs, and continues on her ride.

"She's nice," I say. "And really beautiful."

"Yeah," Steve says simply, shifting the truck back into drive.

"She calls Ronan 'Rony?'"

Steve laughs. "Yeah. She has for as long as I can remember. And he fucking hates it."

"Does she know he hates it?"

"Fuck yeah she does. I think she does it *especially* because he hates it. Randi is just... Randi. She's not great with other people's boundaries. Sometimes that's good, other times not so much."

Ronan

"Hello, hello!" my grandmother chirps as she emerges from the house. Correction, she darts straight past me to welcome Shane, Tori, and Seamus the second we clamber out of the truck this afternoon. Gotta admit, my best friend's arrival makes my visit to the ranch even better than usual.

I just stand there while my grandma pulls first Tori, then Shane into her arms like she's met them hundreds of times.

"You have no idea how wonderful it is to finally see you again, Shane!" she says. Are those tears in her eyes? *Good god. So sappy.* "I always hear so much about you."

Shane flashes his teeth. "Good things only, I hope."

"Definitely not," I deadpan, loud enough for him to hear.

He snorts a laugh while my grandma swats at the air like she's shooing my remark away like a fly. "Yes, only ever good things. Goodness, you are such a blessing to my baby boy. Thank you for being such an amazing friend to him."

Shane turns to me with a foul grin, mouthing *baby boy* like he's memorizing it for future blackmail.

Fuck you, I mouth back, flipping him off.

"Yep, those boys are as close as brothers," Seamus drawls, giving me a fatherly pat on the back.

My grandma nods, all misty-eyed. "Your son is truly heaven-sent. He's always been so good to my Ran," she tells Seamus, giving Shane the kind of fond look usually reserved for puppies and war heroes.

I groan. "Okay, Morai, stop. I still gotta go home and work with this asshole. You're going to make my life unbearable if you keep feeding Shane's ego."

Shane doesn't miss a beat. "Don't be jealous, *baby boy.*"

"Not jealous," I shoot back. "Just concerned for your already-inflated head. Wouldn't want it to pop. You've got a business to run, remember?"

My grandma reaches up and pats Shane's cheek. "Oh, Shane seems to have a very good head on his shoulders."

I blink. "Uhh, you're supposed to be on *my* side, Morai."

Shane slings his arm over my grandma's shoulder like he was born into this family. "Forget it, Ran. She's my Morai now."

I narrow my eyes, smirking. "Careful, Shay. I know where you live, and I'm not above telling Tori about *the donut incident* from when you were fourteen."

Tori perks up immediately. "*What* donut incident?"

Shane's face darkens. "You wouldn't," he growls. "That's take-it-to-your-grave material, Ran."

I just shrug, grinning. "No one's grave is safe, pal."

Seamus's deep laugh reverberates in my chest. "Okay, boys, before the testosterone gets out of hand, how about we drop off the luggage and then someone can tell me where to find the groom."

My grandma launches into her usual welcome spiel, giving the O'Connor guys and Tori a quick tour of the main house before I take them to the cabin they'll be staying in until Wednesday. Five days—that's all Seamus and Shane could spare from work. Restaurants don't run themselves, after all.

"Jack running things at Murphy's?" I ask after we drop Seamus off with my dad and grandpa at the barn that'll serve as the indoor venue for the wedding on Tuesday. Yes, a Tuesday wedding because, one, why the hell not, and two, it's April fourth—supposedly a special date for my dad and Penny. I haven't asked specifics. Don't plan to.

"Sure is," Shane says, an elbow propped on the open truck window as we bump along the dirt road between pastures. "My mom's doing the bank drops and stuff, but Jack's got the rest."

A soft throat-clear emanates from the backseat before Tori's head edges between Shane and me like she's tiptoeing into a minefield. "So uhh, Cat's here, right?"

How is it possible that five simple words manage to throw off my heart's rhythm? Up until this moment I was doing a pretty decent job pretending Cat and I weren't occupying the same space at the same time. And then Tori had to go and say her name—reckless, like lighting a match in a dry field—and just like that, every part of me remembers how desperately I want her. Need her.

"Yeah, I... She should be. I haven't... I haven't seen her yet," I say, my throat tight. I swallow hard. "I... I actually wanted to talk to you guys."

I don't need to look at them to know I have their undivided attention.

I take a deep breath. "I fucked up."

"Duh," Tori mutters.

I resist the urge to roll my eyes. Everyone has opinions about my breakup with Cat, and they're usually not favorable to me.

Shane just nods. "Uh-huh."

"I need to talk to Cat, but—"

"Fuck, Ran, please just tell me you want her back," Shane says.

I try to swallow again, but my throat has gone desert-dry. I nod. "Yeah. I just don't know how badly I fucked it up, how irreversible this is, because I—"

Tori interrupts, eyes wide. "It's not!"

"God, fuck yes!" Shane says, grinning like a cheshire cat. "Jesus, it's about fucking time, asshole." He claps a hand hard against my shoulder.

"Yeah, well, let's just hope she'll take me back."

I didn't need Randi or my grandma to tell me what I already knew—that Cat isn't just someone I love. She's the light I reach for when everything else goes dark. But what I did need was space. Time.

A damn minute to sit with all of it. With my grandma's visit. The revelations from Rashana. Cat's fears. My fears.

Almost two years have passed since the day my mother stopped hurting me. One year since the trial, since she pleaded guilty, and still, I never stopped living like it could all get taken away from me at any second. I never stopped being afraid. The fear just morphed. I was no longer afraid of my mother. I was afraid of myself—*am* afraid of myself, because I don't know who the fuck I am or who I will be.

After my family's middle-of-the-night "pep" talk, they sent me to bed rather than work. But I didn't go to sleep. I sat there in the quiet darkness and did the one thing I've never allowed myself to do before. I imagined my future.

What do you want, Ran? What would make you happy?

I didn't come up with a ton of answers, not with how sleep-deprived I was, but what I do know is it was Cat who made me stop existing and begin living. Those moments and memories I have of being happy are filled to the brim with her. She's there front and center, in my periphery, in the background. Sometimes just her scent or her voice, but she's always there.

It's her. Always has been. Always will be. To me, she's life. *My* life.

Maybe I don't have to take it all on alone? Maybe. Maybe the hurdles between us—hers, mine, *ours*—aren't insurmountable?

"You should talk to her right now, man," Shane says.

I shake my head. "No, the things I have to say can't be said in five minutes. There's a lot she and I have to talk through. This can't be rushed."

Shane nods. "So when?"

I sink my teeth into my bottom lip. "I don't know. Maybe after dinner. If I can get her alone."

I have my work cut out for me. My resolve to unshatter what I've broken comes with the realization that it's time for me to break down every piece of wall I've built over the years. There's no way around it. If I want a future with Cat, if I want to spend every second of the rest of my life with the most perfect girl in the world, then I have to give her all of me. No defenses, no secrets or half-truths, no masked emotions. I have to make myself vulnerable. I have to show her every ugly, sharp-edged piece of me. Let her decide if I'm still something she wants once she understands the depths of my darkness.

As we pull up to the barn, my eyes catch on Miranda sliding the big door shut. I shift the truck into park.

"Whew," Tori says, hopping out. "Good thing Cat didn't hook up with that Levi guy. That would have been awkward."

I freeze. "Wait. What? I thought... I thought she and Vada..." My brain stutters. "I thought she *did*."

Tori stops, brows raised. "No. They hung out with those guys, but Cat told me she didn't sleep with Levi because... well, because she loves you, Ran."

My stomach drops. I was solidly convinced she'd slept with him. To be fair, my intel came from a long, messy game of telephone: my brother heard it from Zack, who heard it from Summer, who heard it from Vada. Classic friend group nightmare.

But now? Knowing she didn't? It makes what I did with Miranda—just yesterday—even worse. Cat made her wariness over my friendship with Miranda more than clear. There's no world in which sleeping with Miranda is forgivable. Still, I have to try. I have to show up—*all* of me—lay myself bare and do what everyone's been urging me to do: let Cat decide.

"Well, shit," Shane mutters with wide blue eyes. "I shouldn't have pushed you to hook up with those girls," he says apologetically.

My brow dips for a second, until it dawns on me that he's thinking of Aubrie and Allie the night Cat and Vada went to hang out with Levi and that other dude. "No, wait, I—"

"Rony!" Miranda bounds toward us, then comes to a stop next to me. Her eyes, though, drift over Shane, slow and deliberate.

I sigh. *This is so Randi.*

"Holy shit, Rony, is this your boyfriend?" she asks, smirking.

In a heartbeat, Tori wraps herself around Shane with a look on her face I can't honestly say I've seen before. "Nope, he's mine."

I tense. I know Randi and her personality. She comes on strong. No damn filter. It doesn't bother me, but Tori doesn't know Randi from Adam, other than what she's heard about Randi, obviously. I'm sure Cat has shared her worries, and knowing how close the girls are, I wouldn't be the least bit surprised if Tori has a preconceived opinion of Miranda.

I clear my throat to ease the rising tension. "Randi, this is my best friend Shane and his girlfriend Tori. Please be nice."

"Jesus. City boys are something else." Miranda doesn't even try to hide the fact that she was eyeing Shane from head to toe.

Tori remains glued to Shane, the crease on her brow deepening.

Shane's eyes are huge as they dart between me and Miranda, who is by far the shortest out of the four of us, and that's saying something. Tori isn't particularly tall, either. "Maybe I was wrong and Cat did have reason to worry about her," Shane says with a quick nod at Randi.

"Wait, Cat was worried about me?" Miranda asks, her attention on me.

I frown. We're wading into waters I have no desire to swim in right now. "Okay, can we not do this? Nobody needs to worry about anyone. Miranda is all talk, no action," I say, mostly for Tori's benefit. The very last thing I need is people not getting along from the get-go.

"No, but seriously? Like, she was jealous?" Miranda asks.

I growl at her. "Stop, Randi. We're not getting into this now."

Miranda turns toward me, her hands propped on her hips. "Here you go again shoving everything uncomfortable down, Rony. You know that's a trauma response, right? And it's one you really need to work on breaking."

Shane grunts. "Yep. Fucking pro at dissociating."

"Good god, you guys are killing me," I groan. "Can we not do this? I'm done being everyone's therapy project for today." I face Tori. "You can stop holding on to Shane like a monkey. Randi isn't gonna try and snatch him away from you. She just appreciates the visual input your shredded guy provides, okay? But she is *usually*"—I throw Randi a sidelong glance—"respectful of established relationships."

Miranda pats my cheek with puckered lips. "Aww, Rony, you sound agitated." She turns to Tori. "He's right, I will behave, though I can't promise not to make comments. I'm like a dude in that regard—if I see a nice piece of meat, I gotta say something. It's like... law. And your man's... a nice piece of man meat. But I won't touch. Promise."

Tori exhales deeply, her lips quirking upward with the admiring glance she tosses Shane's way. "Yeah, he is a nice piece of man meat."

It's shockingly smooth sailing after that. I keep waiting for more tension, but it never comes. Instead, Tori and Miranda completely hit it off, especially when Miranda nonchalantly hooks her arm under Tori's and traipses into the barn with her to show off the three bottle calves Miranda is about to feed.

Shane and I look on, while Tori squeals with delight when Miranda hands over the giant calf nursing bottle. Tori dissolves into a puddle of coos while the mini cow gulps down its meal. And, Jesus, there's even giggling as the girls stick their heads together. *Tori laughing? With Miranda? Shit, okay, maybe this all can work?*

***

I can feel Cat's presence in the house. Her scent lingers in the air. Her energy is everywhere, like electricity under my skin. And I'm a damn bloodhound, trained to detect her in a crowd of people.

I knew it was inevitable, only a matter of time before I'd come face-to-face with the person who's inhabited my heart from the second I laid eyes on her. I tried to brace for it, tried to emotionally prepare myself. But when I finally see Cat tonight, it hits me just as hard as it did that fateful evening in May almost two years ago. I'm just as speechless. Just as overwhelmed.

If there's one thing I've mastered in life, it's avoiding sticky situations. I'm good at dodging people—especially in a place as sprawling as the ranch. I spent the whole day working out of the house, then filled the afternoon with Shane and Tori. Tori's obsessed with ranch life and insisted on helping me muck out the stalls. And even though Shane grumbled about "cleaning up horse shit," I could tell he kind of loved it. It's not glamorous, sure, but it's peaceful. And let's be honest: Shane would do anything for Tori. Anything.

Eventually, though, I ran out of distractions. The sun started to set. My stomach growled. My watch told me it was time to wash up and get ready for dinner at Sterling's.

There'll be seventeen of us. My grandparents and Penny's parents are staying behind with the "kids," meaning my cousins—Riley, who just turned sixteen days ago, stomped off angrily when she was told she couldn't join—Cat's siblings, and the two newest additions to the Soult family tree. The rest of us are supposed to go celebrate my dad and Penny's upcoming wedding.

Celebrate. That's the last thing I feel like doing. I'm a jittery fucking wreck, sneaking from my room to the bathroom and back like I'm on some kind of covert mission or trying to evade a masked serial killer. But nope, I'm just too chickenshit to face Cat.

Of course, my grandma completely ignored my request not to meddle. Instead, she made sure Cat's bedroom is *right* across the hall from mine—barely eight feet between us. I know it's her way of trying to nudge us back together. As much as my grandma couldn't stand my relationship with Miranda, she's doubly invested in ensuring Cat and I find our way back to each other.

And honestly? The thought of walking into Cat's room right now, of looking her in the eyes and telling her how badly I fucked up, it's tempting as hell. I want to hear her voice. I want to touch her. I want to *kiss* her. I want to be near her so badly it physically hurts.

But I don't even know what I'd say. *Hi*? Or better yet, drop to my knees and beg her to take me back because I can't do life without her? Easy enough in theory, except there's a mountain of shit I need to unload on her. Dark, truly unhinged things she needs to know before I'll let myself hope for a future with her. Just the idea of saying them out loud, of dropping my guard, of taking off that mask, makes me want to puke.

I get dressed in record time and am just about to pull on a fresh shirt when I hear Cat's door open. Apparently, my dumb ass decided to tempt fate without even realizing it because I left my bedroom door wide open. Subconsciously, maybe I wanted this. To be fair, it's been a long time since anyone else has stayed in this part of the house. Other than my mother, who actually slept in the bedroom Cat is occupying right now, no girl's slept up here in years. *Miranda sneaking into my bedroom at night doesn't count.*

Instinctively, I turn. And just like that—like that one unforgettable night at the beach house—our eyes meet. Except, it's painful now. Because I know her. I know the sound of her laugh, the sigh she makes when she finally gets that bite of food she's been craving. I know what she looks like when she sleeps. I know her, but I'm not with her when I should be.

She's so beautiful. *God, that hair, those eyes, that mouth.*

She stands there, thunderstruck, blinking at me. Her hazel eyes are wide, filled with something I can't quite name. Pain? Longing?

"Hey," she says softly.

I don't move. I couldn't even if I wanted to. I'm drunk on her. "Hey," I say, still clutching my shirt like it's the only thing keeping me tethered to the floor. Her gaze flicks to my bare chest for the briefest second, then her cheeks flush. It makes the corners of my mouth twitch, but I rein in the selfish thrill. She still feels something, and as much as it kills me, it also sparks a dangerous flicker of hope: that maybe I haven't completely suffocated what once was.

"How was your flight?" I ask, stupidly. Really, I just want to hear her voice again. One more second of her.

"Really good," she says sweetly.

Fuck, I want her back.

I open my mouth, but don't get the chance to respond.

"You ready to go, Cat?" my brother calls from down the hall.

Cat turns her head toward his voice, then looks back at me, her eyes full of emotion. "I'll see you in a little bit?"

Am I imagining things, or do I hear a note of hope?

I nod. "Yeah."

She flashes me the tiniest, shyest smile, then walks out of my sight.

I exhale deeply, trying to shed the tension gripping my shoulders. God, I need to find a way to talk to her alone before the day is over. I can't hold off much longer.

Cat

Steve chauffeurs me to Sterling's. I'm seated in the backseat next to Elias while his dad, Thomas, rides up front, barking directions at Steve—who keeps reminding him that he used to live here. It makes me giggle, and for a few blissful minutes I don't think about that brief, heart-stopping encounter with Ronan.

But only five minutes after I sit down at the long, buffet-style table already occupied by Frank, Penny, Seamus, my parents, Frank's sister, and his brother-in-law, the doors to Sterling's open and in step Shane and Tori, followed by Ronan and—I swallow—Miranda.

It's like my heart has a GPS locked on Ronan and doesn't care that it's supposed to be in recovery. Doesn't care that he shattered it. It thuds traitorously in my chest, fast and desperate, and all I've done is look at him.

He's laughing at something Miranda says—soft, natural, completely unguarded—and I feel the ache of missing him settle into my bones, just like it did an hour ago. Not just the boyfriend part of him, but *him*. The version who used to know how to make me laugh when I didn't want to. The version I used to trust with all the quiet, crumpled parts of me.

He hasn't seen me yet. Good. I need a second. Maybe five.

I force my gaze away and inhale deeply, squaring my shoulders like armor. Tonight is about celebrating Penny and Frank. Tonight, I'll pretend I'm fine. Pretend I don't want to memorize the way he looks at me like I'm the only girl in the whole world. Because tonight, Ronan doesn't get to know that he still owns my heart. Doesn't get to know I'm still desperately, unconditionally in love with him.

I notice Ronan take a seat at the opposite end of the table, as far away from me as possible. I'm simultaneously elated and hurt. *This is so confusing.* Tori, however, plops down in the wooden chair next to me, her face alive. I'm so glad I have her, and Shane, and Steve. Their presence softens the sharpest sting of my separation from Ronan. At least a little.

"Hey," she sing-songs, squeezing me quickly while Shane nods at me from catty-corner across the table—right next to his best friend. Miranda sits on Ronan's other side. Of course, I notice.

"Hey," I say, my eyes locked past her, watching Miranda. There's an ease between her and Ronan, undeniable chemistry. Her face lights up when she looks at him. She's angled toward him, smile unwavering, her posture open and familiar. Even a stranger would be able to tell that the two share a history. Maybe even a present. My heart squirms.

Tori follows my gaze, then looks squarely at me. "Cat?"

I jerk my eyes to her. "What?"

"They're not a thing," she says calmly. "Not a thing." I can't decode the smile dancing in her eyes—whether it's amusement or reassurance.

My shoulders sag with relief. He may not be in love with me anymore, but at least he's also not in love with *her*. I don't think I could handle seeing Ronan be affectionate with her. It would crush me.

"Hey, Randi," Ronan's and Steve's aunt Erin calls from the other end of the table, snapping Miranda—and everyone else—to attention. I take the chance to look at Ronan unabashedly, drinking him in. Those beautiful, masculine features. His full lips and green eyes that always have a way of looking directly into my soul.

"Yeah?" Miranda calls, a bright smile on her pretty face.

"Why don't you get up on that stage and sing something?"

Miranda's gaze drifts to the small, currently unoccupied stage. "Sure!" She pushes up from her chair without a second thought. Jeez, if someone had asked me to randomly perform on a stage in front of everyone, I would've turned beet red and bolted for the nearest exit. Miranda, on the other hand, looks like she was born for this.

"Hey, Reagan," Miranda calls to the young woman delivering round after round of tequila shots. The tip of my mom's nose is already pink, like it gets when she's had a little too much to drink. "Mind if I get up there?"

"I never mind!" Reagan grins. "Let me turn down the music for you."

The country music fades, and Miranda climbs the stage, lowering the mic stand to her height and reaching for one of the guitars. She slips the strap over her shoulder and strums a few lonely chords.

"Okay, people," she says into the microphone, her voice smooth and soulful. "Happy or sad?"

"Start with something happy," Erin calls.

Miranda thinks for a second, then begins plucking gently at the strings. Her eyes close. The first lyrics spill into the room, and just like that, the crowd goes still.

She plays one song after another, switching things up—happy tunes, then heartfelt ballads, even sliding between genres with ease—while Reagan keeps the drinks flowing.

"Okay," Miranda says with a laugh between songs, taking a sip from the glass of water Reagan left near her feet, "I know it's a small stage, but it still feels too big for a little girl like me." Her voice is playful, self-aware.

Then she grins directly at Ronan. "I'm getting kind of lonely up here."

He immediately shakes his head, the crease between his brows deepening as he presses his lips together in a clear *don't you dare* expression.

"You *know* you want to come play with me, Rony," she teases, drawing out the nickname.

Ronan stands no chance against the eruption of cheers, whistles, and applause—not just from our table, but from just about every other one in the room.

Finally—*and obviously reluctantly*—Ronan stands, pushing his chair back with a sharp scrape against the floor. He grits his teeth and gives Miranda a look that could kill, but still, he joins her on stage.

"Fucking trouble, Randi," he mutters, eliciting laughter.

He picks up the second guitar and adjusts the strap. "Just warning you all, this is going to suck," he says to the crowd, drawing more chuckles.

"You got this, bud!" Frank calls out.

"Yeah, yeah. Whatever," Ronan grumbles, then turns to Miranda with an exasperated look. "Fine. What are we playing?"

She only grins and begins to strum.

It takes mere seconds for recognition to light up Ronan's face. His lips twitch into a smile, and before I can brace myself, his fingers are moving, joining hers effortlessly.

Their voices blend in perfect harmony. Ronan's is raw and soulful—low, rich, and magnetic. I realize, with a sharp pang, that I've never heard him sing or play before. I knew he could—he told me his grandfather taught him a few chords—but in our nearly two years together, I never actually saw it for myself. He'd always downplayed it. He sounds incredible.

I don't fight myself. I watch him—really watch him—with an aching heart as he and Miranda perform like they've been doing it for years. She is radiant, open, completely turned into him. Her love for him is so obvious. Maybe Tori was wrong. Maybe Miranda and Ronan *are* something. Maybe he's keeping it a secret, like Steve and his mysterious relationship. Even now, none of us really know anything about the girl.

I just don't know anymore.

I reach for the tequila sitting, untouched, in front of me and throw it back. I shouldn't have come to Montana. Being near Ronan again is like pouring salt into infected wounds. I miss him so much. I want him back. But watching him on that stage, I'm certain I've lost him for good.

Miranda and Ronan finish their song to roaring applause from the bar patrons. As the last notes fade, Miranda leans her head against Ronan's shoulder, a warm smile on her face as she strums the final chords.

"Oh no, you're not done," she says quickly, blocking Ronan's attempt to set his guitar down.

"Come on, keep playing, *Rony*!" Shane calls out, grinning.

Ronan shoots him a withering look. "Keep it up and reap the consequences, man," he says, his voice dry.

Even I can't help but smile at Ronan's obvious dislike for the moniker. *It would be a cute name if Miranda didn't come up with it.*

"Yeah, keep it going!" Erin chimes in from our table.

Ronan exhales dramatically. "Oh, fine," he mutters, then starts playing a slow, haunting melody. Miranda joins him seconds later.

The song is nothing like the upbeat one from before. This one is stripped down, raw, with lyrics about pain, loss, and survival. I've never heard it before, and something about the way the words shift when Miranda starts singing the second verse makes me realize she and Ronan wrote the song together. Ronan has lived an entirely different life with Miranda, a life I know close to nothing about.

When they finish, Shane hollers, "Way to go, Rony!"

Ronan's full lips curve into a sly smile, just like in the photo of him at two years old. Mischief incarnate. "Okay, you're asking for it. Get up here, asshole!"

Shane folds his arms across his sturdy chest, shaking his head with a laugh.

Ronan looks to Miranda. "Randi, we need a drummer, don't you think?"

"What? SheShe plays the drums?" Miranda says into the mic, teasing.

Tori lets out a delighted screech at the brand-new nickname.

"Yep, *SheShe* plays the drums," Ronan says, biting back a laugh. "Come on, get up here, SheShe." That does it. Ronan busts up laughing.

Shane stands and flips Ronan off with both hands. Still, he makes his way to the stage, feigning irritation.

"Alright, SheShe, what are we playing?" Ronan asks, his voice still shaking with laughter. It's always been one of my favorite sounds.

"You made your point," Shane grumbles and takes a seat behind the drum set at the back of the stage.

"Okay, Rony? SheShe? Ready?" Miranda asks, smiling at them both.

"Man, you really know how to emasculate a guy," Shane huffs, though there's no real heat to his words.

Miranda just laughs and strums her guitar again. It takes no time at all for Ronan and Shane to fall into rhythm beside her.

I watch as a familiar ache curls inside me. Seeing Ronan like this—laughing, playing, surrounded by the people he loves—it's like witnessing a memory I'm no longer part of.

And even though I'm sitting right here, it's never felt more like I'm on the outside looking in.

Ronan

My dad ends up calling it a night to collective boos from... the damn adults in the room. Where those of us well under the age of twenty-five appear to be stone-cold sober—or at least aren't stumbling to the bathroom like Cat's mom did a few minutes ago—the parentals are either tipsy or straight-up plastered. Only my dad's gait's steady, his eyes sharp as he scoops a dazed-looking Penny into his arms and starts ushering the crowd out of Sterling's just before midnight.

"Alright, Stevie: you take Cat, Thomas, Elias, and Miranda. Strike that—take Cat, Jen, and Bobby back to the ranch. Ran, you'll drive Seamus, Tori, and Shane." He nods once, like he's giving orders to his squadron at the Air Force. "Randi, are you okay to drive?"

Miranda nods. She isn't lying; all she's had tonight is water.

"Good. Take Martin's truck and take him, Erin, Thomas, and Elias back. I'll take Penny and her sister," he finishes like the lieutenant colonel he is.

Miranda nudges me as she brushes past, aiming a wicked grin my way. "See, your daddy doesn't mind a threesome," she whispers with a naughty eyebrow wiggle.

I groan. Loudly. Then follow everyone out of Sterling's like her little comment didn't just result in a cringe-worthy visual.

It's a clear night, and only fifty minutes later I drop my passengers off at their cabin.

"You still gonna try to get Cat alone tonight?" Shane asks as he opens the back door, ready to hop out of my truck.

I inhale slowly, nodding. My heart's pounding like I'm about to walk into a war zone and I don't even know which side I'm on.

Shane nods, then reaches for my shoulder to squeeze it. "You got this, man. Just... feel. It'll be alright."

I park my truck next to my grandpa's. Neither my dad nor Steve are back yet, their spots empty. Not a shocker. Shane, Tori, Seamus, and I were the first ones back on the road—probably because none of us were fall-over drunk. There's no telling how long it took to coax my giggly aunt or Cat's barely awake dad back into the respective vehicles.

I trudge the fifty yards to the house, my path illuminated by the motion-sensor lights that clicked on with my truck's approach. My understanding is that Cat's siblings are spending the night in the one remaining upstairs bedroom, while my baby brothers are in my grandparents' bedroom. I decide to take a seat on the front steps and wait for Steve and Cat to get here.

It's early April and, not surprisingly, the Montana chill cuts right through me. It takes only minutes before my hands are buried deep inside my jacket pockets and my jaw's clenched tight to keep from shivering. The lights shut off with my lack of movement as I sit in the cold, quiet dark. But the second I spot headlights making their way up the long drive, the cold evaporates under the heat of instant panic.

I watch as Cat and Steve get out of the truck and start toward me. My heart lurches into my throat. I feel the hectic thing slamming against my chest. I swear it makes the spots where my ribs were broken not quite two years ago ache. My mouth is dry, and my shirt sticks to my low back with cold sweat. Weird how my physical reaction now is the exact same it always was when my mother called me into the kitchen. When I knew she was going to hurt me.

And yeah, I'm aware how fucked up that is. Laying myself bare to the love of my life is nothing like getting the shit beaten out of me by my mom. But that's what it feels like—this tight, sick fear in my chest that I'm walking straight into something that is sure to wreck me.

And I'm going anyway.

I stay seated, focusing on my breathing until they're halfway to the house. I stand, wiping my clammy palms on my jeans. I must have gone unnoticed to Steve and Cat until now, because suddenly Cat folds her arms tightly across her chest, her posture stiffening as her pace slows and she begins to trail half a step behind Steve. Almost like she's wary of me.

My brother's cheeks lift with a knowing smile, his eyes warm, encouraging. Much like everyone else, he's made no secret of his dismay over our breakup.

"Hey," I say, my voice rough from cold and nerves.

Cat doesn't answer. She just looks at me. It's not icy. Not exactly. But it's not warm, either.

Steve walks past me up the steps, but Cat stops six feet from me. The physical distance stings.

Her eyes flick past me to Steve.

He glances between us, eyebrows rising expectantly. "You two good if I head in?" he asks, his tone casual.

I nod. "Yeah. Just... wanted to talk to Cat for a sec."

"Don't make it weird," Steve says under his breath, just loud enough for me to hear. He bumps his shoulder against mine, then disappears into the house with a quiet click as the door shuts behind him.

Now it's just us.

Cat stands there, arms still crossed, her frame backlit by the lights mounted to the barn. She looks tired, like she's been carrying something heavy. Like maybe I'm the weight.

"Can we talk?" I ask her, barely above a whisper.

"Yeah," she breathes, matching my volume. The single word brings immediate relief. She's not rejecting me outright.

I take the few steps that separate us like I'm approaching a skittish animal. She doesn't flinch or walk away, and instead lets me take her hand in mine, lets me lead her some yards away from the house. My grandparents and brothers are sleeping downstairs. I don't want to wake anyone, don't want to risk anyone overhearing.

Cat follows me without a word, and I keep her hand in mine like I have so many times in my life because she is what anchors me. And anchoring is exactly what I need right now. I'm about to give life to the darkest, ugliest parts of myself—parts no one knows, parts I've spent months—hell, years—burying deep, deep inside me. And I'm scared shitless. And maybe not so much of the telling, but of the look I'm convinced she'll give me after. The one that says whatever's left between us can't survive the truth.

Cat

Ronan's hand in mine is warm, familiar in a way that guts me. It's like muscle memory. I stare at our joined hands, revel in the steady current that runs from my palm directly to my heart. It's the first time we've touched in months, but the sensation is just as powerful.

Ronan stops maybe thirty feet from the house, then turns to face me. He lets go of my hand to shove both of his into his jeans pockets. Already, I mourn the loss.

"Are you alright?" he asks.

At first, I nod. But he deserves honesty. Heck, *I* deserve honesty. And not just from others, but from myself, too. It's something I've learned about myself these past few months. The catalyst was the breakup, but the revelation came only days ago when I was knee-deep in my research. And suddenly, it all made sense. My past with Adam, my own behavioral patterns, my mom's "apropos" statement. I have codependent tendencies.

Looking back, it's obvious. The signs were all there.

Lack of satisfaction or purpose outside of the relationship. *Check.*

Preoccupation with the other person's thoughts or feelings. *Check.*

Unwillingness to state needs or desires due to fear of conflict. *Check.*

Of course, Ronan never saw it because he was preoccupied with his recovery. And I never recognized it because, well, it was learned behavior meant to keep me safe. I'd been trained since childhood to stay small and agreeable to avoid injury. My dad expected me to be a "good girl," in not so subtle ways tasking me with ensuring others didn't hurt me. Adam, of course, was the case in point, teaching me that defiance results in punishment. So I learned to shrink myself down, to hide certain pieces of me. The last thing I ever wanted was to be abandoned. Especially by the boy I loved... *love* most in this world. Except the steam builds, and the pressure eventually finds a release valve. Ronan was that valve. Everything burst out during that awful fight. After that, everything just... unraveled.

My face contorts with the wave of sorrow rushing through me. I shake my head, unable to dam the tears. "No," I croak. "Ran, I'm so sorry."

"It's okay," he whispers. Somehow, I almost believe him.

I shake my head more vehemently. "No it's not. That kiss should've never happened. I wish I could take it back. I wish I could undo everything. I—"

"I miss you," he says.

I freeze, standing stock-still, unwilling to take even a single breath out of fear he'll take those words right back, will yank them—and my feet—out from underneath me.

He inhales, the sound ragged. "I know I fucked up. I thought I had it figured out, but I honestly have no idea what I'm doing. The one thing I know is that I'm fucking lost without you, Cat." His Adam's apple bobs with his forced swallow. "I never wanted to hurt you. I thought I was doing the right thing. I really just want to keep you safe. You deserve to be happy. You deserve everything you want."

"I want you," I whisper. "You make me happy."

The motion light behind Ronan clicks off, and we vanish into stark night. He waves his left arm once, casting us back into warm light.

His brow is set, his jaw clenched when our eyes meet again.

"I want you, too. Cat, you're... *everything*."

Relief should flood me, should rush in like a spring tide and sweep away all the fear and doubt, but instead, something in his face stops it short. There's weight there. Hesitation. A heaviness behind his eyes that says this isn't the part where we fall back together.

"Then what's stopping us?" I ask. It comes out a whimper.

His gaze drops. "Me." He says it so quietly, I almost miss it.

Elongated silence stretches between us like black tar. I have no idea what to say and instead plead with the universe that Ronan didn't just slam the door on a potential future for us. But then he straightens, shoulders squared, and lifts his eyes to mine with unmistakable resolve.

"Do you love me, Cat?"

I blink at him, at his absurd question. "Yes."

"Okay. Then I need to tell you some things."

"Okay?"

"Okay. And... I'm doing this so you know. Like, really, *really* know."

I have absolutely no idea what's going on, where this is going, but I don't interrupt.

"I want... I'm going to tell you everything. And then it's up to you. What happens to us after? It'll be up to you. And whatever you decide..." he squeezes his eyes shut for a moment. "I don't want to hurt you, but I also can't lie to you anymore, so..." he trails off, his voice cracking.

"Ran, *I* hurt *you*," I say, my voice trembling. "Not the other way around. I kissed that guy at that party and—"

"I slept with Randi."

The words don't register at first. Not fully. It's like a delay in my system, a buffer loading pain. "W-what?" I choke. "What do you mean?"

"I had sex with her," he says, his words like a speeding bullet to my chest.

"When?" I ask meekly.

"Yesterday," he says like he's confessing to murder. And in a sense, he is. He's killing my heart. I *knew* Tori was wrong. I *knew* there was something going on between them. But then why is he telling me he wants me?

"Why?" It's all I can think to ask.

Before he can answer, the light clicks off again.

"Fuck," he mutters, raising his arm to trip the motion sensor.

The lights come on, and I see it. Just behind Ronan, in the tall grass, a flash of movement. Two glowing orbs. No, not orbs. *Eyes*.

I gasp, instinctively stepping back.

"Cat?" Ronan's voice cuts through my panic. His eyes follow mine, and he turns slightly, just enough to look over his shoulder.

"Shit," he breathes.

In quick, calculated movements, Ronan turns his back to me, positioning himself between me and whatever's out there.

"What is that?" I whisper.

"A mountain lion."

The words sink in like ice water. I crane my neck to see past him, and there it is, crouched low, eyes locked on Ronan, muscles coiled. Perfectly still. Perfectly dangerous.

A strangled cry gurgles in my throat.

"Baby, I need you to very, very slowly back up to the house, okay?" he says.

My heart stutters. Not because we're about two minutes away from getting mauled by a mountain lion, but because Ronan just called me *baby*. I'm sure it was a slip-up, an old habit, a relic from our shared past, but still, it results in an overwhelming need to wrap my arms around him and kiss him. Maybe for the last time.

"Keep your eyes on it. Move slowly. Don't run. Not until you're closer to the house," he says, low and steady, though every muscle in his body looks ready to spring.

I start to back away. Two steps, then three. I stop.

"What about you?" I whisper.

His head shakes just slightly. "It's locked on me. I just need you to get to the house, baby. Please."

The grass where the lion crouches shifts and rustles; it takes a tentative step out of its hiding spot, moving in slow motion as if its tempo somehow camouflages it.

I do as Ronan said, backing away slowly, my eyes darting between him and the predator. *God, how far away am I from the house?* The distance feels impossible. Every step is its own little battle against panic. I don't dare go against his instructions, so I keep my eyes fixed on the broad line of his back. His shoulders rise and fall with deliberate breaths, his body taut and still, a living barrier between me and certain, painful death.

It feels like an eternity, but finally my heel knocks against wood.

That's my cue.

I tear my gaze from Ronan, whip around, and bolt for the door. My legs are jelly and fire all at once, and I pray my sudden movement doesn't trigger the mountain lion to pounce and tear into Ronan.

"Help!" I scream the second I slam the front door behind me. "Help! Please!"

I sprint into the living room, headed for the stairs, ready to rip Steve out of bed, or the shower, or wherever the hell he is. But I only make it a few steps before Perry barrels out of his bedroom, Saoirse right behind him in her flannel pajamas, eyes wide.

"What happened?" Perry asks, his voice a rougher version of Frank's.

"Mountain lion," I gasp, pointing a trembling finger toward the door. "Ran. He's still out there."

Saoirse lets out a strangled cry. Perry doesn't waste a single breath. He spins and disappears into his room again. Seconds later, he's back, rifle in hand.

"Where exactly?" he asks, calm but clipped.

"Right outside," I say, voice shaking. "In the grass near the barn. He was keeping it distracted so I could get away."

Perry's already moving, Saoirse on his heels as he pulls open the front door and steps out onto the porch.

I follow, stopping at the threshold. I'm not about to get in anyone's way, not when Ronan's life depends on his grandfather taking the perfect damn shot.

"What's going on?" Steve says, approaching from behind me. He reaches my side, then freezes. "Oh shit."

Ronan is still exactly where I left him, his back to us. But the mountain lion is no longer hidden in the grass. It's fully emerged now, ten feet from him, eyes fixed on its prey.

Perry racks the weapon, the metallic *shick-shick* loud enough to make my heart jump into my throat. Then he shoulders it, and I cease to breathe. This angle is crap, and I pray that Perry is a skilled marksman. One wrong move and Ronan...

"Ran, I got it in sight. Don't. Move!" Perry shouts before he, too, sends a muttered prayer. "God, let my aim be true."

Then everything goes eerily silent, like even nature is holding its breath.

One one-thousand. Two one-thousand. Three one-thousand.

A single shot cracks through the night, a deafening explosion that echoes across the valley. The mountain lion crumples instantly. But Ronan still stands.

No one moves. Not Perry, braced with the rifle still at his shoulder. Not Saoirse, hands clutched to her mouth. Not Steve, wide-eyed beside me. Not me, barely breathing.

Ronan doesn't turn. Doesn't speak. He just stands there, a statue etched in moonlight, like his body hasn't registered yet that he's safe. That it's over.

The silence roars louder than the gunshot.

Then, slowly, his shoulders collapse. Ronan sinks to his knees. And, finally, the rest of us move.

Ronan

I can't find sleep. My room feels like a tomb, the walls too tight, my thoughts too loud.

By the time my adrenaline faded to a bearable level and I managed to walk back into the house only to lower myself onto the sofa, my dad was here. He heard the damn gunshot, got in his truck, and sped to the main house where my grandpa debriefed him.

Even though his military background trained him for high-stakes situations, I could tell my dad was freaking out. His brown eyes were wide, his voice just a little too loud for the hour, his tone clipped when he barked at my grandpa—his own dad. He crouched down in front of me, eyes darting over my face and body, checking for injuries that didn't exist.

"God damn it, Ran," he groaned, raking a hand through his hair. "What's with you and always staring death in the face, bud?"

"It's not like he's doing it on purpose, Frankie," my grandma said, setting cups of tea on the coffee table. One for me, one for Cat who was on the sofa next to me, her leg barely touching mine, but it was enough to ground me, to prove I was still here.

We didn't drink the tea. We couldn't. As far as Cat's and my hierarchy of needs went, tea was the least of our concerns. It took a while, but eventually the quiet returned. My dad went back to his cabin, and my grandma ushered Steve, Cat, and me upstairs into our respective rooms without even the tiniest chance for me to ensure that Cat was alright. Not just because of what happened with that wildcat out there, but because of my confession just before.

All Cat knows right now is that I did the unthinkable, that I slept with Miranda. She doesn't know why. She doesn't know what was going through my head, or the hole I've been living in, or how I've hated myself every fucking second since I've ended things between us.

I didn't get to tell her all the things I still need to get off my chest before we stand even a hope of repairing... *us*. I didn't get the chance to tell her any of it. And it's killing me.

She went into her room without looking back, without saying a word. Without acknowledging me or the gaping rift I caused, the one I had every intention of fixing and somehow only managed to make worse. Fuck that mountain lion for picking that exact moment to show up. Fuck the universe for reminding me, again, that I have absolutely zero control over anything.

A little while ago, I rolled out of bed, then stood outside Cat's door for a solid five minutes like a damn ghost, hoping she'd open it. She didn't.

So now I'm back in the dark, staring at a ceiling I've memorized since childhood, replaying the last hour on a loop, wondering if that one sentence, that one decision, was enough to destroy whatever hope we had left.

I did this to myself.

I deserve the silence.

I deserve the pain.

Sunday, April 2nd

Cat

I'm grumpy.

I knew the second I got on that plane yesterday that it would be an emotional arrival on the ranch. But I *way* underestimated what a rollercoaster it would be.

It was a lot. A total freefall of adrenaline spikes, doubt, longing, anger, disappointment... It's only been one day. One! And already I'm emotionally exhausted.

The house is quiet when I finally crawl out of bed just before ten. I assume everyone's off doing whatever ranch life requires while also somehow preparing for the wedding. I catch the scent of coffee and smile gratefully when I arrive in the kitchen to a full, steaming pot.

I pour myself a cup, then rummage through the fridge for creamer or milk when I hear the sharp clack of bootheels on tile.

"There's caramel creamer all the way in the back of the second shelf." Miranda's voice floats through the space.

My jaw clenches. First of all, why does she have to be *right here* when there are literally three thousand other acres she could be on? And second, how does she even know that I have a weak spot for caramel coffee anything?

I grab the bottle, then close the fridge door behind me. "Thanks," I mutter, not making eye contact.

Something spiky bites my insides. She had sex with Ronan only two days ago. She got to see him in all his masculine glory, got to feel his soft skin on hers, ran her hands over his lean muscles, and probably moaned his name. I'm not usually a violent person, but I won't deny that the idea of decking her isn't all that off-putting.

Miranda moves around the kitchen with annoying ease, pulling a cup from the cabinet with one hand while fishing for a spoon with the other. "So, I heard about your encounter with our resident wildcat. Well, *former* resident wildcat," she says, pouring herself a cup of coffee. "The ranger picked up the carcass this morning."

I don't respond, instead watching the creamer slowly drip into my coffee. Out of my periphery, Miranda takes a sip from her cup, eyes closed. *Is she drinking that black? That's... impressive.*

She smacks her lips with a serene smile. "That was a male, too. The ranger estimated him to be about a hundred and eighty pounds, maybe eight feet long. Rony wouldn't have stood a chance if that thing had decided to ambush him."

I reach for the drawer to grab a spoon, then stir my coffee.

"Need sugar?" she asks, nudging a small ceramic bowl toward me.

The caramel creamer is sweet enough. I ignore the bowl. And *her*.

"Oh, Tori and I talked about maybe going on a trail ride later today," Miranda continues, casual. *Now she's coming for my friends, too?* "You're welcome to join us."

That does it.

My eyes snap to hers, face set in a frown. "You fucked Ran. Two days ago," I say, and march out of the kitchen.

"Oh perfect, just the two people I was looking for," Saoirse says, standing on the threshold, a smile on her lips that looks just a little too enthusiastic to be natural.

Ugh, she probably heard what I just said. Facial combustion in three, two, one.

"I need you two to run a few errands for me. The wedding cake needs to be picked up, as well as the flowers. And since you'll already be in Missoula, I have a list of things I'd like you to grab from the supermarket."

Missoula? Four hours' round-trip in a truck, with my ex-boyfriend's... ex, friend with benefits, side chick? Kinda wish that mountain lion had taken me out.

"Uh, I think my parents nee—"

"Everyone's occupied with work or wedding setup. The boys are all dispersed across the ranch. Tori went into town with Erin and Riley, and your parents went on a hike with your siblings," Saoirse says over my poor attempt at coming up with an excuse for why I can't possibly be gone in excess of four hours. "I'd really appreciate the help." Her gaze swings between me and Miranda.

My shoulders sag. Who am I to turn down Saoirse Soult? "Okay."

She smiles brightly. "Wonderful. You'll need to get on the road ASAP. The bakery closes at two today and is closed on Mondays." Saoirse hands Miranda a list, then takes our coffee cups. "I'll load these into to-go mugs for you."

Miranda nods, smiling. "Okay, I'll just change really quick. I'll be back to pick you up in ten minutes, Cat."

Ah yes, my greatest wish coming true...

***

I might end up with a crick in my neck, but not having to see Miranda even out of the corner of my eyes is worth it. The beautiful landscape flying past the passenger window is an added bonus.

We've been on the road for over thirty minutes now, the awkward silence sitting between us like a third passenger. I can't tell if Miranda is as uncomfortable in my presence as I am in hers, but if she is, she's a hell of a lot better at hiding it.

She's been trying to make small talk and receiving one-syllable responses or plain silence from me. I'm not here to bond over our mutual attraction to the same guy. Kinda funny, now that I think about it: we both want him, and neither of us has him. *Ha.*

"Guess that trail ride's gonna have to wait," Miranda mutters, reaching for the to-go mug nestled in the cupholder and taking a slow, unbothered sip. "Let me know if you need me to stop by a restroom or anything."

I'd rather pee my pants than prolong this trip.

As if she can hear my thoughts, Miranda exhales a resigned sigh. "Okay, Cat, do I need to pull over so you can smack me, or would you rather I just tell you why Rony slept with me?"

There's open exasperation in her voice now.

"Either's fine," she says. "We can hash it out, or you can ask me whatever you want. This one-sided conversation is starting to annoy the crap out of me."

If my neck could creak, it would. I slowly turn to face her. Even though her eyes stay fixed on the empty one-lane highway ahead, her raised eyebrows tell me she's waiting for me to say something.

I press my lips together hard enough to feel the sharp sting of teeth on skin. I don't know that anything she says will change how I feel. She wants Ronan. She's made that clear again and again. And she obviously doesn't care who gets stepped on in the process.

But still, her phrasing hooks me.

Would you rather I just tell you why Rony slept with me?

Honestly? Yeah. I would.

I turn to her, arms folded across my chest.

She glances at me. "Alright, so… no smackdown?"

"No smackdown," I say. "As tempting as that is."

The laughter that bursts from Miranda's lips makes the corners of my lips tug into a smile. At least she's got a decent sense of humor.

"Not a fighter, huh?" she teases.

"Don't underestimate me."

Miranda raises one hand in mock surrender, giggling. "I'd never."

She takes a deep breath, then exhales slowly.

"I love Ronan," she starts.

My spine stiffens.

"I've loved Ronan since we were kids. I was twelve when we met, and let's just say we became really close really fast."

"Yeah, I know that," I say, unable to keep the edge out of my voice.

She doesn't seem to take offense. Instead, she glances at me with a soft smile. "But Ronan *doesn't* love me. He never has." There's something raw in her voice, something that stings my chest in spite of everything.

I shake my head. "You're wrong. He *does* love you. When you called from Tennessee, he dropped everything to get to you. He just up and left."

"That's different. That's Rony being Rony," she says. "Yeah, he loves me. But not like that. He doesn't love me like he loves you, Cat." She pauses, eyes back on the road. "He's never loved a girl the way he loves you. And, Cat, that's still true. Right now. This second. Rony loves you."

Her words slam into me like a ramrod. And maybe it's the fact that it's *her* saying it—when she has every reason not to—that makes me believe it.

"And Friday? When we, you know—"

"Yeah," I mutter. I guess I appreciate her not saying it out loud again.

"Rony and I were talking, and he..." She sighs. "He's so sad, Cat. He's all twisted up inside. His thoughts, his dreams. They scare him. And..." She trails off. "You guys need to talk. It's not my place to tell you everything."

"I'm intimidated by you," I blurt.

Her mouth opens, then closes. "I... That's not my intention."

"I just don't understand your relationship with him. You say he loves me like he's never loved anyone, but you know things about him he never tells me. You had sex with him. He dropped everything to see you in Tennessee. He always answers your calls and steps away to talk to you. He *trusts* you in this way I don't understand. How do you get him to talk about his fears, his dreams, any of it? He doesn't talk to me about those things. He never has. He just tells me he's fine. Even when he's very obviously *not* fine."

The words spill out fast, full of frustration.

"That doesn't make me special, Cat," she says quietly. "It doesn't mean he and I are anything more than friends. The only reason I know those darker parts of him is because I don't let him get away with his bullshit. I don't let him placate me."

"I don't let him get away with his bullshit, either," I snap.

Miranda chuckles softly. I frown, bristling. But her expression sobers.

"I'm sorry, Cat, but... yeah, you do. *You all do.* How do you think he was able to hide the abuse for so long?"

I'm glad her question's rhetorical, because I couldn't answer even if I wanted to.

"He's good at giving you just enough to make you stop asking. Just enough to sound plausible. Just enough to seem okay. And that's not anyone's fault. We're human. It's easier to believe the bruises were from a fall—or whatever bullshit excuse he made up—than to keep pushing."

She looks over at me. "But think about it, Cat. The *one* time he did open up to you—when he told you he didn't want kids because he was afraid of repeating the cycle—what were you doing that made him say it?"

It hits me all at once, like a field of stadium lights blinking on.

"I didn't let him get away with his bullshit."

I remember pushing him. Not backing down when he tried to wave it off.

"Exactly," she says, like a proud parent.

"But we had a huge fight." I frown. "And then he ended things. Is that what I'm risking every time I try to get to the bottom of what's going on in his head?"

She grins knowingly. "Okay, but did he open up and *then* you fought? Or did someone just happen to accuse him of still loving his ex? And didn't someone also suggest he should 'move on' from what his mom did to him?"

My face burns. So Ronan told her about that, too.

"Yeah," I say, voice small. "I should've handled that differently." I wince, remembering the way I twisted the knife right when he'd finally let his guard down.

"Look, Cat, I'm not an expert. But I *do* know Rony. And..." She hesitates. "I can relate to him. My childhood wasn't great, either. We bonded over that. I understand him in ways other people can't. So let me just say this, okay?"

She glances over briefly, then back to the road.

"When Ronan opens up, it's *hard* for him. Really hard. He's making himself vulnerable in a way that terrifies him. You can't take that lightly. Even when you're mad, or hurt, or frustrated—especially then—you've got to learn how to step back from that heat. It doesn't mean you don't get to feel what you feel. You *should*. But when Rony tells you about the dark things in his head, you can't attack him for it or you risk reinforcing what he's learned: that it's not safe to express how he feels. I know it's complicated, but..."

She groans, struggling for words. "What happened to Rony is heavy. And him not opening up to you? That's not about *you*. It's not about how much he loves you, or trusts you, or how safe he feels with you. It's conditioning. It's fear and sadness. It's years of learning to survive by keeping it all locked up. He's only just now learning how to leave survival mode."

She pauses.

"Your life's been pretty consistent, right?"

I nod.

"Yeah. His hasn't. Not even close. And it takes time to adjust. He's still learning. You can't ask him to run when he's just barely learning to walk. I know he's almost nineteen, and sure, in a lot of ways he's a man. But in this—this emotional stuff? He's still just a baby. And Cat? He's scared."

There's a painful lump in my throat. "That... Honestly, Randi, I never... I never thought about it that way." I swallow, shame rising in me like a tide. "I just thought he didn't trust me. Or that maybe he didn't love me as much as I'd hoped."

Her gaze sharpens. "You thought he didn't love you?"

I nod. "Yeah, I… I guess I've got my own baggage. Stuff that played into those fears and—"

Miranda laughs, almost like she's had a realization. "Rony is hyper-independent. He'll die before asking for help. And you are…" She trails off. I can tell she doesn't want to offend me.

But I nod. "Codependent," I finish for her. "Exactly. I keep trying to tune in to him, to understand what he's feeling. I worry about his mental state all the time. I dig and dig because I have this constant need to make sure he won't abandon me."

"And all that does is make Rony withdraw more and more," she says gently. "Leaving you chasing after safety that feels just out of reach."

I blink. "Have you studied psychology?"

Her laugh is light. "No. I barely scraped through high school. But I read a ton. Oof," she groans. "That definitely complicates things."

"You think?" I deadpan.

She giggles again. "I'm a lot like Rony in that way. Hyper-independent. But hey, tuning in to him isn't *bad*. It's only bad when—"

"When I sacrifice my own well-being in the process," I say. "Yeah. I've been reading about that too."

Miranda nods. "Okay, well, it doesn't sound like you're asking for a therapy session, so I'll wrap this up. Rony loves you. He wants to be with you. He and I are just friends. The reason he trusts me with his dark side is because he knows mine. And trust?" She shrugs. "Honestly, it's too strong a word. He only shares because I don't give him a way out. I'm just an annoying pest who won't leave him alone until he talks."

I nod. But she's still left out one huge part.

"So... if he loves me, if he wants to be with me, why did you two have sex two days ago?"

Her eyes flick to me for the span of a heartbeat. "Because I took advantage of his vulnerability," she says, voice quiet. "I knew you two were broken up. And I won't lie, I did want to see if there could be something between us."

She exhales.

"We were at my cabin. He was talking about how he didn't think real happiness was in the cards for him. That he didn't think he'd ever measure up to what you deserve. That it'd be safer if he was alone. I told him he deserved to be happy. And... I made a move."

I squeeze my eyes shut, trying to erase the image.

"He couldn't finish," she says.

My eyes fly open. I stare at her, unsure I heard right.

"He wasn't really with me, Cat. Not emotionally. He was just... going through the motions. Like he used to do when he was fourteen. He was trying to sedate himself with sex. I don't blame him. But he couldn't finish. Because he didn't actually *want* it. He didn't want *me.* He wants *you.* Only you."

I sit frozen, her words heavy and hollow in my chest.

Miranda opens the glove box, pulls out a pack of tissues, and offers them to me. It's only then that I realize tears are streaking down my cheeks.

She gives me a small, warm smile. "You know, when he was in Tennessee, I asked him flat out why he didn't talk to you about his worries. About his grandma. His dreams. All of it. Wanna know what he said?"

My throat is constricted, so I just nod.

"He said your love for him was so pure. That you were whole and unbroken. Not stained like him." Her voice cracks.

I sit in the heavy silence for a moment. "Do you think Saoirse would be mad if we didn't pick up the cake and drove straight back to the ranch so I can find Ran and talk to him?"

Ronan

"Gotta be honest here, Ran, when you said you were gonna talk to Cat last night, I didn't think you meant the animal," Shane says, biting back a grin.

Steve chuckles. "You know Ran and those cougars."

I roll my eyes so hard, it actually hurts. "Wow, guys, you should consider turning Murphy's into a damn comedy club and starring as the headliners."

Tori giggles. "I'd ask what you did to piss that cat off so much, but then you'd be forced to ask me which one I meant."

I nod slowly, lips pressed together. "I see Shane's rubbing off on you. Shame. I really liked you, Tor."

They laugh, and I even manage my usual half-smile, but it doesn't reach my eyes. They don't know that I barely slept. That I spent the hours in bed turning over every single thing that has gone wrong, trying to figure out how I ever became the guy who deserved them. If I'm being honest, last night couldn't have gone worse.

Those couple minutes between Cat spotting the thing behind me and my grandpa landing the perfect shot—I swear I felt the air disturbance from the bullet speeding past my head—stretched on forever. I just stood there, locked in a staring contest with that fucker, praying Cat was doing exactly what I told her to do: get in the damn house.

She did. But I didn't hear much of anything until my grandpa hollered at me to stand still. All I could focus on was that wildcat baring every single tooth, snarling, inching closer like it had already decided I was the perfect damn midnight snack. And here I thought Miranda was the perfect prey. Turns out, it was me. Mountain lions usually ambush their prey from behind, so while I worried mostly about Cat, I'm certain it had its sights on me.

Needless to say, I'm eager to finally get the chance to talk to her. My plan is to get back to the house where everyone's gathering for lunch and pull her outside with me to talk. We can eat later.

But when the four of us walk inside, Cat is nowhere to be seen. She isn't with her family, either, when they join us ten minutes later, faces sun-kissed from what I'm gathering was a nice hike on my grandparents' ranch.

It's when my dad, grandpa, Seamus, Thomas, and Elias seat themselves around the table that my stomach officially drops. Everyone's here, except Cat… and Miranda.

"Morai?" I say quietly while plates are passed around.

She turns her gaze to me, smiling softly. "What, baby boy?"

"Have you seen Cat?"

"I sent her on some errands with Miranda."

I almost choke on my breath. "What?"

It comes out way louder than I meant it to. The entire table goes dead quiet.

My grandma's expression doesn't change except for that sly twinkle in her brown eyes. "I sent Cat and Miranda to pick up the cake and the flowers," she repeats, even though we both know I didn't need her to repeat anything. I needed an explanation.

"Uh-oh," Shane mutters.

I don't spare him a glance. I flex my jaw. "Morai, mind if we have a quick talk?"

I don't wait for an answer. The chair scrapes loudly against the floorboards as I stand, then march out of the dining room.

"You're in trouble now, Mom," my dad chuckles.

"Oh hush, Frankie," she chirps, then follows me into the living room where I'm already pacing. Three steps to the left, stop, turn, three steps to the right. Repeat.

She stands there with an innocent look that we both know she has no business wearing. She's fucking meddling. *Again.*

"Morai," I growl. "What are you doing to me?"

"I'm not doing anything *to* you, Ran. I sent the girls on an errand because those two need to be forced to spend some time together without you fogging up their brains with... well, you."

This is such a bad idea. "What do you mean?"

"They need a good talk."

I stop pacing, exasperated. "Okay? About what?"

"About you, obviously," she says like *duh*.

I pinch the bridge of my nose between my thumb and index finger. "God, Morai, you're such a meddler."

"Baby boy, I have been on this earth quite a bit longer than you. I have a very unique perspective, especially when it comes to you. And my meddling, so far, has done you how much harm?"

"...None," I grit out.

"Exactly. Trust me when I tell you that Cat and Miranda need this. It's clear to me that both girls care about you deeply. Each knows you in a way the other doesn't, and I think this will help ease some of Cat's... worries," she says meaningfully.

My brow creases. I get the distinct impression my grandma knows, or at least suspects, that I... slipped... a couple of days ago. She probably suspected as much when I came back from Miranda's cabin in the middle of the damn night, but that's not the point right now.

"When did you send them out?" I ask, pulling my phone from my back pocket.

She crosses her arms, popping one hip out. "They left at around ten."

I start to dial Cat's number, then think better of it and dial Miranda's instead. Straight to voicemail. Damn it.

"See?" I hold up my phone like I just won some sort of twisted game. "No answer. One's probably dead while the other's on the run. And you know what's worse? I couldn't tell you which one's which."

I'm obviously making an idiot of myself because my grandma starts to laugh. It doesn't exactly make me feel better.

"Oh baby boy," she says, and pats my cheek. "You worry too much."

***

Fuck yeah, I worry. And for good fucking reason. Miranda and Cat? Together? After everything?

I try Miranda's phone twice more, then muster up the courage and dial Cat's number. Gotta admit, I listen to her entire voicemail greeting before hanging up, soaking in her voice like drops off water after days in the desert. I'm fucking pathetic.

I go about my afternoon work dutifully. I show Shane and Tori the literal and figurative ropes, though Tori mostly gets distracted by the calves and foals while Shane helps me fence off a section of pasture.

It's past four. Tori went down for a nap—she's clearly not used to running on minimal sleep like Shane and me—while my best friend is next to me, helping me clean the tack. I've always loved the smell of conditioned leather.

"The contractor said construction should only take a week," Shane says about his plan to reconstruct the small stage at the back of Murphy's. It's been his latest passion project.

"When are they coming in to do that, though? I doubt you want a construction crew wrecking the place while you're serving food."

He nods. "They're coming at night. After we close, they'll work for a few hours, then shut it all down before we open again. We'll wall off that back section temporarily."

"How much will that cut capacity?" I run the waxy cloth over the stirrups, wiping away excess conditioner.

"Four booths and two tables, so thirty-six fewer seats."

"Not bad." I nod. "They starting Monday? Try to wrap it by Friday?" Weekends at Murphy's are always packed. I know Shane doesn't want to touch that cash flow.

"That's the plan."

The distant rumble of an engine cuts through the barn, and Shane's voice fades when I catch a flash of cherry red out the open doors.

Cat and Miranda are back.

I hoist my saddle back on the rack, then turn to Shane, my damn heart thundering in my chest like I'm about to face off with that wildcat again. Different kind of Cat this time.

He takes one look at me and just nods, smiling like he already knows what I'm about to do. "You gonna stand there, or fix what's broken?"

I blink. "Did you just quote... me?"

He grins, shrugs, and goes back to polishing.

I walk out of the barn slowly, listening. There's the slam of a truck door. Then another. Footsteps in the dirt—light, but not quiet. I can tell who's who. Heavy boots clomping? Miranda. The soft pad of well-worn chucks? Cat.

I step into the sunlight and stop short when I see them, standing by the tailgate of Miranda's truck maybe twenty feet off. I need to gauge what I'm about to walk into, assess the threat level like I've done all my life. It's one of the many habits I haven't been able to break in the year and a half since *the end.*

But honestly? I'm not sure anything could've prepared me for this. There's Cat, standing by the open tailgate next to Miranda, and... they're both... smiling? No, they're *giggling* while each pulls a box laden with flowers off the truck bed.

I expected to walk into storm and was met with sunshine.

"I guess I'd appreciate a plant over a flower," Cat says, light and airy. "Flowers have a certain expiration date because they've been separated from their roots. It's kind of a horrible gift, if you think about it."

Miranda nods. “Yep. Flowers die. What a terrible idea. ‘Hey, here’s something pretty you can watch wither away,’” she says, mimicking a dude’s voice.

She sets her box down and pauses, hands on her hips. “You know what? I’ve never actually gotten flowers.”

“Me neither.”

Inwardly, I cringe. Cat’s right—at least when it comes to us. I’ve never gotten her flowers. Maybe that’s not such a bad thing, now that I know how she feels about them… but still. Why didn’t I ever ask? Probably because I assumed all girls like flowers. And yet, I never even gave her that. And now, maybe I never will.

For a moment, panic floods my chest. What does Cat actually like? Have I ever really taken the time to find out? Or have I just been so wrapped up in my own shit that I’ve spent our whole relationship stringing her along? Have I ever actually shown her how much she means to me? That I’d rather take the hit myself than let her hurt, especially if I’m the one who caused it?

I close my eyes, their voices drifting over on a breeze, and I think.

She loves sunsets. Especially at Shane’s mom’s beach house, when the sky turns a burnt orange and the ocean looks like it’s on fire. She loves all things tiny—puppies, kittens, baby penguins… raccoons in clothes, for some reason. Her laugh is the best thing I’ve ever heard, especially when she really loses it, when she’s all breathless and squeaking. It’s so fucking cute that I can’t help but laugh right along with her even when the thing she’s laughing about isn’t actually that funny.

She’s had the same pair of red chucks for years, has glued the sole on the right one twice now. She refuses to toss them because she hates breaking in new shoes. Blisters.

She likes strawberry ice cream and fuzzy socks. She hates being cold, likes her pillows medium-fluffy, and when she’s sad, she orders a caramel macchiato with extra whip at the bottom of the cup.

I wonder how many of those she's had to have since I shattered her heart.

That last thought hits me hard enough to finally get my feet moving.

The dirt crunches under my boots, causing Cat's and Miranda's heads to turn to me.

"Hey there, Rony," Miranda says, but I only have eyes for Cat.

She stands there, that box with flowers still in her hands.

"Would it be okay if we talked?" I ask her.

She raises her eyebrows, something hopeful flashing across her beautiful face. "Now?"

I nod. "Yeah. Now."

I don't know what happened between them during their six hours of forced proximity, but Cat glances at Miranda like she's looking for... what? Permission? Encouragement? Not sure which or why she'd need either, especially from Miranda.

But Miranda grins and says, "Go ahead, I got this. I'll just grab Daddy Soult to come help me move this stuff. Or maybe Stevie... or *both*," she says, obviously for my damn benefit.

I don't acknowledge her statement. I reach for Cat's hand, like it's the most natural thing in the world, then lead her to my truck parked beside Miranda's.

I open the door for her and watch as she climbs in—allowing myself a quick glance at her perfect ass before closing the door behind her and heading to the driver's side.

I know exactly where I'm taking her: the one place that's always been my retreat, my hideout from the world. Somewhere we'll have the privacy I need to finally unpack everything.

Cat

I keep wanting to reach for Ronan's hand as we rumble along a narrow dirt path into a thicket of trees. Back home, back when we were us, it was my favorite way of driving. Ronan in the driver's seat of his Mustang, my hand on his shifter, his hand over mine. But I don't reach for him now. I just fold my hands tightly between my knees, keeping them from even twitching in his direction.

We aren't who we used to be only months ago. I hate how that feels. How my body wishes to bend in his direction, to answer the silent call to be in his arms, yet how much it feels like we're strangers again, separated by a cavernous divide.

The air is thick between us, filled with tension, yet so much familiarity. I conspicuously inhale his scent, glance at his gorgeous profile. The past two months have done nothing to dull my love for him. If anything, his absence from my daily life, though definitely not my thoughts, just made me long for him more.

"Sooo," he says, eyes still locked on the barely-there path ahead. "How was your day?" His voice is careful. I bet he lost his mind when he found out his grandma sent me off with Miranda. I'd have done the same if it were him on some random trip with... *Adam.*

I give him a small smile. "Pretty good."

His eyebrows lift. "Yeah?"

"Yeah. Randi and I had a chance to talk a little bit."

He swallows. His green eyes flick to mine for a single heartbeat, and it looks like he wants to say something. But he just nods, not prying. Not yet, anyway.

Just then, Ronan stops the truck—and I gasp.

Just ahead, tucked between the trees, is a clearing with a beautiful, still lake, its surface sparkling beneath the afternoon light. A long, narrow wooden dock stretches about twenty feet into the water like it's reaching toward something. Or someone.

"Oh my gosh," I breathe, completely overwhelmed. "It's incredible."

Before I realize it, I'm out of the truck. I meet Ronan at the front. Unlike me, he doesn't hesitate. He takes my hand, bold and steady, and leads me down the dock like it's the most natural thing in the world.

"This," he says, gesturing out over the vast expanse of the lake with his free hand, "used to be my hideout. I guess, in a way, it still is."

"It's... Ran, this is..." I have no words to adequately describe how perfect this place is. It's quiet and peaceful, nature in all its perfection. It almost feels like Ronan and I are the only humans on this entire planet.

He nods. "Yeah, I know."

We stand in the silence for a moment, allowing this place to seep into our bones. I feel rather than see Ronan shift beside me.

"Cat, I'm so sorry," he breathes. I turn toward him. The anguish on his face forces my windpipe shut. "I fucked up so badly. So, so badly." He lets go of me only to run his hand roughly across his face.

I part my lips to speak, but he doesn't give me the chance. He turns his body toward me, his gaze locked on mine as if his next words are the difference between living and dying.

"I love you, Cat. I've always loved you, and I will love you until I die. There's no one else for me," he finally says, his eyes serious. "I'm sorry I hurt you. I hurt you in so many damn ways." His breath stutters with emotion.

"I hurt you, too."

It's the truth, but still, my heart stings when he nods. "Yeah, you did. And you know what's weird? Even though I've hurt way worse than that, for some reason, seeing you kiss that guy cut deeper than anything before."

I swallow the boulder-sized lump in my throat.

"I'm so sorry, Ran. I... I wish I could take it back. I wish—"

"Cat," he says, his tone soft. "I didn't end things because of the kiss. It hurt like a bitch, but it wasn't the reason. Not even close. I..."

For a minute, only the sounds of our breathing interrupt the silence around us.

"Please just tell me what you're thinking," I croak, on the verge of tears. I'm so ready for him to bare it all and allow me to bare it all in turn. "Please."

He doesn't respond, letting the silence sink between us like an anchor at the bottom of the ocean. Maybe this will drown us after all.

"Ran, please!" I say more desperately. "We can't keep going like this."

He nods. "I know," he finally says. He inhales deeply, but I don't dare breathe at all.

"Cat, you need to know that I never meant to hurt you. In my head it all made sense. I... I have a really hard time, like, putting the things in my head into words. Part of it is that... I just don't know *how* to say some of the things, and the other part is..." He pauses. "I'm scared of speaking them into existence."

I swallow, but don't interrupt. My gaze stays glued to his, cataloging every emotion flashing across his face. There's mostly pain, fear, and sadness. It makes me want to throw my arms around him, but I still don't dare move.

"I wasn't okay after my grandmother showed up," he says. *Yeah, I knew as much.* "When I was in Montana last year, when my dad called me and told me my mom was forcing a trial, that's the first time I heard that she had been abused by my grandfather. That was the first time I wondered if I was capable of doing the same—if that violence was part of my DNA or something, you know?"

I nod.

"I tried to shove that fear down, lock it away with all the other crap. It worked for a little while." He sighs. "But then my grandmother showed up and... well, you were there for that, so..."

He drops his eyes. "That afternoon, that's when Rashana first made contact with me."

Every fiber in me is wound tightly. I know close to nothing about Ronan's conversations with Rashana. All I know is she wanted to write an article about what he went through as part of her master's degree.

"She told me she had stumbled across my mom's case. She obviously wanted to write about it. I shut her down," he says, stilted. "But when I walked away, she yelled after me, said something about my mom's sister—my aunt."

My eyebrows dip while my eyes widen. I didn't know Ronan even had an aunt on his mom's side. His next words make it clear that, up until Rashana's comment, Ronan didn't, either. "I was so confused. For a second, I considered asking her what the hell she was talking about. But I decided no good could come from knowing, so I just walked away."

He cracks his neck. "I think Rashana's comment was the kindling to my grandma's fucking spark, because that night I dreamed…" His voice cracks.

Ronan slams his eyes shut, his jaw ticking once. Twice. "I dreamed," he starts again. It seems to take all his willpower to say the words.

When he opens his eyes, they're swimming with tears. "I dreamed I was beating you," he chokes.

The breath leaves my lungs.

"I didn't see your face at first. Just the sound. Your voice. Begging me not to hurt you." His voice is barely audible now. "And then I realized it was you. You were in my dad's living room. On that rug…" His voice breaks, tears spilling from his eyes.

I don't think. I just move. My arms are around him fraction of a second later.

"It was just a dream, Ran. Just a dream."

"No, Cat. It's not that simple." He steps out of my arms like he's afraid staying too close might undo him completely. "That rage I felt in that fucking dream… it didn't feel foreign. It felt like something already living inside me. And the worst part?"

He swallows hard. "It didn't go away. I had the dream again. And again. Like it was following me. Like I was becoming a monster in my sleep."

My stomach twists. He broke up with me… because of this? A nightmare? I shake my head. "Ran, dreams aren't real. They don't define you. They don't mean—"

"In January," he says, "Rashana came back." His voice sharpens, like he's bracing for impact. "I told her I wouldn't talk to her. I should've left it at that. I should've left it alone. I should've walked away."

"But you didn't," I say softly.

He shakes his head. "No. I asked her about my mom's sister."

My heart tightens.

"What did she tell you?" I ask, even though I already know that whatever it was, it's about to destroy him all over again.

Ronan presses his lips together. His whole face contorts like he's trying to physically contain the pain. He closes his eyes, just for a second. "My grandfather killed her."

I stagger back a step, like his words are a punch to my chest. "Oh my god," I whisper. "Ran…"

"She was only days old, baby," he croaks. I don't protest his use of his nickname for me, much like I didn't protest it yesterday. "She was in my grandmother's arms when my grandfather pushed my grandmother down the stairs. Always those fucking stairs…" He wipes a hand across his face, muffling the sound of his sob.

"Did your grandfather get arrested?"

This is more horrific than I ever would have thought.

Ronan shakes his head. "No. When my grandma got to the hospital with my aunt, she said she tripped and fell down the stairs with her baby in her arms. They lived in a small community; people were already aware of my grandfather's temper. The cops were suspicious enough to look into things, but my grandfather was chummy with the chief of police. Nothing ever came of it, just like nothing ever came of any of the other shit he probably did to my mom, and her brother, and his wife…" He sighs heavily.

I have no words. All I'm able to whisper is his name as I reach for him, desperate for some physical contact.

He blinks his watery eyes at me. "I broke up with you because I was scared of becoming like them, like my mom and grandfather. Of turning into someone who could destroy his family. If there's even a fraction of them in me, then I'd rather rip my heart out than risk ever hurting you."

I nod, but he speaks before I can say anything. I let him. It's so rare that he opens up like that, I'll be damned if I cut him off now.

"It kept simmering under my skin. That fear. And then, it's like you made the decision for me. You did what my mother had always told me you would do: figure out that I'm not good enough for you. And even though you never said the words, when you kissed that guy—"

I flinch. "No. Ran, no. That's not what happened. I never, not for one second, thought you weren't good enough for me." I swallow, then meet his eyes. "I was just… afraid. All the time. Of losing you."

I press a fist to my chest, like I can keep everything from spilling out. But the words come anyway.

"You're the best thing that's ever happened to me. But somewhere along the way, I started thinking that if something went wrong, it was my fault. That I missed something. That if I just paid more attention, stayed perfectly in tune with everyone around me, I could stop bad things from happening. That if I upset you, you'd leave."

My voice breaks. "I didn't understand why you shut down. Why you wouldn't talk to me about your grandma, or Rashana, or Randi. I didn't know how to read that silence. And instead of asking, I let fear fill in the blanks."

Ronan's mouth opens, but I cut him off gently.

"And yeah, I didn't understand your relationship with Randi. I thought she was a threat. But I didn't talk to you about it because I was scared you'd see me as jealous or insecure and walk away. Even small things, like not getting a key to your apartment right away, felt huge to me."

His eyebrows lift, like *that's* the thing that makes no sense.

"Tori and Vada always told me to just talk to you, that it was okay to ruffle your feathers once in a while, but I was so scared of it turning out bad. I know now that arguing doesn't mean it's the end. I get that. I do. Just like *you* have to get that feeling big things, being angry, doesn't make you dangerous. I mean, you have every right to be angry—at the whole damn world! That doesn't mean you'll turn into a monster."

I move my hand to his cheek, giving in to my need to touch him, to feel his skin against mine.

"I guess, in a way, we both still have some healing to do."

He nods. "I guess we do."

"Yeah," I breathe. "So... what do we do now? Now that we know how fucked up we still are?"

He draws in a deep breath, voice rough. "That's up to you. I told you yesterday, my job was to tell you the truth. The rest... that's yours," he says. "I'm not here to beg you to take me back. Do I wish you would? Abso-fucking-lutely. But it has to be your decision. It has to be what you *want*, Cat. Because here's the thing, I still don't want kids. And I don't know that I ever will, that I'll ever trust myself enough. And I *know* I messed up. I don't expect you to forgive me. I don't expect you to adjust your life around me. I don't expect you to trust me again. Not after... not after keeping so much from you. Not after sleeping with Randi. If I've learned anything in my life, it's that my actions have consequences. All I can do now is try to make it up to you."

I start to speak, but he lifts a hand, his index finger brushing gently against my lips.

"Before you answer," he says, eyes filled with quiet resolve, "I need you to know one more thing."

I still.

"I've been yours, Cat. This whole time. Even over the last few months. Even on Friday. Even when I was with Randi." He says it with weight, with meaning. "I've been yours. And if you'll let me, I'll be yours until my last damn breath. All yours. All in. All the time."

A breath. A heartbeat.

That's all it takes for me to fling myself into Ronan's arms and cling to him like it could somehow make up for the sixty-three days I had to live without him.

"And I'm yours, Ran," I manage to choke out. "I love you."

Yes, we have work to do. Both of us. And I'm sure we'll fall short sometimes. After all, it took a lifetime to build the walls, to harden into these habits, these patterns of silence and fear and self-protection.

But for once, we're not standing on opposite sides of those walls. This time, we're choosing to tear them down. Together.

Ronan takes a minuscule step back from me, his face serious, eyes searching mine like he doesn't quite trust the peace. "Wait... so... you'll... you'll take me back?"

I nod, a slow smile curving my lips. "Yeah. Unless you don't want me to," I tease gently.

He scoffs. "Fuck, Cat, there's nothing I want *more* than this. I guess... I mean, I don't want to jinx myself, but I honestly didn't think you'd let me off the hook this quickly."

"What, like you expected punishment?" I say, grinning. Then I freeze, my hand flying to my mouth. That joke was in bad taste considering Ronan's past.

But he nods. "Yeah, actually, I kind of did." He seems completely nonplussed by my dumb comment. "But then again, I should've known better—you don't have a mean bone in your perfect body, baby."

"That's what you think."

Before I can stop myself, before I even think better of it, I lunge forward and shove him. I put every ounce of strength into moving his solidly muscled body. He topples off the dock, disappearing into the lake with a satisfying splash.

The second my hands leave his chest, I regret it. It's early April; the temperature's barely cracking the mid-fifties. That water has to be freezing. And deep, judging by how long it takes for Ronan's head to reemerge.

The water makes his hair and skin glisten. "Holy fuck, that's cold," he sputters, teeth chattering as he swims to the edge of the dock. "I take back what I said about you not having a mean streak. *Fuck.*"

He reaches for the ledge and tries to hoist himself out, but his hands slip off the planks. His muscles must be seizing from the cold, and his waterlogged clothes probably add thirty pounds of drag.

"Oh god, Ran, I'm so sorry." I drop to all fours, reaching out to him. "I don't know what came over me. That was so messed up."

He grabs my hand—shivering more violently still, his skin already icy—and I try to pull him up.

But there's resistance. My eyes dart to his, and that's when I see it. That gleam in his eyes. The ghost of a smirk on his lips. Before I can react, he yanks me forward. I let out a yelp and plunge straight into the lake beside him.

I surface with a gasp, hair plastered to my face, my mouth full of lake water.

"O-ohh m-my g-god." I'm shivering so hard, my teeth sound like a jackhammer. "T-this is e-even w-worse than I th-thought."

"Yeah," he chuffs, grabbing onto the dock again. I grimace at how easily he pulls himself up and out. He totally faked it before. I should've known. I've seen him do countless pull-ups in the damn gym with a forty-five-pound plate strapped to his waist with a chain.

He drops to his knees and hoists me out of the water like I weigh nothing, like I'm made of air and feathers. We stand there, arms wrapped around ourselves in a sad attempt to retain whatever body heat we have left.

"W-what d-did you d-do th-that f-f-for?" I stammer, teeth chattering.

He grins, though his lips are already suspiciously blue. "You deserved to be punished, too," he says, his entire body shaking. "I wasn't the only one who strayed."

Fair point. Plus, I shoved him in first. What do they always say—don't dish it out if you can't take it?

"Y-yeah, o-okay. I g-guess I d-did." I'm so cold, it hurts.

"Come here." He tugs me toward him, then begins to pull off my jacket.

"What are you doing?"

"We need to get out of these clothes or we'll become hypothermic." He shrugs off his own jacket with effort, then peels off his hoodie and t-shirt like a second skin.

Even though I'm freezing and shaking, the sight of Ronan undressing—muscles taut, skin slick and covered in goosebumps—sends heat straight through me. He pauses, raising his eyebrows with a breathless chuckle. "You, too."

I drag my eyes away as he starts unbuttoning his jeans. I can't let myself get hypnotized while my body temp plummets. I work myself out of my clothes until I'm down to just my underwear.

"Now what?" I ask, shifting my weight from foot to foot.

Ronan's gaze sweeps over me, slow and hungry, a grin curling his lips. His tongue skims across his bottom lip when his eyes settle on my chest. I don't need to look down to know my nipples are stiff beneath the thin fabric of my bra.

I raise my brows, smiling. "Was this your plan all along?"

"Hey, you pushed me in first. But I'm definitely not complaining about where this has led us so far." He grins, collecting our soaked clothes. "Come on, let's get in the truck."

It's not much warmer inside, but as soon as Ronan slides into the driver's seat and tosses the clothes in the back, he reaches behind the seat and pulls out a blanket. I sigh when he drapes it over me.

"Thank you." The words come out as a breathy moan, and his grin widens as he turns the key in the ignition. He turns the heat to high.

"God damn it, it's fucking cold," he mutters, holding his hands to the vent. It blasts nothing but arctic air. It'll be a few minutes before the engine warms up enough to do any good.

He shifts toward me. "You know what really helps in these situations?"

"What's that?" I breathe, though I already know. It's written all over his face.

The smile is gone. In its place is something raw and hungry, like he's starving and I'm the only thing he's ever wanted to taste.

"Body heat," he murmurs, voice low and rough.

And then I'm on the other side of the center console, in his lap, straddling his hips, grinding against him. There's no word, no signal, no decision. It's just instinct.

His mouth crashes into mine, desperate, feral. No hesitation. Just need. Our teeth clash, tongues tangle.

He unhooks my bra, slips the straps off my shoulders, then moves his tongue to my nipple—pebbled with cold and lust—and draws it deep into his warm mouth. My skin is already so sensitive, and the contrast between the icy air and his hot mouth threatens to take me over the edge right now.

I moan and let my head fall back, bowing toward him, my body already aching, already begging.

And god, he's hard. So hard. I roll my hips, seeking friction against my tender, throbbing clit. He groans as his hands find my waist, my hips, my ass, like he can't touch enough of me fast enough.

The cabin is cramped, but somehow, Ronan shifts me back a few inches, my spine grazing the cold steering wheel. I barely register it. He spreads his legs, coaxing mine apart, until I open to him completely.

His green eyes are glossy, pupils blown wide with need when he glides his hand between my thighs. He pushes my lace panties aside, then drags a finger softly across my slick, aching flesh.

Breathy moans tumble from my lips as he does it again. And again. Then his finger dips lower and slides inside me.

"Ran," I gasp, my muscles clenching around him. I need more. Deeper, harder, now.

He releases a sound that's somewhere between a sigh and a growl. "Fuck, baby," he breathes, sliding his finger out of me. "You're already so wet for me." And then, watching me the entire time, he lifts that hand to his mouth and licks his finger clean, slow and deliberate, like he's savoring the last bite of dessert.

My whole body pulses in response, heat coiling in my core. The ache between my legs demands release.

"Ran," I breathe. "If I don't get to have you right now, I might actually die."

I can't take another second without him inside me. Not with the way he's looking at me. Not with the way my body is buzzing with need.

I shift my weight, lift up just enough to hook my thumbs into the waistband of my panties, then somehow manage to wriggle them down my thighs. They're soaked. And not from the lake.

Ronan's jaw flexes, eyes locked on me like he's barely holding himself together. "Fuck," he says under his breath, then shoves his boxers down just enough to free his erection. The sight of it makes my mouth water. He's thick, and long, and so hard.

We don't speak. We don't need to.

I rise up on my knees and grip his shoulders for balance while his hands find my hips, anchoring me. I line myself up, his body heat seeping into my skin.

And then I sink down slowly.

The second he begins to slip into me, relief rips through me like lightning. I gasp as he fills me, stretches me, every rock-hard inch of him sliding home with perfect, aching pressure. My head drops forward, forehead pressed to his, our breaths ragged and trembling.

"Fuck," he groans again, like it's the only word remaining in his vocabulary, the only word powerful enough for this moment.

We move in tandem. It's not soft. It's not slow. We're not here to take our time. We're wild and frantic and grasping. My hips rise and fall in a desperate rhythm, and he meets every thrust with one of his own, each one deeper, harder. His hands dig into my hips while mine tangle in his wet hair.

Our mouths find each other again, messy and uncoordinated, more teeth than lips, more panting than kissing.

I arch my back and brace one hand on his chest, then drag my nails down his pecs, leaving angry red trails in their wake.

Ronan sucks a sharp breath in through his teeth. I freeze, worried I hurt him. But then he thrusts into me harder, his jaw clenched tight, eyes blown wide and locked on mine like I've just lit him on fire.

Oh. I didn't hurt him. I drove him wild.

He slams his hips up and into me again, harder than before, and I gasp, letting my head fall back as my body tightens, barreling toward the edge. I do it again. I drag my nails down his shoulders this time, and he groans, deep and guttural, his grip bruising my hips as he pounds into me like he's chasing something primal.

Every rock of his hips drives me closer to release. I claw at his biceps, somehow trying to ground myself in his skin. "Don't stop," I mewl. "Please, don't stop!"

"I couldn't if I tried," he groans, his voice raw and raspy. "You feel so fucking good."

Every inch of me is on fire with pleasure. He's everywhere. Under me. Around me. Inside me. My thighs start to shake, my body clinging to his with each thrust.

And then I shatter. "Ran," I cry out as my orgasm crashes over me like a tidal wave, relentless, all-consuming. I seize around him, tightening, pulsing with ecstasy.

He buries his face against my neck, groaning as he thrusts twice, three more times before his breath stutters to a halt and he, too, comes, hips jerking, body shuddering under mine.

We don't move. Not for a long moment. Just panting, shaking, skin to skin, Ronan still inside me, his lips pressed to my collarbone.

Somewhere in the haze, I realize the heater must've kicked in. I'm distantly aware of warm air blowing against my back, and for the first time since last night, I'm not cold.

Ronan shifts just enough to meet my eyes. There's a slow, sated smile on his lips. "Well," he murmurs, "I think we've officially beat the hypothermia."

I giggle, breathless. "Yeah. I think we're safe." But my face falls. "From the hypothermia, at least. What are we gonna do when we get back to the ranch?" I fret. Our clothes are drenched. As it stands, I'll have to sneak into the house dressed in a blanket while Ronan sports only his wet boxers. Not exactly subtle.

He raises a brow. "Think we can pass this off as another near-death experience?"

Ronan

We drive back to the ranch, Cat wrapped in the blanket like a delicious burrito, curled in the passenger seat with her legs tucked beneath her, hair still damp, cheeks flushed. And me? I'm driving barefoot, half-naked, wearing nothing but a pair of wet boxers and a damn grin that probably screams I'm fucking floating on cloud nine. Cat and I have found our way back to each other, and we just had frantic, chaotic, mind-blowing sex. What more could I want?

I keep having to blast the damn heat. First the windows fogged up with our damn panting, and now it keeps misting over with damp body heat.

"Oh my gosh, Ran, I'm so sorry," Cat says with a gasp.

I glance over at her, not sure what she's apologizing for. The foggy windows?

She grazes a finger over my chest. It's only then I register the sting, the rawness. I glance down and *yep*. Four angry red scratches rake across my chest, breaking the skin.

"I didn't mean—"

"I fucking loved it," I say, somewhat dismayed. "Sometimes I wonder if there's something wrong with me that I enjoy pain like this."

It's still something I'm figuring out about myself—that a little pain mixed in with pleasure actually does it for me. Not too much. Just enough to heighten everything. Still, it feels... off. Like I should be the last person on earth to get off on pain. But I punish my body in the gym almost daily, chase soreness like a badge of honor, run on empty like it's a competition. So maybe it tracks that getting absolutely fucking feral when Cat scratches the shit out of me feels... right.

She moves her hand to my cheek, brushing a thumb over my bottom lip. My eyes threaten to close with the tenderness of her touch. "There's nothing wrong with you," she says. "I think a lot of people enjoy a little pain during sex, right?"

She lifts her eyebrows in a way that makes me think her question isn't purely rhetorical.

"Yeah, but a lot of people didn't get the life beaten out of them by their mother growing up," I say. "You'd think I'd forever avoid anything even remotely painful. Turns out it's a huge fucking turn-on for me." I make a face. Maybe I need to unpack this with my therapist. *Hey Doc, guess what, turns out my mommy issues go way deeper than we originally thought.*

"Hey, don't be so hard on yourself. You're overthinking this. Just allow yourself to enjoy what you enjoy." She leans over the center console and presses a kiss to my cheek. The soft warmth of her lips makes my chest ache. I missed this. I missed *her*. Touching her without having to second-guess it. Not being allowed to hold her felt like having one hand cut off.

"What happened between us a few minutes ago, that wasn't anything like what your mom did to you. I didn't do it to hurt you." She pauses, eyes flicking to my chest, cheeks going pink. "It just felt necessary in the moment. I was so, so turned on." Her voice drops into something breathy, dangerous. If she keeps talking like that, I might have to pull the truck over again.

"And… it turned you on, too, right?" she asks, her voice laced with vulnerability.

I chuckle. "Obviously. You couldn't tell?" Jesus, it flipped a damn switch. When her nails dug in, all the rational parts of my brain just… *poof.* I wasn't thinking. I was feeling. Moving. Needing.

Her cheeks turn a deeper shade of pink and I swear her whole face follows suit. Her nose, her ears, her forehead. I know she hates it, but I happen to enjoy the crap out of it.

"I could," she says, nodding. Then, more quietly, "I think… I think I like it a little bit rougher, too."

"Yeah, I know."

She blinks at me in surprise. "Really? How?"

I shrug. "Because of the way your body reacts when I go hard. Like, *hard.* I thought I was hurting you earlier. I almost pulled back, but then I realized you were about to come, so I doubled down. And, fuck," I groan, shifting slightly behind the steering wheel. "Nothing gets me there faster than watching you lose yourself to me. You're so fucking hot."

She sinks back into her seat, smiling with a quiet satisfaction.

"But baby?" I say, drawing her eyes back to me. "You have to promise me something, okay?"

She nods, her lips plump, pink, slightly parted. I want to stare at them, want them wrapped around… *Jesus. Focus, Ran!*

"If I ever hurt you in a way you don't want… I mean, like, if I ever lash out at you—if there's even a hint that I might snap—you walk. You walk away and you don't look back. You don't give me another chance. You don't forgive me. You don't take me back, okay?"

She searches my eyes for a long moment. I know she understands what I'm asking, what I'm getting at. I'm not talking about rough sex. I'm talking about abuse, the kind of shit my grandfather did to his family, what Adam did to Cat, what my mother did to me.

She nods, slow and serious. "I promise," she breathes.

I nod once, exhaling deeply. *Enough heavy shit for now.*

We turn the last bend before the main house comes into view. I can't help but laugh. We're half-naked. Soaked. Disheveled. Cat's hair looks like it's been through a hurricane and back, and I've got claw marks down my chest like a wild animal attacked me. Which, technically, checks out. Immediately, my stupid brain comes up with at least ten different wildcat jokes. But now's not the time.

I don't have much hope that we'll be able to sneak into the house unseen, not with my grandmother's weird-ass ESP and the fact that it's just about time for dinner. My grandma is nothing if not punctual. I bet everyone's already gathering at the dining table. Cat and I better use the next thirty seconds to come up with a solid alibi before we walk into the lion's den. Or, more accurately… the wildcat den. *See what I mean?*

Of course, the second Cat and I walk through the door, all conversation cuts out like someone pressed the mute button on a remote. I-don't-know-how-many sets of eyes flicker to us. Jesus Christ, *everyone's* here. Penny's whole family. Cat's parents. Thomas and Elias. Even my baby brothers look judgmental.

Miranda's eyes go wide, her mouth forming an *O.* My brother lets out a snort he barely manages to turn into a cough, and Shane crosses his arms in front of his chest while giving me an approving *hell yeah* nod. Clearly, no one thinks this was remotely accidental.

"What in the *world*?" Cat's dad barks, his voice slicing through the silence. His face contorts like he just bit into something sour. That man has *never* liked me, and walking in soaked and half-naked with his daughter swaddled in a blanket isn't doing much to give him the warm fuzzies.

"Ronan," my grandma says, gentler but firm. She takes the dripping pile of clothes from my hands and disappears into the laundry room, returning a moment later with sweatpants and a clean shirt. She shoves them into my arms like she expects an immediate explanation.

This is the part I've always hated—when my body thinks I'm about to be punished. My heart's pounding, my breathing is quick, and my muscles are tight. My grandma would never hurt me, but try convincing my nervous system of that.

I can't speak. Can't remember the story we rehearsed in the truck. But Cat can.

"Ran showed me the lake," she says, calm and clear. "I tripped on one of the planks and fell into the water. He had to get in to pull me out."

My dad raises an eyebrow, smirking. Yeah, he's not buying it. Not for a second.

"Gosh, those scratches," my grandma mutters, her eyes darting to my chest.

Quickly, I pull the shirt over my head and step into my sweats.

"They're my fault," Cat adds, her voice tight, almost shaking like she's on the verge of tears. "I panicked. I thought I was going to drown." Her performance is fucking flawless. If I didn't know the truth, I'd believe her.

"Oh no, Kitty, that water must have been freezing," Jen says, her voice thick with concern.

I almost feel bad for lying. *Almost.*

My grandma exhales deeply. "Good call getting out of those clothes," she says. "Your body temperatures would have dropped to a dangerous level fast. Stevie broke through the ice once when he was three. Perry and Thomas got him out, but he was already showing signs of hypothermia."

"Oh my god," Penny gasps. "What happened?"

"Well, he and Ran were playing on the ice, even though we'd told them not to. They were little. You underestimate how thin it is. Stevie broke through. You'd think you could just toss him in a hot bath, but no, you've gotta warm up the body slowly. First, get out of the wet clothes. Then wrap up," she says, gesturing toward Cat's blanket. "Warm drinks help. Or movement. Even body heat."

"Body heat," Miranda repeats under her breath, and I don't miss the smirk. Neither does my brother. Shane's trying so hard not to laugh.

I throw a warning look at them. They're going to give us away if they keep this shit up.

"Yeah," Cat says brightly, like it's the most obvious thing in the world. "That's what Ran said. Got me out, told me to get out of my clothes, gave me the blanket, cranked the heat in the truck, then drove us straight back."

Savage. Badass. Always swooping in to save my undeserving ass.

***

Cat and I make our way upstairs. She showers. I change.

Dinner is awkward as hell. No one outright says anything, but the sidelong glances and half-smothered grins from Tori, Shane, my brother, and Miranda are relentless. Shane keeps raising his eyebrows at me every time we make eye contact, like he's waiting for me to tell him Cat and I finally made up. Miranda sends me a text from under the table with only a cat and a fire emoji. And Cat's dad doesn't take his damn eyes off me the entire meal, like he's waiting for me to fuck up so he can finally lay into me like I know he's simmering to do.

But Cat plays it cool. Calm and steady. She may not know it, but she's always been the brave one.

Eventually the table gets cleared, and one by one everyone turns in for the night. I take a long, hot shower, then wait long enough for the house to settle into the kind of quiet that tells me everyone's asleep, that it's safe for me to slip out of my room and into Cat's.

She's already curled up underneath her blanket. The way she smiles at me, not even a hint of surprise on her face when I tip-toe in, tells me she knew I'd come.

We don't say anything. I just crawl into bed beside her, kiss her slow, and start worshipping her body like I have all the damn time in the world. I make love to her—soft and gentle this time. Patient. Like she's something precious. Because she is.

And then I do it again. And again. All night.

No rush. No panic. No frenzy. Just us, and the aching kind of love I've felt for her since the moment I first laid eyes on her.

Tuesday, April 4th

Cat

A loud bang startles me awake, though not hard enough to wipe the smile off my face at the sight of Ronan still sleeping beside me.

He snuck into my room again last night, just like he did the night before—the night after we finally found our way back to each other.

Yesterday, we broke the news of our reconciliation to our friends and families. Some of them reacted like it wasn't news at all. Others pulled us into excited hugs. My dad muttered something dismissive under his breath before managing a half-hearted, "I'm happy for you, Kitty."

After that, Ronan and I spent the day getting busy. Him with ranch duties, me with the final wedding setup for the big day today. The women spent the afternoon setting up chairs and tables, attaching flowers to the little arch where Penny and Frank will exchange vows, and outfitted the barn for the reception with the kind of rustic charm you only ever see in country wedding magazine spreads.

Penny, her sister Piper, my mom, and Ronan's aunt Erin did a lot of clapping and giggling, while Tori, Miranda, Riley, and I mostly exchanged eye rolls and headshakes. Still, I have to admit, their giddy excitement is kind of contagious.

And not just that. Last night at dinner, a random image of my own wedding to Ronan drifted into my head. I let myself sit with it for a moment, allowed myself to look years into the future. I didn't even try to fight the butterflies that came with it. I only snapped out of it when Tori leaned over and asked what was up with the "mushy smile" on my face.

Now, in the quiet of early morning, I lie there watching Ronan sleep. His features are completely relaxed—softer than I ever get to see them when he's awake. The usual seriousness, that subtle tension he carries like he's always bracing for the next shoe to drop, is gone. In sleep, he looks vulnerable. Lighter. Like some part of him still remembers, even unconsciously, what it's like to be unafraid. I know this softness will vanish the moment he wakes up, so I drink it in while I can.

I let my eyes roll over his face—his strong brow, symmetrical nose, soft, full lips. That scar under and around his left eye is so light now, though still visible. It'll never truly fade. A permanent reminder of the war he's fought. But I don't dwell on it. Instead, I let my gaze wander lower, across the lines of his bare chest and stomach. I have an immediate urge to run my fingers over the ridges of his abs. The dull but delicious ache between my thighs reminds me how many times over the past thirty-six hours I've already gotten to enjoy his body, how often we've had sex. I'm sore, yes, but not so much that I don't want him again. We have months to make up for, after all.

I almost give in, too, but Saoirse's voice chimes through the house, loud and clear like the matriarch she is. "Breakfast is ready!"

Ronan's eyes blink open, still heavy with sleep. But the second our eyes meet, he smiles.

We wait a few minutes, listening for footsteps, voices, the scrape of chairs. Once the coast is clear, Ronan slips out of my room without a sound. I take my time getting dressed. By the time I join everyone at the table, Ronan's already in his usual spot, his damp hair suggesting a quick shower, like he's been up for hours.

If we thought we were good at sneaking around, we were obviously wrong.

After breakfast, just before heading to his dad's cabin to get ready for the wedding, Ronan pops his head into my room.

"So, your mom and my dad apparently came to wake us up this morning," he says, that familiar mischievous gleam in his green eyes. "My dad couldn't find me in my room. Your mom found me in yours."

I gasp. "Oh, no."

Ronan chuckles, unfazed. "Yeah. I just got an earful about being more careful if I want to keep paying you nightly visits. Apparently your dad and my grandma wouldn't like the thought of us in the same bed."

I huff. "They can't seriously believe we're not *sleeping* together."

"Oh, they absolutely do," he says, frowning. "As far as they're concerned, we're both untouched virgins. Anyway, note to self: set an alarm tomorrow." He winks before disappearing off to join the guys while the women get ready in the main house.

***

We spend the next couple of hours helping each other get ready. I unzip the garment bag to reveal a silk, tea-length dress in the most perfect ocean blue. It fits like it was made for me, the fabric soft against my skin. The photographer flits around, capturing moments here and there, until a soft knock at the front door lets us know it's time. Penny's dad enters, his eyes instantly teary at the sight of his daughter in her wedding gown.

"Alright, everyone, let's head out," my mom—Penny's maid of honor—calls, and we all step outside to make the short walk. The ceremony is set just beyond the barn, in an open green field under a wide Montana sky. We line up inside it, just out of sight of Frank, who's already waiting.

My face lights up as soon as I spot Ronan. He's standing with his brother and Shane, all three of them in tailored suits. But it's Ronan I can't look away from. As if he can sense me, he turns and his eyes find mine.

"Baby," he breathes, stepping toward me and holding out his hand. "You're stunning."

I blush. Because of course I do. "Thank you. You clean up nice, too."

He's never looked more handsome—fitted black suit, crisp white dress shirt, and a bow tie that somehow doesn't look out of place on him.

"I love the bow tie," I say with a grin.

He groans softly. "Glad someone does. I feel like a penguin," he says, tugging at it like it's cutting off airflow.

"Well, I like penguins."

"I'm aware," he chuckles. "But usually the cutesy type."

"True." I laugh, brushing a kiss to his lips.

"Knock it off, you two," my mom calls, stepping up beside us with Steve, Shane's dad, and Penny's sister. "Time to line up."

We wait for Miranda to start singing. Ronan looks over at me, his eyes bright.

"Ready?" he whispers.

I nod, taking his hand. Together we walk down the aisle, flanked by just our closest friends and family. Miranda's voice floats through the air as she sings, her guitar soft and soulful. The mountains loom in the distance, still snow-capped despite the sun, completing the breathtaking scene. It's like a fairy tale.

I take it all in as we follow Penny's sister, Piper, who's paired with Steve, and then my mom and Seamus in the front. At the head of the aisle stands a beautiful arch, draped with flowers and greenery. Frank waits beneath it, looking sharp in his suit, next to his dad, who's officiating.

I glance at Ronan beside me, and then it strikes me that I could see myself getting married here one day.

At the end of the aisle, Ronan kisses my cheek before we part and take our places opposite each other. Miranda transitions into a new melody, and everyone stands as Penny walks down the aisle on her father's arm. She looks beautiful. Ivory silk dress, intricate lace veil, and a bouquet of warm-colored roses in her hands.

I glance at Frank. He looks absolutely wrecked, in the best way imaginable. His love for her is written all over his face.

Perry begins the ceremony with words about choosing to love each other not just in the easy moments, but through hardship and trial. Sniffles echo through the crowd, my mom dabbing at her eyes. *Good thing she's wearing waterproof mascara.*

Frank's voice cracks as he delivers his vows. "You love my boys like they're yours. I wish they had been. Things would've been better if they'd had you as a mother growing up." He pauses, eyes bright. "Thank you for loving us through our messes. And thank you for blessing me with two more boys. Can't have too much Soult testosterone walking the earth."

Penny laughs through her tears. "That was all you, baby. I just baked them."

She reads her vows next, and to everyone's surprise, Frank actually cries. He's usually so composed, so sure of himself, and seeing him so in love, so overcome by emotion is really sweet.

They exchange rings, simple silver bands, and share their first kiss as husband and wife.

Photos follow, all joy and celebration. Ronan refuses to let go of me as we head into the barn for the reception. A small dance floor is set at the center surrounded by round tables and flickering candles.

"God, this turned out so beautiful," I say to Saoirse as she gives the caterers a few final instructions.

"It did, didn't it?" she says with a twinkle in her eye. "Erin and I wanted to make sure this wedding gave Penny everything she had hoped for. Frankie's first wedding was... forgettable," she says meaningfully. "Small church ceremony and a quick dinner. This one had to be the opposite."

"Love, where's the wine?" Perry calls out as he joins us.

"Oh, still in the house, I think. And the whiskey too."

"I'll grab it," Ronan says. He looks at me. "Want to help?"

"Sure," I say.

"There are a few cases," Perry says. "You might want to bring the truck."

Ronan nods, then motions over his torso. "Nobody minds if I change out of this thing now that the ceremony is over, right?"

"But baby boy, you look so handsome," his grandma says.

"What are you saying, Morai? I don't look handsome in jeans?" he challenges with a chuckle. Before his grandma can respond, Ronan's already pulling me out of the barn with him.

Ronan

Man, what an incredible feeling it is to be on the ranch with Cat by my side, her hand in mine. She looks incredible in her blue silk dress, her hair up, her delicate neck exposed. Her minimal makeup gives her face a glowy hue and beautifully accentuates her hazel eyes. Perfect is honestly not a strong enough word to describe her.

I kept looking at her during the whole ceremony, completely distracted. I barely heard what my dad and Penny said. All I could think about was how much I want to stand at that altar with her one day. For once, that future doesn't feel impossible. It feels like something I might actually get to have. Something safe. Something real.

The house is quiet when we get inside. Everyone's still outside, the reception buzzing in the distance. I shrug off my jacket, moving into the kitchen where I spot the stacks of wine cases lined up by the kitchen counter.

"I'm gonna change out of this thing real quick before we load the truck," I say, tugging at my collar. I've never been a fan of dress clothes. Too stiff, too formal. Give me a t-shirt and jeans any day.

"Aww, but I love you in this," Cat says, pouting.

I raise an eyebrow at her. "You do?"

"I do," she says, eyes sparkling. "You look so damn good in a suit. Your grandma's right: very handsome. Especially with the bow tie."

"Well, I hate it," I say, loosening it.

"Okay, I guess. If you're really tired of wearing it, then maybe I can help you change out of it," she says with a gleam in her eyes.

Oh, interesting.

I grin, leaning back against the kitchen counter. "Oh yeah?"

"Uh-huh." Her fingers move to my belt, unfastening it, and I let her. I let her take whatever she wants. Pretty sure we could be in the middle of an apocalypse and I'd still be standing right here, wanting her more than I've ever wanted anything in my life.

I slide my hands around her waist, resting them on her lower back. I draw her into me, kissing her deeply, tasting her like I've been starving. She answers with a soft moan, her lips hungry against mine. Cat unbuttons my pants, then lowers the zipper. I pull back, head already spinning. I'm not too far gone to remember we're in the kitchen. I don't think this is the best place for what she seems to want. Before I can say anything, she presses herself against me, her mouth claiming mine again.

Her hand slips inside my pants, sliding past the waistband of my boxers, and then—fuck—she wraps her fingers around my cock. Warm. Firm. Perfect. She strokes me with maddening control, her rhythm unhurried, confident. Not gonna lie, this forwardness is new, surprising, and definitely not something I'm going to complain about.

I groan into her mouth, my hips responding on their own, seeking that tight friction. I guess I could make it quick, take her right here against the counter and pray no one walks in. We don't exactly have great luck when it comes to timing. Jesus, I would die if my grandmother walked in right now. Although, the risk almost makes it hotter.

Or maybe I should drag her into that tiny bathroom off the mudroom, press her up against the wall, and give her exactly what she's asking for.

Cat pushes my pants and boxers down just enough to free my cock, and after that, thought becomes impossible. I guess the kitchen's it. I'm throbbing in her grip, aching for her, desperate to be inside her. She tightens her fist, and I kiss her like she's the air I need to breathe.

No time to waste.

I slide my hands up her back, reaching for the zipper of her dress, eager to peel it off her, to let the silky fabric fall off her delicious body and pool at her ankles. But she shifts. I blink in surprise just as she begins to sink to her knees in front of me, steady, deliberate.

Holy fuck.

"What are you..." I pant, breathing hectic with anticipation. Her face is level with my cock, her hazel eyes wide, turned up at me, glowing with mischief and something deeper.

"You always take care of me," she murmurs. "It's about time I take care of you." She parts her lips and takes me into her warm, wet mouth.

"Fuck," I groan, clutching the edge of the counter.

Her tongue swirls over my tip, slow and teasing, before she sucks—gently at first, then deeper, bolder. Her left hand traces up my stomach, fingers outlining my abs, and her right wraps around the base of my cock, stroking in perfect rhythm with her mouth.

I choke on a breath as she drags her teeth down my shaft—not enough to hurt, just enough to make me jolt, my hips bucking involuntarily. I lock my knees, fighting to stay in control, resisting the primal urge to thrust into her mouth.

I slam my eyes shut and focus on her. On the heat, the wet, the rhythm. My hand finds her hair, threading through the strands, guiding her gently, not pushing, just needing to touch her. Do I care that I might be ruining her up-do? Maybe a little. Enough to urge her to stop? Fuck no.

She takes me deeper, until she gags—just once—then pulls back slightly. I look down at her, dazed, breathing hard. "Relax your throat, baby," I whisper, and she does. She swallows me again, deeper this time, and my stomach tightens. I can feel it—the pressure building, pleasure swirling.

"Shit," I breathe, head tipping back as her hand grips my ass, squeezing, steadying me while her mouth works me faster. Her tongue circles, licks, sucks. Her hand joins in again, pumping me with hard, confident strokes.

I can't stay quiet, can't focus on anything but Cat's mouth on my aching, throbbing cock. "God, fuck," I moan, the sound tearing out of me. She's relentless. Perfect. Every movement, every flick of her tongue, every pull of her lips tightens the coil inside me. I'm wound up, chasing it now—my climax.

I'm breathing hard, trying to hold on, but she moans around me and it zaps through my entire body like live-wire electricity. I grit my teeth, my body shuddering, not because it's cold, but because of the way she owns me in this exact moment.

"Baby, you need to stop," I groan, struggling to hang on, to keep a straight head, not to come apart right here, in the kitchen, in her mouth. "I'm gonna come, Cat."

She doesn't stop.

I open my eyes, and she's looking up at me, her beautiful hazel eyes locked on mine, full of fire and determination. *Shit, she wants this.* Her lips tighten. Her hand moves faster. She moans again, the vibration of her hum deep and low. It detonates something inside me, fast and brutal, pleasure slamming through my body.

"Fuck, baby," I gasp as I step over the edge, my whole body tensing, muscles coiled, vision blurring. I thrust once, then freeze, a deep groan tearing from my throat as my orgasm crashes over me. I grip the countertop, knuckles white, eyes shut, lost in the void of sex as I release into her mouth, every nerve alight, every thought wiped away.

My body jerks with the aftershocks, every muscle tight as I ride the tail end of it. Cat takes every drop, gently sucking my tip into her mouth like she's savoring me. I'm fucking wrecked. Breathless, dizzy, still gripping the countertop like it's the only thing keeping me solidly on the ground. When I finally look down, Cat's eyes are glowing, her pink lips swollen, and there's a proud, satisfied smile on her face like she just conquered something.

"Jesus, baby," I breathe, another shiver ripping through me as an aftershock hits.

"Did I do okay?" she asks, grinning up at me, clearly fishing for compliments.

"Fuck, you did more than okay," I say, reaching for her, needing her closer now that I can finally breathe again.

With fresh oxygen and blood finally winning the fight against gravity to reach my brain, reality crashes back in like a bucket of cold water. We're still in the damn kitchen. I exhale sharply, reaching down to tug my pants and boxers back up, fast and clumsy, my hands still shaking. My brain's just starting to reboot, the fog lifting enough to remember that anyone could walk in at any second.

Cat doesn't stop smiling, her thumb swiping across her bottom lip like she's wiping away the last traces of… *me*. Jesus, this girl.

"Sorry for coming in your mouth," I say sheepishly. I should have pulled back, should have held on to a little self-control. Instead, I completely lost myself. I quickly grab a bottle of water from the fridge, handing it to her.

"Don't be," she says with a soft, satisfied smile, taking the water from me. "I wanted you to. I wanted to try this. And…" Her cheeks flush pink. "I liked it. Like, a lot."

My eyebrows rise. I don't have much personal experience in the unloading-in-her-mouth department, but the vast majority of stories I've heard have led me to believe most girls don't particularly enjoy it.

"You have no idea how fucking hot that is," I murmur, thinking of the way she looked up at me, her mouth full of me, eyes on fire. "I've never had an orgasm from oral sex before."

Her eyes widen. "Wait... what do you mean?"

"I mean I've never come while getting head. No one's ever taken me all the way like that."

"Oh." There's a flicker of guilt in her expression.

Cat came into our relationship with zero experience, and it's been a hell of a journey—learning each other, figuring it out together. Oral sex has mostly gone one way, and I've never minded. I *love* getting her off with my mouth—how she tastes, how she sounds, how she melts under my tongue. But she's been hesitant to try it herself, always claiming she didn't know what she was doing. Lately though, something's shifted. She's taken more initiative, gotten bolder. Like back in early January, when I woke up to her stroking me, slipping me inside her before I was even fully awake. Fuck, it was hot.

And then I broke it off. Biggest mistake of my life. One I will never make again.

"No one's ever done that for you?" she asks, eyes soft.

I smile. "Nope."

She hesitates. "What about Randi? You guys were together a while... She never...?"

I shake my head. "Not until I came. It was part of foreplay, never the endgame."

Cat's cheeks flush again, but her eyes are shining with pride. "So this was really a first?"

"Total first," I say, smiling. "You gave me that."

Her grin is so bright it lights up the whole damn kitchen.

"So... can I ask what brought this on?" I ask.

She takes a slow sip of water, then shrugs. "I've done a lot of soul-searching these past couple months. And I realized I've been ignoring my own needs—my own *wants*—to keep other people comfortable."

Her words hit me right in the chest. My stomach twists. I never wanted her to feel like she had to sacrifice anything for *me*. The thought that I might've made her feel that way, even unintentionally, makes me sick.

She must see it in my face, because her hand comes up to gently touch the scar under my eye. "Never you, Ran," she says softly. "By the time I met you, those patterns were already in place. But yeah... I've held back. With my thoughts. My feelings. What I wanted."

I nod, drinking in her words like they're oxygen, letting them sink into my bones. "Please don't hold back," I rasp, suddenly choked up. Post-orgasm crash, maybe. Or just *her*.

"I won't," she says. "You promised me you wouldn't. So I won't either."

"Yeah. Deal."

"Deal," she echoes. "And as part of that: what just happened? That was something I've secretly wanted for a while. I wanted to make you come like that. I wanted to feel you *give in* to me, Ran. I love watching you lose control. You're always so careful, so guarded, but when we have sex... you let go. I see it in your eyes, feel it in your body. The way you tense right before, the way you *give* yourself over? I love it. I love *you*," she says, voice low and thick, pupils blown wide.

Her words send a pulse of heat straight through me. My cock stirs, already waking up again. Jesus. There's no end to this.

"Are you sore?" I whisper, my gaze dropping to where her thighs disappear under that dress. We've been at it like animals, and the last thing I want is to push her past pleasure into pain.

"A little," she whimpers. "But I want you. *Now*."

That sounds like consent to me.

"You have me," I say, my voice raw. "You've always had me."

I scoop her up, hands under her ass, and carry her out of the kitchen and into the small bathroom off the mudroom. What I'm about to do to her can't happen out here in the kitchen.

Too risky.

Cat

Yep, I'm definitely sore now. But it's not painful per se. It's a delicious kind of ache, the kind that comes with repeated stimulation, increased blood flow, muscles stretching and clenching again. And again. And again. Still, I'm nowhere near sated—not after months without Ronan—and neither is he, judging by how quickly he came unglued again once he had me perched on the bathroom counter, my ass teetering on the edge, my legs wrapped around his waist as he thrust into me at a steady but relentless pace.

Eventually, though, the sounds of life outside the house pull us back to earth, reminding us we're not alone on this planet. With flushed cheeks and lingering touches, Ronan helps me straighten up, then disappears upstairs to change into jeans and a t-shirt.

Minutes later, after stealing one last kiss, he loads the booze into the truck and we head back to the barn. It's obvious we've been missed.

"Where the hell did you guys go?" Shane asks as Ronan and I make our way back to the reception, where everyone's gathered around the tables waiting for food to be served.

"We picked up the booze and I needed to change," Ronan says simply.

Shane laughs. "I'm honestly shocked you stayed in that suit as long as you did. Do you remember my confirmation? You were so grumpy in your shiny dress shoes."

Ronan chuffs. "They're the worst. In fact, I've got blisters on my heels right now."

"Dude, the moment I saw the shoes Penny picked out for us, I knew she'd never stepped foot on a ranch," Steve says with a throaty chuckle.

"Did you guys say anything?" Tori asks.

"Fuck no. It's Penny's day," Ronan says quickly. "We can suck it up for a few hours."

And that's one of the many reasons I love him.

"Except the first chance you got, you were out of that getup," Miranda says, strolling to the table and dropping into an empty chair beside Steve.

I've got a whole new appreciation for Miranda—since our talk, since Ronan's and my reunion. She's dressed in a flowing periwinkle dress, her hair loose for once instead of in its usual braid, strappy heels dangling from one finger.

"I could say the same for you," Ronan says, nodding at her bare feet stretched gratefully in front of her.

Miranda shrugs. "Do I strike you as a black-dress-and-heels kind of girl?"

"No," Ronan deadpans.

Miranda frowns. "Why does that offend me?"

"I don't know," Ronan says, unfazed. "It shouldn't. I'm not saying you don't look good—I'm saying you're not usually someone who *chooses* to wear what you're wearing right now."

Miranda seems satisfied with that response.

"I happen to think you look absolutely amazing," Tori chimes in, raising her champagne glass toward Miranda in a casual toast.

"I agree," I say, snagging what looks like an orphaned glass and mimicking Tori.

Miranda smiles widely. "Aww."

"Are you going to sing some more after we eat?" I ask.

"Probably," Miranda says with a quick nod.

"Speaking of singing," Shane says, leaning forward on his elbows, suddenly all business. "You're pretty great on stage," he tells Miranda, then grins at Ronan. "You, too, man."

Ronan squints at his best friend like he's trying to detect sarcasm.

"I'm serious, Ran," Shane says, then turns back to Miranda. "Would you ever consider coming to New York and performing?"

Miranda's eyes go wide, jaw dropping. "Fuck yes," she says without hesitation.

"Nice," Shane chuckles. "I don't know if you know this, but Ran and I work together. My parents own a few Irish pubs in the city and I run one of them."

"Murphy's, right?" Miranda asks.

"Yeah." Shane nods, pride lighting his face. "We've had live bands before, but now that I'm really taking over I want to make some changes. Start featuring more up-and-coming acts, especially on weekends. The place is always packed, and I kinda love the idea of giving new talent a shot, you know?"

Miranda's totally locked in now, nodding along with every word.

"You're pretty fucking amazing on stage," Shane says. "You should come out to New York this summer. Play a few gigs at Murphy's."

"Fuck, I'd *totally* love to," Miranda says, her whole face lighting up. But then it dims. "The only problem is, I'm just starting to get back on my feet. Not sure I could swing it. Isn't New York, like, stupid expensive?"

"Well, yeah," Shane says, "but we could figure something out."

"You could stay with the boys at their apartment," Tori says.

Miranda looks at Ronan, clearly seeking his take.

"Where would she sleep, though?" Ronan asks.

Miranda grins. "In bed with you," she says without missing a beat. Honestly, she and Ronan have *such* similar personalities.

"Randi, I like you, so let me put this gently: *the fuck you will*," I say, grinning.

Everyone cracks up.

"Okay," Miranda laughs. "Maybe the couch then?"

"Dang, Ran, two hot chicks fighting over you," Steve says with mock appreciation.

Ronan flicks a nonexistent speck of dirt off his shoulder. "Well, you know, story of my life."

"Seriously," Tori chimes in. "Like those two girls Shane said you went home with in March."

Ronan's and my expressions shift at the same time into matching frowns. *He did what?*

"What the fuck are you talking about?" Ronan asks.

"Oh, come on, Ran," Shane says with a low chuckle. "Remember those two girls at Murphy's? Really hot, totally made it obvious they wanted to take you home?"

Ronan's face doesn't change.

"Dude, you don't remember? They said they lived nearby, gave you their numbers, told you to text if you were up for some fun."

"I remember," Ronan says. "But I didn't hook up with them."

Shane blinks. "The fuck you mean?"

"I didn't meet up with them, Shay," Ronan says, calm but firm. "I went for a fucking walk."

"Come on, Ran..." Shane starts, but trails off.

"I'm serious," Ronan says.

"Ran, it's okay," I say, resting my hand lightly on his chest. It doesn't hurt, not really, not compared to knowing about Miranda. That was the blow.

"Guys, I'm serious. I didn't hook up that night. I got off work and just... walked."

"But you didn't get home till like seven the next morning," Shane says, brow furrowed.

"Yeah, because I got so wasted I passed out on a park bench. Some homeless dude woke me at five-thirty, said I was in his favorite spot. So I walked back to Murphy's, got in my car, and drove home."

"You passed out on a bench?" Miranda asks, incredulous.

"Yeah." Ronan shrugs. "Not my proudest moment. But I was trashed," he says, then turns to me. "Baby, seeing you at Murphy's that night... fuck, it hurt like a bitch. And then Shane said you and Vada were meeting up with those guys. I just wanted to numb myself."

I think of what Miranda told me, how Ronan used to sedate himself with meaningless sex when he was hurting.

"Did I think about hooking up with those two chicks? Yeah," Ronan says, voice low, eyes locked on mine. "But I stood in front of their building with a bottle of Jack in my hand, and all I could think about was you. So I kept walking. Walked until I couldn't anymore. Sat on a bench. Passed out. Honestly? It's kind of a miracle I'm alive."

"Must've been a less sleazy part of town," Shane mutters.

"The universe was looking out for me," Ronan says. "But no, I didn't sleep with them."

"Jesus, you had a shot at a threesome and *didn't* take it?" Steve asks, eyebrows raised.

"Nope," Ronan says, flashing my favorite half-smile.

"That's love right there," Steve says with a nod.

"Ugh, finally!" Shane groans with the arrival of a loaded plate in front of him. Dinner is served, the kind of hearty, comforting meal that hits the spot after a long day. Once everyone's plates are cleared, Frank and Penny cut the cake to cheers and laughter, then share their first dance as husband and wife under the soft glow of string lights before the floor opens up to everyone else.

"Which one of my boys is going to willingly embarrass themselves to dance with me?" Saoirse's voice interrupts the chatter around our table.

Ronan's hand slides around my waist. "Not me. I'm taken," he says with a chuckle.

"So am I," Steve says grumpily, folding his arms in front of his chest.

"Psh, so you've been saying, but you have yet to provide evidence to substantiate your claim," Shane says dryly.

"Ember does sound suspiciously like a made-up name," Ronan says with a nod.

Steve's mouth opens, then shuts again. Abruptly, he stands from his chair. "I'll dance with you, Morai."

"That's what I thought," Ronan mutters with a sly smirk. Steve flips him off while the rest of us laugh.

"Oh, you know what I was thinking? You all should go for a nice trail ride tomorrow," Saoirse says with a decisive nod before she turns her gaze to me. "You've ridden before, right?"

Ronan doesn't miss a single beat. "Oh, she's ridden before," he says, an unmistakable smirk on his face.

"Rony, pretty sure your grandma was talking about horses," Miranda says nonchalantly.

Saoirse's gasp is drowned out by the sputtering and snorting laughs from Shane, Tori, and Steve. I just sit there and wait for the skin to melt off my face.

"You two," Saoirse scolds, her gaze moving between Ronan and Miranda with a huff. "Unbelievable."

"Sorry, Morai, but you set yourself up for that one," he laughs. He turns to me, only to brush his thumb over the apple of my cheek. "I've always loved how easily your face gives you away."

Saoirse exhales deeply, a small smile tugging at her lips. "Can't stay upset with him for long," she says to me, then hooks her arm under Steve's, ready to take the dance floor. But not before turning back to us. "Take Cat for a ride, Ronan!"

"Will do," Ronan says to her with another chuckle.

"A *horseback* ride." Saoirse shakes her head. "Honestly, Ronan."

As Saoirse and Steve head for the dance floor, the rest of us linger at the table, the air still filled with laughter. Eventually Shane and Ronan ask Tori and me to dance.

I spend the rest of the afternoon and evening in Ronan's arms, swaying under the barn's twinkling lights, and for a moment, everything feels soft and golden—like the universe really *is* looking out for us.

Saturday, May 13th

Cat

“Brady and I are officially broken up,” Vada announces loud and proud when she, Summer, Tori, and I take our seats around a rustic picnic table complete with a red-and-white checkered plastic tablecloth.

The four of us have officially survived our freshman year of college. Summer, Zack, and Vada are back home in New York. We’re buzzing with giddy excitement. It’s the first time we’ve been together in months, and the prospect of a long summer together is almost too good to be true.

Summer snags one of the laminated menus wedged between the salt and pepper shakers lined up at the end of the table. “I feel like you’ve said this before. So when you say ‘official,’ do you mean like, officially official?”

Vada nods. “Officially official.”

“So what made you call off your open, on-again, off-again… whatever that was?” Tori asks, skimming the menu with the name *Pepper’s BBQ* printed in bold Comic Sans across the top.

I love this place. It’s a tiny hole-in-the-wall—well, more like a shack in a dirt parking lot—restaurant Ronan brought me to not long after we started dating two years ago. That was before I knew he didn’t eat beef or pork. I still remember offering him half my rack of ribs and how politely he turned them down. I thought he was just being sweet—and he was—but I had no idea he was probably trying not to gag.

Those ribs? Exactly what I’m ordering today. Along with a giant scoop of coleslaw. I’m starving.

“Commitment-phobia,” Vada says simply.

"You or him?" Summer asks, not looking up.

"Me," Vada says, slapping her menu onto the table. "I'm ready to order."

"Me too," I say enthusiastically.

Summer giggles. "Me three."

Tori clicks her tongue. "Ready to commit to food, but not to a relationship."

"Hardly the same thing." Vada waves her off, laughing.

A young guy I recognize as the owner's grandson comes to take our orders, quickly jotting them down on a notepad before he walks away.

Vada watches him as he walks back toward the building, passing the massive black smoker trailing ribbons of mouthwatering smoke.

"Now him I wouldn't mind being on-again, off-again with this summer," she says, eyebrows raised.

Summer grins. "I say go for it. But speaking of this summer, what do we have planned?"

Tori claps excitedly. "Well, I think the plan was beach camping for a few days around July Fourth."

"Yes!" Vada shouts.

"But other than that, I don't think we have solid plans yet," Tori says, unfazed by the boisterous interruption.

"I honestly just want to spend as much time with you as possible," I say. "I've missed you guys!"

"You don't want to spend every waking second rejoicing in your reunion with Ran?" Summer asks, one eyebrow raised.

I laugh. "I do, and I'm very much rejoicing. But he's still busy with work. And for some reason he signed up for a full class load this summer, so I don't think we'll have all that much time together." I pretend not to know the reason he kept his plate full when, in reality, I know he signed up when we were still broken up, probably to keep himself distracted.

Vada gives a dramatic thumbs-down. "Boo."

"Oh, and Randi's set to visit for a couple weeks in July," I say.

Vada snorts. "I'm still surprised you're cool with that."

I've filled them in on what happened—over many late-night calls, some with all of us on the line. They know about the breakup. About Montana. About the talk Ronan and I had while we were there. Well, most of it. I didn't tell them about his aunt. That's not mine to share.

But even though my perception of Miranda has drastically changed, Vada is still skeptical.

"I mean, I don't really have a choice," I say with a shrug. "Like it or not, Randi is part of Ran's life. And now I get why. They're important to each other. I didn't understand that before, but I do now."

"Plus, Randi's pretty fucking cool," Tori says. "Just you wait, Vada. She'll give you a run for your money."

Vada puckers her lips and lifts her brows. "Guess we'll see," she says, voice low and teasing as our waiter returns carrying a full tray of food. Vada has no shame. "Ooh, look at all that delicious meat," she says, clearly not referring to the food.

"Oh my god," Summer giggles into her palm.

The guy grins at her, teeth flashing. He sets down our plates, and Vada thanks him with a flirtatious smile that's about as subtle as a firework.

As he walks off, she leans forward, eyes gleaming. "Okay, okay, I'm thinking I'll take the opportunity this summer to live a little."

"Or cause chaos," Summer teases.

"Chaos Vada-style. I like it," she says, then tugs the corner of her napkin into her collar, clearly planning to get messy.

I inhale the smell of smoky barbeque winding its way into my nose. My tray is piled high with saucy ribs, thick slices of cornbread, and a heaping scoop of slaw. It's exactly what I wanted. It's exactly what I was craving.

But the second I see it all laid out in front of me, my stomach turns. Like I've been riding a carousel too long.

My appetite vanishes, replaced by a strange pressure in my chest. Like something is out of sync. I blink, frowning at the plate.

"What's wrong?" Summer asks. "Why are you making that face?"

Tori leans closer. "Is there a hair in your food?"

"No, it's just..." I trail off. "I thought I wanted ribs, but now that I see and smell them, I don't know. I feel kind of sick."

I push the plate away slowly.

Vada shrugs. "Well, you're pregnant, that's why," she mumbles, mouth already full.

I shoot her a look. "Haha," I say, my tone dry. "Don't even joke—"

The rest of the words don't come out right, getting stuck somewhere in my throat as a slow, creeping wave of heat rises from my chest to my face. My pulse stumbles over itself. There's a strange ringing in my ears. My hands feel clammy against the table. My breath shortens without warning, becoming shallow and quick like I've just sprinted five blocks to catch the train.

When the hell was my last period?

I yank my phone out of my pocket and pull up the calendar app. I frantically swipe between days and months while trying to breathe.

"I was joking," Vada says quickly.

Summer and Tori have gone still, forks hovering in midair. They're watching me, eyes shifting from amusement to unease.

No, not February. I definitely had one after that.

"Cat?" Tori says gently.

A soft, strangled sound escapes me. "Oh god."

"Kitty Cat?" Tori sets her hand on my forearm as if to draw me out of my mania.

"You're scaring me." Vada's voice is small. So is she, suddenly, her usually loud personality muted.

I swallow what feels like ash. "I'm late," I whisper, afraid to say it out loud, afraid that will make it real. *More* real.

"Are you sure?" Summer asks.

I nod. My heart thuds in my throat like it's trying to punch its way out of my body.

Tori squeezes my arm gently. "How late?"

My eyes fly back to my phone. "I... I don't know." I scroll furiously, trying to somehow reconstruct the timeline, but my brain won't cooperate. All I feel is panic. Just panic. Just static. "Oh god."

My chest is rising and falling too fast. I can't catch a full breath.

Tori gently pries the phone from my hands. Her blue eyes are steady, soft. "Okay, stop," she says calmly—the opposite of how I feel.

I can't form a single coherent thought. Just: *Oh shit. Oh shit. Oh shit.*

"You're probably just stressed," Summer says. "The last few months were hell, and finals don't exactly help. Your body's probably just playing catch-up."

I latch onto her words like they're gospel. I nod. *Yeah, okay. I'm just stressed. That's all. Just stress.*

Vada flags down the waiter with one hand, the other still holding her fork. "But let's just get a test," she says, matter-of-factly. "That way we can rule it out."

The young waiter reappears, and she turns on a dazzling smile. "Could we get some to-go boxes? And feel free to include your phone number," she says with a wink.

I don't know how Vada can flirt right now, but for some reason, I'm grateful she can. Like if she's not panicking, if she can still be Vada, maybe everything isn't crashing down around me. Maybe I don't have to panic, either.

***

"You're still on the pill, right?" Tori asks when we're in the backseat of Vada's car.

I nod, nausea churning in my stomach. I can't tell if it's from the panic or if it's... something else. "Yeah. I never stopped taking it," I say. "But I missed a couple of days when Ran and I were broken up."

Summer turns in the front passenger seat, giving me a sympathetic look. "That's not ideal, but I'm sure you're fine. You've been on the pill for how long? I can't imagine a couple of missed days would immediately undo years of being careful, right?"

I swallow down the bile threatening to rise. "I hope not."

We drive to the nearest drugstore, march to the aisle with the feminine hygiene products, and stare at the wall of pregnancy tests. I had no idea there were so many kinds. Digital, non-digital, early detection, some with fancy displays, others that look like strips of paper.

"Uhh," I mutter, hovering. I have the sudden urge to bolt.

"Let's grab these," Summer says, picking a box with three early-response non-digital tests. "I think these were the ones my brother's girlfriend used during their scare last year. She was negative, so maybe that's a good sign."

I don't have a reason to disagree.

"Where are we going?" Vada asks once we're back in her car.

"My parents are home," I say quickly, shaking my head like that could somehow undo all of this.

"So are mine," Summer says.

Vada glances at Tori in the rearview mirror. "Ran's still in Boston helping Stevie move, right? Is Shane working?"

"Yeah. We could go to their apartment," Tori says. "We'll just need to toss the tests after or the boys will freak."

I'm not convinced throwing them in a random dumpster will prevent said freaking.

Tori has to unlock the apartment because my fingers aren't steady enough to get the key in the lock. As soon as she opens the door, I squeeze past her and rush to the small bathroom, box of pregnancy tests in hand.

I click the lock in place and tear the box open. That little instructional pamphlet is suddenly the most important thing I've ever read. I follow the steps precisely, then set the pregnancy test on the bathroom counter.

I unlock the bathroom door a minute later and join Tori, Vada, and Summer in the living room.

"I have to wait three minutes," I say when Vada peeks at my hands like I walked in already knowing the outcome.

We sit on the couch in silence, knees bouncing, hands fidgeting. The energy is restless, anxious.

"I never realized how long three minutes are," Summer mutters, picking at her nails.

"Same, girl. Same," Vada says.

I jump up from the couch. "I can't take it anymore." I hurry to the bathroom, Vada, Tori, and Summer on my heels, then freeze in the bathroom doorway.

I can see the two pink lines from here. Bold. Certain.

Oh god, it's positive. I'm pregnant. Oh god.

"No," I whimper, stepping closer like maybe distance might change something. I pick up the offending thing, holding it in my hands like it might explode. "No." My voice cracks.

I turn to my friends for help, my eyes huge, hands clammy.

"Maybe it's a false positive," Vada says, always the optimist. "Take another one!" She already unwraps another test and shoves it into my hand, taking the one with the damning pink lines from me.

I do as she says and repeat the process. This time, I don't bother leaving the bathroom. The four of us just stand, staring at the test, watching as one pink line is quickly joined by a second. That test didn't even hesitate. It *knows*. The third and final test, too, turns positive within seconds of me taking it.

I stare at the tests lined up on the counter like they're pieces of evidence in a trial I never meant to be on the stand for. My knees buckle and I sink to the edge of the tub, the cold porcelain biting through my jeans. My breath shudders in and out, thin and shallow, and suddenly I feel like I'm underwater. Like I can't surface.

"Oh god," I say, again. A cracked whisper. I press the heels of my hands into my eyes, trying to squeeze the moment out of existence. "Oh god. What am I going to do?"

No one answers. No one can.

A thought slams into my chest. "How am I supposed to tell Ran?" My voice shakes. With emotion, with fear.

"He's going to think I did this on purpose," I say, panic pulsing through me. "We just had that huge fight. He doesn't want kids. He set a boundary. He made that so clear."

I look up at my friends, my face crumpling, voice breaking open like a wound. "He's going to think I'm trapping him into this."

Tori kneels beside me, her hand on my back. Vada crouches down in front of me, her eyes shiny now. Even Summer looks shaken, helpless.

"He won't," Tori says, low, soothing.

"I didn't mean for this to happen," I say. "I *can't* be pregnant. I wasn't supposed to be pregnant. We were *careful*."

The word feels laughable now. Pathetic.

"I don't know what to do," I whisper. "He's going to be so upset. My parents are going to kill me. And what about school?"

I'm spiraling, and I know it.

"Deep breaths, Kitty Cat," Vada says, soothing. "Everything is going to work out. Ran loves you. You know that. And your parents can hardly be upset unless they want you to call them hypocrites, right? And you have options," she says, heavy meaning tucked between her words.

But that's a decision I know I can't make on my own.

"Do you want to call Ran?" Summer asks.

Tori and I shake our heads in unison. She understands this isn't something to say over the phone. This is something I have to tell him in person.

"Okay... when's he coming home?" Summer asks.

I suck in a shuddering breath. "Not until late tomorrow."

And then I start to cry. Not loud sobs, just quiet, broken sounds slipping out of me like my body's trying to make space for the weight of it all.

I already know I won't talk to him for the rest of the weekend. Not today, not tomorrow. I'll text him quick, casual things that sound like me, but I know I can't risk hearing his voice, or worse, letting him hear mine. He'd know something's wrong. He always knows. He's scarily good at reading body language, listening to inflections. He'd be able to tell something is deeply wrong the second I said "hi." And for some reason, the thought of *not* getting to speak to him, when he's the one person I need most, especially right now, adds a new layer of sorrow.

Monday, May 15th

Ronan

I knew something was off the minute Cat stopped answering my calls Saturday afternoon. The texts she did send were... not her. Short, overly casual, like she was trying too hard to sound normal. At first, I chalked it up to her weekend plans with Tori, Summer, and Vada. She'd been excited about it all week. They had it all mapped out. And I had my own distractions in Boston, helping Steve move from his dorm into his new apartment.

I finally met his *girl*, too, and was looking forward to telling Cat about her. But when she started dodging my calls, when her replies felt like placeholders instead of conversations, I got the distinct impression she wouldn't exactly welcome a long paragraph about Steve's sophomore-year adventures.

I got home late last night. I had half-expected Cat to have changed her mind about waiting for me at the apartment, but was relieved to find her asleep in my bed. Maybe I imagined everything?

Nope. Definitely not. That nagging pull in my chest hasn't gone away. I figured I'd get her to talk this morning, easing in with soft questions—*You alright? Did something happen?*—while we got ready, at breakfast. Nothing. And with every passing minute, the knot in my gut cinches tighter.

She won't look me in the eyes. Won't reach for my hand. Barely tolerates my touch.

After Shane leaves to open Murphy's, Cat disappears into his and Tori's bedroom to "talk to Tori." She's in there for over half an hour. Door closed. Not a sound, which is saying something, considering these walls are practically tissue paper. Trust me, I've had *plenty* of proof. Clearly, their discussion is in hushed voices. They don't want me to hear.

I wander through the apartment in search of something to do, to stop myself from pacing like a fucking lunatic. Laundry it is. I gather all the towels, empty both Shane's and my hampers, and head down to the basement to start a washer. The second I slam the lid shut and drop in four quarters, I pull out my phone and text Shane.

Me:

Did something happen while I was in Boston that I need to know about?

Luckily, Shane doesn't make me wait.

Shane:

No. Why?

Me:

Because Cat's been stand-offish all morning and now she and Tor are in your bedroom "talking." With the door closed.

Shane:

Oh shit.

Me:

Yeah…

Shane:

What did you do?

I frown, quickly hammering out a reply.

Me:

Dude, I have no fucking clue. We were good Saturday morning. Then she stopped answering my calls. Things have been weird ever since.

Shane:

Tor hasn't said anything to me. Do you think maybe Cat's planning something for your birthday? That's in like two weeks.

I pause, considering his idea, but my gut tells me that's not it.

Me:

No. She's just not herself, but not in a "I'm planning something fun" way. Something's wrong, Shay!

Shane:

Ok. I'll see what I can get out of Tor. Don't stress man, maybe she's on her period. Every time I think Tor might kill me in my sleep, turns out she's about to start her cycle.

I actually chuckle at that.

Me:

Sounds wholesome…

Shane:

Keeps things exciting. Do I get homicidal Tori? Cuddly Tori? Horny Tori? Or energetic Tori? It's like roulette, but with knives and teddy bears.

Me:

'Kay, well, if you're able to extract some nuggets of wisdom from Tor, please share.

Shane:

Will do. Don't worry too much.

I send back a pathetic thumbs-up emoji.

When I walk back into the apartment, Tori's by the door, slipping on her shoes. Even though the look she gives me is soft, sympathetic, maybe meant to reassure, it sets off alarm bells in my head. My chest tightens. This can't be good.

"I'm heading out," Tori says, her voice carrying a little too much meaning. Her eyes dart toward Cat who's emerging from the living room with her arms wrapped around herself. *Not. Good.*

"Unless you want me to stick around?" she asks, eyes pinned to Cat.

Cat shakes her head.

"Okay," Tori murmurs. "It'll be okay, Kitty Cat." She walks past me, giving my shoulder a quick, gentle pat, and disappears out the door.

I wait for it to shut behind her, then take a tentative step toward Cat, doing my best to swallow the anxiety clawing at my insides like a trapped animal desperate to escape its cage.

"Okay, baby," I say, my voice low, tight. "What the hell is going on?"

Cat walks back into the living room. I follow, keeping some distance, then watch as she lowers herself onto the couch, her gaze to the floor.

"Did I do something?" It's the only thing I can think of. That I fucked up somehow without even realizing it. Was it something I said the last time we talked?

"No, you didn't do anything. I'm not mad at you, I promise," she says, her voice meek.

"What's wrong then?" I ask her, searching her face for clues.

She doesn't respond, folding into herself instead. She looks so small, so sad. I move, sinking onto the couch beside her.

"We don't do that to each other, remember?" I say softly. "You made me promise to always tell you what's going on in my head, and you promised me the same in return."

More silence. Her shoulders hunch, reminding me of a dog that knows it's in trouble.

"Baby, please," I beg, becoming increasingly worried.

Finally, her eyes lift to mine. "I have to tell you something." She looks absolutely terrified.

What the hell happened?

"You can tell me anything," I say, trying to sound calm even though my heart is racing. Whatever it is, it's big. It's *bad.*

She takes a deep breath. Then another. And another. Her nerves practically radiate off her, and suddenly I feel like I could jump out of my skin with anxiety.

Then her lips part.

"I'm pregnant, Ran."

The words slam into my body, but they don't land. My brain rejects them, shoving them into some dark corner where they can't mean anything. All I know is that my body is reacting while my head stays blank.

I stare at her. "What?"

"I'm pregnant," she says, even softer. Her eyes lock with mine, filling with tears.

The room goes silent. The words settle into the air like lead. Into *me* like lead. Sinking and spreading until I can't breathe.

"Shit," I whisper. Realization slams into me. "Shit," I say again, louder this time. I stand up fast, raking both hands through my hair like that'll help me think.

"Are you sure?" I ask, grasping for the tiniest thread of hope that this isn't real. That it's a mistake. That maybe she's joking, or... I don't know.

"Yeah," she says so quietly I almost don't hear it. But the look on her face—those wide, panicked eyes, the way her arms are wrapped around her body—tells me everything. This isn't a joke. She's not wrong.

Cat is pregnant.

"I took three tests," she says.

"Fuck." I groan, pacing a tight, frantic circle in front of the couch. My mind is a mess. I *can't* think. I *need* to think.

"I thought..." I stop, guilt already creeping in before the sentence is out of my mouth. "I thought you were on the pill."

I hate how that sounds. Like I'm blaming her. Like birth control was only her responsibility. I know better. I *know* that's not fair, but Cat got on the pill pretty much the second we started dating two years ago. We've never used a condom. And when we got back together, I didn't even think twice about it.

Stupid. Fucking *stupid.*

"I am." Her voice breaks, then collapses completely as a sob breaks from her chest. She crumples.

In a heartbeat, I'm back on the couch, pulling her into my arms.

"But I wasn't as careful about taking it when we were broken up," she chokes out, barely intelligible through her crying. "I missed a couple of days. I didn't think it would mess me up this much. I'm so sorry, Ran."

She cries harder, her body heaving in my arms. I'm fucking pissed, but more at myself. I should've asked. Should've checked. Should've known. I shouldn't have assumed she'd stayed on the pill after we split up. I shouldn't have taken it for granted, any of it.

"It's not your fault," I say, trying to ease her guilt, but she shakes her head against me.

"Yes, it is. I wasn't careful enough."

"But birth control isn't just your responsibility," I say. "I should've checked. I should've made sure."

"If you had," she whispers, "I probably would've told you we're fine."

Then she falls silent. Neither of us speak for a good minute, the reality of the situation sinking in deeper with each second that passes.

"Do you hate me?" she finally asks, her voice small.

My answer is instant. Certain. "Of course, I don't hate you," I say. "I love you more than life itself."

Her tears don't let up, and all I can do is hold her. I want to fix it, make it better somehow, but I have no idea how. *God, this is going to change everything.*

"How far along are you?" I ask quietly. My thoughts are racing, head spinning. The version of the future I had allowed myself to envision lately is unraveling at the seams.

"I'm honestly not sure. Maybe three or four weeks? I don't know." She inhales a shaky breath. "What do we do?" Her eyes find mine—wide, pleading, terrified—and I swear she's looking for answers I don't have. But I try.

"Well... I guess we should probably try to get you in with your doctor and make sure everything's okay with you and... and the baby, right?"

Even saying the word feels unreal.

"I have an appointment this afternoon," she says.

I blink. She must have called her doctor while I was in the shower or in the basement, completely oblivious to what she was carrying around with her.

"What time?" I ask.

"At three." She hiccups.

"Okay. I'll tell Shay I'll be late this evening. I promised him I'd work the Monday night shift since he covered for me while I was in Boston, but I can just come in thirty minutes late if I need to."

Cat stares at me, surprise etched into her brow.

"You want to come with me?"

"Yeah. I mean... if it's okay with you," I say. It stings a little that she seems so surprised. "Baby, you're not alone in this, okay?"

She won't go through any of this alone. Not if I have anything to say about it.

She falls against me, fresh sobs bursting from her like a dam breaking. "I'm so afraid of losing you again."

And god, I hate myself. I *really* fucked up when I let her go. No wonder she doesn't trust this. Doesn't trust me to stick around.

I lift her chin gently until her eyes meet mine. "You're not going to lose me. I'm yours. I love you. We're in this together."

I pull her against me and hold her for a long time as neither of us speak.

"In case I haven't told you yet… I missed you while I was in Boston," I say eventually. "Especially when you stopped answering my calls."

"I'm sorry, Ran. I just…"

"It's okay," I say, brushing a strand of tear-damped hair out of her face. "The last couple of days couldn't have been easy."

She looks up at me with red, watery eyes.

"You know you can talk to me, right?" I ask gently.

She nods. "Yeah. But I needed to tell you this in person. I couldn't do it over the phone."

"Who all knows?" I ask. "Tori, obviously… anyone else?

"Vada and Summer," Cat says. "They were with me when I found out."

"I'm glad you weren't alone."

"I still felt alone, though. You weren't there."

My chest tightens. "How do you feel now?"

"Freaked out. Confused. Really scared." She sighs. "But… relieved that you know."

Just like that, in a single conversation, life has changed. Again. And, fuck, I'm scared too.

Cat

The rest of the afternoon passed in a daze with quiet movements, soft touches, a heavy, shared silence. We didn't say much, but Ronan stayed close, orbiting around me like he was afraid to be alone. Or maybe he was afraid of me being alone. I don't know.

When it's finally time, we walk to his car like we're headed somewhere neither of us want to be. The more lights we pass, the closer we get to the doctor's office, the harder my heart hammers in my chest.

Ronan clears his throat. "Have you... have you had any, like, symptoms?" he asks into the thick silence of the car.

I shake my head. "Not really. I mean, I haven't thrown up or anything. The only weird thing was when I went to lunch with Vada, Summer, and Tori."

His eyebrows rise slightly. "Yeah?"

"When the waiter brought out the ribs I ordered, I smelled them and just... couldn't. Like, I felt instantly sick. And you know how much I love ribs."

A small smile tugs at his lips. "Yeah, I'm aware of your rib obsession."

I manage a faint laugh. "But no other symptoms, really. I'm not nauseated, I don't feel extra emotional, my boobs don't hurt, my skin isn't acting weird, my vision hasn't changed, no weird headaches..."

His jaw drops a little. "Those are all pregnancy symptoms?"

"Oh yeah," I say, shrugging. "Just a few of many indicators."

He frowns, almost like the idea physically pains him. "Jesus. I mean, I knew pregnancy wasn't a cakewalk, but I guess I never really thought about all the stuff you go through. Besides, you know... labor."

A flutter expands in my chest. "Are you worried about me?"

He huffs. "Of course I'm worried about you. Fuck, this whole thing is..." He grips the steering wheel tighter, knuckles whitening. "I didn't want this for you. For us. This complicates things so much." There's a roughness in his voice that makes my throat close up.

"I'm so sorry, Ran," I say quietly.

He shakes his head. "Stop apologizing. Pretty sure it took both of us to make this happen," he says, gritted.

My phone vibrates in my lap with a group text from Tori to me, Vada, and Summer.

Tori:

I'm just kind of checking if you're still alive? I just got home and neither you nor Ran are here, sooooo...

My friends have been my lifeline this weekend, anchoring me with distraction and compassion. They helped me through the longest hours, when it felt like I might cry myself into dehydration. And this morning, Tori delivered the pep talk of all pep talks, reminding me it's going to be okay, that I can trust Ronan, trust myself, that I'm not alone and never will be. But after breaking the news to Ronan, I didn't have the energy or the emotional bandwidth to text my friends. I can tell they're concerned by my radio silence.

Me:

Still alive. Ran's taking me to my doctor's appointment right now.

Vada:

And? Reaction?

Me:

He's freaked out, but he's still Ran.

It's all I need to say. I know they'll understand exactly what that means. That he's still *my* Ran, the one who'd lie in front of an oncoming train if it meant keeping me safe.

Tori:

Just like we thought. Keep us posted after your appointment.

"Everything alright?" Ronan's voice draws me out of the group chat.

I nod. "Yeah. The girls just wanted to know if I'd told you. And if your reaction was what I expected."

He keeps his eyes on the road. "What did you expect my reaction to be?"

Guilt wells up in my chest, pressing against the stack of other emotions I've been carrying all weekend. "I thought... I thought maybe you wouldn't want anything to do with this. With me."

His eyes snap to me. I see the hurt in them. "You really thought I was going to just ditch you now?"

I give him a small, one-shouldered shrug. "You made it really clear that you didn't want children. And I thought maybe you'd think I did this on purpose. To trap you into this."

His jaw ticks once. Twice. "That thought hasn't crossed my mind once," he says, voice low, sincere. "Your whole body when you told me? Fuck, I could tell you were terrified. No one fakes that."

He stops at a red light and turns toward me, gaze locked. "Full disclosure?"

I nod, heart pounding.

"I'm not happy about..." He glances at my midsection, despite there being no visible signs of pregnancy. Yet. "I'm scared shitless. But I also know that you're scared shitless, too. And regardless of what happens, I need you to know that I love you. I love you so fucking much it's unbearable sometimes. *I. Will. Not. Leave. You.* Do you understand me?"

I nod, tears slipping quietly down my cheeks.

The light turns green and he turns back to the road as traffic inches forward.

"I messed up a few months ago. We both did. But my feelings for you never changed. And they're not going to change now." His eyes dart to me again, imparting, pleading. "Please believe me. I need you to trust me."

"I trust you," I whisper.

He reaches over and finds my hand, moving it gently to rest on his gear shift, his own palm covering mine.

Ronan

When we finally make it to Cat's doctor's office, we don't have to wait too long to be seen.

"Hey, Cat," her doctor says with a wide smile. "How have you been?"

"Fine, Doctor Simmons. This is my boyfriend, Ronan," Cat says.

"Nice to meet you," Cat's doctor says, and I reciprocate the greeting. Dr. Simmons glances at her tablet. "So you told the nurse you took three pregnancy tests this past Saturday, all positive?"

Cat nods. "Yeah."

"And when was the first day of your last period?"

Cat hesitates, brow furrowing. "I'm honestly not sure. I thought I had a period a few weeks ago, but now that I think about it, it was really light and short. Not normal at all."

She glances at me like she's checking to see how I'm taking this, but I got nothing. I don't know what qualifies as "normal" when it comes to periods. I've never had to think about this stuff before. The more I hear, the more I realize how much I don't know.

"Okay," Dr. Simmons says, setting the tablet aside. "Let's take a look."

Cat shifts on the table, positioning herself for the exam. I look away out of instinct, like I've stepped somewhere private without knocking, like I shouldn't be here. This feels too intimate, too exposed. But then I remember that *I* did this. *We* did this. I don't get to look away just because it's awkward. If Cat's going through this, I'm going through it too. That's how this works.

Still, it's strange. Not because I haven't seen her naked before—I've seen all of her, touched all of her. I've had her come apart under my hands, under my mouth, under my body. But this... this is different. This isn't about pleasure. It's about responsibility. Consequence. Fear. And something else that I don't have a name for yet.

"Your cervix is closed, and your uterus is definitely enlarged," Dr. Simmons says, still mid-exam. "How far along did you think you might be?"

"Four weeks? Maybe?" Cat says.

Dr. Simmons hums. "Hmm. Your uterus is pretty large for just four weeks. Let's do a quick ultrasound and see what we can see."

She pulls a machine closer, lowers a sheet over Cat's legs, and squeezes some clear gel onto her lower belly. Cat inhales sharply.

"Cold?" I ask, and she nods, grimacing.

I move to stand by her side, lacing my fingers with hers as she turns her head toward the screen. I focus on her face for a second, then glance up.

I have no idea what I'm looking at.

There's a blur of gray, then a black void on the screen. At the bottom of that darkness, there's something small. Something that kind of looks like a jellybean.

And then it moves.

I blink. Once. Twice. It wasn't just in my head. The jellybean is wiggling.

"Yes, you're definitely pregnant, Cat. And here's your baby," Dr. Simmons says, cheerful and calm, as she freezes the image on the screen.

My eyes drop to Cat. She's still staring ahead, watching the little wiggling shape inside her with a kind of stunned reverence. I squeeze her hand, and she slowly turns to meet my gaze. I can't quite read her expression. There's definitely shock there, but something softer, too—something achingly vulnerable. Tender.

"There's a baby inside me," she whispers, almost like she doesn't believe it.

I nod, throat tight, swallowing hard.

"And this right here," the doctor says, zooming in on a rapid flicker, "is your baby's heart beating."

She hits a button, and suddenly we can *hear* it—that fast, fluttering rhythm, like hummingbird wings. *Thump-thump, thump-thump, thump-thump.*

Neither of us speaks. We just listen, both of us still, both trying to process what this really means: there's a baby. A real one. Hers. And mine. Ours. *Our baby.*

Dr. Simmons takes some measurements, then grabs a few more stills before glancing up. "You're eight weeks along."

Okay, I know enough that pregnancy math means subtracting a week. Maybe two? I do the math automatically.

Montana. Right when we got back together. Memories flash through my brain—Cat in my truck, in my lap, breathless and urgent. Later in her bed, when I worshiped her slowly, when I thrust into her with deep, long strokes. In the barn when she demanded more, and I gave her everything. Or one of those other wild, desperate moments we stole from the world that week. So many times, like we seemingly couldn't get close enough. I guess we did after all.

Dr. Simmons checks her calendar, then smiles. "How do you feel about a Christmas due date?"

Cat's trying to contain the small smile tugging at her lips, but I notice it anyway. "Really?"

"Really," Doctor Simmons says. "We'll be able to determine the baby's gender in about another seven or eight weeks."

Cat shakes her head immediately. "I don't want to know," she says, then turns to me. "Is that okay?"

"If you don't want to find out, we won't find out." My answer is easy, solid. Of all the things I'm uncertain of right now, I know this one thing for sure: I'll follow her lead. I'll be what she needs. She's the one doing the impossible, the one whose body is already changing, already carrying the weight of something new. The least I can do is carry what's mine.

Honestly, I don't care if it's a boy or girl. I just care that Cat's okay.

"I want to see you again in a month," Dr. Simmons says, already standing and gathering her things. "Until then, try to rest when you can. The nurse will give you some information up front. You'll also need to have your blood drawn before you leave."

She hands Cat a printout with four ultrasound stills. Cat stares down at them for a long moment before quietly taking my hand. I squeeze it, grounding us both, and guide her out of the office.

Cat

I can't even begin to describe how surreal the past few days have felt, how strange this doctor's appointment was. Even after seeing the baby on the ultrasound, hearing its heartbeat, Ronan by my side, holding my hand, it still feels like an out-of-body experience. There's a human growing inside me.

My hands move to my stomach and I rest them there, even though there's obviously no belly yet and no movement can be felt. I feel Ronan's eyes on me and turn my head to look at him.

"I can't believe we're having a baby," I finally say.

"Me neither," he says with a sigh, his voice heavy. "How are you feeling?"

"Scared. Really scared. You?"

"Same. We're going to have to figure out some stuff."

I nod. We sure do. We fall silent then, each retreating into our own heads, into our own anxious thoughts.

The most immediate decision we'll need to make is also the hardest, most difficult. It's all I think about while Ronan navigates the sticky afternoon traffic. I run the scenarios in my head—us with a baby, us without a baby—even when we arrive at home, while Ronan makes us a quick lunch.

"Ran?" I start, gathering every ounce of strength to initiate the conversation I know we have to have. "Do... do you..." I stutter and stumble. "I mean..."

He stops mid-bite, looking at me, brows raised in quiet encouragement. I'm too scared to ask the question outright.

"You know we don't have to keep it," I say with heavy meaning wedged between the words.

"You mean, like, adoption?" he asks carefully.

I nod slowly. "Yeah, or, you know... termination?"

He looks at me again—his eyes searching mine—and then exhales, something unreadable shifting behind his gaze.

"Baby," he says, his voice calm but serious. "I need you to know that my next words are the truth. No hidden meaning. No subtext. No secrets, okay? I know I haven't always been totally open, but I told you: no more bullshit."

I nod, signaling that I understand.

"Whatever you want," he says simply.

I blink.

"Whatever you want," he repeats, firmer now. "I don't want you to hold back because of me. If you want to have this baby and give it up for adoption, then that's what we'll do. If you don't want to carry the pregnancy to term, then I'll be by your side through that. If you want to have this baby... with me... then we will have this baby. It's your body. The only person who gets to decide what happens next is *you*."

I think my heart just left my body, climbed into his lap, and curled up there. "Love" suddenly feels like too small a word for what I feel for him right now.

He looks at me again. "So what do you want, baby? Given everything. What do you truly want?"

I sit with the question for a moment, pretending to think it over. But I already know. I've known since I saw that little worm twitch on the ultrasound screen. Maybe even before that—maybe the moment I saw the two pink lines.

I've weighed every version of this life: one where we walk away, one where we give someone else the chance to raise it, one where we try and fail and break ourselves in the process.

But none of them felt right. None of them felt like *us*.

"I want to keep it," I whisper.

For a moment, guilt wants to nip at me for how easily I say it, for thrusting us into something so utterly life-changing when I know how he's felt, know what a line this crossed for him, even if unintentionally.

"Okay," he says.

I wait. He's not done. His jaw clenches.

"But what I told you in Montana still goes. If I lash out at you or... or the baby, you walk. You *have* to promise me that, Cat. It's the only way I'll be able to sleep at night. I need to know that you're ready to protect yourself and—"

I rest my hand on his right arm. "I'm ready, Ran. I won't need to, but I'm ready."

He exhales shakily. "Okay."

"Okay. And... you'll need to protect me from my dad." The next storm is already building in the distance; I feel my blood pressure rise just thinking about it.

Ronan lets out a dry, humorless laugh. "Only if you'll protect me from mine."

I snort. "Deal."

"Fuck," he mutters.

"Yeah," I whisper. "Fuck."

Ronan

I don't rouse Cat from her sleep. She passed out on the couch about an hour ago. She looks so relaxed, sleeping peacefully for the first time, I imagine, since finding out she's pregnant.

I already texted Tori, asking her to bring back some dinner so Cat has something to eat when she wakes up. She didn't eat much today—probably from the nerves—which can't be good. Especially now.

I slide into my car, call Dr. Seivert's office, and leave a message asking for a callback once she's in tomorrow. I've been slacking on therapy, but if I've ever had an incentive to get my upstairs shit in order, it's this. There's no ignoring the dark family history, not anymore. Before, I could run, could try to hide. No more. It's time to face that crap head-on. I'll be damned if I'm not going to fight my demons with everything I've got.

The nanosecond Shane spots me at Murphy's, he waves me into the office and shuts the door behind us. "Tori's made some kind of vow of silence," he says with a huff. "Wouldn't tell me anything. All she texted me was, 'You'll know when you know.'"

"Yeah, so, I need to talk to you."

His eyes widen. "Oh shit."

"I need a bump in my pay and more hours."

His eyelashes flutter like I just offered to Riverdance on the bar counter. "Okay. I mean, we can talk about it. But...?" He's already bracing for something bigger.

Might as well rip off the Band-Aid. "Cat's pregnant."

Shane blinks. His mouth opens. Closes. His brow furrows. Reminds me a lot of me roughly six hours ago.

"You're fucking joking, right?" he finally says, pressing his palms to the cluttered desk.

"I wish I was."

"Holy fucking shit, Ran. No fucking way."

"Yes, way. Three tests, one doctor's visit, and one ultrasound all confirm it."

"That's... fuck... that's..." He's scrambling for words. "It's yours, right?"

I roll my eyes. "No, it's Stevie's."

"Hey, just checking," he says quickly, holding up his hands. "Oh fuck, dude." His whole vibe shifts, realization blooming in real time, almost like it's happening to him. Yep, exactly how I felt earlier today.

"This is... fuck, this is heavy," he says.

"Yeah. It really complicates things," I say through gritted teeth.

"That's an understatement. Dude, didn't you... weren't you guys using protection?" There's surprise in his tone, probably because he knows how careful I've always been.

"Yeah, she's been on the pill since we got together, but..."

"Shit," he groans, dragging a hand over his head.

"So, yeah. Seeing as I'm about to be responsible not only for making sure Cat's okay, but also feeding and clothing a kid..." The words still feel foreign in my mouth. "I need to either make more working here or find something else. Obviously, I'd rather stay here, but—"

"Dude, no, I got you," Shane says instantly. "What are you thinking?"

"Uh, if I can work twelves on Thursdays, Fridays, and Saturdays, plus pick up Mondays? And if you could bump me a couple of bucks an hour? That would help."

"That would only give you one day off, Ran. You sure?"

I shrug. "I don't think I have a choice."

He nods pensively. "I'll take a look at the schedule, but I'm pretty sure we can make it happen. And I'm sure my dad'll be fine with the raise."

"You know, honestly, all of this might not matter come Friday," I say dryly.

"Why?"

"My grandparents are flying in, and the plan is to tell both our families at dinner. So... I may not survive the night."

He snorts. "That's a very real concern."

I groan, the weight of it all finally breaking through. "How am I supposed to do this, man?" I sink into one of the creaky office chairs and drop my head in my hands. "How am I supposed to—"

God, it hits me like a dumbbell to the chest.

Cat and I are having a baby.

I'm going to be a dad. I'm only turning nineteen in June... I have the unprocessed weight of my mother's dark family history on my shoulders, and I have no idea how to protect Cat, let alone a baby, from what might lurk inside me.

"By taking it one day at a time," Shane says. "There's no point in overthinking this right now."

"Easy for you to say."

He lowers himself in the chair next to me, draping an arm over my shoulder. "Yeah, I know. But you're not alone, Ran. You have Cat and me and Stevie. And, yeah, your families are probably going to freak the fuck out at first, but they'll come around. Try not to stress."

"Dude, have you even met me?" I deadpan. "It's what I do. I stress about shit."

He laughs. "Sorry, forgot who I was talking to for a second."

Somehow, I already feel lighter.

"When is Cat officially moving in?" he asks.

I blink. "Uh, I... I haven't thought that far. Are you sure you want a newborn in your apartment?"

"You mean *our* apartment? It's your place, too. And what, you'd just... put the kid in storage?"

I shrug. "I don't know. Find another place?"

"Fuck that," Shane says. "I'm not about to kick you out just because you couldn't keep your dick in your pants."

I groan. "You're such an asshole."

"But I'm a supportive asshole," he says with a grin. "Plus, your kid can only benefit from spending its early years around Uncle Shane." He pretends to wipe something off his shoulder with a smug look.

That does it. I laugh. "Uncle Shane? You sure about that?"

"Fuck yes. That kid is going to be a badass."

"No doubt about that. I'm just wondering if you're really set on 'Uncle Shane' or if you'd consider something... less creepy-sounding."

Shane always manages to make me feel better about the heaviness in my life. There's a reason why he and Cat are such anchors for me.

"Whatever the kid wants to call me, I'm cool with." That smug but soft-ass look is back on his face.

"Damn, Ran," he says suddenly, eyes wide like it just hit him. Again. "You're gonna be a *dad*."

"Don't say it out loud," I mutter. "It makes it too real."

Friday, May 19th

Ronan

Today's the day.

The day Cat and I march into battle—or at least to the dinner table—armed with a heavy dose of anxiety and the earth-shattering news that my stupid ass managed to get her knocked up. At eighteen. Out of wedlock. Days—maybe even *minutes*—after I somehow, miraculously, convinced her to take me back after I broke her heart in the most spectacular way possible.

So yeah. Should be a peaceful, drama-free gathering. Can't wait. *Insert heavy, soul-crushing sarcasm.*

I didn't sleep at all last night. I don't think Cat did, either. I felt her tossing and turning beside me, heard her sighing quietly in the dark. At some point I got up, paced the apartment, stood in front of the fridge like it might offer me something stronger than water. It didn't. At 5:32 a.m., I gave up pretending I might fall asleep and put on my running shoes instead.

I prefer lifting heavy shit in the gym, but running's good for when I need to *outrun* something—anger, panic, ghosts. Right now, all three are on my heels.

It's been four days since Cat told me she's pregnant, and it still feels like I've been dropped into an episode of *The Twilight Zone.* Like I'm floating just above the surface of my own life, watching the craziest shit go down. None of this feels real. Not really. Except for the tightness in my chest that won't go away. That part is *very* real.

I told Cat I never wanted to be a dad. That I couldn't—*shouldn't*—be one. That I didn't trust myself not to turn into another link in the chain of violence passed down on my mother's side. And now?

Now the universe, in its infinite sense of humor, has decided to make me a father before I'm even old enough to legally buy a beer. And god, I could *really* use one right now. Or better yet, a shot of whiskey. Or seven. *Fuck.*

I push myself harder. Faster. I don't stop until my body's begging me to. And even then, I keep going. Pain makes more sense than anything else right now. But the thoughts don't stop.

First, our living situation. The apartment is too small. Shane says he's cool with a newborn in the place, but we're already on top of each other as it is. I'm not even sure my room can accommodate a crib, let alone a changing table and all the other baby gear I stupidly started looking up on the internet yesterday, only to immediately spiral into a blind panic until I shut my phone off. Like, *off* off. There's so much we need.

Which brings me to my second concern: the money. Yeah, I work. A lot. But I make barely over minimum wage an hour, and the tips aren't a steady, reliable source of income. Some nights I make bank, other nights my tips aren't enough to fill up my gas tank.

I haven't brought any of this up to Cat yet. I can't. Not until I have something solid to offer. What I *do* know is this: I won't let her sacrifice anything. Not school. Not her career. Not the life she's been working for. I won't let her become my mom, stuck in a house with a baby she didn't really want—at least not yet—living a life that wasn't hers by choice.

Which flows nicely into issue number three: who the hell is going to watch this baby while we're in class? Or at work? Our parents? Surely not. Daycare? Those places cost a fortune—definitely more than I make in tips. How does anyone do this? How the hell do actual adults survive it, let alone two broke college kids, one of whom still deals with C-PTSD?

I get back to the apartment just before seven, my body shot to hell but my mind no less frenzied. I was promised a runner's high, god damn it.

Cat's already up. She's standing in the kitchen, a mug of coffee cradled in her hands. She's wearing light blue jeans and one of my fitted t-shirts—oversized on her. She looks tired. Gorgeous. Human in a way that makes my chest ache.

I let my eyes drift from her face—still soft with sleep, hair wild from her restless night but so damn sexy—down to her midsection. Like I'm expecting to see a bump or some other sign confirming that I managed to detonate both our lives in a heartbeat.

Nothing. Not yet.

"How are you feeling?" I ask, peeling off my shirt, which is glued to my skin with sweat. I sling it over my shoulder, then grab a bottle of water from the fridge.

She shrugs. "Like I'm about to vomit, cry, and maybe scream all at the same time."

"Cool. Same." I take a step toward her, resting one hand lightly on the counter beside her. "Did you sleep?"

Another shrug. "Not really."

"Me neither. I bet it's my brain subconsciously making every last living minute count before either your dad or mine—or both—strangle me tonight."

The joke doesn't land. Cat's just as terrified as I am about telling our families.

I take her hand and pull her into the tiny bathroom, shutting and locking the door behind us. Her eyebrows shoot up when I drop my sweats, then my boxers like it's no big deal.

I catch the flick of her gaze—face, chest, dick—and the way she presses her lips together before catching the bottom one between her teeth. If my head were in a better place, I'd drag her into the shower with me, clothes and all.

"I just want you to hang out with me," I say softly, then step underneath the shower's blistering spray. It's hotter than I usually like—Cat's kind of temperature—but right now it feels good. My muscles melt under the heat, like they've been waiting for this moment of surrender.

She sinks down onto the closed toilet lid. "Okay, so walk me through the plan again?"

I squirt some bodywash into my palm, then lather myself up. "I'm getting my grandparents from the airport at four. I'll tell them on the drive back. Hopefully that gives them enough time to go through all five stages of grief and be functional humans by dinner. We're due at my dad's around five. You'll meet us there and... we'll break the joyous news together."

She looks up at me like I just said we're planning a joint government coup. I guess, in a way, we are.

"Together," she echoes.

"Unless you want to run."

She gives a dry laugh. "Do you?"

"Every second."

We fall into a moment of silence. The sound of the water fills the room, steady and loud, drowning out all the things we don't say.

I watch her. She watches her toes draw patterns on the white, fluffy shower rug.

"Hey," I say, breaking into her thoughts. "Whatever happens tonight... I'm not leaving. I'm not bailing. No matter how pissed they get or how loud it gets or what they say. I'm here. You know that, right?"

She looks up at me, eyes glassy, but she doesn't speak. She doesn't trust my words. Doesn't trust that I *will* stick around. I haven't earned it back. Yet.

But I have nothing but time.

***

I'm sitting in the driver's seat of Cat's ancient Subaru Forester. Yes, ancient. Never mind that it's thirty-five years newer than my Mustang. The lack of sex appeal alone adds at least fifty years to its soul. That thing looks like it went through the wringer before her parents even bought it. The paint's salt-faded, the dashboard's cracked, and the leather on the seats is peeling. It still has a cassette deck. A *cassette deck*. I don't think I've ever even seen a cassette in real life. Only in movies. Maybe one day, when we're not about to drop a small fortune on baby essentials, I can spoil her like she deserves.

The passenger-side vent won't stay up. It keeps drooping like it's too tired and depressed to do its job. Guess we have that in common. The one redeeming quality? The interior smells like Cat's lavender shampoo and her caramel coffee.

I gave Cat the keys to my Mustang. It was my dad who insisted I pick up my grandparents in something other than my car. "Bud, do you really expect Morai to climb through the front into your backseat?" he chuckled. I had to admit he had a point. My grandparents in a two-door, classic muscle car, when they're used to crew cab extended-bed trucks? Yeah, that would have been a disaster waiting to happen.

So here we are, my ass in this beige time capsule from circa 2004, while Cat gets to cruise in my Boss. I try not to think about it too hard. As good as she's gotten, she still tends to heavy-foot the clutch and make my transmission cry. I just smile at her, pretend it doesn't hurt, then whisper apologies to my car like she's a wounded war hero. She's very sensitive. My car, that is. Not Cat. Cat's a badass.

I'm at the airport. Well, the parking garage of the airport, to be exact. My grandparents are buckled in beside and behind me, their luggage safely deposited in the trunk. And I'm just sitting here. Not moving. Not turning the key.

My damn heart is about to burst through my chest wall.

My grandparents exchange questioning glances. Here goes.

"What's wrong, baby boy?" my grandma asks.

Ugh, my throat is already tight and I haven't said a single word. "I fucked up," I say, tipping my head back against the headrest while my eyes fall shut.

"What happened?" she asks cautiously, not even objecting to my crude word choice.

I sigh. "Cat's pregnant." The words are still as difficult to form as they were when I told Shane on Monday and my big brother the next morning.

"Oh, baby boy," she says, while my grandpa exhales deeply. "Oh," she just repeats.

"What am I going to do?" I ask desperately. I've asked this exact question a hundred times now.

My grandma's hand is on my shoulder. "You're going to do exactly what Cat needs you to do. You're going to walk by her side through this and you'll figure this out. You're a Soult. You'll be fine, Ran."

"I didn't want this for her," I say. "I didn't want this for us."

"Aww, I know. I know," my grandma says, her voice warm, soft.

"Dad's going to kill me," I say.

My grandpa laughs ruefully. "Let him try. I'll gladly remind him that he had to break similar news to us when he was even younger than you."

"How did you take it when he told you?" I ask, realizing I've never actually heard that story.

"Well, it was certainly a shock in the beginning, but there was no question that we'd support him and... and Rica," he says, hesitating on my mother's name.

"How's Cat doing?" my grandma asks.

"She's scared," I say. "We saw her doctor on Monday and... we saw the baby on the ultrasound. It's so weird..." I trail off, still completely unable to wrap my head around the fact that Cat's pregnant.

"How far along is she?" my grandpa asks.

"Just over eight weeks."

My grandmother sighs. "Ronan Perry Soult. In Montana?"

I'm not a blusher, but it suddenly feels very hot in the car. "Yeah. Sorry," I say sheepishly. "Her due date's Christmas Day," I say for I-don't-know-what-reason, other than to distract from the fact that Cat and I had sex—a lot of it, actually—on the ranch.

"Ronan, listen to me," she says. "I know you're scared. I know. But you're both going to be fine. You're not alone. You are loved. You have each other, you have your dad and brother, you have us, and you have great friends. I will not tell you that it's going to be easy, but it's doable. And... baby boy, you're going to be a great daddy."

Her words make my heart squeeze in my chest.

"I hope you're right," I say quietly.

"When have you ever known me to be wrong?"

I can't help but laugh. "Never, I guess."

"There you go," she says. "When are you planning on telling your dad?"

"Tonight. At dinner. You know, when the whole damn clan is together and joined by Cat's family. What could go wrong?" I immediately feel anxious again. Jesus, what a fucking emotional rollercoaster this is. "Maybe you two could form a human chain and stop him from murdering me," I say, only slightly joking.

"He will do no such thing," she says with a quiet chuckle.

"You're right; it's really more Cat's dad I need to worry about," I say through gritted teeth. "Jesus..." I sigh quietly.

"Sticks and stones, baby boy. Whatever their initial reaction will be, just remember that it's instinctive. It'll be based on shock and surprise and probably a lot of concern for you and Cat. Things will simmer down, they will stabilize, and everything is going to work out. Everything is temporary, even the hard times."

"I've never wanted you to be more right, Morai."

Cat

I've avoided my parents as much as possible this week, spending every single night at Ronan's place. My dad grumbled about it. A lot. But if he thought he had reason to be mad before, boy does he have another thing coming.

The only person I couldn't truly avoid was my mom. She and I agreed weeks ago that, come summer break, I'd work three full days in her office. Tuesdays, Wednesdays, and Fridays. I do enjoy the distraction, but I can't lie, pretending everything's normal while quietly researching prenatal vitamins between scheduling, confirming, and moving around her appointments has been... exhausting. But at least I haven't thrown up on a patient yet. And seeing as I'm halfway through my first trimester already, I'm thinking my chances are good that I dodged it? Fingers crossed.

And now it's past five. My mom's office is locked up, work left behind, as my mom and I walk into Frank and Penny's house. My mom and I are the last to arrive, and not only that, it's immediately obvious to me that Ronan has made good on his plan to tell his grandparents on their way back from the airport. Saoirse wraps me tightly in her arms, then whispers, "If anyone gives you grief tonight, they'll have Perry and me to reckon with."

She pulls back, gives me a wink, then slips away into the kitchen where my parents are deep in conversation with Frank, Penny, and Perry. The only one I don't spot in the kitchen is Ronan. Not a surprise. Of all the places in this house, the kitchen's his least favorite. Or perhaps I should say most disliked. I follow Saoirse down the hallway, then glance right into the living room.

That's when I spot him.

Ronan's on the living room floor, lying on his side next to one of his baby brothers, who's busy practicing the art of tummy time on a colorful ABC blanket. Ronan's talking softly, coaxing him through it, and every so often he gently helps him roll from front to back and then back again, cheering each tiny success like it's the Olympics.

Something inside me cracks. And then it breaks, revealing something new. Like the seed of a different kind of love—something distinct from what I already feel for Ronan—ready to take root and spread through every inch of me. All the tension I walked in with melts into something mushy, something gooey and hormonal and so totally unhelpful. He's so gentle. So focused. So... instinctive.

Good god, it's absurdly, unproductively hot.

I watch Ronan for a minute, drinking in the moment. No way I'm telling him this—yet—but he's going to be an incredible daddy to our baby. I know that like I know that my name is Cat Leighton Stevenson.

***

The energy around the table is familiar, relaxed. My parents chat with Penny, Frank, and Frank's parents like they're all lifelong friends, maybe even family. The smiles on their faces are genuine, warm.

Ronan's and mine? Masks. All forced smiles that don't reach our eyes, all appropriate nods and one-word responses.

Ronan's been pushing food around on his plate like it personally offended him. He stabs at the potatoes, shifts his vegetables, slices his chicken into tiny pieces, but I haven't seen him lift his fork to his mouth once. I get it. I have taken exactly two bites, once again battling the nausea churning in my stomach, once again wondering if it's nerves or that tiny wiggle worm I saw on the ultrasound Monday.

Regardless, I have the odd sensation of being strapped to the tracks, Ronan by my side, watching the train barrel toward us. I know we can't stop this. All I can do is brace for it and hope we survive.

"So, I think Steve and Ember are going to be fine. Steve talked about a potential transfer. Ran just helped him move into his new apartment last weekend," Frank says, continuing some conversation I wasn't even aware was happening. I only register it when the words stop and the silence shifts.

All eyes turn to Ronan, who's still staring down at his plate, eyes distant and unfocused like his thoughts are a million miles away.

"Ran?" his dad says.

I nudge him. His eyes snap to mine, wide for a second, then I nod toward Frank.

Ronan's eyes turn to his dad. "Uh, sorry. What?"

Frank's brow creases.

"What is going on with you two tonight?" my mom asks, like she's just now noticing how quiet we've been. Her gaze moves from me to Ronan, sharp and assessing. "You've both been unusually quiet. Is everything alright?"

Suddenly, the entire table is watching us.

Ronan's hand finds mine under the table, squeezing tight, grounding. He inhales deeply.

"Sorry, guys," he says. "I don't want to ruin your evening, but... we need to tell you something."

His eyes flick to his grandma, whose face softens almost imperceptibly. You'd only catch it if you already knew she knows. But Ronan does. And whatever quiet message passes between them, it's enough. I feel him square his shoulders beside me, like her silent encouragement just injected him with the courage he needed.

He looks at me first, then around the table. Everyone watches him, quiet and waiting.

Ronan draws another breath. Steady. Solid.

"Cat is pregnant."

I'm holding his hand so tight I'm probably cutting off his circulation, but I can't let go. Not now.

The reaction around the table is instantaneous and explosive.

My mom clasps her hands over her mouth to stifle her shocked cry. My dad jumps up from the table, his chair scraping against the hardwood floor. Frank literally drops his fork and knife, and Penny keeps whispering *oh my gods* and *holy shit* on a loop.

Saoirse's eyes sweep the room like a hawk, calculating which threat to monitor first, while Perry wears the quiet, knowing look of someone who's been here before.

"You're joking, right?" my dad bellows, leaning toward Ronan like he might lurch straight across the table and strangle him.

Ronan just shakes his head.

Not satisfied, my dad turns to me—eyes pleading, searching—like he's still holding out hope this is all just some kind of bad joke. But whatever he sees on my face confirms the truth, and he reverts to glowering at Ronan, face red and seemingly steaming.

"Ran, what the fuck," Frank growls. "Haven't I always told you to be careful? How could you do this to Cat? You're eighteen. *Eighteen!*" His voice rises as he gets to his feet.

Both Penny and Saoirse reach for him, a hand on each arm, like they're bracing for whatever he might do next.

"You need to rein it in, son," Perry says to Frank, calm but firm.

Frank stares at his dad, incredulous. "Are you serious, Dad?"

My own dad starts pacing in tight, angry circles. "Jesus Christ," he barks, before stopping to press his palms to the table and glare at Ronan. "So what are you gonna do, son?" he asks, voice low and sharp. "I hope you don't expect my daughter to drop out of college to raise your kid. You better be ready to step up! God damn it."

Frank continues to pile on. "I can't believe you weren't more careful, Ran. I can't believe you let this happen."

"Bobby!" my mom cries, trying to cut through the chaos, but it's too late. The room is a storm of angry voices and she's only adding to the cacophony.

I hate it. I hate how they're laying into Ronan while he just sits beside me, taking it, his hand gripping mine like an anchor. Only, I'm not anchoring him. He's anchoring me. All strength. All quiet, unrelenting support.

"Well, I hope you're planning on asking Cat to marry you soon," my dad roars, face flushed.

"The fuck he is, Bobby," Frank says, turning sharply. "You're not forcing them to get married just because they're having a baby."

"What the hell are you talking about, Frank? You're okay with these *kids* bringing a baby into the world unmarried?"

"If that's what they choose, then yes. I'm not making my son repeat history. It's bad enough he's going to be a teenage dad. I won't make him get married on top of it. Not unless it's *his* decision. Neither of them should be forced to stay in this relationship if they don't want to." Frank's voice rises, heated. This isn't just about us anymore. It's about his own past, obviously still raw under the surface.

"Okay, I think everyone needs to—" Saoirse says, but she's drowned out by my dad.

"That's bullshit, Frank. They're going to be tied to each other for the rest of their lives. This isn't just about *them* anymore. They made the decision to have sex. They didn't use protection. They weren't careful. And now they have to live with the consequences. And that includes making an honest woman out of my daughter. Do you know the kind of shit Cat will face if Ronan doesn't marry her, yet she's forced to raise his—"

"Can I talk?" Ronan interrupts the thundering, his voice clear and steady as he stands.

The room falls silent, every eye moving to him. He stands tall, shoulders squared, his hand never letting go of mine. I sit there, trying my hardest not to melt into a puddle, because the way he's posturing right now—protective, sure of himself—is sexy as hell. Those hormones are *raging*.

"First of all, Bobby, we *did* use protection. We *were* careful. Always. We never wanted this. It's not like I had a one-night stand with your daughter, planning to never see her again. I'm the product of exactly that scenario—teen pregnancy, forced marriage—and let's just say it didn't turn out great for me. So trust me when I say, nobody regrets this more than I do. I know how hard this is going to be—for her, for both of us."

His voice tightens. "I understand the consequences. I know I need to figure my shit out. Fast. I have every intention of being there for Cat every step of the way, for as long as she'll have me."

He looks down at me then, and his expression softens, eyes full of something tender, unshakable.

"This wasn't the plan. We're scared shitless. But yelling at me won't change what's already real. Cat's pregnant. It is what it is. We've decided to keep the baby. So what we need now—what we could *really* use—is your support. You don't have to be happy about it. But don't treat us like kids. I think we all know that Cat and I have been through more together than most people go through in a lifetime."

He pauses, then nods once, firmly.

"So, congratulations. You're going to be grandparents."

Then he sits down again and pulls me into his arms. God, I could cry from how grateful I am for him in this moment.

"You've decided to keep the baby?" my mom says softly, her hand reaching across the table to find mine.

"Yeah," I say, swallowing hard. "It's a piece of Ran and me. I know it's going to be hard, but I also know we have you all." I glance around the table—to my mom, Penny and Frank, Saoirse and Perry—both of whom are smiling gently. And finally to my dad, whose expression has begun to soften.

"How far along are you?" Penny asks.

"Eight weeks. My due date's Christmas."

"Wait," my dad says, blinking as he starts doing the math. "This happened while we were all in Montana? How the hell? When?"

"Bobby," my mom says, her tone warning. "I don't think you want the details of *how* Cat got pregnant."

My dad shoots another glare at Ronan, and Frank and my mom share a look. I know exactly what they're thinking about: the time they caught Ronan in my room. Little do they know, that was far from the only time that week. We were starved for each other after two months apart.

"I'm going to use this moment of lowered tension to remind the adults in the room that Cat and Ronan are hardly setting a precedent," Saoirse says. "If I recall correctly, Jen, you told me you and Bobby had Cat at twenty—a year older than Cat will be by the time she gives birth. And Frankie—my sweet, sweet, beautiful boy—you were *sixteen* when you told me you'd knocked someone up."

Frank chuffs. "How are you so calm about this, Mom? You didn't react like this when I told you about..."

Saoirse smiles. "Your dad and I had a little bit of a heads-up. We had time to process already."

Frank's gaze shifts to Ronan. There's hurt in his eyes. "You told your grandparents before you told me?"

Ronan doesn't flinch. "It's almost like I knew you'd react the way you did, huh?"

Frank nods, his face falling.

"Okay," Penny says, clapping her hands together gently. "At the risk of upsetting my husband and Bobby even more: I'm kind of excited to throw that baby shower."

My mom smiles beside her, and for the first time tonight, it doesn't feel like the world is burning around me.

"Ooh, and I *really* hope you're having a girl," Penny says. "There is too much testosterone in the Soult family tree."

"I actually think it's a boy," I say softly.

Ronan's eyes search mine, and I smile tentatively, full of something bigger than fear. Maybe this is what trust feels like. I'm terrified. But I'm not alone. And somehow, that makes all the difference.

Friday, June 2nd

Cat

"Oh, there she is!" Saoirse calls when I cross the parking lot toward Murphy's this evening.

Despite it being Ronan's nineteenth birthday, he insisted on working tonight, stubbornly rejecting Shane's offer to cover his shift with a gruff, "I need the money, Shay."

So the Soult family decided: if Ronan won't come to the party, then the party will come to Ronan. He has no idea we're currently congregating outside Murphy's, no clue that the plan is to surprise him with dinner—well, we're eating, he's working, but still—then maybe stick around for a few hours, have some drinks, and make a night of it. Jack's been experimenting with alcohol-free recipes just for me. He even created a mocktail, calling it *The Kitten*. "Cat. Pregnant. Kitten. Get it?" he grinned. *Yeah, I get it.* I admit, I giggled.

My parents are here too, much to my dad's visible dismay. Poor guy has no choice but to celebrate the birthday of "my boyfriend," or, as he's recently started calling Ronan, my "baby daddy."

I hate it. Even more than I hate *boyfriend*. There's something so smug in the way he says it, like he's clinging to the role of disappointed father while simultaneously reducing Ronan to a teenage mistake.

I don't know if my dad realizes it, but every time he makes a comment like that a little more of my respect for him erodes. Resentment has begun to settle in its place, hardening like wet cement.

"Oh, this place smells just like O'Callahan's. Remember, Perry?" Saoirse says as she takes in the pub, the scent of which I've always loved. It's a cozy mix of cedar, teakwood, ale, and Irish food. Warm and comforting.

The atmosphere is lively, with people mingling around the bar and filling the tables, music humming in the background. As always, Murphy's is buzzing. Even the bar counter is completely packed.

"I do," Perry says with a chuckle, turning to my parents. "O'Callahan's was a little pub in Killarney, Ireland, where I worked back in the day—until a young woman named Saoirse walked in and stole my heart."

I smile at the story while scanning the room for Ronan but coming up short. I do spot Shane, though. When our eyes meet, he lights up and makes his way over.

"Hey, Cat!" he says, then falters slightly when he notices I'm here with both families.

"Oh, Shane, hello!" Saoirse beams, pulling him into a hug.

"Hi, Mrs. Soult. Sorry, Saoirse," he says, hugging her back. "So good to see you. How have you two been?" he asks, shaking Perry's hand.

"Really well," Perry says, smiling.

"Man, I really want to come back to the ranch," Shane says, laughing.

"Anytime, son," Perry says.

Saoirse nods beside him. "We'd absolutely love to have you. And bring your beautiful girlfriend."

"I'll totally take you up on that. Just don't tell Ran. I want the good food all to myself," Shane teases.

Saoirse pats his cheek. "I make enough for everyone. Truly, you're always welcome."

"Good, because Tori keeps talking about how badly she wants to go back. She wants to see the baby cows," Shane says, bewildered.

"They're really cute," I say, giggling.

Shane chuckles. "I definitely can't compete with that. So are you guys just dropping by to say hi or actually staying for dinner?"

"We're planning to eat. That's if you have a table for us," Frank says in his deep voice, eyeing the crowd. "You guys are packed."

"Yeah, Friday night in summer. This is the vibe for the next three months," Shane says, grinning. "Come on, I have a spot for you."

He leads us to a large table a little deeper into the restaurant.

"Where's Ran?" Frank asks, looking around.

"He's here somewhere," Shane says with a smirk. "Can I get you all started on drinks?"

We rattle off our orders, and I'm as always impressed that neither he nor Ronan ever writes anything down. Somehow, they never get it wrong.

"Great, I'll be right back with those. Want me to let Ran know you're here, or do you want to spy on him first?" he asks with a grin.

"Oh, I'd love to spy on him," Saoirse says with a mischievous smile.

"I see where Ran gets it from," Shane laughs as he heads off to the bar.

Saoirse sighs as she lowers herself into her seat. "I wish Ran had taken the evening off to spend it with us. It's his birthday."

"Yeah, me too," I say. "Shane offered, but Ran was adamant about working. He's really worried about money right now. I hate that he's working so much more. It's only been a couple of weeks and I can already see how exhausted he is—especially now that summer classes have started."

Frank's brow furrows like this is news to him. "What do you mean *more*? How much more is he working?"

"Uh... I think he picked up about twenty extra hours a week," I say, sheepishly. Guilt coils in my chest. I know he's burning the candle at both ends—because of me. Because I'm pregnant.

It's not like I haven't stepped up. I'm in my mom's office every day, putting every penny I earn into savings for baby stuff. But it's nothing compared to what Ronan's pulling in. When I told him how shitty that made me feel a few days ago, he wrapped me into his arms and said, "Baby, you're growing a whole-ass human. The least I can do is work a little more."

"Well, I'd say that's a sacrifice he'll have to make," my dad says. "That's the price you pay when you bring a child into this world at his age."

And there it is again—my dad putting all the weight on Ronan's shoulders. Like this isn't my baby too. Like I didn't choose this just as much as he did.

"We know that, Dad," I snap.

Saoirse doesn't look pleased. "So how much is he working now?"

"Sixty hours," I say.

"A week? Plus school?" she asks, stunned.

I nod.

The sharp look she gives Frank could cut glass. "Frankie, I expect you to have a chat with your son. This isn't sustainable. It's your duty to support him—not just emotionally, but financially. Just like we did for you."

"Mom, of course I'll help with whatever they need," Frank says, jaw clenched. "But Ran... he doesn't accept my help."

"That's because he grew up never being able to ask for it," Saoirse says, voice steady but firm. "And now he's a man who won't. But that doesn't mean you're powerless. He can still learn to count on you. It'll just take work."

"I'm open to suggestions," Frank says, frustrated. "I have a hard enough time just getting him to respond to my texts, Mom. It's not like I don't try!"

"You need to get away with him," Perry says, finally speaking. "Just the two of you. Somewhere quiet. Force the conversation. Ronan's great at avoiding things—you've got to put him in a place where he can't dodge it. Then you lay it all out. Be honest."

"Yeah... maybe," Frank murmurs, rubbing the back of his neck.

"And honestly, Frank," my mom chimes in with a little laugh, "short of locking Ronan in a room with you, just keep showing up for him. Even when he ignores your calls, even when he won't let you help. Keep showing up. Keep doing the shadow work. He'll learn that you're not going anywhere." She softens. "It's a slow process. But if you're consistent—if you're gentle—he'll start to believe you."

I spot Ronan only a moment later and nod toward him as he delivers an overfull tray of food to a large table, then heads back behind the bar to chat with Jack. There's a gorgeous smile on his lips and his shoulders are relaxed.

Then a petite blonde sidles up to the bar, clearly aiming to catch his attention. She twirls a piece of hair around her finger, hops up on the bar stool, and leans in way farther than necessary. She flashes Ronan a smile that's all teeth and cleavage. I know the look. I've seen it a hundred times.

Something squirms in my chest, and this time I know it's *not* my little wiggle worm. It's that dumb little fuzzy monster in my chest that occasionally wants to make me into a jealous girlfriend. But as quickly as it blinked its eyes open, it closes them again—because Ronan just listens politely to the girl, lifts a couple glasses onto his tray, then walks away. Doesn't even look back.

The blonde takes her drink from Jack and struts over to the table directly next to ours, joining four other girls already seated.

"We just got here and Kaylee is already on the prowl," one of them snorts, nodding toward the bar.

"I'd let him wreck me," Kaylee says in a breathy voice, her eyes trailing over Ronan's body like she's mentally undressing him. "God, just *looking* at him gets me wet."

"I'd take a turn," another girl says, sipping her drink like it's a secret. "Or maybe we could share."

I get it. I do. Ronan is stupid hot, which may or may not have been the reason I was late to my mom's office this morning. As if I needed another reason to be utterly attracted to and turned on by him, my hormones are somehow only amplifying everything.

Tonight, he's wearing light-washed jeans sitting low and leisurely on his hips and black long-sleeved shirt hugging every sculpted inch of his arms and back. His V-taper is visible even through the fabric, and his sleeves are pushed to his elbows, begging me to trace my tongue along his forearm veins. His dark-blond hair is tucked beneath his black ball cap, and he moves with the ease of someone who has no idea just how devastatingly perfect he looks.

Saoirse blinks at the table beside us, clearly scandalized. She turns to me. "Does this not bother you?"

I smile. "Not really."

"Really?"

I shrug. "This happens all the time."

"This *obviously*?"

"Oh, this is tame," I say. "You wouldn't believe how handsy some of them get."

"No!" Saoirse gasps.

"Yep. Especially when they're drunk."

"Like... where do they grab him?" Penny asks, totally invested now.

"Wherever they can reach. His chest, his butt, his..." I trail off with a pointed look and a laugh.

"My *goodness*," Saoirse says, shaking her head.

"What does Ran do?" Penny asks.

"He tries to get away. He's polite, sometimes too polite, honestly. He lets them down easy if he can."

"You're so calm about this," Saoirse says.

"There's nothing I can do," I say. "I don't think Shane would appreciate me throwing down in here," I add with a giggle.

"You're not worried he'll give in at some point?" my dad asks with that smug look on his face I've come to expect whenever he makes a dig at Ronan.

I turn to him with a firm shake of my head. "Never. I trust him."

Saoirse smiles gently, and I can feel everyone else at the table quietly acknowledging my dad's *bare minimum* tolerance of Ronan. No one calls him out, though. Yet.

At the table beside us, the blonde—Kaylee—is still going. "I'm gonna ask for his number," she announces.

"Kaylee, guys that hot are always taken, gay, or have serious issues," one of her friends says knowingly, though she's still eyeing Ronan like he's on the menu.

"I'm not trying to *marry* him," Kaylee laughs. "I just want to take him home for a night. Let him ruin me."

"Oh my god," Penny mutters, eyes wide. "No wonder you're pregnant." She leans toward me. "Did you let that boy *ruin* you?"

"Penny!" my mom gasps.

"What? It's a compliment," Penny says, laughing. "Look at him."

"You remind me of my friend Vada," I tell her, laughing too. "She'd say the exact same thing."

But that's enough of this. I push back my chair and get up, my gaze zeroing in on Ronan, who's just come back around the bar. His eyes land on me and his whole face lights up like a kid on Christmas morning. That slow smile spreads across his lips, and my heart does a little somersault.

"Hey baby," he says, but I'm already moving. I throw my arms around his neck and kiss him like it's the only way I know how to tell him how much I love him. I feel him exhale against my mouth, his hands settling on my waist, steady and sure, before he tugs my body flush to his. When I finally pull away, he looks dazed.

"Well. Hello," he murmurs, eyes still on me. "That was a nice greeting."

"Just needed to remind the room who you belong to," I say, brushing my fingers through the hair peeking from beneath his ball cap. "Also, I love you."

He laughs quietly, pulling me closer. "I love you, too. What are you doing here?" He glances past me, eyes widening when he sees the table. "Oh shit, how long have you guys been here?"

"Ten minutes," I say. "Your grandma told Shane not to tell you so she could spy on you first."

He groans. "Of course she did."

I grab his hand, linking our fingers, and guide him toward the table. I don't even bother looking at the group of girls. I can *feel* their disappointment. And it tastes... sweet.

"Hi, baby boy," Saoirse chirps as she stands.

Ronan wraps her in a big, warm hug. "Hi, Morai," he says, quiet with affection.

He hugs Perry next, then gives Frank, Penny, and my parents a polite wave before crouching to peer into the car seats secured atop two highchairs. His baby brothers are still sleeping, pink-cheeked and peaceful.

"They're getting so big," he whispers.

"They smile when they fart," Penny says.

Ronan laughs, tired but full of love.

I slide into my chair, tugging at his sleeve. "Come sit," I whisper. "Just for a few minutes."

Ronan glances over his shoulder back at the bar.

Shane grins, then shouts, "Take a break! We got you, birthday boy."

Ronan takes a seat in the chair next to me, our knees brushing, his arm draping across the back of my chair. I rest my hand on his thigh, grounding him.

He closes his eyes, and, for a moment, he's still. Present. And I let myself soak it in.

He's mine. And I'm keeping him.

Thursday, June 22nd

Ronan

"What the hell? Whose car are you driving?" Shane asks as we walk out of Murphy's together.

It's one of the rare nights we closed the place down together. Usually we tag-team it, switching off between shifts. I take most nights to accommodate my class schedule while Shane handles most day shifts. But tonight we were short on waiters. Summers are usually that way. People get flakey, want to spend the balmy evenings anywhere but at work. I get it. I'd much rather be at Shane's mom's beach house, hanging out with Cat, my friends and brother, than have some drunk assholes short me on tips or keep them from getting handsy with a girl. But I can't afford to act like a nineteen-year-old, can't afford to blow off my responsibilities to have a grand ole time. Time to buckle up.

But getting to work the night shift with Shane was a nice little treat. I still prefer it when we work together. He's been my best friend since we were kids, and honestly, one of the only people I trust with my life.

"Mine," I grumble as I unlock the driver's side of the white RAV4 I picked up today.

Shane stops walking. "What the fuck are you talking about? Where's your Mustang?"

"I sold it." I keep my tone neutral, steady, even though something twists hard in my chest.

He stares at me like I've just confessed to murder. "What? Why? When?"

"Because Cat's having a baby and I can't exactly strap a car seat into the back of a two-door Mustang," I say matter-of-factly. "So, here I am. Driving this... toaster."

"Dude," Shane breathes, moving around the car slowly like it might bite him. "You really sold the Mustang?"

I nod once.

"Fuck." His voice drops. He gets it.

It was a decision I knew I had to make. The Mustang wasn't built for hauling around an infant, and we needed something... practical—four doors, easy access, real trunk space. Still, selling it felt like ripping off my own skin. That car meant more to me than almost anything else I owned. It was mine. My escape. The first thing I'd ever fought for and earned outright. The one thing that didn't come with strings attached or the expectation of pain.

"Plus, I needed the money. This'll take a little pressure off. Enough to breathe a little easier, you know?" Not that I really do. Lately it's like I've forgotten how. Between the panic about becoming a father, figuring out how to support Cat, and the thousand ways I'm convinced I'm going to fuck this all up, I'm drowning most days.

Shane's brow softens with empathy. "You shouldn't have to sell your soul to breathe."

I shrug, not trusting myself to respond to that.

"Who'd you sell it to?"

"Some guy from New Hampshire. Picked it up this morning."

Shane blinks. "Ran, why didn't you tell me? You've been in love with that car since we were kids. Hell, I think you begged my dad to sell it to you before you hit puberty."

"I was thirteen. Definitely had hit puberty by then," I say, trying for some levity.

Shane's right. I was obsessed with his dad's car the moment I saw it in their garage, collecting dust. On my sixteenth birthday, I scraped together every ounce of courage I had and asked Shane's dad if he'd sell it to me.

Made me negotiate, too. Not that I had much leverage or really anything to offer. A couple grand I'd saved from bussing tables. I drained my savings and promised to work for free for months. But the car was mine.

Shane huffs out a laugh. "Still. I wish you'd said something."

"It happened fast," I say, trying to brush it off. "Guy contacted me the second I listed it. No haggling. He just paid what I asked. Now that I think about it, that probably means I should've asked for more. By the time I realized he was serious, he was already on his way. Showed up this morning looking like a kid on Christmas. I swear he had a hard-on just from looking at it; damn near moaned when he sat in it." I wince at the memory. The look on that guy's face still makes my skin crawl. I kind of wanted to punch him. Or maybe beg him not to drive off. Or both.

Shane winces. "Fuck. That had to hurt."

"Like a bitch," I mutter. "I almost didn't let go of the keys. Thought about snatching them back and slamming the door in his face."

"You could've," Shane jokes gently, then falls silent for a second. "But... I get it, man. You're doing what you gotta do."

I nod again, this time more slowly.

Shane studies the RAV4, then opens the passenger door and slides into the seat. "Honestly, it's not the worst. Plenty of room. Great for, you know, hauling diapers and strollers and... existential dread."

"You're a dick," I mutter, but I'm grateful for the grin that tugs at my lips.

We sit in silence for a moment, the weight of that truth hanging between us. Then Shane reaches over and pats the dashboard.

"You know what, Ran? Look at this as you leaving your past behind. The Mustang allowed you to get away. To *run*. No more running. This is a new start. New memories. Ones that will be worth a hell of a lot more. Ones that won't give you nightmares."

I don't respond. I'm too busy trying to swallow whatever emotion just crept up and lodged in my throat.

"Fuck, Ran. I can't believe you're gonna be a dad," he says so quietly it's almost a whisper.

"That makes two of us." I stare ahead, then huff a quiet laugh. "It's weird. Yesterday, Cat was getting into the shower—"

Shane raises a suspicious eyebrow. "Where are you going with this?"

"Calm yourself down," I say, rolling my eyes at him. "Nothing dirty, okay? She was getting into the shower and I swear she wasn't showing the day before. But then, suddenly... there was this tiny bump. Like she just popped overnight. And... I wouldn't have noticed if she wasn't standing there naked, but..." I trail off, remembering the odd warmth that started in the center of my heart and pulsed through every inch of me.

Shane's expression softens as he studies me. "Are you freaked out?"

"I don't know. Maybe?" I pause, searching for the right words. "I don't know what to expect. But she's so fucking beautiful, Shane. And those new curves? Fuck... I kind of like it," I say, scrunching my nose like there's something wrong with me.

But Shane nods. "I've always thought pregnant women were really sexy, too," he says, surprisingly sincere. "It's like the ultimate femininity, right? Soft, curvy, powerful. And when it's your baby in there? That's gotta mess with your head in the best way."

Yeah, it really fucking does. But I'm not ready to admit that out loud. Not yet. Not when the universe has always found a way to fuck with me the moment I had something even remotely good in my life.

Shane chuckles. "I honestly can't wait to get Tori knocked up."

I laugh out loud. "You're so full of shit."

He shakes his head. "I'm serious, Ran. I want it all with her. I want to make her my wife, have a whole football team of kids. I want to grow old with her by my side and die surrounded by fifty grandkids."

"Well, great, get started then so my kid can play with your kid." It feels strange talking about Shane's and my kids playing together.

Shane chuckles, but something in his face shifts and he sobers. "Actually... I've been meaning to show you something."

He climbs out of the passenger seat and heads toward his Jeep. I follow him, then watch as he pops open the glove box. When he turns back around, he's holding a small blue box.

"You've lost your fucking mind," I say, staring at the thing like it might explode.

He swallows, then flips open the lid to reveal a diamond-encrusted ring, the smile stretching across his face half-nervous, half-giddy.

"I've been trying to figure out the right moment to ask her," he says, his voice suddenly quieter. Reverent. "You think I'm rushing it?"

"I mean, I don't think I have any right to tell anyone that they're rushing anything," I say with a quiet chuckle.

I look at the ring, then him. He's holding the box like it's the most precious thing in the world, and I realize he isn't just holding a ring. He's holding a future with the girl he loves.

I study him, his love for Tori practically tattooed on his face. Fuck, I still remember the moment I introduced them to each other... "That being said, no," I continue honestly. "Not when it feels like this."

"Thanks, man." He closes the ring box before safely storing it in his glove compartment. "How about you? Any intention of asking Cat to become Mrs. Soult? Seems logical given—"

"The fact that she's spawning my child?"

"Those weren't the *exact* words I was going to use, but... yeah," Shane laughs. "So?"

I exhale slowly, feeling the weight of that question settle in. "The thing is... if I asked her now and she said yes, I'd always wonder if she only said yes because she felt trapped. She's having my baby, Shay. And her dad's already made it blatantly clear that I should 'make an honest woman out of Cat,'" I say, making air quotes. "And Cat would probably think the same of me. That I'm only asking her because I feel pressured to. I don't want that."

I glance at Shane, seeking his understanding.

"If I ask her to marry me, I want it to be because we both *want* that future, independent of all the outside noise."

He nods. "I get that."

I lean back against the side of his car, staring up at the sky. "The last thing I wanted... *want* is to repeat history. And sometimes... it feels like I'm already on that exact same path. It scares me, Shay. It's like even though I see myself barreling toward the edge, I can't fucking stop it."

"You're always so hard on yourself, Ran." Shane's voice is gentle now, without sarcasm. "First of all, shit happens. Cat was on birth control. It failed. That's not some moral failing on your part. And second, I *know* you're not your mother. Or your grandfather. You'd never hurt Cat. Or your kid. You just don't have that in you."

I shake my head. "You're wrong. I do have it in me. I've been in situations where I've seen nothing but red, Shay, and—"

He cuts me off. "You mean Adam? Dude, that wasn't you losing control. That was you defending Cat. You weren't the god damn aggressor here. You didn't just beat the shit out of him because you thought it was fun. You wouldn't have so much as touched a hair on his head if he hadn't come for the person you love most in this world. Twice! You're not your past," he says, softer now. "Stop looking at every new day like it's yesterday. It's not. This is your tomorrow, Ran. You're already building it."

***

Shane and I take our separate cars home.

This new car is still so unfamiliar. I don't know what to do with my right hand now that the transmission's automatic, so I just let it rest on the shifter like it's lost all purpose. Might as well amputate it.

I don't even use my right hand to jack off. The engine doesn't roar to life the way my Mustang used to. It just... hums awake when I press the button. No key to turn. Not to unlock the door, not to start the engine. Just that dumb little fob sitting in the cupholder, as useless as my hand on the gearstick.

It smells clean. New. Like it hasn't lived yet. No sweat or spilled drinks or spicy backseat memories clinging to the upholstery. No character. I can't even tell if this car's a he, a she, or an it.

And it's white. Not sexy satin-black. Not even a sharp electric-blue or deep steel-gray. Just... white. At least the interior isn't beige. God, I'd have fucking died.

It takes me a solid minute to find the button for the parking brake—of course it's a button—and by the time I climb the stairs to our third-floor apartment, Shane's already inside, the door unlocked behind him.

We don't bother with the lights. I could navigate this place blind by now, it's so familiar. Honestly, it feels more like home after nine months than my dad's house ever did.

I rinse the day off in the shower, quick and mindless, then brush my teeth in the dark. I have no problem with it, with shadows, with silence. They keep you safe. Noise, light? Those only drew unwanted attention, made my mother realize I was around to serve as her punching bag. So I learned to become invisible.

My bedroom's just as dark, just as quiet. I close the door behind me with a soft click, sealing off the rest of the world.

I tug at the towel around my waist, letting it fall where it does. I'll deal with it later. Right now, all I care about is the shape curled up in my bed, the one that makes everything else fall away.

Cat.

She hasn't spent the night with me in a couple of weeks now. Her dad's been giving her a hard time. She hasn't gone into detail, but she doesn't need to. I know he doesn't like me, blames me for... well, everything. Rightfully so, I guess. I told Cat not to pay it any mind, but she's forever a peacekeeper, and as much as she's realized people-pleasing isn't always healthy, I understand why it's much harder to go against your parents than someone on the outside, especially now that we may need to rely on them for help very soon.

But she's here tonight, asleep on her side, facing away from the window she must've cracked open for me. Cool air slips through, giving the room my favorite kind of chill. And, god, she looks so peaceful, so *at home* in my bed it makes something tighten in my chest.

She's the opposite of everything about that new car parked on the curb. The car is sterile. Smooth. Buttoned-up. White, with no personality. Cat is all curves and warmth and chaos and color. She's scent and softness and breath. She's mine, even when my demons say she shouldn't be.

Her right hand rests over her stomach, a pillow tucked under it like she's cradling the tiniest secret. She's barely showing. There's just the faintest swell, something no one would notice unless they were looking for it. But I notice. I notice everything.

She says she's not having many symptoms, that it's all easy so far. Except I notice her fatigue, the frequency of her trips to the bathroom at night, the wrinkling of her nose when something doesn't smell quite right to her. Little tells she probably doesn't even realize I'm clocking.

And then there are the other changes. The ones that get under my skin in all the best ways. She's always been unreal, twelve-out-of-ten, knock-the-wind-out-of-me gorgeous. But lately? Lately, there's this softness, this fullness to her curves that drives me completely fucking insane. And it's not just physical. It's the way she *wants* me. The way she reaches for me, takes the lead, chases her pleasure like it's something urgent.

It's the hottest thing ever.

Quietly, I pad to my side of the bed. My fingers graze the edge of the blanket as I slide beneath it, the mattress dipping with my weight. I inch toward her, slowly, carefully, letting her presence wrap around me before I even touch her. I find her warmth and, *fuck*, she's naked.

My breath catches in my throat as I settle behind her, letting my hand glide to her waist. She shifts slightly in her sleep and makes a soft sound but doesn't wake.

I press my nose to her head and inhale. She smells like lavender and rosewater, and something else I don't have a name for. All I know is it's *her*. It's safety. It's want.

Carefully, I trace my fingers along the gentle dip of her waist, up her side to the arc of her ribs, then under her arm to the warm swell of her breast. She fits perfectly into my palm, like she was made for me. Her nipple tightens under my thumb, and I stifle a groan as I press against her. I'm already so damn hard for her.

I lean in, brushing a kiss over the curve of her shoulder, then up to her delicate jaw. Her skin tastes like sleep and warmth.

She doesn't speak, but I know she's awake by the soft moan that slips from her lips just before her hand moves from her stomach to my hair. Her fingers curl there, and she turns just enough to find my mouth.

She kisses me like she's starving. Like I'm the answer to every question she didn't know she was asking.

I shift even closer to her, desperate to erase every molecule of air between us as my hand glides down her front, slow, memorizing, *feeling* that soft, barely-there bump of her lower stomach. I spread my fingers over it, letting my palm settle there for a moment, allowing the weight of it all to remind me what and whom I'm killing myself for right now. Not my yesterday. My tomorrow.

Then I continue lower, slipping between her thighs.

She parts them willingly, instinctively, and my fingers find the heat of her. *Fuck. She's already so wet.* My middle finger slides through her slickness, parting her softly, circling over her clit with slow, careful pressure. I take my time, learning what her body wants tonight. She's so responsive, every breath a reaction, every thrust of her hips a silent plea.

I dip my finger lower, teasing her entrance, then ease it inside her. She moans into the dark, her fingers still buried in my hair, her body matching the rhythm I set.

I withdraw the finger slowly, savoring the way her heat clings to me, and bring it up to her mouth.

"Open for me," I whisper.

Her lips part without hesitation, her tongue darting out to taste herself from my hand. The sight of it, the feel of her mouth on my finger, the soft suck... *shit*, I almost come right then and there.

"Jesus, Cat," I breathe, the sound wrecked and reverent all at once.

I slide my hand back down between her thighs, this time with purpose. I stroke her again, finding that rhythm she loves—slow at first, precise, then building. I can read her body like a book, every moan, every rock of her hips, every pleading whimper like a poem written only for me.

Her hips move with my hand, her thighs trembling around my hand, and I keep my mouth close to her ear, whispering things I reserve for exactly these moments.

She presses her ass into me, her thrusts more desperate, unrefined, as her breaths morph into shallow inhales of air. "So needy for me," I groan into her ear. "Come for me, baby. That's it."

She tightens around my fingers, her breath hitching high in her chest, and then she's coming, pulsing, her body arching, head tipping back against my shoulder, moaning my name like it's the only word she remembers. And, fuck, it's the only word I need to hear.

Her breathing's ragged, little gasps slipping from her parted lips as her thighs twitch. I keep my strokes steady, easing her down from the high I just took her to. My lips graze her shoulder, her neck, her jaw again. "You're so soft, so perfect," I murmur into her ear. "You did so good."

She shifts, her hand sliding off my head, and rolls forward, moving the pillow that had been tucked under her stomach. Then, wordlessly, she presses her chest to the mattress, her spine a graceful curve, her back arching, her ass tilted up and toward me in open invitation. Her head turns, just enough for her eyes to find mine in the dark, and the look she gives me—glossy, wrecked, wanting—is almost too much.

"Holy fuck," I whisper, not even trying to hide the desperation in my voice.

I kneel behind her, dragging my hand from her shoulder along her spine, slow and deliberate, like I'm tracing a path of worship. I settle at her hips, hands resting there as I take a breath, trying—and very much failing—not to lose my mind.

"You want it like this?" I ask, even though we both know the answer.

She gives the barest nod, followed by a breathy, desperate, "Yeah."

I line myself up, guiding myself with one hand while the other rests gently on her waist. And then I pause. Just for a second.

Her doctor said it was safe. That I wouldn't hurt her. That I wouldn't hurt the baby. But there's still a part of me—a loud, terrified part—that worries I could do damage just by wanting her too much. By needing her the way I do.

So I go slow, shaking with restraint as I push forward, easing into her inch by inch, every part of me tuned to her, the smallest shift in breath, the slightest sound. My body screams at me to possess her, to bury myself deep, to let go completely. But I don't. I can't. I won't hurt her.

Cat's impatience, however, tells me she doesn't care for careful. She exhales sharply, hips pressing back, greedy for more. I give it to her—still steady, still mindful—until I'm fully, deeply inside her, surrounded by heat and softness and that impossible closeness that makes the rest of the world fade away. I hit the edge of her, the very limit of what she can take, and stay there.

"God, Cat," I breathe, the words rasping from my chest. "You feel... fuck."

She makes a sound—half-gasp, half-moan—and I pause, just to let myself *feel*. The way my hands tremble on her hips, not from hesitation, but from how vulnerable I am, how completely undone. How utterly, deeply, unconditionally in love I am.

I start to move, each thrust a long, deep stroke meant to savor her. To honor her. To hold her gently from the inside out. She moans, her fingers gripping the sheets, her back arching. I glide my hands over her waist, down to her hips, grounding myself in the feel of her skin, in the way her body yields and takes me in again and again.

But it's not enough for her.

She pushes back into me harder, meeting my thrusts, trying to take more. Her breath stutters, her voice ragged. "Harder, Ran. Please, *please*—just..." she moans.

Her desperation undoes something in me.

She doesn't want careful. She wants *everything*. And she wants it now. Feral. Wild. Needy.

I grip her hips tighter, let go of the tension coiled in my spine, and give her what she's begging for. My pace breaks. No more holding back. My body answers hers thrust for thrust, deeper, harder, meeting every roll of her hips with mine. She moans like she's lost in it, hair falling in waves around her shoulders, her breath breaking on every exhale.

She's taking what she needs, and fuck, I *want* her to.

She moans loudly, no care that the walls are paper-thin, no care who might overhear, like she *wants* to make her pleasure known. Like she's claiming it.

There's no hesitation left. No fear. Just this rhythm we fall into. Sweat and skin and breath and need. Her body, wrapped around mine. Her moans, her heat, her strength. The way she commands it, commands *me*. Not with words, but with her body, with the way she opens for me, the way she *trusts* me to meet her right here, in the thick of it.

Every thrust is a vow. Every gasp, a prayer. This isn't just sex. It's devotion. It's trust. It's everything I've never known how to ask for. And somehow, still, everything she gives me freely.

Friday, June 23rd

Cat

I wake up warm, tangled in sheets and memory and the delicious ache of satisfaction still pulsing under my skin.

Despite the obscene hour we finally passed out, I feel... good. Great, actually. I feel rested and loose-limbed and sore in a way that makes my toes curl just thinking about it. My thighs ache. My lower back. Even my hips where his hands held me so tightly last night. It's the kind of soreness that doesn't ask for relief. It begs for a repeat.

But the bed is empty next to me.

Ronan's already up.

Of course he is.

He never seems to need sleep the way I do, and lately I seem to need twelve hours plus a nap to be functional.

And I also need more of Ronan just to feel sane.

Wanting him isn't new by any means. I've always wanted him. But lately it's not just want. It's need. Deep in my bones. In my blood. There's a low, constant hum of desire threading through my days, tugging at the edges of my thoughts like a live wire. Sometimes all it takes is a glance. Sometimes it's nothing, maybe just the memory of his voice, the smell of his skin, the way his hand looked on the curve of my thigh last weekend.

And when he touches me? It's like my body short-circuits. I come apart so fast now, like I'm primed for him, always on the cusp of falling.

I even asked Doctor Simmons about it at my last appointment. Half-embarrassed, half-desperate to understand what the hell was happening to me. She just smiled knowingly, like she'd heard it all before, and told me that, while some women don't want to be touched at all during pregnancy, others experience increased arousal. Heightened sensitivity. Higher need.

"Increased blood flow," she'd said, like that explained the way I'm constantly on fire.

I don't think Ronan minds. I mean, he hasn't complained once, always giving me exactly what I ask for and when. But sometimes it's a little... inconvenient.

Like Sunday, when we went to the movies. I don't even remember what we saw. Something loud and long and action-packed. All I remember is how I couldn't stop staring at his hands, the shape of his mouth in the dim light. How, by the time the credits rolled, I was practically vibrating. I dragged him out by the arm, told him to drive us somewhere—anywhere—then climbed into the backseat of the Mustang before the car had even cooled. Then I rode him hard and fast until I found the release I had been craving.

Oh, the Mustang.

I swallow, my throat tightening a little. I tried to talk Ronan out of selling it, but it was already too late. He only told me after he had listed it. It was a sacrifice I didn't want him to make. I know what that car meant to him. I saw it in his eyes yesterday, the way his jaw tensed when the middle-aged guy with the receding hairline showed up to take it. I watched Ronan hand over the keys, his fingers lingering just a second too long, like maybe he'd change his mind. Then the Mustang was loaded onto a transport truck and gone.

We stood there on the sidewalk for a long time afterward. I wrapped my arms around him from behind, held him while he stared down the street like he could still hear the rumble of the engine. I didn't try to cheer him up or talk it away. I just stayed with him. Allowed him to feel the loss.

All for me. For *us.*

My fingers brush the small swell of my belly, just barely a curve now, but real. Growing. Present. I exhale, my palm resting there a moment like I'm grounding myself.

I only entered my second trimester a few days ago, and already the changes feel impossibly fast. I didn't expect to *see* anything this soon, but my body's doing its own thing, and I'm learning, slowly, stubbornly, to let it. Like I have a choice...

I slide out of bed and tug one of Ronan's shirts over my head. It's loose on my body, soft against my skin. Even better? It smells like him. I pull on a pair of his boxer briefs too. They're stretchier and more forgiving than my own underwear. Comfort wins this round.

My bladder doesn't wait. Another lovely pregnancy feature: everything on me is growing, including my libido, but my bladder has apparently decided to downsize. After I pee, I brush my teeth and run a brush through my hair, then shuffle into the living room where I find Ronan and Shane hunched over Ronan's laptop like two overly serious CEOs. They're so unlike what I'd expect other nineteen- and twenty-year-olds to be like. No video games. No sports. Just full-on business mode.

I settle on the couch beside Ronan and he immediately curls an arm around my shoulders, pulling me against him like I'm just another part of him.

"Morning, baby," he murmurs, kissing the side of my head.

"Hey, sweet boy," I say, voice still raspy from sleep. "What are you guys working on?"

"Going paperless," Shane says without looking up. "We're updating our systems to make it easier for customers to order, close out, and pay. Ran and I are just talking through the strategy for the rollout."

"Shane's going all techy," Ronan says with a small smirk. "Always messing around with something new."

I smile, honestly impressed. "You two never stop. You're already more responsible than most people I know."

Shane scoffs. "Tell my parents that."

Ronan squeezes me. "How are you feeling this morning?"

"Fine, just... you know, busy growing a whole entire person inside me," I say with a grin.

Ronan's hand flies to his chest, eyes wide. "What? Why haven't you told me? You're pregnant?"

I roll my eyes, but the smile on my lips remains.

Shane grunts, unimpressed. "Not your best, man."

Ronan shrugs, deadpan. "Like you're so fucking funny."

"Funnier than you," Shane fires back.

"Sure, whatever keeps you from crying yourself to sleep at night," Ronan mutters, then turns his attention back to me. "What do you want for breakfast?"

"I'm good with some scrambled eggs and bacon. Oh, and can I get an English muffin with—"

"Strawberry jam," Shane says, cutting me off. "Same."

I laugh.

Ronan narrows his eyes at his best friend. "Not you. You need to watch your waistline."

Shane looks deeply offended. "I *am* the waistline standard."

Ronan snorts. "Of a dad in his fifties, maybe. Dude, my grandpa's more ripped than you."

Shane's mouth drops wide open. "You take that back right now unless you want me to challenge you to a gentleman's duel."

Ronan just laughs, shaking his head like he can't believe Shane sometimes, then shuts his laptop. "Come on," he says, standing and offering me his hand.

I take it without hesitation, letting him pull me up from the couch. His fingers stay laced with mine as he leads me into the kitchen, where the morning light casts a soft glow through the window above the sink.

He moves with purpose, already pulling out eggs and bacon while I head for the coffee maker. My lifeline. My doctor said I didn't have to cut it out completely, that a cup or two a day was fine. Thank goodness for that. I don't know how I'd function without it.

"Ooh, will you make a cup for me, too?" Tori's voice floats into the kitchen with a half-yawn as she peeks her head around the corner. Her bed hair is even wilder than mine.

"You got it," I say with a smile.

"Want breakfast?" Ronan asks her.

Tori nods gratefully. "If it's not too much of a bother."

"Nah." Ronan waves her off, and Tori disappears to join Shane in the living room.

The bacon starts to sizzle just as Ronan's phone buzzes against the counter. He glances at it, then answers.

"Hey, Dad," he says. "Hold on, let me put you on speaker. I'm trying to do a thousand things at once." He taps the screen and places the phone down, resuming his bacon-cooking duties as he cracks eggs into a small bowl.

"I found him, Ran," Frank says simply.

My eyebrows pull together; the words mean nothing to me. But Ronan's whole body stills.

"Are you for real?" he asks, frozen in place, his hands hovering in midair.

"Yeah. He's still alive, bud."

I piece it together. "Your uncle?"

Ronan nods, pale, swallowing hard.

I step closer, gently take the tongs from his hand, and nudge him aside. He needs to focus on this conversation.

"Hey, Cat," Frank says, noticing the change.

"Hey, Frank," I say quietly.

"Where is he?" Ronan asks.

"Camden, Maine. He changed his name though, goes by Mac Johnson now."

"Are you sure it's him?"

"I'm sure. Double- and triple-checked. It's him, Ran."

"What... what do you know about him?"

"Well, he's married. Took his wife's last name. They have a son—Mark. He's your age. Looks like they run a small family business. No criminal record, clean background. Not even a speeding ticket, aside from a parking violation or two. He looks like a good guy, Ran."

Ronan lets out a short, dry laugh. "Yeah, well... I'm sure if someone looked at our family from the outside, it would've looked good, too. Military dad. Nurse mom. Two sons. Nice house. No arrests. No way to see what was really happening behind closed doors."

"Fair," Frank says.

"I need to see for myself," Ronan says, tone solid.

"Wait," I say, looking at him. "You want to go see him?"

He nods. "Yeah."

"What's his address?" he asks into the phone.

"Forget it," Frank says. "You're not doing this alone."

"Dad—"

"Don't start. That was the deal. I'm going with you. End of debate."

Ronan sighs. "Fine. When can we do this?"

"Are you working tomorrow?"

Ronan turns to me, surprise flickering across his face. "I'm supposed to work the day shift tomorrow, but I'm sure Shane will let me work a double for him today."

"Totally," Shane calls from the living room.

I can't help but laugh. Eavesdropper.

"Alright," Frank says. "I'll pick you up at seven. It's about six and a half hours to Camden, and we'll stay overnight. You can sleep in the car. Sound good?"

"Yeah," Ronan says, his voice caught somewhere between relief and dread. "Thanks, Dad."

"Ran, I got your back. Always. We all do," Frank says. "I love you, bud."

"Love you, too," Ronan says quietly. "I'll see you in the morning."

I wait until he hangs up, then glance at him. "So, were you going to tell me about this, or...?"

He looks at me with those beautiful green eyes. "Eventually," he says, sheepish. "I asked my dad to help me find my uncle when we were... when we were split up."

"Why?" I ask gently.

He takes a deep breath. "I was so fucking stuck in my head about... well, you know."

"I'm pretty sure you still are," Shane shouts from the living room.

Ronan shakes his head but doesn't argue. "Anyways, I was talking to Randi one day. It was actually her idea. She thought finding him might help me with this fear I have... that I won't be able to break the cycle." His eyes stay on mine, searching, as if trying to see if I understand. I do. "She said that even if things turned out badly—if it turns out he's an asshole, too—it doesn't change anything for me because I'm already assuming that whole side of the family is rotten. I realized she's right—I have nothing to lose and everything to gain," Ronan says, his voice cracking slightly. He sounds like he's still trying to convince himself.

I nod, encouraging him to keep going.

"I asked my dad if he could help me find him back in March. Right after... right after I saw you at Murphy's."

"Are you scared?" I ask softly.

Ronan hesitates. "Yeah. A lot. I'm worried that if he's a shit human, too... it's gonna fuck with my head."

"Ran, I want to go with you," I say, worry bubbling in my chest.

But he shakes his head fast. "No, baby, I need you to stay behind."

I frown. "Why?"

"I know you want to be there for me, and I love you for that. But I need to do this without you. I honestly don't even want my dad there, but he's obviously really insistent."

I stare at him, feeling that familiar pang. "Because we know how you get, Ran. You'll shut down, you'll lock it away, pretend you're fine. And I can't lose you again, sweet boy."

I rest my hand on my stomach, on that tiny baby bump, invisible under Ronan's shirt. "I've always needed you... but I *really* need you now."

He places his hand over mine. His voice is thick when he says, "You won't lose me. I promise. I'll talk to you about it. If it's bad, I'll tell you. But I need to do this. Alone. Or at least—"

"Without me," I finish for him.

"Please don't take this personally, baby. I love you. You're my fucking world. I want to be everything you need me to be. I want to be everything our *baby* needs me to be." His voice breaks slightly on *baby*, and it makes my eyes sting.

"I need to know that I can face this. And if it turns out like shit, I need to be able to process this for a minute before I pick myself up off the ground and keep on keeping on, okay?"

I nod. "Okay." Then I throw my arms around him, needing to feel him close. He wraps his arms around my waist, holding me like he means it.

"Just remember, if it turns out like shit, that says *nothing* about you," I whisper. "You aren't capable of the things you worry about. I know it. *Everyone* knows it. I get why you need to find out, but fight the urge to spiral, okay? Please, Ran, fight!"

"I will," he promises me.

***

He finishes making us breakfast, and we eat together with Tori and Shane, the four of us squeezed around the tiny kitchen table like some weird little chosen family. Afterward, I get ready to put some hours in at my mom's practice while Ronan throws a few essentials into his backpack so he won't have to do it in the middle of the night. He leaves before I do to pick up some supplies, then head into Murphy's to open the place up. It'll be a long day for him. He'll be there until at least two in the morning.

Once the door closes behind him, I glance toward the kitchen, where Tori and Shane are already loading dishes into the sink.

"What do you guys think? About Ronan finding his uncle?" I ask.

Shane sighs. "I don't know. I always worry about him. Ran's real good at acting like nothing touches him, but we all know he gets stuck in his own head. Deep."

"I'm so worried," I say, the words slipping out with a weight I hadn't planned to voice. "What if it goes wrong?"

"Then we'll do what we always do," Tori says calmly. "We'll help him pick up the pieces."

I shake my head, my chest tightening. "Yeah, but he didn't leave you two. He left *me*. And I can't—" My voice cracks. "I can't lose him. Not now. Not ever."

I rest a hand on my stomach. "We have a baby on the way. I can't do this without him."

Tori steps forward and gently places a hand on my arm. "He's not going to leave you again," she says with steady conviction.

"No way in hell," Shane says. "Ran already figured out that breaking up with you did nothing but make you both miserable. Look, he's back in therapy, yeah? And he's actually talking more. I've seen him trying not to shut us out. That's real progress."

He gives me a half-smile. "I'm gonna give you the same advice I give him all the damn time: don't go down the rabbit hole. Don't live in your head too much."

I let out a shaky breath, grateful and still scared.

"It'll be what it'll be," Shane says, more softly this time. "Let's just hope—for once—it turns out okay. Ran needs a win."

I couldn't agree more.

Shane chuckles. "Sooo... I don't know if this is a good time or whatever, but I feel like you should know—I've got a pot going."

My eyebrows shoot up. "For what?"

"Bets," Tori says with a small shrug. "On whether you're having a boy or a girl, and when you'll actually give birth. I said girl. January second."

I laugh. "Are you serious?"

"I would *never* joke about something as serious as a bet," Shane says, completely straight-faced, making me laugh again.

"It's a twenty-dollar buy-in," he says. "The winnings are split fifty-fifty. Half goes to you guys, half to the winner."

"Well, that's... interesting," I say, still smiling. "So who all's in on this?"

"Well, Tor and me, obviously," Shane begins. "Stevie, Vada, Zack, Summer, and basically everyone at Murphy's—except Cadance, because apparently her religious beliefs don't allow gambling. Jack bet twice—boy *and* girl. Smart-ass," he says with a chuckle.

I shake my head, grinning. "Oh my god, Shay."

He shrugs. "Are you sure you don't want to find out and maybe just... tell me?"

Tori swats his shoulder. "Hey! If anyone gets to know, it's me. I was *there* when she found out she was pregnant."

I laugh, watching them bicker fondly.

"Doesn't look like either of us is getting lucky," Shane says with a throaty chuckle.

"Nope," I say, still smiling.

"I don't think I could handle the suspense." Tori starts wiping down the counter. "I'd *have* to know, just so I could prepare properly."

"Why don't you want to find out?" Shane asks, his tone sincere now.

I shrug. "I don't know. I just... don't. I want to be surprised. Like everything with Ran is always a surprise," I say with a laugh, and Shane chuckles too.

"Do you have a preference?" Tori asks.

"Ran said he doesn't care either way," Shane chimes in before I can answer. "He just wants you and the baby to be okay."

That makes me smile. "No preference," I say honestly. Then, after a pause, "But I *do* think Ran would make a great girl-dad. Don't you?"

Tori and Shane both nod without hesitation.

"How about names?" Tori asks. "Have you guys thought of anything?"

I shake my head. "We haven't really talked about it, to be honest. I think we're still just... processing everything."

"Well, you know," Shane says, deadpan, "*Shane* is a great name for a boy."

I laugh again. "Oh, for sure."

"And *Tori* is a great name for a girl," Tori says, grinning.

"Oh yeah," I say, grinning back. "Definitely. Top of our list."

Saturday, June 24th

Ronan

I didn't get much sleep last night. Hardly any, to be honest.

Murphy's was *fucking insane*, and I'm not even exaggerating. We were slammed most of the day, but the evening? Total chaos. We had several birthday parties and *two* separate bachelor parties—one of which turned into a full-on disaster. It took Jack, two of our waiters, and me to kick out five drunk assholes who decided a bar brawl was the perfect way to liven things up.

I didn't get home until almost four in the morning. It took forever to clean up the mess, document the broken chairs and busted table, and make sure Tyler—one of the waiters who helped me throw those guys out—was okay. He got nailed in the head with a beer bottle and ended up needing stitches. One of the other guys drove him to the ER.

I called Shane around midnight to give him a heads-up. He'll have the absolute *joy* of dealing with the insurance today—both liability and workers' comp. I hate when this shit happens on my shift. Shane and his dad trust me to handle things, and I always feel like I've let them down when people act like idiots and ruin the night for everyone.

It was an exhausting night after an already long day. But still, I couldn't sleep.

Even after I dragged myself into bed, I just... couldn't shut my brain off. I kept thinking about the trip. About my uncle. About what I might find in Camden.

Cat wasn't at the apartment when I got home—she stayed at her place last night. It made sense. I got in late, and I was heading out early, but still... I would've loved to crawl into bed next to her. Just to feel her warmth. To hear her soft breathing.

There's no one and nothing that calms my nerves quite like Cat. She's always been medicine for my soul.

As promised, my dad was outside the apartment by seven. We hit the road a few minutes later. I crashed pretty hard in the passenger seat and slept most of the way.

I only wake up when my dad gently nudges me.

"Bud, let's eat something. What do you think?" my dad says as I blink awake and squint at the morning light.

"Okay, sure," I mumble, my voice rough with sleep. I rub my eyes. "How far out are we?"

"A couple hours, maybe." He eases the Tahoe off the freeway. "You slept quite a bit. How was your night?"

So, I tell him. About the packed bar. The back-to-back parties. The idiots who thought a full-on brawl was a solid way to end the night. I talk about Tyler and the beer bottle. About staying until almost four to deal with the aftermath.

My dad lets out a low chuckle as he pulls into a dusty parking lot in front of a small roadside diner. He throws the Tahoe in park and turns to me. "I was one of those idiots once."

I stare at him. "Are you serious?"

He laughs, already opening his door. "Dead serious. I was maybe twenty-one, stationed in Germany. Got absolutely shit-faced with a few officer buddies one night. Tried to make a move on this gorgeous German girl—blonde, blue eyes, *perfect* ass."

"Jesus, Dad. Too much info," I groan, laughing despite myself.

He grins as we both get out. "Hey, I'm just sharing my worldly wealth of knowledge with you. I'm not in intelligence for nothing."

"Oh, sure. So documenting women's bodies around the globe is part of your official duties for the U.S. military?"

"Well, it's not *technically* in the job description, but I like to think it's implied," he says, walking toward the entrance.

I shake my head, still chuckling. "Right. Got it."

"Anyway," he says as he holds the door open for me, "turns out this girl had a boyfriend—Hans or Otto, probably—and he *really* wasn't cool with me hitting on her. Me, being a dumb twenty-one-year-old with more testosterone than sense, thought a fight was a brilliant idea. Didn't end well."

"You got hurt?"

"Black eye. Bad concussion. Two of my buddies needed stitches. It was a whole ordeal—and then came the discipline," he says, chuckling again. A waitress gives us a nod, and my dad points toward a small booth by the window.

We slide into the worn leather bench seats across from each other. I grab a menu from behind the salt and pepper shakers.

"I have to say, Dad... I'm kind of enjoying hearing about this stuff," I say as I flip it open.

"Yeah?"

"Yeah. I mean... this might sound weird, but I feel like I don't really *know* you," I say, brow creasing.

My dad presses his lips together and nods slowly. "I feel the same way about you, Ran. I guess... that's what I get for not being around while you were growing up." His voice is low, full of regret.

"I guess so," I murmur, and we both fall quiet, our eyes scanning the menus but clearly not really reading them.

The waitress comes by to take our orders, and once she leaves my dad excuses himself to use the restroom. I watch him walk away, then pull out my phone and send Cat a quick update.

He returns a few minutes later, sliding back into the booth just as his phone starts to ring. He answers it immediately.

"Hi, baby," he says with a smile. Penny, I assume. "Yeah, we're about two hours out. Ran and I just stopped to grab something to eat... How are the boys?"

He chats with her for a few more minutes, his voice warm as he talks about my twin half brothers, and I try not to listen too closely.

When he finally hangs up, he pockets his phone and looks at me. "Penny says hi."

"Okay," I say. "How is she doing?"

"She's good," he chuckles. "Wasn't thrilled about me being gone tonight. She still gets overwhelmed being alone with both boys. It's a lot, especially now that they're both rolling around like little maniacs. One of them is always trying to off himself."

"Oh, yeah?"

"Yeah. Dean's the main culprit. Kellan's more relaxed, but Dean? Total second-born energy."

He shakes his head, smiling. "The other day he somehow army-crawled under the armchair and couldn't get back out. Penny was freaking out because she couldn't find him—called me in a full panic. Eventually Dean started whining and she found him wedged under there like a grumpy little burrito."

I can't help but laugh.

"Honestly, Dean reminds me so much of you. You think you've got it figured out with your first kid—nice, mellow, follows the rules. And then the second one comes along and he's just... absolutely feral."

"*I* was feral?" I ask, raising an eyebrow.

"Hell yes. You were a menace. Constant energy. You climbed before you could walk, and, shit, you were on top of everything. Chairs, ladders, the banister. You tried to ride a bull calf when you were, like, eighteen months old. Morai said Athair had to rescue you more than once from near-death situations."

"I have *zero* memory of that," I say, shaking my head.

"You were tiny, man. And you never slept. Up till all hours, then awake again at five or six."

"Huh. I guess not much has changed," I say, half to myself. Cat literally mentioned that just yesterday—how I seem to function on less sleep than humanly possible.

"Apparently not. I know Morai always brought you downstairs with her once they got up at three-thirty. You'd just hang out with her," he chuckles. “But yeah, I see a lot of you in Dean. And I see a lot of Stevie in Kellan. I just wish I had shown up for you and your brother like I get the chance to show up for Kellan and Dean now.”

“Yeah,” I say flatly.

“Ran, I—” he starts, but the waitress shows up with our food, placing steaming plates in front of us.

I take the out and push back from the booth. “Gonna hit the bathroom real quick,” I mutter before walking off. I’m not ready to go there with him. Not now.

When I return, my dad gives me a cautious glance as I slide back into the booth.

“So... how’ve you been doing, kiddo?” he asks. “You’re really busy these days.”

“Yeah,” I say. “I’m trying to knock out some classes now so I’ll have more flexibility in the spring. I want to be around to help Cat as much as I can.”

“And you’re working a ton, too.” He watches me closely, his face serious. “Don’t forget to rest, Ran.”

“I don’t really have a choice, Dad,” I say. “I’m just doing what I need to do to make sure Cat and the baby are taken care of.”

He smiles at me, something soft in his expression. “I’m proud of you.”

That catches me off guard.

“For what?” I ask, my brows drawing together. “Following in your footsteps and procreating before I hit twenty?” I ask, sarcasm sharpening my words.

He laughs. “For the kind of man you’re becoming, Ran. I know you don’t see it, but... you had all the odds stacked against you. And still, at barely nineteen, you’re more mature, more responsible, more considerate than I was even in my thirties.” He chuckles a little, though there's something heavy behind it. “I should’ve been more like you when you and Stevie were born. I shouldn’t have left.”

My shoulders tighten. I can tell he's hoping this trip will open some kind of door between us, give us a chance to really talk. To connect. The truth is, my dad and I have never spent this much time alone together. Ever.

And despite everything I've worked on with Dr. Seivert... despite how much I want to let go of all the resentment... I still can't seem to let him in. I feel myself resisting every time he tries to reach for me. And it's not even about what he's saying now. It's not about what he's doing. It's about everything he didn't do before.

"Dad, can we not do this right now?" I say, voice quiet but tense. My brow furrows. And as soon as the words leave my mouth, I feel guilty. "I'm sorry. I just... I don't—"

I don't know how to talk to you. I don't know how to not feel this way. I don't know how to let this go. I don't know how to move on from my feelings of being abandoned by you.

"I just don't want to talk about it."

"No, it's okay, Ran. I'm sorry for bringing it up." He sounds sincere. "I don't want to upset you."

"You're not upsetting me, Dad. It's..." I rake my hand through my hair. "Ugh. I don't know. I just don't want to talk about it."

"No problem," he says gently.

We fall silent again. And just eat.

When we finish eating, my dad pays for the food and we climb back into the SUV to continue the drive to Camden. We talk only occasionally, the conversations light and forgettable. I try to close my eyes again, but I'm too restless now. The closer we get, the more tightly wound I feel.

"So, it looks like he owns a building supply store in town," my dad says as we drive through downtown Camden. "I figured we'd check there first. A little more inconspicuous than sitting outside someone's house for hours," he adds with a chuckle.

"Probably," I say, but my voice is tight. The nerves are pressing in on me now.

Camden's a nice town, from what I can tell. Actually, "nice" probably doesn't do it justice. It's pretty. Picture-perfect, even. There's that small-town postcard vibe: people walking along the sidewalks, popping into cafés and shops, enjoying the warm weather and the sunshine. It's pleasant, but not stifling like back in the city. We're already melting in New York, and I thank Shane every damn day that he had the good sense to find us an apartment with actual A/C instead of just cheap coolers. Total lifesaver.

The streets are lined with storefronts—flower shops, bakeries, boutiques. I focus on them as we drive, trying to anchor myself to the details instead of the pressure cinching my throat shut.

"How's Cat doing?" my dad asks, clearly trying to make conversation. Maybe distract me.

I turn to look at him. "Pretty good. She's getting some of her energy back. She was completely wiped for a while, but she's been feeling a little better lately."

He nods. "Penny was the same way during her first trimester. The second one was easier. But the third..." he chuckles. "That felt like it lasted nine months all on its own. Especially for her."

"I bet," I murmur. "I have to admit, I never really thought much about what women actually go through during pregnancy. But then Cat started telling me about the symptoms, and now, just watching her deal with all of it..."

"They're pretty badass," my dad says, nodding.

"Yeah. And she does it all looking fucking stunning," I say without hesitation.

He smiles. "You really love her, huh?"

"Love isn't a strong enough word," I say. "Worship is probably more accurate."

He chuckles. "Sounds about right. When's her next doctor's appointment?"

"Thursday." I glance out the window again, but I'm not really seeing anything now. "I still can't believe we're having a baby," I say, shaking my head. "It's so damn surreal. I honestly thought she was joking when she first told me. I *hoped* she was... but then I looked at her face... and I just *knew* she wasn't."

I can still picture that exact moment. Her wide eyes. The way her voice trembled just slightly. The way everything shifted in an instant. "Talk about an oh-shit moment," I mumble.

"I know what that feels like," my dad says with a nod, his expression tightening.

Just then, he slows the car and eases into a parking spot across the street from what looks like a hardware store.

"Alright," he says, peering out the driver's side window, "that's the place."

I unbuckle and lean forward to get a better look. The store sits at the corner, front painted a dark navy blue. The black door has a small glass pane with an *Open* sign dangling in the center. It's nothing flashy. Just another neighborhood supply store.

But my pulse starts pounding anyway.

"So, what do we do?" I ask him.

"Reconnaissance," my dad says, eyes still trained on the building.

"I'm sorry, what?"

He chuckles. "We observe and surveil to obtain information."

"You're right back in your element, aren't you?" I ask dryly.

That makes him laugh. "It's what I do, Ran."

"Uh-huh. So, we just sit here?"

"*You* are going to sit here," he says, already popping his door open. "*I'm* going inside to see what I can see."

"No, I want to—"

"Ronan," he says sharply. "Stay put. For now, okay? Please."

I exhale loudly but do as I'm told. He crosses the street and disappears into the store. It's maddening just sitting here alone with my nerves while my dad scopes the place out. Every second stretches too long. But still, I wait.

He comes back ten minutes later with a small bag in his hand.

"You bought something?" I ask as he tosses it into the backseat.

"Had to make it look legit, right?" he says with a half-smile that's basically a carbon copy of mine. It's weirdly comforting. People say I look like my mom—light hair, green eyes—but the shape of my face, the way I move, even some of my facial expressions... that's all him. And I've heard more than once now that I sound like him, too.

"So?" I ask. "What kind of intelligence were you able to gather, Lieutenant Colonel?"

That earns a real laugh. "Cormac is in there," he says, and I swallow hard. "Go inside, take a look around. You're looking for a guy in his early forties, short dark-blond hair, average build, khaki pants, and a fitted navy shirt. Oh, and buy something. Zip ties or whatever."

I raise an eyebrow. "Okay, but just to clarify: why do you want me to buy zip ties? Are we planning to kidnap this dude?"

He laughs again. "Go ahead, Ran. Go check him out."

I open the door and step out, my stomach tight as I cross the street. When I push open the shop door the overhead bell jingles, and I spot Cormac behind the counter. My dad's description was dead-on. He doesn't look up as I walk in.

I stand there for a moment, watching him, trying to detect traces of my mom in his features.

"Do you need help finding anything?" a voice says beside me.

I flinch and turn toward the girl—probably about my age—who's suddenly standing there, waiting.

"No, uh... yeah," I stammer. "Where are your zip ties?"

Smooth.

"Right this way," she says cheerfully.

I tear my eyes away from Cormac and follow the girl as she gestures down an aisle.

"Are you looking for a particular size?" Her gaze flicks to my jeans, then back up. She swallows. "Eight inches? Nine?"

I blink. *Was that a sexual innuendo?*

"Uh, do you have a variety pack?" I ask, thinking quickly.

"Yeah, we have one that ranges from four inches to eighteen," she says as we stop in front of a shelf.

"Perfect," I say, grabbing the plastic container stuffed with about 500 zip ties in assorted colors and lengths.

"Anything else I can help you with?"

"No, I think that's it," I say, feeling like such a fucking idiot for some reason.

"Great. I can ring you up," she says, leading the way to the register.

I glance sideways toward Cormac, who's still absorbed in whatever he's doing behind the counter.

"Do you want a bag?" the girl asks, smiling as I hand her a twenty.

"No, I'm good, thanks," I say. Then, stalling, "Hey, do you guys have a recommendation for a good seafood place around here?"

That gets Cormac's attention. He finally looks up, eyes narrowing as he takes me in.

"Are you not from around here?" the girl asks, her tone flirty.

"No. New York."

"City?"

"Yeah."

"Well, you've come to the right place for seafood," Cormac says, still eyeing me like I'm a puzzle. "You really can't go wrong anywhere in Camden, but this is my personal favorite." He walks over and hands me a business card.

"Thanks." I glance at it, then back at him. He's still studying me. I wonder if he sees my mom in my face. Or maybe his dad. I've always hated how much I resemble her.

"Yeah, no problem," Cormac says with a nod.

I pocket my change, grab the zip ties, and head out, feeling their eyes on me the whole way.

"We're set on zip ties for a while," I mutter when I get back in the Tahoe, slam the door behind me, and toss the container onto the backseat.

"I can't believe you really bought zip ties," my dad laughs. "Did you see him?"

"Yep. Talked to him, too."

"You what?"

"I talked to him," I shrug.

"Damn, Ran. You'd make a great undercover officer. What'd you talk about?"

"Seafood. I asked for restaurant recommendations."

"And?"

I hand him the card. "He said it was his favorite."

"You're killing me, Ran," my dad laughs. "Alright, so, Cormac closes up at four. We've got about an hour. We can either stay here or go wait at his house."

"How far is it?"

"GPS says five minutes."

"Okay. Let's head there and wait. Better than following him home, right?"

"It's always better to be in place before your subject arrives," he says, grinning.

"You're really having fun with this, huh?"

"Maybe a little," my dad admits as he shifts the SUV into drive.

***

We pull up to a white, two-story home just a few minutes later. Two cars are parked in the driveway. I take in the large unfenced yard, the red front door, and the rose bushes blooming under a wide bay window facing the street.

"Nice home," my dad says simply.

I nod. "Yep."

"Looks like Cormac's son and wife are home," he says. "That Subaru is registered to his wife. The blue GT belongs to his son."

I grin. "Kinda love that he drives a Mustang."

My dad chuckles. "Yeah, I bet you do."

We sit there for what feels like forever. About an hour and a half later, he nudges me with his elbow. I look up just as a white GMC pickup pulls into the driveway. We watch silently as Cormac parks, climbs out, and disappears into the house.

"So... now what?" I ask. "More reconnaissance?"

"Yep," my dad says, leaning back.

But there isn't much to see. Just shadows moving behind the windows now and then.

"I'm gonna go talk to him," I say suddenly, already reaching for the door handle.

"Woah, woah, Ran, are you sure?" my dad asks, gripping my arm.

I look him in the eye. "Yeah, Dad. I need to do this."

He studies me for a beat, then exhales. "Fine."

We both get out and walk across the street. My heart is hammering. When we reach the front door, I knock twice. I glance at my dad. He squeezes my shoulder, giving me a quick nod just as footsteps approach.

A guy around my age opens the door—and it's wild how much of myself I see in him. He's shorter by a few inches, not as broad, but the resemblance is unmistakable. Dark-blond hair, light eyes—steel blue instead of green—but the same mouth.

"Yeah?" he says, eyeing us warily.

"Hey, you're Mark, right?" my dad asks when I can't seem to get words out.

"Can I help you?" Mark asks, suspicious now. I don't blame him. If two random guys showed up at my door and knew my name, I'd be on edge too.

"We're actually here to talk to your dad," my dad says, keeping his voice warm and steady. He's trying hard not to come off like the military guy he is—hands tucked into the pockets of his jeans, posture relaxed.

"Uh... okay," Mark says slowly, not taking his eyes off us. He leans back slightly and calls into the house, "Dad? There are a couple of dudes here asking for you."

"Who is it?" a man calls back. Then footsteps, and a moment later, Cormac appears next to his son.

He stops short when he sees us. His eyes land on me, and something flashes in them—fear? Disbelief? Recognition?

"Hey, Cormac," my dad says calmly.

Cormac's brows pull together. His eyes flick between us, like he's trying to connect the dots.

"Who are you?" he asks, pulling Mark a little closer to him.

"I'm Frank Soult," my dad says, and rests a hand lightly on my shoulder. "And this is my son, Ronan."

Cormac blinks. "Wait... you—" He stares at me. "I saw you earlier. At my store."

"Yeah, you did," my dad says. "Ronan's your nephew."

Silence follows as the words sink in. Cormac stares at me again—really stares—his eyes scanning my face, lingering on the scar around my left eye.

"You're my sister's son?" he finally says. His voice is thick with disbelief... and something like love, I think.

I nod.

"Jesus. You look just like her. And... and my dad," he says quietly.

"So I've been told," I say.

"How old are you?"

"Nineteen."

Cormac frowns. "That would've made my sister... seventeen?"

"Yeah," my dad says. "We had our first son, Steve, at sixteen. Then Ronan came the year after."

Just then, a woman descends the stairs behind Cormac—presumably his wife. "What's going on, Mac?"

Cormac turns to her. "Ashley, this is Frank." He motions toward my dad. "And this is Ronan. Rica's son."

Ashley's mouth falls open. "Rica's son? Your nephew?"

Cormac nods, lips tight. "Apparently so."

"Oh my god," she breathes, stepping closer. "Please, come in!"

We follow them into the house. Cormac leads us to the living room, and the five of us sit down.

The house is bright and tidy, with worn hardwood floors that creak slightly underfoot. Light furniture, heavy white curtains, and the faint scent of flowers fill the space. A blue sofa and matching loveseat frame a wooden coffee table stacked with oversized books on Bauhaus architecture. Family photos cover the mantel and shelves.

We never had photos in my house.

Cormac gestures for my dad and me to take the loveseat while he and Mark take the couch.

"Do you want water? Coffee?" Ashley asks as she disappears briefly into the kitchen.

"Water would be great, thanks," my dad says, his hands resting awkwardly on his knees.

"Nothing for me. Thanks," I say, and glance around the living room. It's so... restful.

"You built that coffee table?" my dad asks, nodding toward the slab of walnut wood with hairpin legs in the center of the room.

"Yeah." Cormac motions behind us. "That built-in, too. It started as a sort of hobby, until I had an entire woodworking shop in my garage," he chuckles.

"No kidding," my dad says. "Looks great in your home, too."

"Ashley's the design buff," Cormac says. "I just build the stuff she wants."

Mark grins. "That's pretty much their whole dynamic. She dreams it, he builds it."

Ashley reappears with glasses of water and a plate of cookies. "Don't let them fool you. Mac has impeccable taste."

Cormac leans back on the couch, his smile fading into something quieter as he studies me again.

"When I saw you at the store earlier," he says, "it was like looking at a ghost. You looked so damn familiar... I just couldn't place it." Then his voice softens. "How is she? Rica. Is she... is she doing okay? I haven't spoken to her in a long time. I think about her all the time."

My dad clears his throat, glancing at me before answering. "Far as we know, she's okay. But... I haven't seen or spoken to her in over a year."

Cormac frowns.

"Your sister... she's in prison," my dad says.

Ashley gasps, clutching her husband's arm. "Oh my god. What happened?"

But Cormac is still looking at me. His eyes drop to the scar below my eye, then the much-smaller one on my top lip. His jaw tightens.

"She gave you that," he says quietly.

My shoulders stiffen. I nod. "Yeah."

"God," he sighs, closing his eyes. "I don't even know what to say." He looks back at me. "How bad was it for you?"

I hate talking about it. Hate remembering. "Bad," I say, staring at the floor. "Really bad."

"Can I ask what happened?" Mark asks, ignoring the look his mom shoots him.

I look at him. Like, really look at him. There are no scars. No bruises. No cuts. No signs at all that his parents ever laid a hand on him. His eyes are bright, his face relaxed. His shoulders don't look like they bear the weight of the world. He doesn't come across as wearing heavy armor, always anticipating the next fight, the next hit. He looks like he had a great upbringing, was loved and doted on by two caring parents. His body language is open and inviting, rather than closed off and protective, as he sits next to his dad. I wouldn't be caught dead sitting next to my mom.

I could leave this house right now, never asking a single question, and still I'd know, without a shadow of doubt, that Cormac managed to do what I so desperately want for myself.

He broke the cycle of abuse for his family.

"She beat me within an inch of my life almost two years ago," I finally say. "I was in a coma for a week."

Ashley gasps.

"Rica beat Ronan so badly," my dad says, "he had over twenty broken bones. Collapsed lungs. A ruptured spleen. I wasn't sure he was going to make it. That's when I found out what had been happening... that she'd been abusing him his whole life."

"God," Cormac mutters, rubbing his chin, lost in thought. "I never imagined she would... that she..." He shakes his head.

"Your mother came to my house last November," my dad says.

Cormac's head snaps up.

"She stopped by after visiting Rica in prison. Said she wanted to talk to Ronan. To tell him about Rica's past. About what your dad did to her... and to you."

Cormac's expression hardens. He says nothing for a long moment, lips pressed into a thin line.

"My dad was abusive, and his dad before him, and so on," Cormac sighs. "My baby sister..."

Ashley's hand moves to the back of his neck, gently stroking. She knows. She's always known he had another sister.

Cormac swallows hard. "My dad would hit Rica and me pretty regularly. It was always about respect and obedience. If we talked back, if we got bad grades, if we made him look bad in any way—he'd lash out. And he hit my mom, too. If she tried to defend us, he'd turn on her. If I stepped in, it just made things worse. He loved using the broom handle."

My jaw tightens. "My mom hit me with the broom handle, too," I say quietly.

Cormac meets my eyes and nods with a look that holds nothing but understanding. No shock. No pity. Just empathy.

"My sister and I... we were never good enough for him," he says. "I gave up trying pretty early, but Rica didn't. She kept trying to meet his impossible standards. She was obedient. So smart. A hard worker. Sweet—so damn sweet. I loved her more than anything."

He pauses, rubbing his hands together as if trying to warm himself.

"I tried to protect her. But every time I did, he'd just hit her harder. Hit me harder. It didn't stop anything. Just made it all more brutal."

Cormac leans forward slightly, voice quieter now. "On my eighteenth birthday, we had a bad fight. He wanted me to enlist in the military. I refused. I knew it would provoke him, but I couldn't keep doing what he wanted. He called me a worthless screwup, said I'd never be anything, and then he tried to beat me into submission. Pretty sure he broke a couple ribs. Two fingers. Probably my nose. I had a cut under my left eye."

He touches a small scar on his cheekbone.

"That night, I left. I packed what I could, took the little cash I had, and drove off. I didn't say goodbye. I just... left. I sold my car at a junkyard, bought a piece-of-shit replacement, and drove until I landed here in Camden. I started going by Mac instead of Cormac. Took Ashley's last name when we got married. I never looked back."

He breathes in deeply, voice shaking.

"I thought about Rica all the time. I wanted to check in, to make sure she was okay, but I was terrified. I didn't think I could survive going back to that life. And I left her behind."

Ashley speaks gently beside him. "It took Mac a long time to open up about everything. He didn't tell me until I got pregnant with Mark."

Cormac swipes quickly at his eyes. "I was so scared of becoming a dad. I thought—what if I'm like him? What if that violence is in me too?"

The silence that follows is dense. I stare down at the coffee table, at the candlesticks and the glossy books that haven't been thrown or broken or used as weapons. My throat tightens.

"My girlfriend is pregnant," I say, not looking up. "And I'm really scared I won't be able to break the cycle."

My dad shifts beside me and pulls me into his side, his arm coming around my shoulders. The pressure of his body steadies me.

"Oh, honey," Ashley says, her voice warm and soft.

Cormac leans forward, eyes locked on mine. "Let me guess," he says. "You have dreams where you hurt her. You worry constantly about what kind of father you'll be. You try to keep it all bottled up, thinking that maybe if you say nothing, feel nothing, it won't come true."

I nod.

"You probably even thought about breaking things off with her to protect her."

I glance at him. "I did. I broke up with her," I say, my voice small.

Cormac offers a knowing, rueful smile. "I did the same thing. I kept telling Ashley she deserved better. That I wasn't good enough. But I kept talking to her. I went to therapy for years. And eventually, I made a choice."

He pauses, lets the words settle.

"I made the choice that I wouldn't be like my father. I knew I loved Ashley more than anything. And when Mark came into the world, I loved him even more. The thought of hurting either of them made me sick. And that's how I knew—I wasn't capable of it. I wasn't him."

Mark speaks up then, sudden and sure. "My dad has never put a hand me." His voice is clear. Strong. "Well, that's not true," he adds quickly, grinning. "He's a hugger. Constantly hugging me."

Ashley laughs softly.

"He coached my T-ball team. My little league team. He never missed a single game, even though he embarrassed the hell out of me cheering. Took me to the park every weekend. Or let me hang out in the shop until I was old enough to help. He was always there. Always."

Mark looks directly at me.

"He still calls me like a million times a day. And he never lets me forget how much he loves me. Even when I screw up—and I screw up a lot—he never even yells."

I swallow thickly, blinking hard.

"I'm... Honestly, this helps a lot," I say.

My dad glances at Cormac. "A few months ago, Ronan decided he wanted to find you. No one even knew if you were alive, but he was determined."

"Why?" Mark asks.

I take a deep breath. "Because I needed to know if it was possible to change things," I say, my voice low, cracking. "I needed to know if someone like me could break the cycle. I thought... maybe if you escaped it, if you turned it all around, then maybe I could, too."

Cormac's expression shifts, pained but deeply understanding.

"Ronan," he says gently, "you're the one who gets to decide what kind of man you'll be. That decision isn't made for you."

He pauses, steadying himself.

"I know what it's like to feel powerless. I felt that way for most of my childhood. No control over anything, not even my own body. If I spoke up, if I said the wrong thing, it meant pain. So I kept it all inside. For years."

Ashley's fingers tighten slightly around his.

"A lot of the time after the abuse ends," he continues, "you're left trying to figure out who you are without it. Without the fear, the violence, the shame. It's hard. It's confusing. For a long time I thought maybe I was just broken. That maybe the only thing I'd ever be was what he made me."

He takes a breath.

"But eventually I understood that what happened to me isn't who I am. It's not my identity. I'm more than his son. I'm more than the bruises and broken bones. I'm not my father."

Ashley leans her head against his shoulder, and Cormac's voice softens.

"I'm Mac Johnson. I'm Ashley's husband. Mark's dad. I've built a life for myself that has nothing to do with him. I have my own business, my own home, my own family. And all of that... I chose it. I made that life for myself."

He looks over at me. "Everything before I left happened to me. But everything after? I made it happen. And it's a damn good life."

Ashley smiles up at him, full of quiet pride.

"How far along is your girlfriend?" she asks me gently.

"A little over three months," I say.

She nods, still smiling. "How long have you been together?"

"Just over two years," I say. "It wasn't... really planned."

Cormac lets out a low chuckle. "Yeah, it rarely is when you're young. It wasn't planned for Ashley and me, either. We had Mark when we were twenty-one."

He glances between me and Mark. "Actually, Ronan, when's your birthday?"

"June second," I say.

"My birthday's May twenty-fourth," Mark chimes in, grinning. "I just turned nineteen, too."

"Crazy to think Rica had her first baby at sixteen," Cormac murmurs, his voice heavy.

"It wasn't exactly planned by us, either," my dad says with a sheepish smile.

"I bet," Cormac says dryly. "I bet my father lost his shit."

"He did," my dad says. "Kicked her out."

There's a moment of silence. Something shifts in Cormac's expression—something tentative and raw.

"I think... I think I should go see my sister sometime," he says quietly.

Ashley nods, her hand brushing gently over his arm.

"Frank," Cormac says, turning toward my dad. "Do you happen to know which prison she's in...?" But his voice fades, the question unraveling halfway through. Just saying the words seems to undo him.

My dad answers softly and writes down the name and address. While he does, the rest of us sit in silence. Ashley's fingers gently rub Cormac's back. Mark stares at the floor. I watch Cormac fold the paper in half, like it might tear if he isn't careful.

"Are you guys driving back to New York tonight?" he asks, finally breaking the quiet.

"No," my dad says. "We're staying at a motel overnight. Heading back in the morning. It's a bit of a drive."

Cormac nods slowly. Then, almost shyly, "Why don't we all grab some dinner?"

He glances at Ashley, who smiles without hesitation.

"We could check out that seafood place I mentioned earlier," he says, his eyes landing on me now, soft and open.

My dad shifts a little, his voice polite. "We'd hate to inconvenience you."

"Not at all," Ashley says, waving him off with a warm grin. "After all, you're family."

Cat

I've been an anxious, restless mess all day.

From the moment I woke up, my chest has felt tight with nerves, my thoughts looping endlessly, obsessively. I've spent the whole day hoping, wishing, praying that Ronan would find what he's been looking for—peace, answers, maybe even a sliver of hope. Something. Anything to lighten the weight he's been carrying for so long.

I know today is going to change things. Hopefully for the better.

Shane's right—Ronan needs a win. Desperately. And I've been clinging to that thought all day, trying to keep myself distracted. I haven't texted or called him once, though I've wanted to. My fingers have itched to dial his number, my hand constantly reaching for my phone to check for missed calls or messages.

I've tried to give him space—to let him do this on his terms—but the longer the silence stretches, the more I feel like I'm crawling out of my skin. By the time nine o'clock rolls around, I'm practically vibrating with anxiety.

Finally, I give in and call Shane. He answers on the first ring.

"Have you heard from him?" I ask, skipping the greeting.

"Nope. I was hoping you had," Shane says, his voice tight.

"What does that mean?" I ask, bracing myself for the worst.

"It means nothing," he says. "They might still be talking, or maybe they're just decompressing. Try not to freak out."

"Excellent advice," I say sarcastically.

"I've been known to offer that from time to time," he jokes, and I smile despite myself.

"Uh-huh. And are you taking your own advice?"

"Definitely not."

"Ugh, this is killing me," I groan.

"Yeah, me too, but—"

"Shane, it's Ran," I say as another call comes through. "He's calling me. I'll call you back." I hang up without waiting for a reply.

"Hey, baby," Ronan says the moment I pick up, his voice velvety and warm.

I smile instantly. "Hi," I breathe, curling up on the bed, my hand absently rubbing my stomach.

"How are you two?" he asks gently.

My heart stutters.

You two.

Something about the way he says it—soft and sure and already folded into this new future we're building—makes my heart expand in my chest. He doesn't hesitate. Doesn't flinch. It's not just me he's asking about, it's *us.* Me and this little person growing inside me. His child. Our baby.

I blink hard, my throat tightening. This is the version of Ronan I always believed was in there, even when he couldn't see it himself—the protective, gentle, loving boy... *man* who talks to his unborn baby without even realizing he's doing it. The man who's already showing up.

It makes something in me melt. God, I love him.

I press my palm more firmly over my stomach, my smile deepening.

"We're good," I say, voice soft with emotion. "We're resting."

"Good. How was your day?"

"Busy. I took Sammy to get mani-pedis—she's a diva, obviously—and then hung out with Tori, Vada, and Summer for a bit." I pause. "But more importantly... how was your day? How are you?"

"I'm okay," he says, and even though I can't see him, I can feel something different in his voice. Calmer. Less guarded.

"Did you see him?"

"Yeah. I actually talked to him. For a long time."

My breath catches. "And?"

"It went better than I could've hoped," he says, and I feel the relief wash through me like a tide.

"Yeah? Are you okay talking about it?"

"Yeah," he says, and he tells me everything. About the drive, the wait, the hesitation. About seeing Cormac. About the stories, the hurt, the history. I listen—fully, completely, the way I always try to. And when he repeats the words Cormac told him—that he gets to choose the kind of man he becomes—I feel something soften in my chest.

"So, how do you feel now?" I ask, voice low.

"Lighter," he says, and I can hear the honesty in it. "And hopeful. And a lot less stressed."

"God, Ran, I'm so glad," I exhale. "You needed this."

"I did." A pause. "Baby... I want to be good to you. And our baby."

My heart gives a little flutter. "Sweet boy," I say, voice warm. "You are good to me. You always have been. And you're going to be amazing to our baby. I know it."

"When are you heading home tomorrow?"

"Probably late morning. I think I'll stop by Murphy's when we get back, but I want to see you. Will you come by in the evening? I need to recharge my battery."

"Your battery?" I tease.

"Yeah. You recharge my emotional battery, baby. Ever since I met you. When I'm not around you for too long, I can feel it draining."

"Really?"

"Really. Is that weird?"

"No," I whisper, smiling so hard it hurts. "I love it."

Hope blooms in my chest. It's tentative, but real. I want to hold onto it, to let it fill me completely. But hope has hurt before. Hope has made promises it couldn't keep. So I let it in gently, carefully... like something wild that might run if I move too fast.

Sunday, June 25th

Ronan

Dinner with Cormac and his family last night felt... surreal. But good. I sat across the table from a man who, not long ago, was just a name, a blurred silhouette. But last night he was all presence and voice and gentle wisdom. And hope.

The hours passed in a haze of warmth I still don't quite know how to hold. The conversation drifted between Mark's and my college classes, the best clam chowder on the coast, and a long, dramatic retelling of a T-ball game Ashley swears was the peak of Mark's athletic career. Everyone laughed. Even me. Even my dad. And Cormac—Mac—sat across from us, talking about the best type of wood for framing, about the kid he once was and the father he chose to become, like it's not a miracle. Like healing doesn't have to be loud to be real.

Later, in the stillness of the motel room, I lay on the bed staring at the ceiling. The quiet settled differently than it used to. Not heavy, not hollow. Just quiet. I thought about Cat. About her laugh. Her beauty. Her strength. About our baby, a blur of cells and possibility, already reshaping me. And I thought about Cormac. About how he hasn't erased the past, but he hasn't surrendered to it, either.

And then something stirred in me. Not certainty. Not peace. It was Cat's words, and Shane's, and my grandparents', and my therapist's. It was a small, stubborn belief that tomorrow doesn't have to echo the worst parts of before. That I can *choose* something different. That this life I'm building, still imperfect, still unfinished, is not just another yesterday.

***

Even now, in the quiet hum of morning light spilling through the car window, that feeling lingers. It sits in my chest like a foreign object I'm afraid to poke too hard. What if it dissolves under pressure? What if I imagined it?

My dad hasn't said much since we hit the road. We've been driving for over an hour, the highway stretching out like an old scar—cracked, familiar, unchanging. I can tell he's thinking. So am I.

We're overdue for a talk. We've been dodging it. Well, I've been dodging it, shutting him down the moment he even hinted at getting too close to something real.

But I have a sneaking suspicion the time has come. The road ahead is looking pretty damn empty. And there's nowhere left to hide.

Sure enough.

"I am so sorry, Ronan," my dad says into the silence.

I turn my head to look at him, not sure what he's apologizing for. Everything, probably. *Everything.* But I don't ask—I wouldn't even know where to start. So, I wait.

"I'm sorry I wasn't a dad to you and Stevie. I'm sorry I left you. I'm sorry I didn't protect you." The words spill out like he's been holding them in for years. "Sitting there yesterday, listening to Mark talk about what an amazing father Mac is, I realized how much I've failed you—and Stevie—but especially you. I shouldn't have left you guys."

"Dad, you did what you could," I say, out of habit more than belief.

"No. Actually, I didn't." His voice goes stern. "Things could've been different if I'd been man enough to do what was right."

He takes a deep breath, then exhales through his nose. "I left Morai and Athair just a few days after I turned sixteen."

I nod. I've always known he left the ranch that young, though I never really understood why. Montana has always felt like a refuge to me.

So, I ask: "How come? Why'd you leave?"

He glances over, and there's a heaviness behind his eyes that startles me. I recognize it—the same fractures I saw in Cat's eyes the night I met her. The same darkness I see in my own reflection.

"I just... couldn't stay," he says. "I needed to leave. For me. And I swore I'd never step foot on Montana soil again."

I don't get the chance to press further.

"I grew up knowing I'd inherit the ranch. That I'd take over the family business. Until one day, I couldn't bear the thought of it. Of staying. At sixteen, the only way out I saw was the military."

I listen, more intently now. I've never heard this part.

"I knew I couldn't enlist until I was seventeen. I knew that because the day I turned sixteen, I took Athair's truck and drove to Missoula. Walked into a recruitment center and they told me they'd love to have me... *next year.* Man, I was pissed," he says with a dry laugh. "So, I decided I'd leave anyway. Started working whatever jobs I could find, sleeping wherever I could crash. Sometimes there wasn't even that."

He shakes his head, like he's watching it all play back in real time.

"I made my way to New York two weeks later. Met some people, crashed in their apartment for a bit. One weekend, we went to the beach—it was brutally hot—and that's where I met Rica. It was her sixteenth birthday. She was in the city with some girlfriends. We started talking, hit it off, and... well, we kind of just snuck away from the group and—"

"Yeah, no need to share details, Dad," I say, grimacing.

He chuckles. "I'll spare you." He sobers a little. "We exchanged numbers, but as shitty as it sounds, I had no intention of calling her. She was obviously a beautiful girl, but I wasn't in that headspace."

"Where *was* your head?" I ask.

He grins. "I was sixteen, Ran. Living away from my parents in a big city. My mind was on parties and sex and all the dumb stuff you get caught up in when you think the world owes you something."

"Shit. Sorry I asked."

"Oh, please. I've heard you weren't exactly a saint before Cat," he says with a laugh.

"Okay, fair enough," I say. "So... when did you find out about Stevie?"

"Your mom called me about three months later, out of the blue. Asked if she could see me. I thought we were gonna hook up again, but she showed up at the apartment and it was obvious that wasn't why she came. She told me she was pregnant. God, Ran, I was such an asshole to her. I tried to deny it. Said it wasn't mine. She was just bawling, swearing I was the only person she'd ever been with."

He stares out the windshield.

"I took her virginity during a one-night stand. How fucking shitty is that."

"Definitely shitty," I say. It's something I've always worried about—being someone's first when I had no intention of sticking around. I remember how much it meant when Cat trusted me that way. How it changed us. Changed *me*. I wouldn't want to do that to someone I'd just met, someone I'd never see again.

"Yeah," he says quietly. "She told me her dad kicked her out. She completely broke down. Told me her dad had been abusive. We stayed up all night talking, and I realized I needed to step up. But, Ran?" He looks at me again, eyes steady. "I'm going to be honest with you, so try not to judge me too hard: I hated it. The idea of being a dad. I felt trapped. I was sixteen. I didn't love her. I didn't want to raise a family. I wanted to *live*. I wanted to *go places*."

"You sound like every sixteen-year-old guy ever," I say, because... yeah. I get it.

"Rica stayed with me for a bit. We tried to make it work, but we couldn't stay. The guy I was crashing with didn't want a baby in the place. I had no way to support her or the baby. So, I bit the bullet and called my parents. Morai cried when I told her. But within minutes, she had a plan for us to come back to Montana. Rica's parents wanted nothing to do with her. And I couldn't do it on my own."

He exhales like the memory still stings.

"So back to Montana we went. We got married. And I was *so fucking resentful*, Ran. I didn't want any of it. Not Montana, not the ranch, not the marriage, not fatherhood."

He stares out the windshield, jaw tight.

"But then Stevie was born," he says, softening. "And, god. That moment you hold your child for the first time... it's like your heart breaks wide open."

I nod slowly. "Still didn't stop you from leaving."

"No. It didn't." He pauses. "I told Rica and my parents that I was still going to enlist. The plan was that once I got stationed somewhere in the U.S., I'd bring Rica and Stevie to live on base with me. But... Rica got pregnant again. Right before I left for basic training."

He swallows. "She called me crying. Told me she was expecting you. I wasn't there for any of her pregnancy. Not the doctor visits, not the ultrasounds. I completed basic, then technical training, then went overseas for a bit. Ran, I didn't meet you until you were six months old."

That one stings more than I expect.

"Can I ask you a weird question?" I say.

He glances at me. "Sure."

"Were you... faithful to Mom? Before Penny, I mean."

He exhales long and deep, then shakes his head. "No. I wasn't. I was a shitty husband to your mom. Just like I was a shitty dad to you and your brother."

"Did you love her?"

"I had love *for* her—as the mother of my kids. But I didn't love her like a husband should. Not like I love Penny. Not like you love Cat."

He looks at me again, eyes glassy but steady. "Ran, I am as much to blame for what happened to you as your mother. I may not have laid a hand on you, but I didn't protect you, either."

He looks back to the road, knuckles tight on the wheel.

"I remember Morai telling me, over and over, that she was worried Rica didn't have much of a bond with you. She told me once she saw Rica hit you. I confronted Rica. She blamed it on stress. Said she was overwhelmed. I bought it. I *wanted* to believe it, because it meant I didn't have to look closer. And I didn't."

He goes quiet, and I let the silence hang.

"When it was time for me to move to Georgia, Rica was going to stay in New York. Her parents helped with the house. Things *seemed* stable. So I didn't push. The only reason you guys ever lived with me that one year when you were five or six was because Morai guilted me into it. Rica hated it. She wanted to go back to New York. So you did."

I breathe in slowly. "Why did we go back to Montana?"

"Ugh, it was always such a push-and-pull. Morai honestly wanted you guys there. They wanted me home. They wanted you boys close. When I tell you your grandparents love you, Ran, that's not enough to describe the kind of love they have for you and Stevie. You are obviously her favorite," my dad chuckles. "Pretty sure you have been from the moment you took your first breath. I remember her calling me just after you were born. I was stationed in Okinawa and she was crying, telling me about you, how you had a strong cry. Said you were little but already feisty. And she said she thought your name should be Ronan. After her dad."

He smiles at the memory.

"So Rica and I argued about you three moving back to Montana. She gave in, gave it a really good shot for a couple of years, but then you obviously came back to New York. Then I moved to Montana, was stationed there for a hot minute and brought you guys back to the ranch while I was in Great Falls. But, then I was in Virginia for a few weeks and I met Penny..."

I know where this is going.

"Her husband Cade and I had been friends since basic. They had only been married a couple of years when I met her at a military function. And, fuck, I fell for her right then and there. Hard. Ran, I had never felt anything like it. The moment I laid eyes on her, I was completely lost to her."

I nod because I get it. I get the earth-tilting clarity that comes with seeing someone and just... knowing. "I know exactly what that feels like."

He nods like he knows who I'm talking about. But the smile dies too fast. There's a sharp twist in my stomach as I brace for the rest.

"I couldn't stand being away from her. So I went back to Virginia, and I had you guys move back to New York so I could still see you. Ran, I feel so bad about it all. I never realized what I was putting you through."

Because you didn't look. Not when I needed you to. Not when she was hurting me.

"I didn't think about the repercussions of all the moving, not really. And I know that if I'd paid closer attention, I would've seen Rica was hurting you. But I didn't look, because, well... things were going great for me. Penny and I were serious. We'd talked about spending the rest of our lives together."

"Did you think that would include Stevie and me?" I ask flatly.

"I hoped it would. But you were old enough by then that I figured you'd make the call. Stevie was about to head to college. I knew you had your life in New York—your friends, Cat."

My heart stutters at her name. Fuck, I'm still devastated by this girl, and I have a feeling it'll only get worse as the years go by.

He exhales. "So I found a divorce lawyer. I saw her a couple of times before I pulled the trigger. She had everything ready and was going to file that Monday after... after Rica hurt you."

I stare straight ahead. *After she hurt me.* That's such a gentle phrase for what she did. I was barely alive. Actually, no. I know there were at least a few seconds where my lungs had ceased to breathe and my heart had stopped beating. For all intents and purposes, I was gone. If it hadn't been for Steve...

"That Friday night, I just started feeling so much fucking guilt..."

He keeps talking, and I hear the words, but they blur around the edges. My heartbeat is too loud in my ears. He's explaining why he didn't want to blindside my mom with the divorce, how she "sacrificed so much," how he thought it wasn't fair. *It wasn't fair to me, either.* But he didn't know that. Not then.

"I told Rica I was coming home, that I was leaving her, that I was going to grab some stuff and then leave for Virginia for good. And, well, you know the rest of the story," he sighs.

Yeah. I do. *Too fucking well.*

He swallows, hard. "When I pulled up... there were cop cars. An ambulance. I threw my car in park and just ran. A cop stopped me in the hall, but I saw you on the floor. EMTs shocking your heart."

His voice starts to crack.

"I just fucking stood there, trying to comprehend what the fuck was going on. Rica was kneeling on the floor, Stevie was, too, blood all over himself, Zack beside him. For a moment, I thought something had happened to Stevie, too. I couldn't understand what the hell had gone down." He inhales a shaky breath. "The EMTs got your heart going again, intubated you right there, and rushed you to the hospital. I rode with you. I was asking questions but they didn't know much—just said it was blunt force trauma, suspected abuse."

He shakes his head, clearly ashamed. I blink, but everything in me goes still. The way he says it yanks me back into it—the struggle for air, for breath, the panic when it didn't come, the burning pain. Everywhere. Inside and out. The sound of Steve's voice shaking. The taste of blood in my mouth. The fingers of darkness, of sweet numbness pulling me under until there was nothing but quiet peace.

"It wasn't until Steve and Zack made it to the hospital that I began to understand what the hell had happened," my dad says. "And then

Shane... he told me that you had confided in him, at least a little bit. He said you had told him that your mom had hit you before. That he had seen the bruises. God, my world just crumbled."

He clears his throat, voice barely hanging on.

"The cops gave me more info at the hospital. Your surgeon took me aside and told me the scans showed signs of old fractures—injuries that had never been properly treated. Signs you'd been hurt before. Multiple times."

I swallow hard, bile rising. I feel exposed, cracked wide open, and it's not even my dad doing it. It's the truth itself, dragging its fingernails down my spine.

"You were in surgery for almost eleven hours. When we finally saw you... you were unrecognizable. Your face was just... gone. Swollen, bruised. I didn't think you'd make it. I sat with you all night, just telling you how sorry I was. Telling you I loved you."

He pauses, swallowing the memory.

"Every day, Cat, Shane, Vada, Tori—they were all there. Taking turns. Talking to you. Holding your hand. That moment when you opened your eyes..." He breaks off.

I remember waking up and seeing them. I remember how heavy everything felt. I remember the light hurting my eyes and Cat holding my hand so gently, like I'd break if she gripped too hard. I remember thinking it was too late, that I was already broken.

"You're so unbelievably strong, Ran. Such a fighter."

I flinch. Not visibly, but it's a jolt inside. I don't feel strong. I've never felt strong. I felt like a ghost for months.

"But we all saw what it cost you. You weren't the same. Your soul was just... tired. And when Dr. Seivert said you were contemplating... you were—"

He doesn't finish the sentence. I just sit there, letting him talk. Letting it settle.

"I talked with Morai and Athair every day when you were in Montana, especially those first few months. They were so worried. Said you wouldn't get out of bed. That you weren't eating. They argued with me and Doctor Seivert about how to reach you. I kept saying to trust your therapist. But... I guess Athair took matters into his own hands," he chuckles softly.

I raise an eyebrow. "What do you mean?"

"Well, I guess he messed with his truck so you'd have to fix it. Just to get you out of bed. Out of the house. Out of your head. So you'd have a problem to solve."

"I fucking *knew* it." I laugh, but sober quickly. "Honestly, it worked. I still remember walking outside, how fucking bright the sun was, how sharp the air felt. It really was the moment things started to shift. Before that, I was just... stuck. I can't even explain it. I felt like I was buried in cement. Exhausted doesn't even cover it. I had nothing left. Nothing mattered. Everything was too heavy. And it's so weird, because I never felt like that even when things were bad. When Mom... When things were bad at home... I never felt that way. But once it was over, once I was safe, it was like everything collapsed all at once."

"Because you held it together for so long, Ran," he says gently. "Your adrenaline kept you going. It was pure survival. That's what happens in combat, too. You survive the battle and only once you're safe do you realize how badly you're hurt. That's when the real fight starts. And it did for you. Coming back from that... that's a war in itself. And you've been so goddamn strong."

I shake my head. "I don't know about that, Dad. I've messed up a lot. I still get stuck in my head. Still have nightmares. Panic attacks. I broke up with Cat because I'm so fucking screwed up."

He looks at me, eyes soft. "Kiddo, you can't be so hard on yourself. This healing business..." He exhales, like the words weigh more than he expected. "Rica broke you down piece by tiny piece. For seventeen years. No one comes back from that overnight. Nobody expects you to be healed yet. I understand it takes time... trust me. I know."

His voice dips, something knowing and wounded in it. Something lived-in. I suddenly realize how little I know about my dad, not just as my *dad*, but as Frank Soult. He's someone with his own scars and secrets. I can see it written all over his face. Maybe someday I'll get the chance to find out what shaped him, what made him run, who he really is.

"And..." he trails off, voice rough. "I also know it takes time to forgive."

My brow lifts, cautious. *Forgive who?* Myself? My mom? Him?

"Ran, I know you're angry... at me. And you have every right to be," he says. "I failed you. In every way. I left you to fend for yourself for a long time. You fought with no one by your side, no one to protect you. I can't begin to tell you how sorry I am... for all of it. For living a secret life with Penny, for abandoning you and Stevie. For not seeing the signs. I should've known. I should've protected you. I should've done a hell of a lot differently. I'm sorry, Ran," he says, voice low. Then again, firmer: "I am sorry."

Silence.

Suddenly, he merges across two lanes of freeway and pulls onto the shoulder. The tires crunch against gravel as he throws the Tahoe in park. He flips the hazard lights on. Then he turns full body in his seat to face me, his gaze locked on mine.

"Ronan," he says, eyes steady. "I'm sorry. I love you. I need you to *hear* that. I love you. There was never a time in my life when I didn't want to be your dad. When I didn't love you."

I lock eyes with him, jaw tight. I'm not used to this version of him, the one who owns his shit. It hits me then that he's been trying to, and I just... haven't been willing to listen. He's been making these quiet little attempts for a while now. He always answers the phone when I call, no matter how late it is or how many of his calls and texts I've ignored. He shows up at Murphy's when he knows I'm working to check on me, always asks about Cat. He keeps trying, even when I give him nothing back but silence or sarcasm or make him run straight into my carefully built emotional brick wall.

I've been so angry. He left. He looked the other way. He kept running while I was stuck, made a whole other life while I lived in the wreckage of the first one.

But still... he's here. When I told him how much it mattered to me to find Cormac, he dug. Probably used his military security clearance to find him, then insisted he go with me. And I'm glad he did. He showed up.

No fanfare. No big gestures. Just showing up. And maybe that matters. Maybe that counts for something. It should, right?

It twists something in me. Not forgiveness, not yet. But it cracks the door.

He swallows. "I want to be in your life, Ran. I've missed too much of you. And... I want to be in my grandbaby's life, too."

I blink, heart hammering in my chest. It still feels surreal when people say it out loud—that I'm going to be a dad. That there's going to be a tiny human who's half me and half Cat. *Fuck.* I'm going to be a father before the year is out. And to say I have a hard time wrapping my head around that would be a fucking understatement.

"Even though I'm clearly way too handsome and young to be a grandfather," my dad adds with a grin.

I huff a laugh in spite of myself.

He looks at me, a smile tugging at his lips. "Seriously, Ran. Do I look like a grandpa?" He puffs his chest out, flexing so hard I worry about the integrity of his already-very-fitted shirt stretching across his pecs.

"Not really," I say, chuckling.

"Exactly. I'm too damn hot to be a grandfather. Shit, I'm only turning thirty-seven next month."

"Yeah, sorry, Dad," I say sheepishly.

He just shakes his head with a smile. "It's alright. It's what we do, right? You come from a long line of men who couldn't keep it in their pants."

I snort. "At least I made it to nineteen."

"Athair was only thirty-six when he became a grandfather." Then he pauses, more thoughtful now. "Speaking of which, I refuse to be called 'Grandpa' or any of that nonsense."

"Oh yeah?" I smirk. "What do you want to be called, then?"

"I don't know." He shrugs. "Haven't figured that part out yet."

"Well, Athair is taken, so that's a no-go."

He nods. "We'll have to think of something."

"You still got some time," I say. "It's not like this baby's showing up tomorrow."

"No, but six months will fly by, Ran."

"Yeah," I breathe. "God, I'm not ready."

The weight of everything presses in on my chest again like it always does when I think too far ahead. I don't have the faintest idea how I'm going to make it all work.

My dad squeezes my shoulder lightly. "It's okay. I'm here. Whatever you guys need. I mean it."

I look at him, unsure what to say. For so long, I didn't think I *could* count on him. I still don't know if I can—not truly—but maybe... maybe this is the start of something different.

"Do you know what you're going to do about your living situation?" he asks.

"Not really. Right now we're still in the apartment. Cat and I haven't really figured it all out yet, but Shane thinks he'll be fine with a newborn crying all night." I shrug. "Whatever Cat wants, I'll try to make it work. I just want her to be alright. I'm trying to save up as much as I can."

"Whatever I can do to help, Ran, please let me know. You're not alone, okay? If you need help, financial or otherwise, it's no problem."

I shift uncomfortably. "I appreciate that, Dad, I do. But it'd feel weird as hell asking you for money."

"Why?"

I shrug. "I mean… I managed to get a girl pregnant, but I still need to ask Daddy for help? Feels pathetic. Like, if I can fuck around, I can step up."

He huffs a quiet laugh. "You seem to feel strongly about this."

"I do."

"But Ran…" His tone softens again. "I know you've never had anyone you could rely on, not really. But I'm telling you now: I'm here. You and Cat don't have to do this alone. Please, ask for help when you need it. You don't have to carry the whole weight on your shoulders."

"I'm not," I say. "Cat's already carrying more than her fair share. The least I can do is make sure she and the baby have what they need."

He nods. "And that's exactly why I want to help. So you can focus on being a good… boyfriend… a good partner to Cat, and a good dad. Let me be a part of this, Ran. Let me show up this time."

For a second I just sit there, staring at him. His ask is simple, but it lands hard, like a boulder plummeting into water, and all I can feel are the ripples spreading out from where it hits.

I want to hold onto the anger. I want to say it's too late. But the truth is… I don't think I believe that anymore.

My throat feels tight. My chest too. I don't say anything, just lean forward, dragging a shaky breath through my nose as I press my forehead to his shoulder.

And then his arms are around me. Strong. Solid. Familiar in a way that makes my heart ache. He hugs me like he's been waiting to, like maybe he needed this just as much as I did.

It's awkward and cramped and the console digs into my ribs, but I stay there anyway. For the first time in a long time, I don't fight him. I let myself stay.

"I missed you," I mutter, voice thick. "I've missed you so much… for so long."

"I missed you too, bud," he says into my hair. "So damn much. But I'm here now. And I'm not going anywhere."

Sunday, August 13th

Cat

"Does it make me a terrible, horrible son that I really don't feel like having dinner with the whole damn family every freaking Sunday?" Ronan mutters as he ties his shoes.

I stand next to him in the hallway, one hand on my stomach. I've definitely started to show. The bump is noticeable underneath my clothes now—much to Tori's, Vada's, and Summer's delight, all of whom keep asking if they can touch my belly—and just yesterday I realized I was no longer able to button my jeans. I know it comes with the territory. I know it's a change I have to accept. After all, this baby's nowhere near done growing. But still, I cried to Ronan about it yesterday. I kept yammering about how soon I'd be so big he wouldn't be attracted to me anymore. Of course, that boy did everything in his power to convince me otherwise. He finally managed to when he laid me down on his bed, then descended between my thighs until the only sounds I was able to make were mewling whimpers and moans.

"Not really," I say. Ronan's right. These dinners aren't just dinners. They're inspections, check-ins, our parents' way of ensuring they have an eye on us. Ever since we told them I was pregnant, they've been hovering. Cooking elaborate meals. Making casual but loaded comments. Offering advice we didn't ask for. Always with that thin smile that says, "We're just checking in." But the eyes say, "We're worried. We're watching you."

And the silly thing is? I still live at home. Granted, I'm at Ronan's apartment more often than not, but I spend at least two to three nights at home, in my own room. And I see my mom at work every day. Apparently that's still not enough.

I tug at my white sundress. It's clingy in all the wrong places. Maybe a corset top wasn't the best idea.

"I don't really feel like going either, but it makes them happy." I fan the back of my neck. "Is it me or is it hot in here?"

Ronan chuckles. "It's you."

I turn around to inspect the thermostat, even though I already know they keep the apartment cold for me—cold enough that poor Tori's taken to wearing Shane's hoodies and wrapping herself up like a burrito anytime she's over. Even Ronan's started throwing on extra layers in the mornings, but he never complains. Not once. He just shivers and kisses me and asks if I need anything.

I twist my hair into a knot at the crown of my head and let the cooler air hit my neck. It helps, a little.

"You're always so damn hot, baby," Ronan says from behind me, and then his lips brush the curve of my shoulder as his arms slip around my waist, just above the gentle rise of our baby. My eyes flutter closed. I lean back into him, helpless against the pull of his touch, his warmth.

He trails kisses along my neck, and I feel his breath against my skin, feel the way his hands settle—protective and claiming all at once.

"I'd tell you to stop being so horny," I murmur, "but I don't really want you to."

He hums into my skin, and I melt just a little more. "Let's just skip dinner," he mutters. "We can eat at home."

"And what are you going to eat, sweet boy? Me?" I tease with a light giggle.

"Uh-huh," he groans, his hand gliding down the front of me, slipping beneath the hem of my dress. He strokes back up along my thigh before settling between them, the heat of his palm pressing right where I'm already aching for him. Moist heat pools there so fast. It's always like this. I'm always needy for him.

My breath quickens as he slips one strap of my dress off my shoulder, then pushes the top down, exposing one breast.

"We're going to be late," I whisper, my voice barely a breath, already dizzy from the sensation of his mouth—licking, kissing, sucking—while his thumb circles my nipple.

"Want me to stop?" he rasps, his mouth still warm against my skin. I can tell he has no intention of stopping. And honestly, neither do I.

"No," I whimper, almost ashamed of how fast the word leaves me.

His hand leaves my breast and dips down again, sliding under my dress to hook his fingers in the waistband of my panties. He eases them down to my ankles, then rises, gliding both hands up my thighs as he bunches my dress up around my waist.

"Fuck," Ronan growls, his hand splaying over my bare cheek. "That ass is so delicious. Everything about you is. I can't get enough of you, baby."

His hand slips back up, cupping my breast again, thumb dragging slow, taunting circles over my nipple. I gasp at the sensation shooting straight down my spine, settling hot and deep between my legs.

His other hand glides lower, between my thighs, to my most sensitive flesh. *God.*

His fingers part me just enough, and he finds my clit like he's mapping constellations. He draws perfect, maddening little circles with that familiar, practiced pressure that makes my knees weaken.

I brace a hand against the wall, the other gripping his wrist as I try to press into him, into more, but he keeps it measured, deliberate.

"Ran," I breathe, my voice breaking around the hunger in me.

"I know, baby," he says, mouth still at my neck, voice low and raw. "You're already primed for me."

It's true. I'm soaked, drenched, and the slow drag of his fingers over my slick, throbbing skin makes me want to sob with need. He doesn't push in, doesn't let me fall apart. He just keeps stroking, circling, teasing.

He's relentless.

My hips start rocking on instinct, chasing friction, but he moves with me just enough to keep me teetering, never tipping. Pleasure coils tighter and tighter, like a wire pulled taut. My breath is coming in gasps now, thighs trembling, nipples peaked and aching under his touch.

"Please," I whimper, shameless. I'm so wound up, I'm not sure I could stop even if Tori and Shane suddenly walked in.

"Not yet," he says, his voice like gravel. "You're so fucking beautiful like this. Desperate for me."

His words make me wetter, make me throb. I want him inside me so badly it's blinding. I ache for it, for him, for the way he fills me and makes me feel whole, like I'm not just carrying his baby but his entire damn universe inside me.

He moves his hand again, just enough to slide one finger into me. I moan, sharp and needy, my hips jerking at the sudden intrusion. He pumps once, then twice, then adds another, curling them to stroke that spot inside me that makes me see stars.

My head falls back onto his shoulder, and he growls into my ear, "You're doing so good, baby."

His fingers curl again inside me, slow and deep, and then he pulls back, just enough to make me cry out.

"Ran," I gasp, hips rolling back into him, frantic. "Please—"

"Not yet," he murmurs again, lips brushing my ear. "I want to hear it."

I whimper, shaking with want. "Hear what?"

His hand moves again, that cruel, perfect pressure over my clit resuming—tight, deliberate circles that make my whole body clench with need.

"What do you want, Cat?" he asks, his voice low and wrecked, every word laced with hunger. "You have to tell me."

I can barely breathe. The words stick in my throat, thick with embarrassment and want and everything else that makes him feel like home and danger all at once.

His fingers pause, just enough to make me whine. I'm so close, so damn close, but he won't let me reach the peak.

"Use your words, baby," he says, pressing a kiss behind my ear. "Tell me what you need. I want to hear you say it."

I swallow hard, too far gone to care about shame. I press back against him, shuddering, desperate.

"I want... I need to come, Ran," I pant. "Please. I need it. I need you."

"That's it, baby," he growls. Then he's moving again, his hand between my thighs working me with devastating precision. The other pinches my nipple just enough to send a bolt of lightning through me. "You're so fucking ready, aren't you? So wet, so close. Just from my fingers."

God, why is this so hot? I'm unraveling. I'm fire and need and his.

And when he curls his fingers deep inside me and presses down on my clit in that perfect rhythm, I shatter, moaning his name, my body pulsing and squeezing around him, the orgasm ripping through me so fast and so hard it feels like I'm tearing at the seams.

He holds me through it, his muscular front pressed to my back, whispering praise against my skin as I fall apart in his arms.

"Fuck," he groans, voice ragged. "I love making you come, baby."

I glance over my shoulder, my body still slick and sensitive, and catch the hunger in his glossy eyes, the flush high on his cheeks. He's so turned on, barely holding on.

"You need to be inside me," I whisper, pushing my hips back, brushing against the solid length of him through his jeans. "Don't you?"

His answering groan is all primal need.

"Go ahead, sweet boy," I coo, hinging forward at the hip, hands braced against the wall. "I took what I needed. Now it's your turn." I watch him over my shoulder as he makes short work of things. He unbuttons his jeans, then yanks them down just enough to free himself. He fists his cock at the base, the tip glistening. God, it makes me want to run my tongue over it. I know how he tastes, know what it does to him when I pleasure him with my mouth, what it does to me in return. I wish I hadn't waited so long to try it, but I plan on spending the rest of my life catching up.

He grips my hip with his right hand, while he guides himself to my entrance with the other. "Tell me to stop if I'm too rough, okay?" he grits out. Then he thrusts into me in one smooth, brutal motion, burying himself so deep he's hitting the very edge of me. I gasp, arching into him, my hands bracing against the wall as he begins to move—fast, hard, needy. Every stroke is thick with desperation, the slap of skin on skin echoing in the hallway.

Nope, not too rough. Perfect. "Yeah, Ran," I cry, "just like that."

"Jesus, baby," he growls. "I hope you don't mind a quick one because I'm not going to last."

I can feel him losing control, hips stuttering as he drives into me, his breath coming in broken, uneven pants. He's already close. So close.

I push back into him, loving the helpless sound he makes when I clench around him.

"You gonna come for me, Ran?" I murmur, glancing over my shoulder. "You gonna come for me like a good boy?"

He groans, loud and guttural, and his rhythm breaks.

"God, Cat," he gasps, "don't say shit like that unless you want me to... Fuck..."

"Do it," I whisper, filthy and sweet. "Come for me, Ran. Be a good boy and let me feel you."

With a ragged groan, he drives deep one last time and loses himself inside me. I feel every pulse of him, every desperate twitch, and it lights a spark in my chest, something hot and tender and a little unhinged. And powerful. I know it's trust that allows me to explore what I enjoy. Trust that Ronan won't hurt me, that he'll stop when I ask him to stop, that he won't judge when I try myself out.

We stay like that for a long moment, still connected, hearts racing. I wait for Ronan's aftershocks to subside, for his breathing to slow a little, then straighten. Ronan slips out of me and the fabric of my dress falls over my waist. Then his arms wrap around me again, tight and protective.

"I'll never get enough of you," he whispers.

Ronan

We get to Cat's parents' house only ten minutes late, which honestly isn't bad considering what we were up to before we left my apartment.

I throw the car in park, then dramatically jab the engine button—I'm still not used to this thing—before slouching back in the seat. I can think of a thousand better ways to spend my evening with Cat than having dinner with our parents. But at least we're not at my dad's tonight.

"Thanks for suggesting the change of locale," I say with a half-smile to Cat. "I still don't love going to my dad's." It's not that I don't enjoy the people. I do. Well, with the exception of Cat's dad, who stares at me like I got Cat pregnant only to spite him.

It's the house itself. It's the pain I associate with the place—especially the downstairs, the damn kitchen and living room. It's where the worst shit happened, and sitting down for a roast chicken and polite conversation in the middle of it just... fucking sucks. I'm always rushing Cat through the meal, desperate to get the hell out.

Cat could obviously tell, and last week she finally suggested dinner at her parents' house instead.

She tucks a strand of her hair behind her ear. "Yeah, I know. It's nice being here," she says sweetly, and reaches for the door handle. "This place is safe. Smells like garlic bread... and memories of you taking my virginity."

She giggles and hops out of the car.

Thirty minutes later, we've survived—or really, *Cat's* survived—the weekly belly touching and barrage of overly personal questions. Weird cravings? New aches and pains? Strange pregnancy symptoms? When Penny leaned in and asked Cat if she was "leaking colostrum yet," I bailed and took my spot at the dinner table, pretending I didn't just hear the word "colostrum" come out of Penny's mouth. She followed it up with how she used to soak through shirts during her second trimester with my baby brothers, and... yeah. That was my cue.

We're at the table, eating beef stroganoff—I'm picking out every morsel of beef I can spot—when Jen turns her attention to me.

"So, Ran, Bobby and I were talking and we thought it might be a good idea if you moved in with all of us," she says with a smile.

Uh, that sounds like a terrible fucking idea to me.

I'm completely caught off guard and look to Cat for help, but she only shrugs like she's hearing this for the first time, too.

"We just thought it would be good once the baby is here," Jen continues. "Bobby and I could help you guys. I work a flexible schedule, and Bobby is home in the afternoons."

She turns to Bobby for backup, but his expression doesn't exactly scream enthusiasm. If anything, he looks like he'd rather stick his fork into his eye socket than have me live with them.

"Jen, that's so sweet," Penny says, her voice full of encouragement. She looks at me. "It's a great idea, Ran. You should take her up on the offer!"

And just like that, my walls slam up. I feel completely overrun, boxed in, like this whole thing was decided for me before I even walked in the door.

Luckily, Cat is so in tune with me she picks up on my apprehension instantly. She reaches for my hand under the table and gives it a soft squeeze.

"I don't know, Mom," she says sweetly. "Ran and I were thinking of living at his place. We don't want to burden you and Dad."

I don't deserve this girl.

Her dad lets out a dry, condescending laugh. "Come on, Kitty. You'll need help when you have that baby. You'll be sleep-deprived, busy taking care of a newborn. Who's going to take care of you while you're taking care of the baby?"

No he fucking didn't...

"I am," I growl.

He chuckles again and glances around the table. "Ronan, with all due respect, do you expect me to believe you'll be able to give Cat and her baby everything she'll need? There's laundry, meals to cook, errands to run, cleaning. Babies require a lot of care—there won't be time to go out and party."

I seriously wonder who the fuck he thinks I am.

"Bobby, I'm sure Ronan will be able to handle all those things just fine," Jen says in a calming voice, but Bobby just lets out another derisive laugh.

"He handles things, Bobby," my dad says, clipped. "He's plenty responsible."

"Yeah? You call getting my daughter pregnant at eighteen responsible?" Bobby asks, his anger finally breaking through the sarcasm.

"Jesus, Bobby, that was an accident," my dad growls.

The air in the room turns sharp.

"Some accident," Bobby mutters. "Seems Ronan's prone to those. First he breaks Cat's heart, then he gets her knocked up. Look, Ronan, I'm sure you're a good kid, but I just don't trust you with my daughter. And I sure as hell don't know if I can trust you to take care of her and my grandbaby."

"Dad, stop!" Cat says, anger threading through her voice. "You don't know what you're talking about."

"Don't I?" He rises from his chair. "How can you be so sure Ronan's good for you, Cat? Last I checked, you didn't have the best track record picking good guys."

He's talking about Adam. That smug, controlling asshole who hurt her more than once. And the fact that Bobby's comparing me to him?

That's the last fucking drop.

"With all due respect, Bobby," I say, repeating his words, my jaw so tight it hurts, "I would never lay a hand on Cat. And you keep talking about Cat's baby—your grandbaby—like you forgot that the child she's carrying is also mine. I have every intention of taking care of her and our baby."

"Ronan, do you even know how to make a sandwich?" Bobby shouts. "Do you know how to do a load of laundry, boy?"

"I do," I say, calm but steely. "I've been doing my own laundry since I was eight. Been cooking, cleaning, handling my own shit for a long fucking time—because if I didn't, my mother would've beaten the living crap out of me."

Bobby recoils, his face softening just a little—maybe remembering who the fuck he's talking to.

"I get that you're pissed at me. I fucked up. I admit that. And I'll probably fuck up again, in one way or another. And yeah, Cat is too fucking good for me—believe me, I know that. But she chose me. For some insane reason, she picked me. And I will never stop being grateful. I will do everything in my power to take care of her the way she deserves. I love her, Bobby. More than anything or anyone in this world.

"I don't know what I can do to change your opinion of me—and honestly, I don't care to. You can think and feel whatever you want. The only thing that matters to me is how Cat thinks and feels. If she wants me to move in with you guys, I will. If she wants to stay at my apartment, then that's where we'll be. Fuck, if she asked me to build her a goddamn hut in the forest and go completely off-grid, I'd do it—because that's how much I love her.

"Whatever happens, I'm going to make damn sure Cat and our baby are taken care of."

Silence.

Then I add, a little softer, "You might also consider trusting your daughter a bit more. She's pretty fucking smart. Her being hurt by some motherfucker doesn't mean she's bad at choosing good men. Abusers don't walk around with signs telling you they've got rotten souls. If they did, my mother wouldn't have gotten away with what she did for seventeen years."

I turn to Cat. Her hazel eyes are glassy, full of emotion. She's still holding my hand under the table.

"I'm done with this dinner whenever you are," I say quietly.

She nods. "I'm ready to go," she says, her voice cool, eyes locked on her dad. I'm glad I'm not on the receiving end of that death stare.

"No, guys, please don't go yet," Jen pleads, smacking Bobby's shoulder hard as Cat and I rise from the table. "You're an ass, Robert."

I lead Cat out of the dining room.

"Give me five minutes. I'll be right back down," she says, brushing past my dad on her way upstairs.

"Ran, you don't have to leave," he says, his voice low. "Yeah, Bobby's being a dick, but he's just overreacting. He's being a dad."

"I get it, Dad. He's protective of her. But so am I," I say, keeping my tone even. "It's probably best we just leave. Let things cool off for a bit, okay?"

He sighs. "Okay. For what it's worth, bud, you're doing great. I know you're going to be a hell of a dad."

He squeezes my shoulder, and I nod, grateful.

A moment later, Cat comes down the stairs with a backpack slung over one shoulder and that look on her face, the one that says she's made up her mind and God help anyone who tries to change it.

Cat

Ten seconds ago I was all anger, but the second Ronan closes the passenger door behind me, I dissolve into sobs. I can't believe how difficult, how obtuse, how *mean* my dad is. And maybe I *am* extra emotional these days—hormones pushing me from the highest highs to the lowest lows—but this isn't hormones. This is my dad's blatant disrespect for the boy I love more than life itself.

"Baby," Ronan says gently as he gets in and sees me crying. "No, baby, it's okay." He reaches for me immediately, pulling me into his arms.

"No, it's not," I sob against his chest. "My dad is so mean."

"Yeah, he's kind of a dick right now," Ronan says, brushing my hair back with his left hand. "But he's just worried about you."

"Whatever," I choke out. "He doesn't have to be such an asshole about it."

Ronan chuckles softly. "Guys aren't exactly known for emotional intelligence."

"I'm so sorry he's being so rude to you," I say, pulling back to wipe my face.

"I'm more annoyed with how rude he is to *you*." Ronan strokes his thumb gently across my cheek. "And I'm sorry I put you in a situation where you're fighting with him."

"Sweet boy," I say, heart aching. "This isn't anything new. He's been difficult from the moment you and I started dating."

"Yeah," Ronan sighs, leaning back a little. "He's definitely not my biggest fan. Maybe it's just a dad thing."

"Well, whatever it is, it's not fair," I mutter. "And it makes me not want to be around him."

He turns his head to look at me, eyes soft. "Baby, I don't want to come between you and your dad."

"You're not," I say. "*He* is. You haven't done anything wrong."

We sit in silence for a moment before I ask, quietly, "Do you think I could stay with you for a while?"

Ronan looks at me again, something tender lighting in his eyes. "Baby, you can stay with me as long as you want. There's a reason you have a key."

I nod, letting out a long breath. "I think my dad and I need some space. If he can't accept that my heart is yours—that we're in this together—then... I need to step away for a bit."

Ronan huffs a dry laugh. "These Sunday dinners are gonna be awkward as fuck from now on, huh?"

"They were already awkward as fuck," I say, still half-laughing through the tears.

"Facts," he nods, grinning. "So... that means we don't have to go again for a while, right?"

"Yep. That's what that means."

"Perfect," he says. "Honestly, I'd much rather spend Sundays in bed with you anyway."

"Oh yeah? Doing what, exactly?"

"I can't say it out loud. The baby might hear," he says solemnly.

I giggle, then cup my stomach. "There. Now the baby has earmuffs."

Ronan laughs. "Okay, well, I'd much rather kiss every inch of that perfect body of yours, suck your beautiful pink nipples into my mouth, run my tongue down your stomach and between your legs, taste your sweet honey—make you come, baby," he growls, voice dark with heat.

My face flushes. "Yeah... that does sound a lot better than Sunday dinner."

Ronan chuckles, that mischievous spark in his eye. "It's not too late to make that happen."

I grin. "Okay. But can we stop by the store real quick? I think I forgot to pack underwear."

He raises an eyebrow. "Oops. Stores are closed. Guess that means... no underwear for you."

I giggle. "All the stores?"

"Every single one."

"Shame," I say, grinning.

"Oh yeah. Just awful," he deadpans.

I laugh out loud but stop with the sudden jab in my stomach. My hand moves to it, like every time I feel the baby move inside me. I remember the first few flutters, like butterfly wings or perhaps like goldfish bumping against their glass bowl. But this baby's getting stronger by the day and the little karate kicks are downright startling sometimes.

"Oh my gosh, are you trying to break out already?" I giggle.

Ronan's brows dip with confusion.

"The baby," I say. "It's awake. Probably heard the entire no-underwear conversation we just had."

Ronan chuckles. I reach for his arm, then place his hand on my belly where I just felt the jab. I've done it before—placed his hand on my belly whenever I've felt the baby move, but the flutters weren't powerful enough for Ronan to feel anything from the outside. Still, I keep trying.

We wait in the silence of the car.

Jab. My eyes snap to Ronan's. Instantly, I can tell he felt it. His eyes are wide, locked on mine, jaw dropping.

I grin widely. "Did you feel it?"

He nods, awestruck. "Yeah," he breathes.

Right on cue, another kick exactly where Ronan's warm hand rests against my stomach. Like the baby is saying "hi."

Ronan's hand stays firmly on my tummy while his eyes close. He lowers his head, focusing. The baby gives one more little one-two punch, leaving me teary-eyed at the emotion in Ronan's eyes when he opens them.

"Holy shit," he whispers. "That's our baby?"

I nod.

"God, baby... you're incredible."

I lean over and kiss his cheek. "Let's go home."

Thursday, August 24th

Ronan

Eleven days. That's how long it's been since Cat started staying here full time. Technically it's supposed to be temporary—just until things cool off with her dad, just until we figure out what to do once the baby comes. But the longer she's here, the more often I wake to the sound of her humming while she brushes her teeth, the more often I fall asleep with her stealing my pillow to wedge between her legs and even out her hips, the more I *want* this. Us. Together. In this apartment. With my best friend and my best friend's girl.

It's cramped as hell—two bedrooms, four people, one tiny-ass bathroom and an even smaller kitchen—but I wouldn't change a thing. I love knowing who and what I come home to. There's no guessing, no analyzing anyone's mood beside Cat's current pregnancy craving.

Cat has appointed herself the designated grocery shopper, relieving a grateful Shane and guaranteeing her most random craving can be satisfied anytime. Shane, on the other hand, has prohibited Cat from doing any laundry; he thinks she shouldn't have to schlepp an overfull basket down four flights of stairs, then stoop and bend in front of washers and dryers. Tori keeps slipping Cat little self-care things—fancy lotions, herbal teas, some noisy pillow filled with clay beads that gets warmed up in the microwave. So basically, Tori and Shane have appointed themselves Cat's backup support team while I'm at work, and even if I haven't said it out loud yet, I'm so fucking grateful. We don't have everything figured out, not by a long shot. But I look around this cramped, noisy apartment and all I can think is: we're going to be okay.

And thank god summer classes are finally over. I took my last final yesterday and now I get a whole week without lectures, quizzes, or cramming during my ten-minute breaks at work. Sleep, here I fucking come. I swear, if I could crawl into a dark cave and hibernate for seven days straight, I would.

"Hey, sweet boy," Cat calls softly from the living room when I finally come through the door tonight. It's past two-thirty in the morning. I'm surprised she's still awake.

I drop my keys on the entryway table and make my way over to her. "Hey, baby." I press a kiss to her forehead. She's curled up on the couch, a blanket draped over her, eyes heavy with exhaustion.

"Why are you still up?" I lift her legs to sit down before laying them back across my lap.

"I can't sleep," she says, voice gravelly. "My back hurts."

"Want me to give you a back rub?"

She smiles at me gratefully, then shifts upright, turning her back to me. I start to knead gently, working my thumbs in slow circles.

"Lower," she says, and I follow, my hands gliding beneath her shirt. Her skin is warm and soft beneath my fingers. I've touched her a thousand times, but somehow I still can't get enough.

"That feels nice," she sighs, her head dropping forward.

"How was your day?" I ask, my voice low. Between classes and back-to-back night shifts, I've barely seen her except when she's asleep. So even if it's the middle of the night, I enjoy this quiet moment she and I get to share.

"It was alright," she says groggily. "I missed you." She turns to me, brushing her lips softly against mine.

"I missed you too," I murmur against her lips, then slip my tongue into her mouth, tasting her. My body reacts instantly—like it always does with Cat—and I carefully guide her down onto the couch. Her hands are already tugging at my shirt. I pull back just long enough to yank it over my head and toss it to the floor.

"Where's Shane?" I ask, breathless against her mouth. My hands slide under her shirt, greedy to feel her skin.

"He and Tori went to bed hours ago," she says, her breathing already uneven as my thumb brushes over her nipple.

I sit up, pull her shirt over her head, and let my gaze trail down the curves I can never get enough of. Her breasts. Her stomach—not flat and toned like it used to be, but full and tight and round, her skin stretched over the unmistakable swell of the baby growing inside her.

"God damn," I whisper. "I never get over how fucking beautiful you are." I lean in to kiss her—first her lips, then her neck, then lower, over her collarbone, across her chest. I take my time at her breasts, licking each nipple before sucking it gently into my mouth. She tastes like heaven. And I hadn't expected it, not really, but her pregnant body drives me absolutely wild. Every curve, every soft new edge of her—it's like my body is permanently dialed to crave hers.

She lifts her hips, letting me slide her panties down to her knees. She kicks them off, and I waste no time sliding my hand up her thigh, between her legs. She's already worked up, and it makes me smile. I tease her slowly, letting my fingers sweep over the spot I know she likes, again and again. She moves with me, grinding into my hand with a rhythm that sets my pulse racing. Watching her unravel beneath me, hearing her moan my name—it undoes me every single time.

She comes hard, her body arching, her breath catching in my ear, and all I can think is: I'll never get tired of this. Of her.

"That was fast," she breathes, dazed. She flashes me that smile that always kills me. "Your turn, sweet boy."

She unbuttons my jeans, pushing them and my boxers down. I kick them off and let my eyes fall closed for a second as I slide into her. Her warmth surrounds me, and I exhale like I've finally come home.

She pulls me close, her arms winding around my shoulders as I begin to move. God, I love this—being surrounded by her like this, her hips rising to meet mine, like she can't get enough of me. Like we're both starving.

And we are. I need more of her. More of this. Every thrust just makes me want her deeper, closer, until I'm fighting to stay grounded, to hold on just a little longer. But I'm already on the edge.

"Baby," she breathes, nails digging into my back, dragging hard as she rakes them upward. The sharp pain against all that pleasure—it tips me over. I lose it completely, groaning her name as the wave crashes through me. And even through the haze I feel her body tighten again, feel her tremble as she falls over the edge with me.

God, she has the most perfect post-sex glow: flushed cheeks, heavy-lidded eyes, lips parted, catching her breath. Her mouth is too irresistible not to kiss, so I do. Once, twice, then again. Slow and lingering.

We stay there like that for a while, wrapped up in each other, slowly coming down.

Cat

I've been uncomfortable all day, shifting restlessly behind the front desk at my mom's office—sitting, standing, then sitting again. It was mostly my back, this weird, aching pressure I couldn't relieve no matter what I did. Eventually my mom noticed how miserable I was and sent me home around two.

I went straight to Ronan's apartment, drew a warm bath, and soaked for the better part of an hour before finally reemerging. I slipped into a fresh pair of underwear and one of Ronan's t-shirts. The place was empty. Ronan and Shane were both at Murphy's, and Tori was still working her shift at that bagel shop near campus. I spent the rest of the afternoon sprawled on the couch, watching mindless TV and occasionally reheating the clay bead pillow Tori gave me—the one that's supposed to relax sore muscles.

Tori got home a little after six. Shane around 8:30, carrying takeout containers like a hero, as usual. But much to their concern, I barely touched my food.

"You're growing a human in there; shouldn't you be eating more?" Shane asked, nudging the container toward me.

I shrugged. "I'm not that hungry. My back's bugging me—it's kind of messing with my appetite."

"Have Ran give you a back rub when he gets home," Tori said. I reminded her that Ronan had the late shift—he wouldn't be back until after two.

It didn't matter. I couldn't sleep anyway. I lay on the couch watching more mindless TV, too restless to settle. But the second I heard Ronan's key in the door, everything inside me softened. It always does when he's near. Seeing him is still the best part of my day, especially lately, when we haven't had much real time together.

And once his back rub turned into something more? I wasn't complaining. Say what you want about orgasms—they're underrated for pain management. For the first time all day, the ache in my back finally disappeared.

We stayed curled up on the couch for a while, limbs tangled, skin warm. When I felt him start to doze off, I suggested we move to the bed. He carried me into his room, laid me down gently, then pulled on a pair of sweatpants before crawling in beside me, shirtless and warm. I fell asleep with my head on his chest, lulled by the slow, steady rhythm of his heartbeat.

I can't have been asleep more than forty-five minutes when I wake up with a jolt—my lower back screaming in pain, sharp and sudden and nothing like before. I sit up abruptly, blinded by both the dark and the intensity of it. The pain wraps from my spine all the way around to the front of my stomach, tightening my abdomen like a vise.

I press a hand to my belly, breathing through it. After about a minute the pain lets up, and I exhale shakily.

"What the hell was that?" I whisper into the dark.

A moment later, I feel a different kind of pressure, lower. I shift in bed, ready to climb out and head to the bathroom when suddenly, *oh no*, a warm gush floods between my legs. I freeze.

Something's wrong. Something is *very* wrong.

I fling the blanket back and my breath catches in my throat. Blood. Bright, red blood, pooling between my thighs and soaking the white sheets beneath me.

"Oh god," I gasp, my voice barely registering past the rising panic. My hand shoots out and grabs Ronan's shoulder, shaking him.

"Ran, wake up," I say, voice trembling.

He stirs, groggy, voice thick with sleep. "What's wrong, baby?"

"I'm bleeding," is all I manage to say.

It hits me then—how clammy my skin feels, how my shirt is soaked with sweat. I'm freezing and burning at the same time. Ronan jolts fully awake, immediately reaching for the light. When it flicks on and his eyes land on the blood, I see the panic flicker across his face—but his voice stays steady.

"Are you having any pain?" he asks, already climbing out of bed and coming to my side.

I start to shake my head, the word *no* already forming—when another wave of pain tears through me. I suck in a breath so sharp it cuts, every muscle in my body locking up as the contraction hits.

"Baby," Ronan says, dropping to his knees beside me and taking my hand. His grip is warm, grounding, while I try to breathe through the storm inside my body. I'm only halfway through this pregnancy. I haven't taken any classes, haven't learned how to breathe for labor—I'm just trying to survive this moment.

"I think..." My voice shakes as the pain fades again. "I think I'm losing the baby."

The words make the fear real. My vision swims. I feel faint.

"I need to lie down," I whisper, collapsing back into the pillows, my fingers still tangled in his. "I'm really tired..."

"Don't you fall asleep right now!" Ronan snaps.

The sudden command slices through the fog in my head.

"Get up." His voice is fierce, unrelenting.

I frown at him, tears welling. *I can't.* I'm too weak. Too tired. My body hurts in places I didn't know could hurt.

"Ran, please," I whisper.

But he's already pulling me upright. "I'm taking you to the hospital." He scans the room, frantic. "Do not lie back down." He points a finger at me before sprinting to the hallway. "Shane! Wake the fuck up! I need your help!"

He's back a moment later, yanking open his closet. He tugs a plain white shirt over his head and grabs a pair of black sweats.

"Come on, baby," he says, his voice gentler now. He kneels in front of me again, steady hands guiding mine. "Let's get these on you."

He threads my legs carefully into the oversized pants, his hands brushing against my knees, his eyes never leaving my face like he's willing me to stay awake, to stay *with him*.

"What the hell is going on?" Shane asks, suddenly standing in the doorway in just his boxers, his chest bare and his face still puffy with sleep.

"I think Cat's hemorrhaging. I need to get her to the hospital right now," Ronan says, urgent but level.

Shane's eyes dart to the bed, to the pool of crimson blood. "Holy shit." He doesn't hesitate. "What do you need from me?"

"Grab my keys. Help me get her to the car."

Ronan sweeps me into his arms, cradling me like a baby. I cling to him, barely holding on.

"You sure you don't want me to call an ambulance?" Shane asks as he dashes out of Ronan's room ahead of us.

"They'll take too fucking long." Ronan's already striding out of his bedroom. "She's too pale, and she's cold as fucking ice, Shay."

Another contraction hits me like a train, snuffing out all rational thought, shooting straight through my spine and curling around to my front like barbed wire. I tense so hard I think I might pass out.

"Stop, please—" I gasp, teeth clenched against the pain.

Ronan halts instantly, arms tightening around me, holding me solidly against his chest. I bury my face in his shoulder and try to ride it out, breathing hard.

"Are you okay, baby?" he asks, his voice raw.

I can hear how scared he is. But his arms are strong. He hasn't let go of me once.

"No," I whisper, tears stinging my eyes. I cling to Ronan's neck like I'll slip away if I let go.

Shane rushes ahead, grabbing Ronan's keys. He throws open the front door and Ronan carries me out, careful with every step down the three flights of stairs.

The hot night air hits my damp skin as we step outside. It should feel good, but I'm still trembling, my whole body cold and clammy. I hear the click of the car door unlocking, then Shane swinging it open.

Ronan lowers me into the passenger seat as gently as if I were made of glass.

"Baby, listen to me," he says, his green eyes locked on mine. "I know you're tired right now. But you can't fall asleep, okay? Please don't fall asleep on me."

I nod, barely.

He closes my door, takes the keys from Shane, and mutters something I don't catch. I rest my head against the cool window as we pull away from the curb. The streets are empty. Everything is so quiet, except the roaring inside my body.

Each contraction tears through me like a storm surge. I drift in and out, fading, my limbs heavy, my breath shallow. The seatbelt presses against my stomach and I can't tell if it helps or hurts.

It feels like the drive lasts hours. Maybe it does? *Don't fall asleep*, I chant, or maybe it's Ronan's voice? I can't tell, and it scares me.

"Come on, baby, wake up. Cat, please." Ronan's voice echoes through the haze, desperate and cracking. I blink, barely, catching the shape of him through blurry eyes. He's already pulling me out of the car.

My arms don't move. My hands tingle. I'm freezing.

His chest is warm against my cheek.

"What happened?" a voice I don't recognize asks.

I try to answer. I can't. My head lolls against Ronan's shoulder, and everything begins to slip sideways.

"She just woke up bleeding," Ronan says, his voice tight with urgency. "She's twenty-two weeks pregnant. Contractions are coming about every minute and a half."

I want to look at him, tell him how incredible he is for tracking that when I couldn't even keep my eyes open, but another contraction steals my breath. My body locks up, muscles straining so hard it feels like I might rupture from the inside.

I can feel how soaked Ronan's sweatpants are with blood, the fabric clinging to my thighs, sticky warmth running down my legs. I know what that means. I know what's happening. But I can't focus on it, can't focus on anything except the next wave of pain crashing over me.

Suddenly I'm being lifted from Ronan's arms, and I whimper in protest, trying to reach for him. My fingers twitch, grasping air.

He's right there. His green eyes meet mine, stricken and scared, and I want to say something—anything. That it'll be okay. That I just need to rest. That I'm sorry.

But my body gives out before my voice can catch up.

Everything goes black.

Ronan

I am a fucking mess.

I'm sitting in the waiting room of the ER—the same hospital where I woke up almost two years ago to the day—and the smell alone hits me like a punch to the gut. The sterile sting of antiseptic and something metallic and sour. It grabs me by the throat, yanking up memories I don't want, but I shove them down hard. I can't afford to fall apart. Not right now. Not when Cat needs me.

I followed the three nurses pushing her stretcher like my legs were on autopilot, moving faster than I could think. I'd driven here like a maniac, flooring it through red lights, flying over potholes, not caring if I wrecked my shitty car or got pulled over. Every second mattered. Every single fucking second.

As soon as Cat told me she was bleeding and I saw the sheets—saw how much blood there was—I knew we were in real trouble. I might still be learning, but I knew enough that this wasn't spotting. This wasn't some harmless pregnancy symptom.

She was hemorrhaging.

She was pale, drenched in sweat, her skin clammy and cold, and by the time I pulled up to the hospital, her lips were tinged with blue and she was barely conscious. The sweatpants I helped her into were soaked through.

The entire drive, I kept whipping my head between her and the road, trying to time her contractions. I could see them coming, how her body would go rigid, how even half-unconscious she'd moan in pain. I kept pressing harder on the gas like I could outrun the clock, outrun what was happening to her.

I held her hand all the way through until they made me let go. Until they wheeled her into the treatment area and told me to stay behind. One of the nurses asked me questions in that too-calm voice they use when they're bracing for the worst: Cat's age, how far along she was, if I was the father.

Then she asked if Cat and I had been in a physical altercation.

Like maybe *I* had done this to her.

I almost lost it. My fists clenched, jaw tight enough to crack a molar, but I kept my voice steady when I said, "No. I would never."

She made me sign some papers, consent for emergency surgery, blood transfusions—as if I'd get to make decisions like that for Cat. But I signed away like my damn life depended on it. It does. Cat's life is my life. She has to make it through this.

And then I was left here. Alone. On a hard black plastic chair that feels like it was designed to make you more aware of your body just so you can suffer inside it. An entire fucking hour now. I sit. I pace. I sit again. I try to call Jen to tell her what's going on, but I hang up when her voicemail kicks in. She can't find out that her daughter's in the hospital from a message like that.

She needs to hear it from me. And I need to be able to *say* it.

I've tried my dad a few times, too. No luck. Everyone's probably still sleeping.

But I'm wide awake.

Wide awake and terrified.

I'm restless and on edge, jittering with adrenaline and dread. I feel completely out of control, like I'm trapped in a nightmare with no way to wake up.

Finally, a doctor approaches me. Her face is kind, and I stand quickly from my chair, my body coiled and ready—braced for either relief or devastation.

Her voice is warm, gentle. She's clearly trying to soften the blow, but even before she speaks, I know it's not good news.

"Cat has suffered a severe placental abruption," she says.

I frown, blinking at her. The words mean nothing to me. Abruption. It sounds violent. Wrong. My brain can't connect the dots, can't keep up.

Her hand comes to my shoulder, settling there gently. "We did an ultrasound," she continues softly, "and unfortunately, we were unable to detect a heartbeat. I'm so sorry."

Heartbeat.

The word hits me like a wrecking ball. I stare at her, waiting for my mind to make sense of what she's saying. Is she talking about Cat? Or the baby? Or both?

"It's rare, but not unheard of," she says, her tone apologetic, like she wishes she could change what's already happened. "The severity of the abruption deprived the baby of oxygen."

The baby. Not Cat.

I start to understand.

I feel my heart lurch and falter, like it's skipping beats, trying to keep pace with the flood of realization. The baby didn't make it.

"I'm so sorry," she repeats. "We're prepping Cat for an emergency C-section to deliver the baby and get control of the bleeding. Would you... would you like to see your son after delivery?"

My son.

A boy.

The air leaves my lungs. My knees give out and I drop back into the chair.

"I... I don't know," I whisper. Everything's spinning. I drop my head into my hands, trying to hold it together, trying to stop the world from crashing down around me.

The doctor lowers herself into the seat next to me. "That's alright," she says gently. "I have to get back to your wife. I'll come find you afterward. Give you some time to decide."

My wife. My son.

Fuck.

I manage a slight nod, the weight of her words crushing me.

But then a thought slams into my chest. I reach for her, stopping her mid-stride.

"We were intimate a few hours ago," I say, my voice barely above a whisper. "We... we had sex. Could that have been the reason for—"

She shakes her head before I can finish. "No. You don't have to worry about that. Sex and orgasms can sometimes trigger contractions, but this wasn't caused by that. Cat's abruption was severe, and not related to anything you did. These things... sometimes they just happen." Her expression softens. "We'll run tests, see if we can determine a cause. I'll come find you once she's out of surgery."

She offers a small, sympathetic smile—meant to comfort—and then she's gone, off to save the woman I love more than anything.

The moment she disappears, I bolt out of the ER, crashing through the doors like I can outrun the grief clawing at my insides. The cool morning air hits my lungs hard. I gulp it down like I'm drowning.

I pace. I rake my hands through my hair, across my face, over and over again. I want to scream. I want to run until my legs give out. But I don't. Of course I don't.

So I just keep pacing—back and forth on the sidewalk—until I calm myself down enough to go back inside. Back to the waiting room. Back to *waiting*.

My eyes burn from exhaustion, but I don't dare close them. Not until I know Cat's okay. I keep checking my watch. Then my phone. Then my watch again. Twenty minutes since I last spoke to the doctor, but it feels like fucking hours.

Then my phone buzzes in the pocket of my sweats. It's Shane.

"How's Cat?" he asks. No hello, just urgency.

I sigh, dropping my elbows to my knees, tipping my head forward as I press the phone to my ear.

"I don't know," I say, my voice fraying. "She's in surgery."

"What happened?" Tori's voice now. I must be on speaker.

"Cat... her placenta abrupted. The baby didn't make it," I say. "They're doing an emergency C-section now. Trying to control the bleeding. And... deliver the baby." My throat tightens around the last words. "It was a boy," I choke.

Tori gasps.

"Ran, I'm so sorry," Shane says, and his voice cracks.

"Shay?" I breathe, reaching for the only thing I can. His voice. My best friend.

"I'm here, Ran."

And thank god for that!

"They asked if I want to see him. After he's delivered." I swallow hard. "I don't know what the right thing is."

There's a pause. I hear him inhale shakily, and I can picture him sitting up, pressing a hand over his mouth, steadying himself for me.

"Don't think, Ran. Just feel. Don't worry about what's right or wrong right now. What do *you* want? If you want to see him, see him. If you don't, that's okay too. This isn't anyone else's decision. I'm so fucking sorry."

We fall silent for a moment, each of us struggling with the heaviness of the moment.

"What can I do?" Shane asks, his voice thick with emotion.

"Nothing," I sigh, feeling completely drained.

Just then, I see Cat's doctor emerge from the double doors and I shoot to my feet.

"Shane, I gotta go. Cat's doctor is coming to talk to me. Hey, can you try to get in touch with Cat's mom? Or my dad? Or both? I haven't been able to reach anyone."

"Sure thing, Ran."

"Thanks," I murmur, hanging up and shoving my phone back into my pocket as I move toward the doctor.

"How is she?" The words tumble out as soon as I reach her.

She rests a hand on my shoulder and begins guiding me gently toward the double doors. "She's out of surgery. We were able to stop the bleeding, and we've been giving her blood transfusions. She's going to be okay."

The air rushes from my lungs. Relief hits me like a wave, giving me enough strength to speak the next words. "I'd like to see him."

The doctor nods, offering a small, warm smile that somehow makes the whole moment even more unbearable.

She leads me down a wide hallway to an elevator.

"Were you able to figure out why this happened?" I ask, my voice strained. "I mean, is there anything we need to do differently the next time... wait, will she be able to have kids? She wants kids."

"We're going to run some tests," the doctor says, her voice calm, practiced, kind. "But yes, she will be able to have children. She'll just need to be monitored more closely next time. Once complications like these arise, the risk can be higher in future pregnancies. But that's something her primary doctor will watch for... once she's ready to try again. Right now, she just needs time. Time to rest. To heal."

The elevator doors open. We take it up to the third floor where she leads me into a small room.

The morning sun spills in through a large window to the left of Cat's bed. I walk straight to her, taking her hand into mine.

She's sleeping. Peaceful now. Her face no longer contorted in pain. The cold sheen of sweat is gone, wiped clean from her skin, but she's still too pale. Ashen. Her lips barely pink. There's an IV feeding her donated blood. I catch the sticker on the bag: A negative. I never knew her blood type. I make a mental note, filing it away just in case that's info I'll ever need to have on hand.

"We'll keep her for a couple of days," the doctor says. "She should be able to go home on Saturday." Her hand touches my shoulder again, soft, comforting. "The nurse will be up shortly to let you see your son. I'm so sorry for your loss."

I nod. Or at least I think I nod. And then she leaves.

I pull a chair next to Cat's bed and sit, still holding her hand. My thumb drags along her soft skin, still too cool. I let my forehead rest against her arm, and for a moment, I just breathe.

It hits me then. All of it. Everything I've been forcing down to survive the last few hours—terror, adrenaline, helplessness, grief—rises at once, leaving me shaking.

I almost lost her. I almost lost the only person I've ever been certain of.

Even in the months we were apart, I still belonged to her. I always did. I see that now, with painful, piercing clarity.

A soft knock at the door draws my head up. A nurse steps in, gently pushing a small hospital bassinet toward me.

My breath catches. Or disappears entirely. I can't tell which.

She brings it to a stop beside me.

My heart—if it's still beating—feels like it's moving underwater.

Inside the bassinet is a tiny bundle, wrapped in a white blanket with pale pink and blue stripes. There's a matching hat on his small head. He looks like he's just sleeping.

"Can I hold him?" I ask, barely above a whisper.

The nurse nods and lifts the baby—*my son*—into my arms.

He's weightless. Fragile. Perfect. Lifeless.

His skin is grayish, almost translucent. Still… he's *mine*.

"I'll give you some time," the nurse says softly. "Just press the call button when you're ready." She leaves quietly, shutting the door behind her.

I retake my seat beside Cat, cradling our baby in one arm and holding Cat's hand with the other.

"I'm holding our son, baby," I say, my voice strange in the quiet. "He's already beautiful."

My vision blurs. Tears rise and spill over. I don't stop them. I don't even try. I just let myself *feel*.

I look down at the baby, studying every inch of him. His delicate mouth. The slope of his nose. The closed lids over eyes I'll never get to see open. Cat's hazel? My green? Or maybe something else entirely? A color that belongs only to him?

"I'm so sorry," I whisper. "I'm sorry for everything."

The words come in waves.

"I'm sorry I wasn't excited about you at first. I was scared. So fucking scared I wouldn't know how to love you right."

But I did. I *do*. I realize it as I say the words—I've loved him for weeks.

Every time we heard his heartbeat at the doctor's office. Every time I saw the ultrasound pinned to the fridge. Every time my hands rested on Cat's belly and felt him move underneath.

I loved him more than I knew.

And now it's all been pulled out from under me, leaving nothing but this aching, hollow quiet.

"I wanted to be so good to you. And to her," I whisper, my throat burning. "But I wasted so much time worrying, being afraid... I didn't enjoy any of it. And now I'll never get the chance to."

A sob shudders out of me, raw and broken. I hold on to Cat and to him—our son—as the grief pours out.

When the tears slow, I stare down at his face again, memorizing it. Trying to make sense of this moment. Trying to give it something—*him*—meaning.

"I don't know if I'm supposed to name you," I murmur, blinking past the blur. "We never really talked about names. But you feel like... like you deserve one."

I study him again, wondering if I can see any of myself in him. Or maybe he's all Cat. Maybe he's both of us, all tangled up in this small, silent life.

And then it comes to me.

"You deserve a name that means something. Something real. You were here. You mattered."

My throat tightens as I speak his name aloud for the first—and maybe only—time.

"What do you think of Ronan?" I whisper.

I gaze down at him, letting the words settle around us. It feels... heavy. And right. Like something inside me shifts.

Gently, I move to place him in Cat's arms. His little body, light and still, nestled against hers. Safe. Sound. She should get to hold him. *She should've held him first.*

I step back, just a little, and pull out my phone. I take a picture—Cat, asleep, her face soft in the morning light, with our beautiful boy resting next to her.

I don't know if she'll want to see it. Maybe not now. Maybe not ever.

But I'll have it. A piece of this memory. Of him. Of *us*.

Forever.

***

I held my son for close to an hour before I called the nurse, reluctantly turned him over to her, and watched her take him away from me. I needed to focus on the now, on the living, breathing love of my life. I didn't want to risk her waking up to him in my arms. She'll need to be eased into our loss.

Exhaustion gnaws at me as I sit with Cat. I have been awake for twenty-seven hours now, with the exception of that hour or so when Cat and I went to bed at three in the morning. But I can't find any rest, only closing my eyes here and there to stop them from burning. They feel raw and dry and swollen, partially from the lack of sleep, partially from the tears I've shed this morning.

Just after nine-thirty, the door creaks open, and I look up, startled. Jen. My dad. Penny. They rush in, faces pale, anxious. Jen is at my side in an instant, pulling me into a hug as I rise unsteadily to meet her.

"What happened, Ran?" she asks, her voice muffled against my shoulder. "Shane showed up at my house an hour ago. He said you had to take Cat to the hospital. I'm so sorry I missed your calls." Her voice breaks. "He said… he said Cat lost the baby?"

Lost the baby. No. More like he was ripped from her, stolen by something violent and sudden.

I nod, my shoulders heavy. "Yeah. She woke up bleeding last night and her contractions came on strong. I just grabbed her and drove," I say, too tired to lay out the excruciating details. "They rushed her into surgery to stop the bleeding. The baby..." I pause, swallowing hard. "He didn't make it."

Everything goes silent, like the room itself is holding its breath.

He.

"It was a boy." My voice barely holds. My eyes sting again, hot and unrelenting. I don't think I've ever cried this much in my life.

"Oh, Ran," Jen chokes and takes a small step back to look at her daughter. "Did the doctor tell you how this could have happened?"

"No. They're running some tests," I say, my voice strained. "I have no idea," I sigh, resting my head in my hands.

"How is she?" my dad asks, his deep voice low. He steps beside me, placing a hand on my shoulder. Solid. Warm.

"She's been asleep this whole time. The doctor said she'll be okay. Physically," I say, and Jen nods, her eyes swimming with tears. "She'll be able to go home Saturday."

"How are you holding up, bud?" he asks.

"I don't know," I say. "Overwhelmed, I guess. Scared. Tired."

I don't leave Cat's side for the next few hours. I just sit there holding her hand, watching her face like it's the only thing tethering me to the earth. I memorize it—every freckle, every line, every inch of skin I almost lost last night.

Jen and Penny step out to speak with the doctor and come back about twenty minutes later, whispering to my dad. Their voices blend into a dull hum. I'm too tired to make out their words.

Steve calls—Shane must've told him. I hand the phone to my dad without saying anything. I'm done explaining. Each time I say it out loud, it feels more real. More painful.

At eleven, Shane and Tori show up. Shane squats down beside me, resting a hand on my shoulder.

"How are you, Ran?" he asks softly.

"Fine," I say, eyes still locked on Cat.

"You're not a good liar, you know that?" he says with a small smile. I nod. "Don't worry about anything. I've got you covered at work. Take all the time you need."

He steps away, joining my dad and Jen at the back of the room.

Half an hour later, Bobby rushes in. "I came as soon as class let out and I got your message," he tells Jen, slightly out of breath. Then his eyes cut to me. "What happened?" he asks rapid-fire, like he's demanding answers, like this is something I could've prevented.

But I can't deal with him. Not now. I barely have the energy to stay upright.

Thankfully, Jen and my dad step in. They answer his questions quietly, ushering him away so I can stay beside Cat without interruption.

***

I'm drained, but restless—wired with something jagged. I want to get up, resume pacing, claw my way out of this stillness. But I can't bring myself to let go of Cat. So I force myself to stay seated, holding her hand, watching her breathe, waiting.

Finally, just after noon, she opens her beautiful hazel eyes.

They find mine instantly.

There are deep shadows under her eyes, stark against the ghostly pallor of her skin. Even her lips have lost their soft pink hue, dulled by blood loss and shock.

"Hey, baby," I say, my voice breaking as I cradle her hand in both of mine. The emotions in my chest are merciless—grief and relief tearing at each other.

Out of the corner of my eye, I see Jen and Bobby step toward the bed, but they stop short. They keep their distance, giving us a pocket of quiet. She's their daughter, but this loss belongs to both of us.

"Hi," she whispers, her voice barely there. But she's awake. She's here. She's alive.

"How are you feeling?" I ask gently.

"Tired..." Her face twists with pain. "And empty. Am I still pregnant?"

Her voice is already breaking. She knows the answer instinctively. Her body knows.

I shake my head, squeezing her hand more tightly. Her tears spill immediately.

"I lost our baby," she cries, dissolving into sobs.

I move without thinking, shifting from the chair to the edge of the bed, wrapping her in my arms.

"I'm so sorry, baby," I whisper, my own grief surging violently as hers collides with mine. The pain is too big for one body. So we hold it together.

"I lost our baby," she sobs again, her whole body shaking. "I couldn't keep it safe."

"No, baby. No," I rasp, forcing the words through clenched teeth. "You didn't do anything wrong. It's not your fault."

"I didn't even get to see it... I don't even know if it was a boy or a girl," she chokes out.

I inhale shakily, then meet her eyes. "It was a boy." My voice fractures. "He was beautiful, baby."

She cries harder. I hear the quiet sobs behind us—Jen, leaning against Bobby, and Penny wrapped in my dad's arms. But all I can focus on is Cat.

"I knew it was a boy," she weeps. "I felt it."

"Yeah. You did." I kiss her hair and pull her against me, just trying to keep her from falling apart completely, holding the last pieces of her heart together.

"It hurts so much, Ran," she whispers. Her pain is so sharp, so real, I swear I feel it in my own chest like a blade. "Please... make it stop."

I just about lose it then and there.

"I'm trying, baby," I whisper, my voice thick. "I'm trying. I love you so much."

I wish I could take it all from her—the ache, the fear, the unbearable weight. But all I can do is hold her while she cries. For minutes. For what feels like hours. I speak to her in quiet fragments, telling her it's going to be okay even if we don't believe it yet.

Eventually, her sobs soften. Her face slackens, what little energy she had in her drained for now. I ease her back against her pillow and she slips into sleep almost immediately. I thank the heavens for it. Sometimes sleep is the best medicine, the best way to shut off the pain. At least temporarily.

Gently, I slide my hand out of hers, then turn around to face our parents.

"Can you... can you guys stay with Cat for a bit?" My voice catches. "I need a minute."

"Of course," Jen says, giving me a quick squeeze before she moves to take my place beside her daughter.

"Ran, are you—" my dad starts, but I hold up a hand to cut him off. I already feel the pressure rising behind my eyes, in my throat.

If he asks me how I'm doing, if he tries to pull me into a hug, I'll break apart. Right here. Right now.

"I'm alright, Dad. I just need some air," I say quickly. Then I bolt out the door, down the stairs, and into the sweltering New York summer heat.

And it all comes crashing out of me.

The fear of losing Cat.

The loss of our baby... our son.

The emotional chaos of these last few months.

All of it barrels through me like a wave I can't outrun.

I didn't want children. I made a big fucking deal about it. I broke up with the love of my life over it, so sure of what I didn't want, so damn certain I was protecting both of us.

But I was wrong.

Seeing Cat pregnant, watching her carry a future that belonged to both of us, changed everything. It made me fall even more in love with her. It made me *want* the things I swore I didn't.

I started to picture it: holding our baby in my arms, watching Cat smile at him the way she smiles at me, being a dad. I knew it wouldn't be easy—I knew myself—but I wanted it. I wanted *us*.

And now it's gone. Ripped away the second I let myself believe we could have something good, something whole.

I can't breathe.

This helplessness, this dizzying, crushing lack of control, wraps itself around my ribs and squeezes. It's not new. I've felt it all my life. But I'd started to believe I'd outrun it. After the trial, after everything, I thought maybe I could finally have a life that wasn't just about surviving.

But right now?

Right now, I feel like the universe is laughing at me.

Like I was a fool to think it would ever let me have peace.

I rake my hands over my face, shaking, gutted, but... I'm breathing. I'm here. And so is Cat. Maybe I can't control the universe. Maybe I never could. But I can choose what I do with what's left. I can be there for Cat. I can keep showing up, even when it hurts. I can keep healing. Keep fighting for the life I want with the girl I love. That part? That's still mine. And I'm not letting go.

Cat

I spend most of my time in the hospital asleep, waking only to make sure Ronan is still there. It's like my body needs proof—his hand in mine, his gorgeous face beside me—before it lets me rest again. He never leaves, always in the same spot when I blink awake, just long enough to see him before I drift off again.

I can't begin to describe how exhausted I am, but I guess that's expected. My body went through labor and delivery, though I don't remember any of it. I was unconscious—too much blood loss, they said—and everything's a blur. I remember Ronan's arms around me, the contractions tearing through me, how cold I felt. And then nothing.

I was pregnant one moment... and the next, I wasn't. But there was no baby in my arms.

That aching absence is what settles deepest in my chest.

There's a soft, hesitant knock on the door sometime later. A nurse steps inside, her presence calm, unintrusive. Ronan sits up beside me, his hand still wrapped around mine.

"Hi, Cat," she says gently. "I'm so sorry for your loss. I wanted to ask... would you like to see your baby?"

The air goes still. My heart stutters. My stomach twists. I feel the blood drain from my face. I notice my parents shifting in the corner of the room, but I glance at Ronan, panic rising in my chest. His eyes meet mine with quiet understanding. He doesn't pressure me. He never would.

I look back at the nurse. My mouth opens, then closes. The air in the room feels too thin.

"I..." My voice catches. "I don't know."

"You don't have to decide right this second," she says softly. "Take your time. But we'll only be able to keep him with us a little while longer."

Ronan squeezes my hand. "Whatever you need, baby. It's okay. Either way."

I swallow thickly. The idea of seeing him, holding that tiny body in my arms, memorizing a face I'll never see again, terrifies me. A part of me aches for it. But a bigger part knows I'm not strong enough. Not yet. Maybe not ever.

"I just..." The words break out of me, heavy with guilt. "I feel like I should. Like I *have* to. That if I don't hold him, I'm not showing him I love him."

Ronan's face softens, grief in every line. He shakes his head. "Baby, you already held him. You carried our boy for almost five months. He knew you loved him. Every time you talked to him, every time you touched your belly—he knew. And... you held him after, too."

My breath catches. I blink at him. "You... you saw him?"

He nods.

"And you held him in your arms?"

Another nod. "And so did you, baby. When you were still sleeping. I put him in your arms. I thought... I thought you should get to." His voice breaks. "You already held him," he says, choking on the words.

And just like that, I know. He's giving me permission to let go of the guilt. To listen to my heart.

I turn to the nurse, tears blurring everything. "No," I whisper. "I can't. I can't see him."

Ronan's grip tightens gently. No judgment. Just quiet grief. "Okay," he says. "It's okay."

The nurse nods with understanding. "Would you like us to make a memory box? His footprints, a photo, a blanket? You don't have to look at it now... but maybe someday."

I nod, tears spilling over before I can stop them. "Yes. Please."

The nurse gives me a warm smile, then steps away.

When she's gone, I bury my face in Ronan's chest and cry harder than I have since I first woke up. He holds me tightly, whispering that he's here, that I'm safe, that I'm not alone.

I don't know if I made the right choice. Maybe there isn't a right one, only the one that hurts a little less in the moment. I couldn't bear the idea of holding my baby only to have him taken away again. Ronan's right. I did hold him. I did love him. And nothing I do now will change that.

My heart aches with the loss of our son. And I know Ronan feels it too. I see it in his face, hear it in his voice when he asks me how I'm doing, if I'm hungry, if I need water. He looks as tired as I feel, but I don't think he's slept at all, probably not since before everything happened, except for that hour, just before our world was ripped apart again.

Our parents spend a few quiet hours at the hospital, talking in hushed voices until my mom gently insists they give us some privacy.

"Kitty," she says softly, bending to hug me, "your doctor said you'll likely be discharged on Saturday. I'd like it if you came home to recover."

Her voice is thick with emotion. She's been crying as much as I have, her eyes puffy, cheeks tear-stained. Even my dad looks grief-stricken. I haven't been home more than a few minutes here and there since that Sunday dinner, since my dad tore into Ronan and I made it clear how disappointed I was in him. My mom wasn't the issue. Never has been. She's always loved Ronan, has always seen how good he is to me—how loving, respectful, and devoted he's been from the beginning.

Even when we were broken up, she never spoke badly of him. She just kept reminding me that everything would work out, that Ronan loved me, that we'd find our way back once he had worked through whatever he needed to.

"Baby, I think that's a good idea," Ronan says quietly from his seat beside me. "I don't want you to be alone right now, and I've got to go back to work, and classes start up again soon." His voice is hoarse with exhaustion. "I want you to be taken care of."

"Please come home, Kitty," my mom says, her voice cracking.

My dad steps forward and takes my left hand in his right. "I'm sorry," he says quietly. "For how I've been acting. I never meant to push you away..." His voice trails off as he lowers his gaze.

"Okay," I whisper, nodding. I glance over at Ronan, noting the deep, dark circles under his eyes, the scruff on his jaw. "Will you drop me off at my parents' when I'm discharged?"

"Yeah. Of course," he says, steady as ever. Always showing up for me.

"Thank you, Ronan," my mom says, walking over to him. She wraps him in a hug as he stands. "For taking care of my baby. I'm so sorry." Her voice is muffled against his shoulder. "I love you both so much."

That evening, Shane and Tori stop by with Vada, Summer, and Zack in tow. They drop off dinner and spend some time with us, providing quiet, steady support to Ronan and me. Steve calls, and I cry fresh tears when speaking to him.

Ronan stays with me all night, curled awkwardly in the uncomfortable chair beside my bed, legs kicked up beside me, trying to find some rest.

I wake a few times during the night when the nurse comes to check on me. She smiles when she sees Ronan still there.

"He doesn't leave your side, huh?" she says while she hooks me up to a fresh bag of saline.

"No," I whisper. "He's a keeper."

Saturday, August 26th

Cat

It's late Saturday morning when I get released from the hospital.

Despite the transfusions to make up for the severe blood loss I suffered, I feel weak and tired when Ronan helps me out of the wheelchair and into his car. My body aches all over, but especially my lower abdomen, where an inches-long incision will soon become a scar. A permanent reminder of what happened. What we lost.

I can't even walk upright, each of the three steps from the wheelchair to the car slow and hunched over.

I would've preferred going back to Ronan's apartment, but between his classes and work, I know he wouldn't be around much. My mom wants someone to keep an eye on me at all times for the next couple of weeks anyway, and I don't have the strength to argue.

Luckily, I don't anticipate having to miss much school—a week at most, since there are no classes next week and the fall semester of my sophomore year in college starts the week after that.

"Do you have to work tonight?" I ask Ronan as we pull up to my house just before noon.

He hesitates, chewing on his bottom lip. "Well... technically, no. Shane offered to cover for me. But..." His eyes flick to mine, cautious. "If it's okay with you, I'd kind of like to go in. I could use the distraction."

He says it like a confession. Like something he's ashamed to admit.

And as much as I want him here—want him beside me every second—I get it. He's hurting, too. Devastated. And he copes by moving, by doing, by distracting himself. Healthy or not, I'm not about to lecture him on grief when I haven't even figured out how to handle my own.

"Yeah," I say softly. "Okay."

Ronan gives me a small, grateful smile, then rounds the car to help me out. The moment I'm upright, he scoops me into his arms and carries me to the house.

My parents are already waiting.

My dad opens the door for us, greeting us both with a warm smile, his whole demeanor radiating a kindness toward Ronan I haven't seen in... well, ever.

"I put fresh linens on your bed, Kitty," my mom says sweetly, already moving to lead us upstairs.

"Ronan," my dad calls after us, "I'd like a quick word with you once you've deposited Cat upstairs."

Ronan nods, then follows my mom up the stairs to my room, carrying me like I weigh nothing. He gently lowers me onto my bed, adjusting me against the stack of perfectly fluffed pillows.

"Be right back, I guess," he says with a touch of skepticism.

As Ronan steps out of the room, my mom trails after him, thankfully leaving the door wide open. Which means I can hear *everything* my dad says to him next.

"You know," my dad begins, his voice low, "I really wanted to hurt you when you broke up with Cat."

My heart stutters. I frown, already shifting in bed, tempted to make my way downstairs and tell him to knock it off.

"I don't blame you, sir," Ronan says, calm and sincere. "It was a stupid move on my part. Probably the dumbest thing I've ever done, because Cat... she's the best thing that ever happened to me."

There's a pause. A long one. And when my dad finally speaks again, his voice has softened. "Yeah. She is."

Another silence settles between them, heavy with all the unsaid things.

"I wasn't sure I could forgive you for hurting her," my dad says. "Even after she did. I was hell-bent on hanging on to that grudge. You didn't see her cry herself to sleep every night for two months. And as a father... watching that, knowing there was nothing I could do to take her pain away? That was hell. Pure and simple."

Ronan doesn't rush to respond. When he does, his voice is thick.

"I'm sorry," he says. "I know it doesn't make a lot of sense, but I never wanted to hurt her. I only ever wanted to keep her safe."

"I believe you," my dad says without a hint of doubt. "I know you've been through a lot. Things no kid should have to go through. And I know that stuff shaped you. How you think, how you love, how you protect. Your heart was in the right place, even if your choices didn't always reflect that."

Ronan is quiet. I can almost picture him standing there, eyes lowered but listening closely.

My dad clears his throat. "I wasn't able to wrap my head around that until now. I was hurt for Cat. You see, Ronan, the thing is that I, too, want nothing more than to keep my children safe, and I wasn't so sure that Cat's heart was safe with you. She'd already been through something awful with that other guy, and then you came along. And damn, she fell so fast and so hard for you, only to have her heart ripped out of her chest again. As a dad, that pissed me off enormously. And then you two got back together, but I guess I wasn't so quick to forgive you. I was cautious, you know?"

"I could tell," Ronan says earnestly.

"I bet you could." My dad chuckles dryly. "I was hard on you. I'll admit that. From the moment I heard about you over two years ago now, I decided I wasn't okay with you in Cat's life. I judged you before I ever met you. I'd heard about your past, and instead of giving you a chance, I focused on every little thing that could confirm what I'd already decided: that you weren't right for her."

He pauses again, this time longer.

"And I ignored everything that showed me how wrong I was. I didn't want to see the truth. I didn't want to see that you were good for her. Really good. And when you told us Cat was pregnant..." He laughs under his breath, low and rough. "It's a good thing there were witnesses, because I was about ready to strangle you."

He chuckles again, but this time it's tinged with something softer. "But even then, I admired the way you took the heat. You didn't flinch. You stepped up. Over the last few months, I've watched you work your ass off. You've taken the weight off Cat's shoulders. You've gone to every doctor's appointment, made sure she had what she needed, was taken care of, all while juggling work and a full course load at school."

My chest tightens with love for Ronan. My dad's right. Ronan did step up. No hesitation. No question. Despite the clear boundary he had set, he didn't let his fears prevent him from being the softest version of himself with me.

"What really impressed me," my dad goes on, "was how you kept your cool when I lost mine. I laid into you more than once. I lashed out at you, but you never retaliated. And slowly, I started to see the truth. You're a good guy, Ronan. A good *man*. A really good man."

His voice falters for the first time.

"Then the hemorrhage happened. And I saw it—your fear of losing her. It was written all over you. The way you held her hand for hours, never letting go. You didn't rest. And when she cried..." He clears his throat again, voice thick now. "You were the one who held her together, even though it was clear your own heart was broken. You'd just lost your son, and still, your first thought was Cat. You fought for her. You'd fight for her with your dying breath. And that... that's all a father could ever ask for his daughter."

There's a moment of silence, then my dad says, a little unsteadily, "I'm glad you held your son, Ronan. And I'm glad you told her to listen to her heart. You gave her that permission to let go. So... all that to say, Ronan, I forgive you." My dad releases a sound, a strangled mix of a sob and a chuckle.

There's a rustling kind of jingly sound, and then he says, "Here."

I have no idea what's happening.

"You're working tonight?" my dad asks.

"Yeah," Ronan says.

"What time are you done? Two-thirty?"

"Yeah, around then. Fridays and Saturdays usually run later. Takes time to clean up and get the stragglers out."

"Okay, well, if you care to, just let yourself in," my dad says. "I can't say I'm a huge fan of the two of you in the same bed before you're married, but I guess that ship has *very* obviously sailed. So I might as well accept the reality of your relationship with Cat."

There's a pause. His voice softens.

"And the reality is that she needs you right now. So if you're comfortable, just stay with us until Cat's back on her feet and the two of you can figure out your next steps."

Another pause, then more briskly: "But, please—for my peace of mind—leave the door to her room open."

"Sure, no problem," Ronan says with a quiet chuckle.

When he rejoins me a couple of minutes later, he holds up a silver key, his expression a mix of disbelief and awe.

"Your dad gave me this and told me to let myself in when I get off work tonight," he says, sitting down beside me and kicking off his shoes. He pulls his legs up and settles in next to me like he's been doing it forever.

"Yeah, I heard," I say, grinning. "Sounds like he's coming around."

"Or it's his way of trying to control the situation," Ronan says.

I burst out laughing. "Probably both. So, are you coming back here after work?" I ask hopefully.

"That's the plan," he says, pulling me into his arms.

I lean into him, breathing him in—that familiar mix of sun, ocean air, and clean laundry. He goes quiet, and I can tell he's thinking hard about something.

"Penny for your thoughts?" I say, watching his beautiful profile.

He smiles a little. "I don't know if this is a good time to bring it up," he says, turning to face me.

"It is," I say, nudging him. "Whatever it is."

He laughs. "Of course it is. You never think there's a bad time."

"Because there isn't."

"Alright," he says, then looks me dead in the eye. "I want you to move in with me."

I blink. "I thought I already kind of... did?"

"No," he says, grinning. "I mean *really* move in. None of this back-and-forth stuff. I want all your crap and all my crap in the same place. I want my apartment to be your home. And if you don't want to live with Shane and Tori, we can look for somewhere else. But I want to wake up next to you and fall asleep next to you every single day."

His words are so sweet, my stomach feels like it's full of fluttering wings.

"My dad is not going to love this," I tease.

"Baby, with all due respect, I don't really give a shit what your dad thinks," Ronan says, eyes intense and unwavering. "What matters to me is *you*. What you want. What you need. I already broke your heart, and then I got you pregnant. I'm not sure how I could possibly fuck up more, so I'm willing to risk it."

"Wow," I say, mock-swooning. "So romantic."

He grins. "Admit it, you're swept off your feet."

"Completely," I say. "And because you're *so* romantic, I will absolutely move in with you."

"Sweet." He kisses the top of my head. Then he glances across the room and frowns. "But... you can't bring that thing." He points to the porcelain doll propped up in my rocking chair.

"That belonged to my great-grandmother," I say, mock-offended.

"That's great. Really. But that thing *definitely* comes alive at night, and I'm not having it in my place."

I start laughing so hard, my C-section incision hurts. "You've seen too many horror movies."

"Honestly, that doll scares me more than my mother ever did," Ronan says with complete sincerity, and I lose it. I can barely catch my breath, clutching my stomach to hold my insides in place.

"You are unbelievable," I manage between gasps, my voice high and wheezy.

"I really think Sammy would love to have this doll," he says, deadpan. "You should definitely pass it down. You know, since you're such an amazing big sister and all."

"I can't with you," I say, tears streaming down my face. "You really don't want me to bring it?"

"I'm one hundred percent serious. Baby, I will burn that thing if you even think about packing it."

"Oh my god, Ran, stop."

"Not until you promise not to bring Annabelle," he says, and I collapse into another round of laughter.

"But I was really hoping to give her a special place in our bedroom," I say, voice breathless and giggly.

"Did I say 'move in with me?' I meant I think we need to end our relationship for good. This just isn't going to work out between us."

My laughter spirals out of control again, my abs screaming from the effort, but it's the best I've felt in days. It's the kind of laughter that empties you out and fills you back up at the same time. I needed this. I needed a little levity, even though part of me feels guilty at the burst of joy after I just lost my baby. Like I don't have a right to feel happiness. Not yet. Not for a long time.

"Okay, okay," I wheeze. "I won't bring the doll. I promise."

"Good deal," Ronan says, satisfied. "I'd really hate to have to murder a doll, but a man's gotta do what a man's gotta do."

"I can't breathe," I say, still shaking with laughter.

"That's not good," he says with a mischievous grin. "Need me to give you mouth-to-mouth?"

"Hmm, yes, I think I might." I lean back against my pillow as his lips find mine.

His kiss is slow, soft, his tongue brushing against mine in a way that makes my whole body hum. It's deep and warm and comforting. It's everything I need.

Ronan

I feel bad about leaving Cat, torn between staying by her side to make sure she's okay and needing—desperately—to distract myself from the weight of everything we've just lost. I know running off to work probably isn't the healthiest coping mechanism, but the alternative—sitting still, wallowing, spiraling—is worse. I don't trust my brain to be left unsupervised right now.

I'm tired. Bone-deep exhausted. Emotionally and physically drained, even though I managed a few hours of sleep at the hospital last night. It's funny how exhaustion finds a way to let you sleep anywhere, in any position. I remember those days of crashing in class after my mom's last act of violence, my body too heavy to hold up my own head, my mind too weighted down to concentrate. I know that kind of exhaustion well. It's the same kind of exhaustion I feel now. I know what it means when even breathing feels like work. Life has a brutal way of reminding you how little control you actually have.

So I do the one thing I know how to do: lock it away. Focus on something else.

"Hey, man, what are you doing here?" Shane asks as I head behind the bar at Murphy's.

"Working," I say simply.

He frowns. "Where's Cat?"

"She's at her parents'. They discharged her this morning. Her mom insisted she stay with them while she recovers." I pull out my wallet, phone, and keys, ready to stash them in the small office.

"Dude, I told you not to worry about coming in. I've got you covered," Shane says, trailing me.

"Yeah, I know. But, Shay... I *want* to be here."

He watches, eyes narrowed. "Don't you think you should be with Cat right now?"

Oof, heavy on the guilt.

"I'm going back after I close. She's not alone. She's taken care of." My voice tightens. "Please, Shane. I just need a few hours. Please."

He studies me, his eyes roaming my face, even my body, like he's expecting to see some gaping wound. But no, the injuries are only emotional this time.

"Have you talked to your therapist?" he suddenly asks, catching me off guard.

"No," I say, shaking my head.

"Okay. Before I let you work, you have to call her. *Right now*," he says, firm.

"What?"

"Ran, I've known you all my life. I've *seen* you spiral. I saw you at the hospital. I know what you're doing. And I'm not letting you disappear again. Call her. Now."

I stare at him, trying to gauge if he's serious. "Dude... it's Saturday."

"She doesn't have an answering service that can connect you in case of emergency? Which this is!"

My mouth opens, then shuts again.

"I'll call your dad and have him drag you out of here if I have to," he says, arms folded over his sturdy chest.

"Jesus, Shay. Fine." I grab my phone from the desk, unlock it, and dial Doctor Seivert's number. I hold it up for him to see. "Here. I'm calling. Now get out. This shit is supposed to be confidential."

He grins and backs out of the room, shutting the door behind him.

As expected, only Doctor Seivert's answering service picks up. I let them connect me to her personal cell phone, making this only the third time in two years that I've bothered her at home or grocery shopping or whatever she's doing with her time when she doesn't have to deal with asshole patients like me.

"Hi Doc, it's Ronan," I say when she answers the phone. Judging by the background noise, she's in her car.

"Oh, hi Ronan," she says jovially. "How are you?"

"Well, I want to say I'm fine, but I'm sure you wouldn't believe me anyways."

She laughs quietly. "Especially considering that you're calling me on the weekend."

"Yeah, I guess that, too."

"So what's on your mind, Ronan?" she asks, her voice warm.

"Cat suffered a stillbirth two days ago," I say, sitting down in one of the office chairs.

"Oh no." She sighs heavily. "Ronan, I'm so, so sorry to hear that. Listen, this warrants my undivided attention. I'm on the road right now, but I'm only about five minutes from my house. Let me call you back in a few minutes, okay?" she says, her tone compassionate.

"Sure."

She calls back as promised, and we talk for forty-five minutes. I tell her about Cat's hemorrhage, the loss of our baby, how fucking scared I was of losing Cat, too, how it feels like nothing is within my control, like I can't hold on to anything good. And Doctor Seivert does her best to help me work through it, at least enough that I can breathe again.

"Ronan, why don't we see each other face-to-face next week. Do you have any time on Monday or Tuesday?"

"Yeah, either day is fine. I don't have class next week. My days are wide open," I say, feeling drained after our conversation.

"Great. Why don't you pop in Monday? Let's say at eleven. I have a two-hour block for you, okay?"

I agree to the plan and we end our call.

When I finally come out of the office, Shane's waiting behind the bar.

"So, did you talk to your therapist?"

"No, I spent the last hour jerking off," I deadpan.

He bursts out laughing. "Well, at least you did *something* to take your mind off things. But seriously, how's Cat? How are you?"

"Physically, I'm fine. Cat... she looks like a ghost, but she'll be okay. Emotionally, we're both kind of fucked."

"I can imagine," Shane says quietly, a crease settling on his brow.

"Hey Shay, did you... my mattress?"

I left Cat's and stopped by my apartment to shower and change. I braced myself on the walk down the hall, trying to prepare for what I knew was waiting in my bedroom.

But when I opened the door, I froze.

The mattress was gone.

In its place sat a brand-new one, covered in clean, white sheets so bright they almost hurt to look at. For a moment, I just stood there, gripping the doorframe, my brain slow to catch up. No dark stains. No rumpled blankets. No reminder of the blood and the panic and the worst night of our lives.

It should have felt like a gift. A relief.

Instead, my chest tightened. Because if I didn't know better, I could almost believe it never happened. That Cat never endured that pain. That we never lost him.

Shane's voice pulls me back. "Your dad and I," he says, studying me. "He dropped by this morning, and we went and got you a new one. He didn't want you to have to see... didn't want you to have to deal with it, so he hauled the old one off to the dump."

I swallow the truth settling in. My dad—showing up again. Not in a loud way. Just quietly working in the background, taking care of things I didn't even know I needed.

I nod, pushing past the heaviness. "Anyway," I say, "have you figured out when you're going to pop the question to Tori?"

His eyes go wide, and I can't help the grin that spreads across my face.

"Nope," he says. "And that damn ring is burning a hole into my pocket."

"What's holding you back?"

"Pure, unfiltered fear she'll say no."

I blink. "You seriously worry she'll say no?"

"I do."

"Wait, how long have you guys been together now?"

"Like three and a half years."

"Uh-huh, and in all that time has she *ever* once made you think she didn't want to be with you?"

"Not really."

"Not really?"

"Okay, no, she hasn't."

"Perfect. There's your answer. Grow some balls and ask her," I say. "You don't need a special occasion to do it. You just need to do it."

Shane straightens up, puffing his chest out, taking on a determined expression. "Okay."

"Okay?"

"Yeah. You're right, I just need to do it."

"There you go," I say, clapping him on the shoulder.

"You'll be my best man, right?"

I chuckle. "Sure, but maybe ask her first."

I adjust my ball cap and make to get to work, only to stop dead in my tracks and turn back to him. "Oh hey, just a heads-up, Cat's officially moving in with us."

"I thought she already had?" Shane says, confused.

"What the hell? No, she hadn't," I say, shaking my head at Shane's reaction—so similar to Cat's earlier.

"She hadn't?"

"No. Not officially. But now it's officially official."

He laughs as I finally head off to start my shift.

Monday, December 25th

Ronan

I wake at the crack of dawn, the sun barely strong enough to suggest morning through the heavy snow clouds pressed low in the sky. I don't even need to look out the window to know it's snowing. The world is quieter—cars, footsteps, everything muffled like someone laid a blanket over the city.

I'm not sure what woke me. Maybe nothing. Maybe everything. But I'm not ready to move. The bed is warm. Comfortable. Familiar.

Cat is curled beside me, still sound asleep. I smile when I become aware of her body, her perfectly shaped ass pressed against me, one of her legs tucked between mine, the other peeking out from beneath the blanket. She's wearing her favorite sweater. Technically mine, the dark-green one I wore when we first met. She "borrowed" it two years ago when I lived in Montana and conveniently never gave it back. Aside from that, she's only in a pair of black lace panties.

She came home late last night from her parents' place, waking me just long enough to whisper that she was home before climbing into bed and rubbing her cold feet against my calves.

I worked the night shift at Murphy's. You'd think Christmas Eve would mean the place is dead, that people would want to be at home with their families. But it was busier than expected. Luckily, Shane told me to close early, so I made it home just after ten. The apartment was quiet; Shane and Tori were with his parents and their new partners at the beach house. Honestly, I admire how well his family has come together. Blended but still intact. Good for them making an effort.

Steve's home for a few days, but I didn't see him yesterday. I guess he had a low-key day at my dad's, who was out of the house, having

Christmas Eve dinner at Penny's parents' house with Penny and the twins.

The plan for today is to head to my dad's place, where Cat's family will meet us. But that's still hours away, so I decide to stay here, unmoving, just soaking in the peace while I can.

It's been a hard few weeks. Harder for Cat than for me, though I don't say that to minimize my own grief. Just to name the truth of what I see in her. Today was supposed to be her due date. I know it's been on her mind. She hasn't mentioned it much leading up to today, but I feel it in her body. Hear it in the way she sighs when she thinks I'm not listening. See it in the way her eyes linger on things. There's a heaviness in her I don't know how to lift. I try to give her what she needs when she needs it—whether that's space or closeness, distraction or silence. Her grief moves in waves, crashing and receding without warning. Sometimes she's filled with gratitude for what we have. Sometimes she's gutted. Devastated. Sometimes both at once.

Two nights ago we were curled up on the couch, halfway through some movie neither of us was really watching, when she got up and disappeared into our bedroom. When she came back, she was holding the memory box from the hospital, still unopened. She'd kept it tucked away in our closet, untouched until now. She sat beside me with the box cradled against her chest, crying. We opened it together for the first time. We didn't say anything. We just sat together, hands brushing, breath syncing, remembering.

I scoot closer to her, sliding my arm over her waist and nuzzling my face into her hair. I inhale deeply. God, she always smells so good. I could pick her out of a crowd with my eyes closed, just by her scent.

She sighs softly when I kiss her, but doesn't wake. I linger there for a moment, tempted. Too tempted. Her body is warm against mine, and if I stay like this I'm not going to be able to stop myself from touching her. And I don't want to wake her. Not today.

So I ease out of bed, take my time under the hot spray of the shower, then dress quietly and make my way into the kitchen to start breakfast.

"Hey you," Cat says about half an hour later. Her voice is soft, a little sleep-rough, and I turn to see her still in that green sweater. My eyes drag up her bare legs to the hem of the hoodie. It's just long enough to hide the delicate lace of her panties and the soft V hidden beneath it. Being denied even a glimpse makes my pulse spike. Jesus. She wakes up looking like this?

"Hey you," I echo, smiling as she walks over and kisses me. Her lips are soft, warm. "You hungry?"

"Yes," she says, stepping around me to reach for a mug. "The smell of the coffee actually woke me. You know, for someone who doesn't drink coffee, you make it really well," she says with a giggle, reaching for the pot.

I grab her wrist before she can pour and tug her gently back toward me. "I just know how you like it," I murmur, my voice low now, the shift in atmosphere almost immediate as I rest my hands on her hips. It's not urgent, not hectic, but quiet. Sacred.

"Yeah," she breathes, eyes darkening. "You always do."

I kiss her again, deeper this time, coaxing her lips apart so I can taste her. I sweep my tongue over hers, savoring, reverent. She melts into me as I back her up against the kitchen counter, already sliding my thumbs into the waistband of her panties. She wiggles them down, stepping out of them just as I lift her easily and set her on the counter, my mouth never leaving hers.

God, I'm so in love with her, am so wholly, completely hers. Always have been. Always will be. The sight of her like this, the feel of her warm skin under my hands, it makes me want to drop to my knees and worship her.

I push her sweater up, exposing her perfect breasts, my eyes lingering for a second before I bend to take one nipple into my mouth and suck gently. Her fingers tangle in my hair. She tips her head back against the cabinet with a breathless sound that makes me ache.

My hand slides down her side, over her hip, down her thigh. Then I reach between her legs, touch her gently, soft, slow. She gasps and arches toward me. I keep working her, teasing her, stroking her in ways I know will drive her to the edge. When I finally slip one, then two fingers inside her, curling them to stroke her inner walls, she whimpers quietly, desperately.

She's so wet already. So warm and tight. I'm completely lost in her, focused only on the way her body reacts to mine. Her hips move in rhythm with my slow fingers, breathy moans bursting from her lips. Until I hear it. A key in the lock.

"Nooo," I groan, withdrawing my hand and scooping her off the counter. Her legs immediately wrap around my waist.

Shane's voice filters in as the door opens. Tori's laugh follows. Perfect fucking timing. I swear, two and a half years later and people still can't seem to stop barging in on us.

"My underwear is still on the kitchen floor," Cat giggles against my neck, her moist heat seeping through my jeans. All I want is to sink into her slowly.

"Well, Merry Christmas, Shane," I mutter, hurrying down the hall with Cat in my arms. I kick the bedroom door shut behind us before I slow and move Cat onto the bed.

I don't want to rush her today. So I move quietly, intentionally as I rid myself of my clothes, then peel off her sweater. Her skin is warm and soft beneath my palms, and she watches me with wide, trusting eyes as I undress her like I'm unwrapping something precious. I am.

I kiss her collarbone to her shoulder, the swell of her breast to her nipple. I lick it softly. Her breath catches, her hands finding my face, my jaw.

But I don't linger. I work my way down, kissing and nipping at her soft skin, letting my tongue trail the landscape of her body until I arrive between her thighs.

"Hmm," I groan, and run my tongue along her sensitive flesh, tasting her.

She moans quietly, fingers threaded through my hair as she thrusts against my face slowly. I glance up at her. Cat's eyes are closed, cheeks rosy, her head tipping back against the pillows while her chest rises and falls with labored breaths.

I hold her gently, hands stroking her hips, her thighs, anchoring her as I devour her. I let my tongue move in slow, teasing circles, learning the rhythm of her breath, the catch of her sighs. I savor every sound, every shift of her body, the way her knees bend around me like she's cradling something sacred.

I slip a finger inside her, then a second, curling them, stroking her inner walls as she clenches around me as though her body is seeking more, is beginning to become one with mine. But I stay there, tongue circling, fingers moving.

She's trembling now, breath coming in tiny stuttering gasps. But I don't push her. I hold her steady and love her slow.

When her thighs start to shake, when she lets out a soft, broken moan, I hum against her in encouragement. She comes with a sigh and a shiver, pulsing around me, squeezing and thrusting and so damn perfect.

I kiss her inner thigh, then her hip, then the space just below her navel, crawling up her body slowly. Her eyes are still glassy, her lips parted. She tugs at my shoulders, urging me up. "Come here," she whispers, and I do.

She reaches between us, wrapping a warm hand around my erection as I slide between her thighs, careful, cradling her face as she guides me inside her with a soft sigh. I groan against her lips like I've finally come home.

I move inside her with long, deep, slow thrusts she meets with her own. God she's beautiful—a light sheen of sweat between her perfect breasts, her lips plump and parted, cheeks flushed with lust. Her soft moans are rhythmic, secret declarations of love, of trust.

I kiss her mouth. Her jaw. The tear that slips from the corner of her eye.

"I've got you," I whisper, and she nods, curling her arms around my neck like I'm her anchor.

When release finally comes, it comes quietly, like a sigh into the night, like soft waves rolling against the shore. Cat's warm and tight and everything. I hold myself over her, forehead resting against hers, trying to breathe through the intensity. It's not just the way her body feels—it's what this means. Today. Us. Still here. Still holding on.

When the aftershocks finally subside, we're still tangled together. I'm breathless. She's smiling. It's all I want: to see her smile.

"So... breakfast?" I manage.

"Sure," she giggles, but makes no move to unwrap her legs from around my hips, keeping me trapped against and inside her in the best way.

I kiss her softly. "I love you, baby," I murmur against her lips.

"I love you, too," she breathes, kissing me back deeply, her hands wrapping around my neck.

"Okay," I say, laughing a little when we finally part. "You're gonna need to let me get off you unless you want a round two."

She laughs, her legs sliding off me. "So horny," she teases.

I sit back and watch her climb out of bed. "It's all your fault," I say, grabbing my boxers and jeans.

"How's that?" she asks, heading to the closet.

"Uh, because you're unspeakably hot and *really* fucking good," I say, giving her an exaggerated *duh* look.

"But *you're* the one doing all the work," she muses, stepping into a navy-blue thong, then slipping into a pair of light jeans.

"Trust me," I say. "You're doing plenty."

We finish getting dressed and step out of the bedroom to find Tori and Shane in the kitchen. They're both grinning like assholes the second they see us.

Tori holds out her hand, Cat's black lace panties dangling from her finger. "Good morning," she sing-songs.

Cat blushes violently, snatching her underwear out of Tori's hand with a mortified groan.

"Good morning *indeed*," I say, stretching and grinning, feeling loose-limbed and thoroughly satisfied. "We weren't expecting you guys back."

Shane smirks. "Clearly."

"I was gonna have Cat right here on the kitchen counter," I say casually, "but your ass decided to walk in."

"Ran!" Cat scolds me quietly, making Shane laugh.

"We're heading to Tori's parents' house here in a minute, but we wanted to change and grab the Christmas presents," Shane says, still grinning at us while I retrieve a couple of plates from the kitchen cabinet to finally eat breakfast with Cat.

"Right. Well, do you guys want to eat with us?" I ask.

Tori shakes her head. "We're going to have brunch at my dad's house," she says. "But hey, that means you *can* have Cat in the kitchen." She giggles, watching Cat's blush deepen.

"I wouldn't hate that," I say sincerely.

"Okay, can we stop talking about me and Ran having sex?" Cat asks.

"Why?" I ask dryly. "It's one of my favorite subjects. Hobbies. Things to do. It's what I live for, actually."

Shane nods appreciatively. Tori giggles. Cat rolls her eyes and flees to the bathroom.

"So, what's the plan for you guys today?" Shane asks with a chuckle.

"Oh, you know, just going to have the time of our lives hanging out with the whole damn family. Not just mine, but Cat's, too."

"Oh, yeah, you're just chomping at the fucking bit," Shane laughs.

"You know it."

"Oh, come on, Ran. Both of your families are great," Tori says.

"Okay, my brothers are great, I give you that," I say. "And Cat's mom is awesome, and so are her siblings. And, I guess, Penny's nice, too..."

"It's the dads that are the issue, huh?" Shane says knowingly.

"They're alright, I guess. They're just kind of overbearing, and one in particular after being absent the vast majority of my life. In fact"—I pull my vibrating phone out of my back pocket, glancing at the screen—"here's my dad now, probably wondering where the fuck we are." I let his call go to voicemail.

Shane studies me amusedly, then asks, "How's therapy going?"

"Dude, you know as well as I do that there are some things even therapy can't fix. Look, I'm trying, okay?"

"I know you are, Ran. But maybe at least answer his phone calls. Just a suggestion." Shane nudges my shoulder. "He's a good dad. He's making a hell of an effort. Let him in, dude."

"Sage advice, as always," I chuckle.

"I'm your best friend for a reason."

"Clearly."

A few minutes later Shane and Tori head out, arms full of presents and the mountain of Christmas cookies Tori and Cat baked a couple of days ago. That process had mostly involved Tori smacking Shane's hands away every time he tried to steal one still warm from the oven.

I'm ignoring yet another buzz from my dad when I stop at the bathroom door.

Cat stands in front of the mirror, still and quiet. Her gaze is distant. Her hands rest on her stomach, and my chest tightens. I step inside and wrap my arms around her from behind.

"How are you today?" I ask softly, knowing full well the weight this date carries.

She sighs, leaning back into me. "I don't know," she says quietly. "I think I'm okay, but... I get sad."

"Yeah." I hold her tighter, neither of us moving for a long moment. "I love you, baby. I wish I could make this easier for you."

"You do," she says with quiet conviction. She turns in my arms and presses her lips to mine.

Cat

If things had gone the way they were supposed to, I'd be holding Ronan's and my son in my arms today. Or maybe I'd still be waiting, expecting to meet him any day now.

But then again, if things had gone the way they were *supposed* to, I probably never would've gotten pregnant in the first place. I don't know.

Most days I feel okay. And physically I *am* okay. My clothes fit the way they used to. My cycle's back to normal. With the exception of that three-inch scar on my lower abdomen, there's no trace left, nothing to show that, just over four months ago, I was growing a baby inside me.

But the memories haven't gone anywhere. And sometimes I swear I still feel phantom flutters in my belly. Little kicks that never were. Reminders of everything I lost, of everything *we* lost.

Even though things are good now, even though I'm happy—*really* happy—I still get sad. I still wonder what today would look like if I hadn't lost our baby. Would we be bleary-eyed and exhausted, our arms full of this tiny new life? Would we be late today for a whole different reason?

Ronan has been everything I didn't even know I'd need. I thank the stars for him every day, his steady presence, the calm he brings into any room. The way he loves me so openly, so easily. He always knows what I need, even when I don't. Most of the time it's just him, just his arms around me while I let whatever feeling has crept in run its course.

Like this morning. He held me without asking questions, without needing explanations, just... held me.

I don't know how I'd do this without him.

We take our time getting ready. Neither of us is eager to rush over to his dad's house, where both of our families are already congregating in a too-small space. My mom's already called twice and texted four times asking for our ETA.

"Do we have everything we need?" I ask out loud, mentally going through my checklist as Ronan holds the apartment door open for me. I'm balancing a tote bag stuffed with small presents.

"You're with me, so... yeah," he says sweetly.

I glance back and smile. "Ugh. You know *exactly* what to say to make me go all weird in my head."

I walk out with him, feeling a little lighter.

Not surprisingly, the house is packed by the time we arrive twenty minutes later. Frank beelines for us the second we walk through the door.

"Oh boy," Ronan mutters. "Watch him lay into me about ignoring his calls."

But instead of the chewing-out I expect, Frank's mouth pulls into a tentative smile. "Do you two have a second?"

"Uh... yeah?" Ronan throws me a quick glance as Frank gestures for us to follow him upstairs.

At the top of the landing, Penny emerges from their bedroom. I blink. She looks pale, a light sheen of sweat on her forehead.

"What's going on?" Ronan asks, his eyes bouncing between his dad and Penny.

Frank clears his throat, sheepish. He reaches for Penny's hand. "Yeah, so... I know today probably isn't the best timing, but we won't be able to keep it under wraps. Not with Penny feeling the way she does..."

My jaw drops. I already know where this is going. And judging by Ronan's face, he does too.

"Oh shit, Dad," Ronan groans. "Ever heard of pulling out?"

Frank chuckles, the tension in his shoulders easing. "I'm not about to discuss my pull-out game with my son."

"'Cause you clearly have no pull-out game," Ronan deadpans.

Frank smirks. "Oh, didn't realize I was talking to the *master.*"

"Oh my god," Penny laughs. She turns to me, her expression soft. "I'm sorry. I know this isn't ideal timing. I've just been feeling pretty sick the last few days."

"We thought it was a stomach bug," Frank says.

"Yeah, but then I took a test two days ago..." Penny sighs. "I didn't feel this awful with the boys."

"Maybe that means it's a girl," I say, feeling a small spark of giddy surprise catch fire in my chest.

Her smile widens. "Maybe. We weren't going to say anything yet, but I've been running to the bathroom every fifteen minutes. Hard to hide that. We wanted you two to know first. We didn't want to be insensitive."

"No, really, this is *so* exciting," I say honestly. And it is. It surprises me how genuine my joy is.

"What's your goal here, Dad? Repopulate the earth with Soults? Build your own little army?" Ronan jokes.

"I make good-looking kids," Frank says with a shrug. "Why should I stop?"

"Huh, guess you have a point," Ronan grunts.

The four of us make our way back into the living room where Penny and Frank announce the news of their pregnancy to everyone, which is met with delighted squeals from my mom and hugs from my dad. I giggle when Steve proceeds to roast his dad just like Ronan did.

"God, Dad, for a man who kept hounding Ran and me about using protection, you fail pretty epically," he laughs.

"Hey, I'm thirty-seven," Frank says, puffing his chest out. "I'm not a kid anymore."

"You were sixteen with Stevie," Ronan mutters behind a fake cough.

The room erupts with laughter.

The excitement lingers for a while, everyone peppering Frank and Penny with questions about the due date—no idea, they don't see her doctor until after the new year—and whether they want to find out the gender—absolutely.

My mom approaches me in the kitchen a little while later, concerned that Penny and Frank's news may have added to my sadness today. I assure her that I'm alright, and actually really happy for them. She hugs me for a long time, talking to me sweetly, telling me that Ronan's and my time will come when it's right, that things will work out for us just like they always do.

Eventually we all manage to gather in the living room. My siblings are playing with Dean and Kellan, who I swear are moments away from taking their first steps. They keep pulling themselves up on anything they can reach, balancing with wide-eyed determination before plopping backwards onto their diapered butts.

"Can we open presents now?" Benny yells, eyeing the bag of neatly wrapped gifts I stashed beside the sofa.

We give in and let the kids go first, which turns the room into a tornado of paper and squeals. Afterward, the adults exchange gifts.

Ronan had already surprised me a couple of weeks ago with a weekend trip to a fancy resort.

"Early Christmas present," he told me at the time. "Because we desperately need to get away."

He wasn't wrong. Four days of sex, incredible food, spa treatments, and zero interruptions? I'd never felt more relaxed or connected to him.

Which should make today's surprise even more satisfying.

"Okay, you have to follow me," I tell him once everyone's opened their presents, barely containing my excitement.

"Where?" Ronan asks, confusion etched into his gorgeous features.

"Stop questioning and just follow her," Frank says with a grin on his face.

Ronan does as instructed, following me into the kitchen. I stop in front of the garage door, my heart pounding so hard I swear he can hear it. This has taken me months to make happen, and I can't wait for him to see it.

"Alright," I say, beaming at him.

"Alright what?"

"Open the door!" I huff, stepping back to let him reach for the handle.

He pushes it open and then just stands there.

His Mustang—sleek, satin black and gleaming under the garage light—sits pristine and perfect, like no time has passed at all.

He doesn't speak. Just stares. Then he turns to me, his face full of emotion. "Cat... is this... how did you..." he breathes, unable to finish his thought. Wordlessly, he walks down the three steps and over to the car. He runs his hand along the smooth curves, over the roof and to the hood like he's afraid it might vanish.

I follow, fishing the key out of my pocket.

"Merry Christmas, sweet boy," I whisper.

He takes the key from me, unlocks the door, and slips into the driver's seat. His hands settle on the steering wheel, feeling the supple leather under his fingers. He looks around the interior like he's stepped into a dream.

"I don't know what to say," Ronan murmurs, getting out of the car. He swallows hard, his eyes watery. He doesn't say anything more. He just pulls me into his arms and kisses me so deeply my knees almost give out.

"How did you even make this happen?" he asks breathlessly when he finally pulls away, glancing back at the car in awe.

"I may have snooped in your phone a little. Found the guy you sold it to."

"You went through my phone?"

"Relax. No porn. No sketchy texts from girls named Ashley or Brittney or Chelsey or something else that ends in *ey*," I grin.

"Yeah, well, I use a burner phone for that," he deadpans.

"I figured as much," I say, mimicking his dry tone. "Anyway, I called the guy and he definitely wasn't interested in selling it."

"So, how did you get it? Wait, baby, are the cops going to show up to arrest your ass because you committed grand theft auto?"

I look at my watch. "Any second now."

"Alright, get in the car. I'll drive," Ronan says with a sigh.

I giggle at him. "I just kept calling. And eventually, a few weeks ago, I told him the whole story. About you. Why you sold it. What it meant. And, well... I can be *very* persuasive."

"Oh, I *know* how persuasive you can be," he says, flashing that mischievous half-smile I love.

"I'm serious. Yesterday, when you thought I was at my parents' all day? Stevie and I actually drove up to New Hampshire to get it and bring it back. Tada!" I throw my arms out.

"You are fucking amazing, baby." Ronan scoops me into his arms. "But how in the world did you pay for this?"

"I sold my own car. It wasn't quite enough to buy your Mustang back—"

"You don't say." He grins.

I pretend I didn't hear that. "—so your dad, Stevie, Shane, and my parents all chipped in," I say with a huge smile. "I told them that I was sure you'd let me have your RAV4."

"Done." Ronan fishes the keys from his pocket and hands them to me. "It's yours. I'll sign the title when we get home."

"Are you happy?" I ask, curling my fingers around his.

"Are you kidding me? Fuck yes, I'm happy. Baby, this is *insane.* I don't deserve y—"

"Nope!" I press my hand over his mouth. "Don't finish that sentence. You do deserve me. And I deserve you. Got it?"

He smiles against my palm.

"Nod if you understand, Mr. Soult."

He nods.

I drop my hand and he immediately kisses me again—deep, consuming, perfect.

We stay like that for a while, wrapped up in each other. When he finally tucks the Mustang's key into his pocket, he reaches for my hand again.

"Let's go," he says softly, lacing our fingers together.

We head back inside to join our families, where everyone is eagerly waiting to hear Ronan's reaction to the most epic Christmas present he's ever gotten.

Ronan

Cat has absolutely outdone herself.

I can't believe my eyes when I open the garage door and find my Mustang—*my* Mustang—parked there like it never left. Pristine. Perfect. I take one look at it and immediately know: she pulled off something major. And when I find out she sold her car, and then hustled not only my dad, my brother, and Shane, but got her parents to pitch in, too? I mean, I know I'm not supposed to say it out loud, but nobody can stop me from thinking—until the end of my days—that Cat is *way too damn good for me.*

Naturally, I handed her the keys to the RAV4 the second she told me.

Cat tells me about her little mission yesterday, how she enlisted my big brother's help. She and Steve drove all the way to New Hampshire, picked up the car, and drove it back home to park it in my dad's garage.

"The guy you sold it to hadn't even driven it," Steve chimes in. "He was a collector, Ran. Just kept it in a giant garage like some museum piece."

I couldn't have wished for better news. My Mustang is in almost exactly the same condition I sold it in—no changes, no damage, just a little over 600 miles more on my odometer, clean, cared for, and waiting for me. Waiting for *her* to bring it home.

Cat and I spend much of the day hanging out in the living room, chatting with Steve, entertaining my brothers and Cat's siblings. But my attention keeps drifting. My eyes keep finding Cat. I don't know how to describe what's happening inside me other than this: I'm completely overwhelmed by her. Always have been.

When she disappears into the kitchen to help her mom and take over for Penny, who had to bolt to the bathroom yet again, I go to help set the table for dinner. Something's stirring inside me. I need something to do or I might combust from whatever is rattling around in my chest.

Fifteen minutes later, we're all gathered around the table, passing plates of food. Again, my thoughts drift. When Penny suggests my dad say something before we dig into the food, I stop him just as he's about to open his mouth to talk.

"Dad, actually, do you mind if I say something?"

"Sure, Ran, go ahead," he says, as everyone looks at me with quizzical expressions.

My heart slams against my ribs like it's trying to make a run for it. My hands are sweaty. And yeah, I've been through some terrifying shit in my life, but somehow this is the scariest thing I've ever done.

I look at Cat, and everything else falls away.

"It's been a hell of a couple of years," I say. "Actually, it's been a hell of a *life* so far, but we're not gonna talk about that today. Because all those years before you? They don't really matter anymore." I pause, laugh awkwardly. "Shit. I suck at this. Sorry."

Everyone chuckles. It gives me just enough air to keep going.

"I know today's hard for you," I say. Cat nods, already tearing up. "I wish I could make it better. I wish I could take away everything that's ever hurt you. I wish I could undo all the shit I put you through. But then again... maybe I wouldn't. Not really. Because even when things were bad—and *fuck*, some days felt like the whole damn world was caving in—you were always the part of it that felt like home. You're still the best, most unwavering, most *real* part of me."

I swallow hard. "You make it easier. Always have. From the moment I met you, I knew it was you or no one. You have this way of easing the weight I carry. You make unbearable shit feel bearable. And when things got really bad at home—like, the kind of bad you don't talk about in polite company—you were the reason I didn't give up. I don't mean to put that on you, but you need to know that you were the reason I fought. You were the reason I *lived.* You kept me breathing when I didn't think I could anymore."

Cat watches me, unspeaking, eyes wide and shimmering.

"And even after everything, you were there. After the trauma, after the trial... you loved me through it. Even when I left. You loved me over distance. Steady. Never judging, always telling me I'm worthy of love, even when I couldn't believe it myself. I still think you're full of shit most of the time, but I promise, I'm working on that."

More quiet laughter from the table, but I don't look away from Cat.

"For a moment, it felt like maybe we'd turned a corner. Things were good. But then my grandmother showed up, and there was... I learned some truly unnerving shit. And I spiraled. I spiraled and pushed you away in the worst possible way. Baby, I know I left. I left *you.* Emotionally, mentally, I checked out. More than once. And I almost didn't come back. But, god, Cat, I always wanted you. I always loved you."

My voice cracks on the memory like stained glass.

"I promise, I tried to get better, tried to figure it all out somehow, tried to... find myself. And you let me do that. You never demanded anything. You just let me heal."

I pause, locking eyes with her.

"I still have healing to do. I know that. I probably always will. But you need to know something, Cat: *you* were never something I needed to heal from. You were, and are, my healing. You are the safest place I've ever known."

She chokes on a sob, and I step closer.

"I'm just glad that you took me back, baby. I half-expected you to have moved on, to have fallen out of love with me. But you welcomed me back and then... well, the last nine months happened. And honestly, some days it feels like we can't catch a damn break. Like the universe keeps testing us and testing us and testing us again."

I take a deep, cleansing breath.

"I don't care anymore. I don't need any more tests. I spent an entire lifetime lost. And then you found me, which in turn allowed me to find myself. It took me a minute but... I know what I want. I know *who* I want. I want you. Forever."

I pull the simple gold ring from my pocket, the single oval diamond grabbing all the attention, and get down on one knee. "And I want forever to start now."

"Bobby, what is he doing? Is he proposing?" I hear Jen gasp somewhere behind me, but it's like I have blinders on. All I see is Cat, her hands covering her mouth, her eyes wide and locked on mine.

"Baby, marry me. Please!"

She laughs and cries all at once. "Of course I'll marry you, Ran!"

"Are you serious?" I ask, in complete disbelief.

"Yes," she laughs again.

I slide the ring onto her finger before pulling her into my arms and kissing her like it's the last breath I'll ever take.

It doesn't take long before we're surrounded by everyone, giving and getting hugs. Jen and Penny swoon over Cat's ring, which honestly cost me a small fortune. I figured since we didn't end up having to buy all the baby essentials, I might as well spoil her.

"Bobby, did you know about this?" Jen asks him loudly when she catches sight of him grinning widely.

He chuckles. "Sort of. Ronan had *the talk* with me a few weeks ago."

Cat looks at me, her eyes brimming with tears and emotion. "You talked to my dad first?"

"Only to give him a heads-up," I say with a grin.

I had actually bought the ring the day after Cat came home from the hospital, her nineteenth birthday. Yeah, I know we're young, but we've been through so much shit together, that alone has matured us by at least twenty years. I know I want to spend the rest of my life with her. The only thing I wavered on was the timing of my proposal.

I didn't want to overshadow the heaviness of our loss. I didn't want to make Cat feel as though I was rushing that process. I wanted to give us time to grieve. And, yeah, I wanted to talk to Bobby.

It wasn't about permission. Cat isn't property. She doesn't need anyone's permission but her own. But given Bobby's and my rather tense relationship in the past and how much better things have been between us lately, I thought I should at least provide him with the illusion of control rather than blindsiding him.

So on a Saturday morning a couple of weeks ago, I dropped Cat off at her parents' home so she and her mom could go Christmas shopping together. I pretended to use the bathroom, lingering way longer than necessary so I could catch Bobby alone.

I waited for Cat and Jen to head out, then went to find Bobby. "Do you have a second?" I asked when I finally came back downstairs.

"Sure, what's up?"

"I wanted to talk to you really quick."

Bobby's expression changed immediately. He nodded. "You're going to ask me if you have my blessing to marry Cat, aren't you?"

I fully expected him to launch into a tirade about why he didn't approve of me asking Cat to be my wife, but he surprised me.

"I have been wondering when this would happen. You guys are so young, Ronan. Only nineteen. Are you sure?"

I almost reminded him that just months ago, he'd been trying to pressure me into "making an honest woman out of Cat." But I figured now wasn't the time to point out the hypocrisy.

"I've never been surer about anything than the fact that I want to be with Cat for the rest of my life."

"You know, Ronan, when Cat was born and I held her in my arms for the very first time, I knew, absolutely, one hundred percent *knew* that no guy would ever be good enough for my daughter."

He hesitated for a second.

"But I was wrong. I know it took me a while to come around. When Cat cried after losing her baby... your baby... she sought your arms. Not her dad's."

He quickly swiped at his eyes, trying to hide the emotion.

"I guess I finally understood that there were things I couldn't fix for her, that there was pain I couldn't take away. But you can. You did. You do. That was a hard pill to swallow, because when she was little I was able to make everything better. Even with that bastard Adam. But what Cat has with you is on a different plane. She needs you, and, more importantly, she *wants* you. You're now the one she goes to first when she's happy, or sad, or angry. You're her safe space. You're her person. She loves you. I see it. And I see how much you love her. I know you'll keep her safe."

He took a deep, steadying breath.

"So yes, you have my blessing to ask her to marry you."

"Thank you, sir." Even though his approval wasn't a prerequisite to me proposing to Cat, I was still relieved. It was still nice to know we had his support after he had been less than supportive of me for so long.

He grinned. "What would you have done if I had said no?"

I gave him a one-shouldered shrug. I was ready to give him *some* control. Not all of it. "I'd have asked her to marry me anyway, but she would have been pissed at you, I'm sure."

He laughed. "Fair enough. Do you know when you're going to do it?"

I shook my head. "No idea. I figure I'll know when the moment is right."

"Do you have a ring?"

I nodded, reached into my pocket, and pulled out the dainty piece of jewelry. Cat's not a flashy person, so I made sure the band was simple—thin, delicate—just enough to seat the sparkly oval diamond. I'd been carrying it with me everywhere I went, constantly afraid of losing it but too paranoid to leave it at home or in my car, where I was sure Cat would find it in five seconds flat.

I hadn't told anyone else about it. Not my brother. Not my dad. Not even Shane. He'll probably give me shit for it later, be in his feelings about not knowing, but I didn't want the pressure. Didn't want the opinions or the teasing or the weight of anyone else's expectations stacked on top of my own.

So I waited. Just waited. Waited for my heart to tell me when it was time.

And tell me, it did.

I spent my whole life anticipating pain, hiding, running, waiting for the other shoe to drop. But now, for once, I'm not bracing for impact. I'm not waiting for the fall. I'm reaching for the future. I'm reaching for happiness.

I'm reaching for Cat.

This is the end of Ronan and Cat's story... for now.

Acknowledgements

As always, I have to start by acknowledging the one person without whom this series would never have lived anywhere but inside my head (and maybe on some forgotten path on my computer): my husband aka my favorite person, my ride-or-die, my better half, my... well, you get the point. Baby, I know I'm not the most expressive person in this world, but you need to know how much I love and appreciate you. Thank you for being my sounding board, for listening to the roughest of rough ideas, for being my Ben Affleck to my Matt Damon (and vice versa), for sitting with me at Peggy Sue's Diner and helping me come up with the most unhinged plot ideas. I wouldn't want to do any of this without you by my side.

To my dad, brother, and SIL – ich vermisse euch! Hab euch ganz doll lieb.

To my bookish fam – there are so many of you who support and inspire me, who make this author journey worthwhile, and who give me the encouragement to keep going even on the days when it all feels overwhelming or futile. A special "Thank you" to Ashley, Chelsey and the Bookgrubbers, Jess, Jenn, Carol, Nancy, Lindsey, Lacrissa, and Diana (aka MommaD) for being incredible hype people! Please know that this list is very much *not* exclusive, my brain is just too fried to list everyone who has loved on or shouted about my book babies. Honestly, I love you all!

To Tyler — Amanda — HelloHappyGoodMorning — my Canadian bestie: I thank the universe every day for connecting us. I can't believe the journey we've embarked on. I mean, seriously, from me watching one of your reels to us starting a bookish podcast to meeting up in Las Vegas a year later? Absolutely crazy! Can't wait to see where we go from here.

To my ARC readers – thank you for putting eyes on my babies before the rest of the world does, for your feedback, your energy, support, love, and warranted criticism. I appreciate you more than I can adequately express.

To Shavonne at MotifEdits – you're the true MVP! Thank you for all your input, grace, and constructive criticism. I thank the stars for you every day.

To all the bookish content creators, illustrators, narrators, and readers who have interacted with me and my stories – please know that you have touched my life in a deep, meaningful way. Thank you!

And last, but most definitely not least: to my babies – watching you grow into full-fledged people with opinions and tastes is the most incredible privilege. We have the best conversations. I am so proud of who you are. I can't wait to see what the future brings for each of you. I love you more than all the stars in the sky. As always, I just hope your mommy makes you proud.

About the Author

J.V. Reese lives in a very sunny and very hot part of California (think Death Valley, except less "deathy") where she escapes the demands of everyday life by lifting heavy things, going on little getaways with her favorite people, and writing stories.

Stay in Touch!

Sign up for my newsletter and receive updates on future releases and giveaways.

www.subscribepage.io/jvreese

www.JVREESE.com

I would also love to connect on social media.

You can find me on

Instagram – jvreeseauthor

TikTok – jvreese.author

Facebook – J. V. Reese Author

Made in the USA
Monee, IL
29 September 2025

30569543R00312